PRAISE FOR
THE DAUGHTERS OF BLOCK ISLAND

"Christa Carmen celebrates the gothic in this twisty, spooky tour de force that ticks all the boxes with panache and style! This love child of Barbara Michaels and John Harwood has written a chilling page-turner guaranteed to keep you up all night. *The Daughters of Block Island* is a top-notch read!"

—Nancy Holder, Lifetime Achievement Award Winner,
Horror Writers Association

"I have been a Christa Carmen fan since reading her collection, *Something Borrowed, Something Blood-Soaked*. I knew she could tell a hell of a short story and her novel, *The Daughters of Block Island*, does not disappoint. The mystery leaves the reader feeling like they are trying to escape a twisted haunted dollhouse without knowing what is real or imagined. Lovers of gothic fiction should pick up this book that contains a wealth of nods to the genre, but also discusses personal horrors like addiction, abuse, and mental health."

—V. Castro, Bram Stoker Award–nominated author of
Goddess of Filth and *The Queen of the Cicadas*

"Christa Carmen's *The Daughters of Block Island* is a tantalizing love letter to gothic fiction, imbued with rain-soaked atmosphere and scandal-ridden mysteries that unravel to reveal the dark beating heart at the center of a mysterious island mansion. Readers of gothic novels will delight in nods to classic works and the way the past continues to haunt the present in White Hall. Filled with intrigue, this book is the perfect addition to your bookshelf, tucked in beside Radcliffe and du Maurier!"

—Jo Kaplan, author of *It Will Just Be Us*

THE
DAUGHTERS
OF BLOCK
ISLAND

THE
DAUGHTERS
OF BLOCK
ISLAND

A NOVEL

CHRISTA CARMEN

THOMAS & MERCER

Published by Thomas & Mercer, Seattle

www.apub.com

Amazon, the Amazon logo, and Thomas & Mercer are trademarks of Amazon.com, Inc., or its affiliates.

ISBN-13: 9781662512988 (paperback)
ISBN-13: 9781662512971 (digital)

Cover design by Caroline Teagle Johnson
Cover image: © shunli zhao, © ANGELGILD / Getty Images;
© Nic Skerten / ArcAngel

For Eleanor . . . I love you all the whispering leaves in the trees and all the thunder crashing, lightning flashing in the skies.

Prologue:
The Spider and the Fly

The letter arrives on a Thursday, along with several pieces of junk mail and a postcard from their dentist. Thalia Mills notices the light-brown envelope, soft and expensive-looking, sticking out from the scattered pile her girlfriend, Laura, brought up from downstairs. There's no return address, her own address is hastily scribbled, and the handwriting is unfamiliar. Thalia places the novel she was reading beside the steaming teacup on the counter and picks the envelope up. A smudge of ink mars the clear space below the zip code, but the Block Island postmark is perfectly legible. At the sight of those two words, the hometown she's not set foot in for over a decade, a current of unease runs up Thalia's back and spreads like ocean water across her shoulders.

Laura is unloading the groceries, yet to realize something is amiss. It's that type of gloomy February evening in Boston where the sky is the same steely gray as the buildings spread out beneath it. Rain is in the forecast, but the temperature has remained north enough of freezing to avoid much snow.

"You start work on the new case yet?" Laura asks. Across the kitchen, a pile of legal briefs looms like a sentence, awaiting Thalia's analysis, her judgment. When Thalia doesn't respond, Laura looks up. "Thal? Are you okay?"

"Were you expecting something from Block Island?" It's a foolish question. Thalia's name is on the envelope. But her brain balks at the possibility of receiving anything from anyone on that island.

"Was *I* expecting something?" Laura says. "Of course not." She steps closer. "Could it be something from your mother?"

Thalia frowns. "No." She doesn't bother reminding Laura why she can state this with such conviction, only takes a breath, slips a finger beneath the seal, and tears the envelope open. She hears, rather than sees, Laura go back to sorting groceries. Thalia considers reaching for her tea, prolonging the discovery of whatever's contained within this unexpected parcel, but her stomach is already queasy.

She removes two pieces of paper. The first is a handwritten letter dated February 4. She checks the envelope; it's postmarked February 5. Today is the eighteenth, and while a frisson of annoyance courses through her, she doesn't bother chastising Laura; despite it being her partner's unofficial job to bring in the mail, she *never* does it in a timely fashion.

Dear Thalia, the letter begins . . . *They say that truth is stranger than fiction, and while I've never been inclined to believe this before, I'm afraid that, now, I'd have to agree.*

"Is it from your mother, after all?" Laura asks, but Thalia barely hears her. She continues reading:

> *I'm writing to you from Block Island, a place I under-stand you no longer visit, and I'm not finding it hard to see why. This place is a dark and dismal one. It's full of secretive coves and more secretive people . . .*

"Anything important?" Laura presses.

"I . . ." She's about to say *I don't know*, but her voice falters. Her eyes skip over the lines cascading down the page, catching random, strange musings: *I'm a fly who's placed one thin leg onto a strand of spiderweb, and the house, the weaver, felt the vibrations, heard my thoughts.* She flips the letter over, and her eyes alight on the closing lines:

> Sincerely,
> —Your sister, Blake Bronson

With shaky fingers, Thalia sets the letter aside and reaches for the second piece of paper. The seal in the bottom left-hand corner gives away the type of document before she even reads the heading: CERTIFICATION OF BIRTH. Her eyes skip down again:

Date of Birth: April 22, 1992
Name: Blake Thalia Mills
Sex: Female
Mother's Name: Maureen Mills
Father's Name: Unknown

At the sight of her own mother's name printed on the document, Thalia's eyes burn, not with tears, but with a shock so absolute, her body can find no other way to process it. Her gaze is drawn to the counter, to the novel she'd set aside after Laura tossed her the mail. It's a new release, a popular thriller author's take on the gothic novels of the Victorian era. The book is all right, Thalia supposes, but it doesn't hold a candle to the classics her mother read to her as a child, when they'd engage in the one pastime during which Thalia could pretend Maureen was *normal.*

"Who's it *from?*" Laura insists, and Thalia jumps. Her girlfriend has abandoned the groceries and is walking over.

Thalia forces herself to meet Laura's eyes, feeling as though she's plunged to the bottom of an oceanic trench and cannot swim out. "It's from . . . my sister," she says. The words are salt on a scorched tongue.

Laura scrunches her nose. "You don't have a sister."

Thalia holds up the birth certificate. In a voice as thick and strangled as if she were choking on seawater, she says, "Apparently, I do."

In a sudden, violent burst of movement, Thalia drops the birth certificate and reaches into her back pocket for her phone. She googles "Blake Mills," then "Blake Thalia Mills"—still not letting herself fully internalize that this younger sister she did not know she had was given Thalia's first name as her middle one—but nothing comes up. She grabs for the letter and rereads the name with which it was signed, then googles "Blake Bronson, Block Island." The news articles display across the screen in a neat row, but Thalia only sees the first, brief, surreal snapshot before her sweaty fingers lose their grip, and her phone smashes to the tile floor. She does not flinch or bend to retrieve it.

"Thalia," Laura says, and there's naked worry in her tone, "what on earth is going on?" Thalia says nothing, only stares.

"Thalia!" Laura grips her by one shoulder and gives her a little shake.

Finally, Thalia picks up her phone. She reopens the Safari browser, clicks on the article, and holds it out for Laura to see once it loads—and once she's checked the date on which it was published: February 6.

Body Discovered Yesterday in Block Island B and B Identified as Twenty-Six-Year-Old Mainlander Blake Bronson. Laura's eyes jump from the screen to Thalia's face. "I don't understand."

Images—a desolate stretch of beach backdropped by red-clay cliffs; rows of boarded-up houses; her mother, standing on the porch as a storm descends, her face its own storm cloud, yelling at a ten-year-old Thalia to get in the house—parade through Thalia's head, and she shakes them away. "I have a sister," she says. "She sent me a letter two weeks ago today." Thalia points to the article on the phone she's still holding up like a flag. "One day later, she was found dead. *On Block Island.*"

Thalia pushes back from the counter and hurries across the kitchen. Outside, the sky darkens to an ominous urchin-black.

Laura follows. "Where are you going?"

Thalia doesn't slow her pace. "First, to get my laptop so I can do a *lot* more research." The clouds open. Thunder rolls in the distance.

Thalia stomps through the Back Bay apartment and disappears into her home office.

"And then where?" Laura sounds panicked.

Thalia pops her head out of the office to address her: "And then I'm checking the Point Judith schedule for ferries to New Shoreham." Despite her shock, she feels electrified by the prospect of it, after almost thirty years of her mother having closed herself off to Thalia, to everyone, years during which Thalia understood her mother about as much as she did a stranger on the street. And now this letter. This clue to Maureen's walled-off personality, her rigidity, her cold, impenetrable nature. This clue to *Thalia's* personality, formed like a piece of sea glass by a childhood as capricious as the waves.

"I'm going to Block Island," Thalia declares. "To find out what happened to Blake. To *my sister*. And why my mother kept her a secret."

Thalia spins back into her office and goes to her computer, trying to envision where in her closet she stashed her small waterproof suitcase.

Beyond the big bay windows of the safe, cozy apartment, it begins to rain.

PART I

Chapter 1

Blake knows she's in a gothic horror novel the moment she steps off the rain-slicked ferry. The terminal is as dark and deserted as if each of Block Island's one thousand winter residents has hunkered down to escape the storm. Upon closer inspection, she sees a lone, somewhat decrepit taxi, its headlights turning raindrops into will-o'-the-wisps. Ducking her head against the whipping wind, Blake sprints across the lot. The rippling, flint-gray puddles are smaller versions of the twelve-mile stretch of ocean she's just crossed.

The taxi driver is no older than thirty, with shoulder-length black hair and features that remind Blake of her Taiwanese American room-mate. When Blake knocks on the window, the woman almost drops her phone in an effort to unlock the doors. "I didn't really expect anyone tonight," she says once Blake has climbed in and stuffed her soggy backpack between the seats. "I'm glad I came out, though, or you would have been a heck of a lot wetter than you are now."

She holds a roll of paper towels through the glass partition, and Blake takes one gratefully and wipes her neck and brow. The sense of surrealness she experienced on the ferry has extended into the taxi, like she fell asleep in her apartment in South Boston and has since been in the midst of one long, illogical dream. She slips a hand into her jacket pocket and fingers the aluminum medallion, tracing the embossing on either side of it. Maybe illogical dreams are what everything in early sobriety feels like.

"Where to?" the driver asks.

"One sec." Blake pulls her hand from her pocket and digs around in her bag. She unearths a tattered paperback and finds the piece of paper stuck within its pages. "Seventeen-oh-one Mansion Road," she reads. There is silence, and Blake looks up to find the taxi driver staring at her in the rearview mirror. She double-checks the address. "One-seven-oh-one Mansion Road." She fans the book's pages, but that's the only piece of paper she has. "Is that not right?"

The driver puts the car in reverse. "No, no, that's certainly an address. You're going to White Hall, then? It's unusual for someone to be staying at the B and B this time of year." She catches Blake's eye in the rearview again and gives her a smile that's meant to be reassuring.

Blake isn't reassured.

She sits back against the seat and closes her eyes. That sense of surrealness—maybe even wrongness—increases. She can almost hear the old-timers in her Monday-night home group, can see them exchange knowing, disappointed looks as she trudges up to exchange her thirty-day medallion for yet another twenty-four-hour one. *We told you this was a bad idea,* they'll say, voices low, shaking their heads at her pallid complexion and trembling hands. *We told you not to go anywhere stressful, anywhere that would threaten your sobriety. There's a reason you're not supposed to make major life changes during the first year of recovery.*

Does this trip constitute a major life change? Only if it has a certain outcome. Otherwise, it's further proof of her inconsequentiality, her lack of belonging. And there would certainly be no change there.

Rain has been pummeling the windshield since they left the terminal, and the driver increases the speed of the wipers. The sound relaxes her, reminds Blake of the old droning chaos that used to vibrate within her skull. Too quickly, however, the driver is tapping the brake and bringing the wipers in line with the taxi's sudden crawl.

"I just pulled off Corn Neck Road, and I've got to take this part slow," the driver says. "Fiona keeps saying she wants to have Mansion Road paved, but Aileen insists it'll ruin the aesthetic. I'll tell you one thing that'll ruin White Hall's aesthetic a heck of a lot faster than fresh pavement, and that's someone careening off this mud path and over the side of the neck."

Blake has no idea what *over the side of the neck* means, or who Fiona is, though Aileen rings a bell as possibly the person with whom Blake corresponded to book her room. Any chance of replying to the driver is eliminated by her shock at the ghostly-white edifice ahead of them, looming up from the glistening, jumping pavement like a ship from a rippling sea.

It's framed by two brick entry pillars at least twenty feet high, each topped with a great stone globe. Beyond the pillars, white fences stretch the length of the drive, barely holding back forests of beach roses, switchgrass, winterberry, and arrowwood shrubs. The mansion itself is a pile of ornate splendor, entirely out of place on an island very much one with the culture of New England. It lords over the beach like an errant queen who's lifted her heavy skirts and settled down beside a neighborhood tavern. The mansion is split into two bilaterally symmetrical sides and separated by a massive three-story central hall. A domed cupola glares down from a dizzying height like an owl's static, yellow eye. Without question, that cupola has usurped the moon.

Blake tries to force the macabre comparisons from her brain. It probably doesn't help that she read a few chapters of *The Mysteries of Udolpho* on the ferry ride over. People—from her earliest caregivers at the orphanage to an endless rotation of foster parents, from boyfriends (and girlfriends) to various AA sponsors over the years—were always telling her to get her nose out of those melodramatic novels. And Blake can't deny she has a bit of a proclivity for the melodramatic. At seven hundred pages, even the physical book is melodramatic. But this is different. *This place* is different. The comparisons persist, no matter how hard she attempts to displace them.

It is the Castle of Otranto. Ambrosio's abbey. Manderley. Udolpho. Every setting from every novel that has held her rapt and terrified over the years. It will hold her within its walls until her reason for coming to the island disintegrates beneath her. It is claustrophobia and decay and tragedy too intense for her fragile, newly recovered self to take.

"It's rusticated wood," the taxi driver says, startling Blake from her dread-filled reverie. "Not stone like people think. It's what gives the mansion that ethereal glow. In 1890, when Edward Searles had it built for his wife, the architect dubbed it 'Dream House.' But everyone on the island has always called it White Hall. Or Searles' Folly. It's—" The taxi driver stops when she sees Blake's expression in the mirror. "Is everything okay?"

Blake pushes down the certainty that she should throw a few twenties into the driver's lap and beg her to turn around. "Fine," she says. "It's a little intimidating, that's all."

"It doesn't look like it does on the website, that's for sure. Not in February, anyway."

Blake can imagine the moment, at the end of summer, when cheerful, multicolored umbrellas disappear from the wide, white expanses of sand. She can see the ocean turn from blue to gray and screeching gulls replace friendly fishermen and bobbing boats. It's not the thought of Block Island in the winter that chills her, the isolation and bleak weather. It's that, now that she's here, that isolation feels like home.

"Well, don't worry," the driver continues cheerily as she pulls the taxi beneath a marble overhang at the mansion's entrance. The sudden cessation of rain makes Blake's left eye twitch and her head thrum with a warm, dull ache. "While the inside is just as overwhelming, it will be warm and quiet and dry. And Aileen will set you up right quick with a nice cup of mulberry tea."

Blake fishes a crumpled bill from her backpack, mumbles a thank-you, and climbs out of the car. She watches the driver maneuver the endless, flooded driveway until the taillights wink out beyond the pillars. Then, gripping the door handle with as much breathless trepidation as she would the next page of *The Mysteries of Udolpho*—which she swears she's not going to read another word of while on this island—Blake shrugs her bag higher onto her shoulder and opens the door.

Chapter 2

Ten minutes later, Blake is perched on the edge of a burgundy velvet settee. Her hostess, Aileen Searles, is going on about how it's such a horrible night for travel. Blake is only half listening, stealing glances back into the cavernous foyer, where twin mahogany staircases stretch up into the starry, diffuse light of a chandelier.

The hardwood in the parlor is of varying shades and types; Blake struggles to work out whether the patterns of light and dark form odd, long-petaled flowers across the floor. The flower shapes stretch beneath brocade chairs and entryway dressers with tarnished brass handles, darting out of and under her periphery, never existing in their whole, unbroken forms. When Aileen punctuates a question with her name, Blake is forced to pull her gaze from the floorboards. "Sorry, what was that?"

"I asked . . . ," Aileen says in a voice like pebbles dragged by the tide, "what brings you to Block Island in the dead of winter? As you can see, there aren't many people hankering for a room in the off-season."

Aileen gestures at the mansion around her, and Blake finds herself pulled away from their conversation yet again. The room, separated from another by frosted, multipaneled windows, seems to be breathing around them. A mantel clock beats from over a stone fireplace, and a second, smaller chandelier drips illumination from cloudy prisms. Above ornate oak paneling, wallpaper depicting farm life and woodland scenes creeps as if on a slow-moving conveyor belt. Blake squints against these intrusions and grits her teeth, focusing on the question Aileen has asked.

"It's kind of a long story." Her clothes haven't dried much from her sprint across the terminal, and she shivers.

"And listen to me, plying you for information while you sit here, soaked to the bone and chilled. If you're inclined to tell me, you can do so tomorrow." Aileen checks her watch. "It's past the normal time I serve dinner, but I can bring you up something small if you're hungry."

"I'm okay, Aileen, thank you."

"Then let's get you to your room. I put a fresh stack of towels on your bed before you arrived. They'd just come out of the dryer."

That the mansion would have something as modern as a dryer strikes Blake as unexpected, but she's not about to argue with the prospect of disappearing into the safety of a room free from questions and—with any luck—ticking clocks. She follows Aileen back into the foyer and up the right-hand staircase. Halfway up, her hostess nods at a black-and-white portrait; the woman captured within its frame wears a half-pernicious, half-playful expression. Her hair is glossy and pulled into three distinct, wavy coifs, and the bodice of her dress features satin buttons, gimp embroidery, and a collar of Alençon lace.

"Mary Frances Sherwood Hopkins Searles," Aileen says, a note of pride in her voice. "My great-great-grandaunt on our mother's side, sister to Great-great-grandmother Susanne. No Searles woman for five generations has changed her surname."

Blake's quad muscles burn as she continues to climb. The eyes of the woman in the portrait follow her up the stairs.

"Here we are," Aileen says, after they've reached the third floor and traversed a hallway as long as a fairground. She unlocks the door on the left.

"The rooms lock from the outside?" Blake asks. "Isn't that . . ." *Claustrophobia inducing?* ". . . weird?"

Aileen sighs, apparently used to being asked this question. "Weird for a B and B in this day and age? Yes. Weird for a mansion built in the nineteenth century? No. I'll be leaving the key with you, of course, and you can lock the room whenever you're not in it. There's a hook-and-eye latch on the other side of the door, and in addition to the towels, you'll find a bottle of mulberry wine on the nightstand."

At what must be Blake's deer-in-headlights expression, Aileen presses on. "You might not remember from the website, but White Hall is a fully functioning vineyard and winery in addition to a B and B. We have fifteen acres of mulberry trees and press about sixty-seven hundred gallons of wine a year."

Blake stumbles across the threshold and drops her bag onto the floor next to the bed. The bottle of wine sits harmlessly on the polished wood, the liquid inside so dark it appears almost black. Blake reaches out sluggishly, as if submerged beneath lake water summer-tepid and thick with sediment. The familiarity of her fingers around the bottle's neck causes a school of minnows to splash around in her gut.

Give it, her mind commands. *Hand it to the nice B and B propri-etress.* The bottle stays suspended in her sweaty fingers.

"If you'd like a different kind—" Aileen starts.

"It's not that."

"I know the dark hue can be a turnoff for some," Aileen continues.

Blake forces a measure of confidence—however thin—into her voice. "It's a nice gesture, but I won't be able to accept it. I gave up drinking. Recently, actually." Paradoxically, inexplicably, Blake does not extend her arm toward Aileen. The bottle remains six inches from her rib cage.

"Oh! I'm so sorry," Aileen exclaims. "Fiona—she's my sister—insists I take the nondrinkers into account, but I always forget to ask when taking reservations. Here, let me have that. I'll put it back in our storeroom right away."

Aileen's embarrassment and concern send shame ricocheting through Blake's chest. How is she going to navigate the painful conver-sation she came to Block Island to have if she can't even decline a bottle of wine without causing offense? She shakes her head and forces herself to meet Aileen's gaze.

"You know what? It's fine. Wine was never really my thing. It's not a problem to keep it in the room. I'll take it home when I check out, and it'll make a great gift the next time I'm invited to a party. I'll put it in one of those skinny foil bags like normal people do."

Aileen's dark eyes narrow. She's not exactly stout, but she's a solid woman, and when she places a hand on one hip, she gives the impression of a schoolmarm about to discipline a roomful of rowdy students. "Are you sure? It's no trouble to take it back to the storeroom. I'm down there several times a day as it is."

Blake forces a smile to her lips and walks deeper into the room, noticing for the first time the slightly musty smell of the mansion. The room's curtains have not been drawn, and the sight of the rain pelting the glass causes goose bumps to rise along her forearms. She places the bottle on the far left of a doily-covered lowboy, then smacks the wood beside it with an open palm to indicate the matter is closed.

"I'm certain," she says. "Honest. Don't trouble yourself thinking about it another minute." The sense that she is the heroine of a gothic novel returns to her unbidden.

She'd been eight when she'd read her first, a glossy-covered copy of *Jane Eyre* handed down to her by a girl who'd returned with it after an unsuccessful stint with foster parents. Blake wouldn't know it then—destined as she was to devour the battered, dog-eared copies from the sagging shelves that functioned as the orphanage library—but it would be the most pristine book she'd ever get her hands on. She'd read it by flashlight under the covers over two sleepless, transcendent nights, awestruck by both the cruelties Jane survived and the heights to which she aspired. From that moment, she was hooked, far from the first overlooked and neglected little girl to become lost in classic literature. Was it a cliché to have seen herself in Jane Eyre, or the eponymous Rebecca, or in *The Castle of Otranto*'s Isabella? Of course, but imagining herself as the heroines of those stories allowed Blake to survive her childhood.

She meant what she said to Aileen about having no intention of tapping into the wine, so why does she feel like Emily St. Aubert from *The Mysteries of Udolpho*, spirited up to the castle's highest chamber to await her inevitable undoing?

A scream rips loose in her mind, and she revels in its vibrations. Noise, whether real or imagined, blunts the edges of her sobriety-induced intrusive thoughts. When the unnerving silence returns a moment later, she walks toward the bed with feigned self-assuredness and lays her hand on the stack of fresh towels.

"Thank you again, Aileen. White Hall is a dream. That's what they used to call it, right? Dream House?"

Aileen titters, and Blake relaxes slightly, now that she's put the woman at ease. "I see Sarah Liang has been entertaining her passengers with White Hall lore and legend," Aileen says. "Yes, that was one of the mansion's many monikers." She takes a step back and gives an awkward little bow. "But I should let you rest. I sincerely hope you enjoy your time here, Miss Bronson. And remember, breakfast is served at eight."

Blake thanks her again, secures the rather flimsy hook-and-eye latch, and rests her forehead on the cool, carved wood of the door. It's only eight o'clock, but the darkness outside the windows is as thick as paint. Exhausted by a journey that began almost twelve hours earlier, Blake turns to the damask-patterned bedspread and flops down without taking off her jacket or shoes. She lets the drumming of the rain on the roof dispel the reel of the day. A minute passes. Then another. Blake falls asleep.

She dreams she is lost at sea in a bathtub, nothing in sight but endless black water. The ocean is a tempest beneath her, the sky a demon above. Cyclonic winds toss the tub about while torrential rain fills the makeshift raft. She sloshes water from the vessel, but the endless volley refuses to let up. Just as Blake decides to chance the waves rather than go down with the cast-iron coffin, something pulls her out of sleep and back to the bedroom.

The rain has already been relegated to the background, as innocuous as a landscape painting. Blake listens to the sounds of the room *beneath* the rain and blinks disorientation from grainy eyes. Before she can lift her head from the feathery pillow, a muffled click comes from across the room. This is it. The sound that roused her from sleep. Blake's blood turns as icy as she imagines the rain is. She takes a breath like inhaling smoke and pushes herself up in one smooth but terror-filled motion. The room is vague and shadow-steeped and creepier than the sum of its parts.

As Blake stares, a shape in the corner by the rolltop desk coalesces into the silhouette of a woman. Or, is there not a desk in that corner at all but a larger piece of furniture that would explain the upright figure? Blake can't remember the exact layout of the room. If it *is* a woman, she appears to be wearing long, full skirts and perhaps a veil to obscure her features. Blake stares so hard that the image gets blurrier rather than sharper. Just when she decides she's acting even dumber than usual, allowing herself to become frightened over nothing, a ghostly voice floats across the bedroom:

"Blaaaaaakke."

The silhouette glides backward, to where the room cuts into an L, and out of her sight. Blake gasps and scrambles from the bed.

"Aileen?" she calls in a hoarse whisper. "Is that you?" Maybe the woman gave her too many towels or forgot to leave a bar of soap. Latching on to this feeble explanation, Blake rushes forward and sees a hint of movement in front of the bathroom door, a change in depth as if the intangible shape has just passed through it. She lurches in that direction, both numb with fear and crackling with adrenaline. The door is angled so that she can see nothing of the inside of the room.

"Aileen?" she whispers again. No response.

Blake pushes open the door, practically trips over the threshold, and fumbles for the switch. A heartbeat later, the bathroom floods with bright, beautiful light. She scans the space once, twice, three times, four, her eyes unblinking and wild. Then, finally, she gains control of her breathing and stares at her own reflection in the gilded baroque mirror.

The room is empty and pristine, modest in relation to the rest of the mansion: just the mirror, a clawfoot bathtub, toilet, and sink. Four smooth walls of eggshell white, and no windows or doors besides the one she's come through. Blake can see every nook from floor to ceiling without turning her head. There's not even a cabinet in which someone could hide. Whatever black, shifty shape she saw—or imagined—is gone like a raven in the mist.

Blake turns off the light and crosses the room. She shrugs out of her jacket and kicks off her shoes. She pauses long enough to scowl at the bottle of wine on the dresser, then climbs onto the mattress and pulls the covers over her head.

Chapter 3

The next morning, Blake makes her way to the kitchen just after eight, following the smell of cinnamon and vanilla once she descends to the foyer. When she steps into the kitchen, she is struck yet again by the splendor—and antiquatedness—of her surroundings, as well as the idea that there might be guests besides her staying at the B and B. Aileen had said something about the lack of demand for rooms in the off-season, but how else to justify this lavish spread?

The stove stretches over a distance of at least twenty-five feet, with interconnected cast-iron vents extending up from each of five different ranges. On one, a bulging omelet sits like a tightly rolled haystack. On another, a teapot is leaking steam. Across the marble-topped island in the center—which matches the stove in length—bowls of fruit, baskets of muffins, and tiers of jellies, butters, and preserves tantalize Blake with mouthwatering colors and scents.

Aileen stands before an extralarge mixing bowl, whipping cream to spread over almond-encrusted french toast. She gestures to a sideboard behind her, and Blake responds with an involuntary *Ahh* at the sight of a coffeepot and waiting mug.

Aileen finishes whipping the cream and carries the bowl from the far-right range to the island. "The dining room is through those double doors," she says, and nods toward the back of the kitchen. "Make a plate. I'll join you in a moment."

Blake does as she's told, though her breakfast usually consists of little more than a cup of coffee and—up until a month ago—an unfiltered cigarette. The goat-cheese-and-asparagus omelet, hash browns fried to perfection, and grilled bagel with blueberry preserves look too delicious to resist. She carries her cup and plate through the doors and sets them down on a table that could accommodate every member of her AA group with room to spare. Aileen comes in with the french toast and a small platter of tea, milk, and honey. She pulls out the chair directly across from Blake.

At first, they sit in silence, slicing, spreading, and stirring their respective breakfasts. Blake looks up from her bagel and says, "This is to die for, Aileen. Really. It's not every day I get to eat in a room fit for a queen." She sips her coffee, keeping her hands around the cup despite the sting of the heat through the porcelain. "As delicious as everything is, the coffee's the best part."

Aileen dabs her mouth with a napkin, and when she looks up, her eyes widen ever so slightly, then narrow the way they did when Blake insisted on keeping the bottle of mulberry wine. "Us islanders are known for our bluntness, so I'll just come right out and say it: you look like you need the caffeine."

"I didn't sleep well last night," Blake admits.

"I hope it wasn't anything Fiona or I could have alleviated. Heat too high or water pipes too creaky? We actually have a couple of those sound machines lying around if you'd prefer whale song to the pops and echoes of a hundred-thirty-year-old mansion settling."

"Nothing like that," Blake assures her. "Though, I'm not sure I would have heard the water pipes even if they were creaky. Not through all that rain." She looks out the window. "I see not much has changed in that regard."

"It hasn't been all that cold of a winter, but the rain's been god-awful. I think this is the most I've seen in one stretch since I was skipping along in knee socks on my way to primary school." Aileen chuckles. "Thirty-some years ago."

Blake pushes away the rest of her bagel and takes a small bite of omelet. She regrets piling so much food onto her plate. The desire to refill her coffee and retreat upstairs is as intense as an opioid craving. The day has the potential to be the emotional equivalent of a torn Achilles, and she needs time to get her admittedly scattered thoughts in order and prepare.

Despite this, and despite hearing a voice in her head that sounds an awful lot like Chris, her sponsor—the leather-skinned, AA-adage-spouting South Boston woman whose years of sobriety exceed those that Blake has been alive—saying, *It's not only acceptable, but* preferable, *to leave well enough alone,* Blake puts her fork down, clears her throat, and says, "Aileen, you didn't happen to go into my room last night, did you? Maybe to drop off a bar of soap or, I don't know, check the heat, like you said?"

Aileen gives her a strange, searching look, as if she'll find her response in the curvature of Blake's face. "Fiona and I have a policy not to go into guests' rooms during their stay. Housekeeping and turndown service only leads to trouble when it's an operation as intimate as this."

Blake nods, and feels that rush of shame again. Why does she constantly do things that make her feel so foolish? "I understand." She grasps for something else to say, but Aileen is watching her more curiously than ever.

"Is something missing from your room? I'd be happy to help you look. This house has a habit of . . . obscuring belongings."

Of course it does, Blake thinks, *because it's not a house—it's the setting of a Radcliffe novel. Next she'll be telling me there's a ghost who haunts the attic, or a secret passageway beneath the foundation.*

"No, nothing like that," she says, because Aileen is waiting for an answer. "I thought I saw someone when I woke up from a nap. When I followed the woman—the shadow, really—into the bathroom, there was no one there."

Aileen's expression turns from inquiring to alarmed, and Blake's usual self-deprecating internal script grows more severe. Here she is, worried that Aileen and Fiona would think her unstable, yet the shape wasn't a shadow; it was an intruder! She allowed someone who broke into the mansion uncontested passage right through her room. So much for being clean and sober, for being responsible. She can't even rely on her own senses. Why is she such an idiot, so passive and oblivious? And then, the bitter conclusion, the point she always lands on eventually: *No wonder my mother gave me up for adoption.*

But Aileen's next utterance is neither accusation nor reprimand; it's a statement, matter-of-fact: "It sounds like you saw the resident ghost of White Hall. That of the great-great-grandaunt I was telling you about, Mary Hopkins Searles, who weeps tears of arsenic and mourns her long-lost love."

Blake sits back hard in her chair, one elbow coming close to knocking her mug from the table. She grabs for it, a flash of anger replacing her anxiety. A ghost, after all. Aileen must have seen the way she looked around the mansion, the way she worried that the rusticated wood and gilded surfaces might reflect the contents of her soul and manipulate the doubt there. Aileen is mocking her, working as a conduit for the mansion's self-serving objectives.

But Aileen's eyes are guileless, and her mouth smiles kindly. *Us islanders are known for our bluntness,* she had said. Is it possible Aileen *isn't* messing with her? Blake tempers the acidic words forming on her tongue, but her brain feels muddled. A door opens behind her, followed by sharp, quick footsteps. Blake turns to see a tall, slim woman marching over the marble toward them.

"Let's leave the ghost talk for later, eh?" Aileen whispers. Then, "Hey, Fi. What brings you to Wine Wing this early?" Aileen turns to Blake. "The staircases in the foyer go all the way up to a third-floor belvedere, separating the mansion into 'His' and 'Hers' wings. Each wing consists of an identical floor plan and eighteen identical rooms. I call this one Wine Wing, because it contains the entrance to the underground wine cellar. Fiona calls it Arsenic Wing because it's where Great-Great-Grandaunt Mary tried to poison her deceitful would-be lover with arsenic-spiked mulberry wine." She looks back at her sister and rolls her eyes. "Allegedly," she adds.

Despite a second reference to arsenic poisoning, Blake can focus on little more than the lack of physical evidence that the two women before her are sisters. Aileen has chestnut hair and hazel eyes. Fiona is blonde, blue-eyed, and fair-skinned. Though Blake admits they both have strong cheekbones and a rather prominent nose, these features give Aileen a harsh, rugged look, while Fiona appears polished, almost regal.

Having acknowledged neither Blake's presence nor Aileen's banter, Fiona looks at her watch. "I'm heading into town. Where's the outgoing mail?"

Aileen drains her tea, tosses her napkin on the table, and fixes Blake with a knowing smile. "Excuse me, Miss Bronson. There's a gorgeous old wooden letter organizer on the parlor wall that's held White Hall's outgoing mail since before the Prohibition era. If my sister's asking for our mail, it means she has other business matters with which to pummel me under the guise of locating the bills. Is there anything you need before I go? The number for a taxi or a map of the island?"

"I'm fine, thank you," Blake says, and picks up her mug. "I'll probably just take a refill on the coffee."

"Help yourself. Oh, and while we don't do lunch, dinner is served at seven thirty. Will seafood cioppino be okay?"

Blake nods and tries to smile, but the thought of having to make it through the next ten hours in order to return to this room for dinner produces an instant headache. Fiona walks out. Aileen gives a final wave and bustles out of the dining room after her sister.

Blake sits for several minutes, working up the energy to head to the kitchen for that second coffee. She hears the sisters' muffled voices, maybe in the foyer or by the parlor. It sounds like Fiona is angry. Did the trim, posh woman overhear Aileen trying to scare their only guest? Because that's what Aileen had been doing, right? Like those opportunists who turn real-life tragedies into tourist attractions—Lizzie Borden's

Fall River home comes to mind—to drum up interest in an otherwise straightforward place?

With a concentrated burst of effort, Blake stands, hooks a finger in the handle of her mug, and trudges toward the kitchen. She will bring her cup of—what does *The Haunting of Hill House*'s protagonist, Eleanor Vance, call it? Her cup of stars?—upstairs, and work out her plan for the rest of the morning. Though it doesn't feel like it in this moment, Blake knows she'll have more stamina for not having had a mimosa or Bloody Mary, knows she won't need a midafternoon nap or chemical pick-me-up to make it through the day. She focuses on this small victory as she carries her too-full cup (*of stars!*) up the mountain of stairs.

Yes, the mansion inspires disquiet, and yes, she feels as if she's trapped here, but Blake has never been one for believing in ghosts. The best gothic stories always have real-world explanations for the supernatural. Still, when she passes the painting of Mary Hopkins Searles, she keeps her eyes averted, too fearful she'll see something of last night's silhouette in the slope of the woman's neck or the bounce of her hair.

Chapter 4

Two hours after breakfast, two and a half decades after their last encounter, Blake is on the way to the restaurant at which her mother works. As the taxi—newer than last night's but manned by a driver far less interested in conversation—pulls onto Corn Neck Road, and White Hall recedes in the background, Blake can't help but feel as if she's escaped. It doesn't matter that there is nothing actually holding her at the mansion—nothing but her own ridiculous notions of moving wallpaper and sentient shadows. She fidgets and reminds herself that she has something far more pressing to consider.

"This is it?" Blake asks when they pull up in front of the restaurant, and the driver nods. She pays with a credit card, wanting to hold on to her cash in case she needs to make a quick departure. "Thanks," Blake says after the card is—mercifully—not declined. The driver takes off the moment Blake shuts the door. Without an umbrella, she has no choice but to go inside.

A bell above the door announces her entrance, and while there are a few waitresses milling about, only the hostess is inclined to turn her head. "Table for one?" she asks. When Blake concurs, she leads her to a small table in the corner of the restaurant.

Martin's Above the Rocks sits—true to its name—above a section of particularly rocky coastline. There are framed, old-fashioned portraits on the wall that remind Blake of the one hanging above White Hall's stairs. Brass lanterns throw shafts of light across the bar, and there's a large oval mirror mounted horizontally above the shelves of scotch and whiskey. The mirror reflects the lantern light, causing the whole bar to hum with an arresting amber glow. The floor and tables are dark wood, and gray brick curls around tall arched windows. There's a fireplace cut into a back wall, the stone of which juts and stretches like distorted faces.

It takes a second for Blake to determine what unsettles her about the restaurant, but the candelabra and velvet-backed chairs decide it for her: it's as if a section of White Hall successfully liberated itself from the mansion but was stopped above the jagged, salt-worn jetty before it could escape the island. Blake feels as if she can't breathe here, let alone ask questions that have been more than two decades in the making.

"Something to drink?" an impatient voice asks, and Blake jumps. She searches the waitress's face, but it's not her mother.

"A Coke, I guess."

"That it?"

"And . . ." Blake feels the morning's breakfast, heavy as driftwood, in her stomach, but she needs a reason to sit here long enough to figure out if her mother is working. "A slice of cherry pie?"

The waitress takes her menu. "Be back in a few."

Before she turns to head for the kitchen, Blake glimpses the waitress's name tag. "Annie? This might be an odd question, but is Maureen Mills working today?"

As soon as the words are out of her mouth, Blake cannot believe she's said them. She wasn't planning on drawing attention to herself until she observed Maureen long enough to get a feel for her general demeanor. Maybe her birth mother is as curt as this woman is. Maybe she loathes talking about her personal life while at the restaurant. Maybe the digging Blake did back in Boston was completely misguided, and Maureen doesn't work here at all.

Annie's expression shifts from impatient to distrustful. Blake's inhalations are tiny waves cut short by an outgoing tide. "I'm staying at

White Hall," she blurts out. "Aileen said that she knew Maureen and to tell her she said hi."

The waitress's lips remain twisted, and her eyebrows crease. "That's funny," she says. "It's been two leap years since I've laid eyes on Aileen, but Fiona's in here every day. I wonder, if Aileen wanted someone to say hi to Maureen for her, why she didn't have her sister do it."

Blake lets out a little grunt as if to agree that yes, Aileen's actions were incredibly funny. She looks around before remembering she just placed her order, and there's nothing on the table with which to busy her hands. "Does Fiona work here too?" she asks, knowing she's making it worse but unable to help herself.

Annie snorts. "She owns White Hall; she's got more money than God. Even if she didn't, Martin would never let her work at the restaurant." She gestures at the sign, visible out the windows. "*Martin's* Above the Rocks. Fiona is Martin's girlfriend."

So much for keeping a low profile. "I see," Blake says ridiculously. "I'm not sure why Aileen said to say hi to Maureen then. Maybe I misunderstood her."

"Maybe," Annie says, and raises an eyebrow. "At any rate, Maureen is right over there."

Blake nods woodenly and watches Annie go. She *feels* the woman Annie pointed to in her periphery rather than sees her. Tears well in Blake's eyes, and, keeping her chin angled so they don't fall, she turns her head.

Maureen Mills stands before a table, taking a couple's order. She is of average height, with sharp, bony shoulder blades that tent the black fabric of her collared dress shirt. She wears scuffed leather shoes and tailored black pants. Her hair is the exact same shade of brown that Blake's was before she dyed it. Though the couple is talking at length and pointing to the menu, Maureen doesn't write anything down. Dark liner rims her eyes, and she is pretty but weary-looking. Blake tries to conjure up the memory of this woman looking down at her in a fluorescent-lit delivery room, the feeling of Maureen's arms around her, and then the void their absence creates when she is pulled away. But of course, these efforts are in vain.

Without warning, Maureen spins from the table and walks in Blake's direction. Blake's throat closes, and her hands flutter like startled birds. Her brain is caught between fight and flight; should she push herself up from the table and run, or wait to see if Maureen talks to her? In her jerking indecision, she sends a napkin-wrapped set of utensils flying across the table and onto the floor.

Blake doesn't lean down to retrieve it so much as she collapses against her knees, and when she sits back up, Maureen has passed. She is entering something on the computer screen across from the hostess station. Blake releases a sigh she's been holding since she was six and first understood the concept of adoption. Annie appears from nowhere, sets down a sweating glass, and strides away without saying anything.

Blake sucks down cold, greedy mouthfuls of soda, the wish that it was something stronger blooming in her blood and traveling, like an infection, to her brain. When she sits back, lantern light dances over the bar, the flickering shadows inverting her vision like the instant after a flash of lightning. A black shape, like a shadow, like the specter from her room the night before, materializes. Blake looks up to find that Maureen is on the move, coffeepot in hand. She passes Blake a second time and goes to a table in the opposite corner.

"Hello, Tom," Maureen says to the elderly gentleman staring out the window. "How's the coffee treating you? Want me to warm her up?"

Tom lifts his gaze. "That'd be nice," he replies, and holds the cup out with a shaky, liver-spotted hand.

Maureen takes the cup in order to top it off, then places it down before him. "There you are," she says, and Blake feels a tug in her chest at the warmth in her mother's voice. "How's Angie doing?" Maureen continues. "Her and Josh moved to Framingham, I heard. You see your grandkids lately?"

The old man smiles so broadly, Blake can see the sheen of his wet, pink gums. He nods over and over, closing his eyes while he gathers his thoughts. Maureen waits for him with the patience only a waitress—or a mother—could muster. Though, as Blake watches, Maureen's eyelids flutter and her head dips slightly. It's a gesture she's seen a thousand times in clinics and AA meetings, the "nod" of an addict who's partaken in some sort of downer, though, of course, Maureen must be overcome with exhaustion rather than narcotics.

"I have," Tom says finally, in a voice full of pride. "Boy, are they something else. In college now, all of them. Even the youngest. It cheers—and breaks—my heart to see it. But you'll be getting a taste for what that's like soon enough. How old's your daughter now? Going to be having kids of her own soon, I bet."

Blood whooshes in Blake's ears. This man knows about her! How? The taste of cola goes sour on her tongue. Is he someone special to her mother, to where she has told him of her family? Or does everyone on Block Island know Maureen Mills has a daughter?

"Oh, Thalia," Maureen sighs. "She's twenty-nine. Who knows when that daughter of mine is going to settle down. She's been in Massachusetts, what, ten years now? She never comes back to see me."

Blake's body goes cold.

Maureen shifts the coffeepot from one hand to the other, orienting herself slightly toward the kitchen. Blake sees her catch the eye of a young, aproned woman balancing two salads on a tray. *One sec,* Maureen mouths, and the bus girl nods.

"But that's not the worst thing we could do, is it, Tom?" Maureen says, patting the elderly man's arm with affection. "Getting a kid off the island?" Her tone is light, but Blake catches something darker, more serious, in her words. Maureen's eyelids flutter again, ever so slightly, and she starts to walk toward the bus girl. "Enjoy your coffee," she calls over her shoulder. Blake averts her gaze.

Thalia. Thalia. Thalia. Who knows when that daughter of mine is going to settle down. Thalia, Thalia, Thalia! The restaurant spins around her. Her palms are sweat-slicked, and though her mouth is a beach baked by a noonday sun, she isn't sure she can order her muscles to guide the glass to her lips. She needs to focus. Needs to make sense of this. Of Maureen Mills's other (*only!*) daughter. Maureen Mills's older daughter. Nowhere in her research had Blake come across evidence that she had a sister.

During a prior short-lived period of sobriety, Blake saved the almost ninety dollars for an AncestryDNA kit, but when she reached out to her only match—a second cousin—the woman never messaged her back. Several years later, on a cocaine binge in Providence with a man she met at an NA meeting, Blake discovered her hookup-of-the-moment worked in the Vital Records Department of City Hall.

All Blake's foster homes had been in Rhode Island, and she always figured that—with two major hospitals in the city—the odds of her sealed birth certificate being somewhere in Providence were the greatest. Now, as at the time of their interaction, Blake likes to focus on the (heavily cut) bags of cocaine with which she bribed the vital records worker as opposed to the other favors she granted him. Ironically, she'd found out only later that Rhode Island was one of ten states that granted orphans the unrestricted right to their birth certificates once they turned eighteen. Either way, it was worth it when he handed her the record. The record she now carries in a protected, inner pocket of her backpack.

Even with her birth mother's name, Maureen had been hard to find. Blake finally located her via a property records search in Block Island after exhausting every other town and city in the state. Still, nowhere in her search for "Maureen Mills" had a "Thalia Mills" surfaced.

Blake strains to recall the pages of records. Was it there, in the countless internet searches, and she hadn't looked hard enough? Or had the fact that she'd lubricated her trips to the library with Percocet and vodka meant she'd simply missed this detail completely? Blake wilts with self-disgust that she could overlook such a vital piece of information. At least the discovery of her mother had helped instigate her return to Alcoholics Anonymous. This momentary respite from shame is overshadowed by another question. If Maureen Mills had *two* daughters, what reason could she possibly have had for only keeping one? Who keeps one daughter but gives away the second as if they were donating a goddamn sweater?

The tinkle of glassware and muffled conversation distend into a roaring, angry ocean. Blake stands on seasick legs and zeros in on the exit. The rain has never looked so inviting. She can disappear into it, slip beneath its cover of mist and silence. She remembers to throw cash on the table for the soda and pie, then starts, head down, across the dining room. Maureen Mills does not reappear by the time Blake makes it to the door.

She does, however, look up to find Fiona Searles staring at her from a dimly lit hallway. Beside her stands a tall, dark-haired man in a black jacket. Fiona says something to the man, and his eyes flick to her quickly, but then his gaze returns to Blake. Those eyes are dark and unreadable, and they shine at her like black seashells winking out from a stretch of pale sand.

Chapter 5

Blake walks the length of the beach across from Martin's Above the Rocks until her sneakers are caked with sand and flecks of seaweed. She can't determine where her tears end and the rain sluicing mascara from her eyes begins. A colony of seals lies on the sand, heads cocked in what seems like judgment. She cuts to the street, pulling out her phone with the idea to call another taxi, but changes her mind and pushes it back into her pocket. The dreadful wind and rain are keeping her tethered to the earth. Without them, she fears she'll float out of her skin and up over the island like a discarded balloon.

She walks the three miles to White Hall as desperate as she's ever felt. She went to the restaurant hoping to find justification—however trivial—for introducing herself to her mother. Instead, she's come away feeling as if this trip was the worst idea of her life. No wonder she spent her childhood being shuffled from one unloving foster home to another; Blake has met lots of people from whom drugs and alcohol had robbed all reason, but she has to be the stupidest person who's ever endeavored to get sober.

Did she think she was going to introduce herself to her mother twenty-six years after she was born and say, *I know you gave me up for adoption, but can we build a relationship?* She had, up until the moment Maureen had uttered another woman's name after the words *daughter of mine.* That her birth mother had kept a daughter before her, a daughter over whom—regardless of whether she saw her often or not—she'd maintained maternal rights, means Blake's prospective conversation with Maureen is elevated to another level of volatility.

So Blake walks, letting the rain numb her. The sky is a luminous periwinkle rimmed white along the horizon, and the wind blows excess water off the blades of beach grass that line the road. By the time White Hall grows up from the tangle of island fauna, Blake is trembling and her skin is raw.

Before she steps inside, something flashes to her left. It's a man, hunched against the rain and dressed in thick, dark clothing. Water drips from his long beard and the ends of his disheveled, shoulder-length brown hair. He doesn't wave. He doesn't smile. He stares at Blake from beneath a dogwood tree. Unsettled, she raises her hand in greeting, but the man turns and skulks away. She watches the trees, but he doesn't reappear.

Inside, the foyer is empty, but before Blake can reach the stairs, Aileen appears in the arched doorway of the parlor. Blake's face burns with humiliation at her bedraggled appearance.

"I . . . ," Blake says, but tears spring to her eyes.

Aileen nods, as if a nervous breakdown from her only B and B guest is expected. "Go change into something dry," she says kindly, "and meet me in the kitchen. I'll make something hot to drink."

Blake climbs the stairs, turning in the wrong direction before realizing the mansion's mirror-image wings have tricked her. She backtracks and trudges to her door. Inside the stuffy chamber, she changes into a sweatshirt and soft black leggings, but the dry clothes don't make her feel any better. On top of everything else, she feels the presence of the wine on the dresser as keenly as if there's another person in the room.

Why didn't I return the bottle to Aileen when I had the chance?

One hand is on the doorknob when her cell phone vibrates. An unknown number parades across the screen. Blake swallows an exasperated groan and answers the phone.

"Who's this?" She tries to sound businesslike rather than flustered but fails as miserably as she does at everything else.

"Angela Lynch."

Blake says nothing, and the woman continues, "Your court-appointed lawyer."

Shit. "Of course. How can I help you?" Why did she pick up?

"I'm calling with an update on your case. Mr. Stevenson and his son are doing better. Mr. Stevenson had a third surgery yesterday, this one to insert a plate into his leg where the bone was crushed. There will be additional surgeries, and months of physical therapy, but the doctors believe he'll walk again."

Blake swallows and nods, then realizing the woman can't see her, says, "Good." The word is a croak, so she tries again. "Good. I'm really glad to hear it."

"Still, I'm not sure his recovery will have the effect you hoped for. Mr. Stevenson's lawyer is pushing for the maximum sentence."

Blake sinks onto the bed. "And what would that be?"

"If you're convicted of a DUI with serious bodily injury, and the case is charged as a felony—a possibility, due to the graveness of Mr. Stevenson's injuries—it's six months to ten years in state prison. It would also be a two-year revocation of your driver's license and fines of up to five thousand dollars."

Blake's vision goes black except for a pinprick of light at the center. The lawyer's voice is coming to her as if from under a dozen layers of sand. She forces herself to loosen her grip on the phone.

"You're lucky in that you have no DUI criminal history. A misdemeanor conviction on this charge will have slightly increased penalties as compared to a standard DUI, but far less than those for a felony."

Blake whispers, "I understand."

"The date for your preliminary hearing is next Monday at nine a.m."

"I thought every division of Boston's court system was backed up, like, a year."

"They are. Apparently, Walton Stevenson's brother is a judge in Essex County."

Of course he is. She stifles a bark of manic laughter. She has to get off the phone before this lawyer figures out how unstable she is. "I see. Monday at nine, then. I'll be there."

"If you weren't, it wouldn't go well for you."

"Is that everything?"

"Everything for now, Miss Bronson."

Blake hangs up and pushes her phone under a pillow. Shrieking brakes and imploding metal threaten to encroach on the silence of her sober mind. The wind picks up, and the walls of the mansion groan.

I know you're hungry, she tells the house. *So what are you waiting for? Part the floorboards and swallow me.* Another laugh threatens to bubble up the dry corridor of her throat. *Get it together.* She pulls a shiny new journal from her bag and jots down the day and time of her court date. The exercise calms her, and she gives Chris—who gifted her the journal—a begrudging nod of respect. She places the journal on top of the brick of *The Mysteries of Udolpho* and pushes the stack to the back of the nightstand drawer.

Blake descends the two flights of steps at a jog and arrives, out of breath, in the kitchen. Without the lights on above the stove, or the colorful array of fruits laid out for breakfast, it's a dimmer, more melancholy place. Aileen drags a stool over to the island and entreats Blake to sit while she fills the kettle.

"I saw a man outside," Blake says to fill the silence. "Did another guest check in?"

Aileen's forehead wrinkles, then smooths. "Ah, that would be Monty Daniels. Our resident groundskeeper and overall handyman."

"I waved, but he ignored me."

"He's a little standoffish with guests but friendly enough once you get to know him. He's probably salty due to this weather." She drags a second stool across from Blake's and groans as she climbs onto it. "And aren't we all? A real gully washer it's been as of late. My back's hell in this dampness, like a tree trunk that's liable to snap. But enough about me. I asked last night what brought you to Block Island in the dead of winter, and I had a feeling it was something important. Now you show up this afternoon looking like you've been tossed around the yacht basin of Old Harbor."

Aileen reaches for the tea tray and organizes it so that every other label is upside down, allowing the tea bags to fit more closely together. "You want to tell me what's going on?" she asks, after Blake has become almost hypnotized by the flicking movements of her fingers. "I'm a real good listener."

A gust of wind rattles a windowpane. Blake wants to retreat inside herself, yet she's also tired of carting this mammoth secret. She wants to heave it into someone else's lap, if only for a moment. She's a storm cloud that wants to *rain*.

So Blake tells Aileen Searles why she came to Block Island. She tells her of the thirty-day AA chip—the longest stretch she's had—and of the way sobriety has turned her feelings over being given up at birth from the drawn-out pain of a daily dose of poison to the bite of a sharpened razor blade across a vein. She tells her she wanted to know her mother, wanted answers, wanted some sort of explanation for who she is, for who she might someday be. But then she went to that off-putting, off-kilter restaurant, and everything—her hope for an even remotely positive outcome—changed in the space of a sentence.

She doesn't tell her about hitting Walton Stevenson and his seven-year-old son while the man was in the breakdown lane changing a tire, or the phone call from her lawyer. Blake wishes this is because she isn't sure *what* to think, but deep down, she knows hitting Walton is why she's sober in the first place. The accident was akin to her letter from a mysterious baron, her invitation to a strange castle in a foreign land, the inciting incident for the narrative that—even now—is unfolding.

Blake dabs her eyes with her sleeve. "I feel like this house, this mansion, knows why I've come here. It feels, I don't know, foreboding or something. Like it's enlisted even the weather to conspire against me. I know that sounds stupid."

"It doesn't. I feel that way sometimes myself. Like this place surmises the secrets of each person who stays in its rooms."

Blake manages a weak smile. Aileen reminds her a little of the addicts she's met in the basement of Saint Monica's Parish. Say what you want about their pasts, but no one listens without judgment quite like another member of AA. Though, maybe Aileen's not *entirely* without scrutiny; she is looking at Blake sort of funnily.

"Do you know Maureen?" Blake asks, anxious to shift the subject away from doomed-damsel-in-creepy-castle.

"Everyone knows everyone on this island. But I don't know her well, and I'll tell you something else, I sure don't remember a scandal—how old did you say you were, twenty-six?—twenty-six years ago, any instance of Maureen being pregnant and then there not being a baby. I know she had a fling with a tourist from the mainland that resulted in Thalia, the daughter you heard her mention. You know . . ." Aileen trails off. "Never mind."

"Please, if there's anything you can tell me, I need to know."

"That's just it, see. *I* can't tell you anything. But there might be someone who can." Before Aileen can get any further, the whistle of the teakettle lifts her from her seat.

Blake grits her teeth until the scream dies away and Aileen pours the boiling water. When she finally sits again, Blake cannot keep the impatience from her voice. "You were saying there might be someone who can help me?" She pauses, then says, "Just to be clear, I'm trying to limit the number of people who know why I'm here. Maureen must've kept me a secret for a reason. I don't want to upset her by allowing that secret to get out."

"I understand. And I'm only saying I know someone who's privy to an awful lot about everyone on the island," Aileen clarifies. "You could ask him your questions, and he might be able to help you decide if introducing yourself to your mother is a good idea."

"Who is it?" Blake asks. She grabs her mug. Tea sloshes over the edge, but she makes no move to wipe it up. "Where can I find him?"

"It's Martin," Aileen says. "Owner of Martin's Above the Rocks and about a dozen other businesses and properties around the island. He's the town selectman and owns the *Block Island Times*, our modest fifty-year-old newspaper. If anyone's going to tell you anything worth knowing about Maureen Mills, it's Martin Dempsey."

"I saw him when I was leaving the restaurant," Blake says. "At least, I assumed that's who it was. He was standing with your sister, and he looked less than thrilled by my presence."

Aileen waves a hand. "Martin and Fiona have the same personality. I call it the three *a*'s: *aloof*, passive-*aggressive*, and *always* right." She cackles. "Sometimes I change it to the four *a*'s, and throw *asshole* into the mix. Anyway, he was just here with Fiona, but he left right after you got back. Said he was heading over to the *Times* to touch base with his editor. If you went there now, you could probably catch him."

"I'd have to wait for another taxi," Blake says.

"You can borrow the Jeep."

"Why the he—" She swallows the expletive. "Why would you do that for me?"

Aileen pushes back her stool and busies herself clearing their tea things. "It's hardly a monumental act of charity," she says. "And besides, it's miserable out." She glances at Blake's hair, which still falls in wet waves across her shoulders. "Take the car. I'm not going anywhere in this weather."

It's been two leap years since I've laid eyes on Aileen. That's what Blake's waitress had said this morning. The B and B proprietress doesn't seem like a woman about town. Blake wonders why Aileen owns a car at all. Still, she hears the voice of her sponsor, Chris, grumbling in her ear: *Don't look a gift of recovery in the mouth.*

"Thank you," Blake says. "That's very kind. I'll be extra careful in this weather and get the car back as soon as possible."

Aileen waves her hand again. "As long as you ask first—and Fiona's not around—I don't care if you use the car for the duration of your stay."

Blake's heart swells with gratitude for this woman she wasn't sure she'd liked upon first meeting. "Thank you again. I can't tell you how much I appreciate this." She doesn't bother asking why Fiona shouldn't be present if she's going to borrow the vehicle. There are probably insurance liabilities to consider, and it's clear Fiona is the pragmatic one while Aileen's the sister who keeps things lively and pleasant. Blake stands. Aileen goes to a drawer and removes a set of keys.

"There's a built-in GPS in the dash. I'd write the address for the *Times* down, but it's 123 Ocean Avenue. Next to impossible to forget."

Blake laughs. She feels lighter than she has since before last evening, when she stepped off the ferry and into a world where the rain never stopped and mothers were brutes who auctioned off their children. No matter that Martin might not be able to tell her anything; she has hope. A sliver of a chance with Maureen.

When she slides into the front seat of Aileen's boxy Jeep, she is further buoyed by the sight of a sturdy-looking umbrella on the passenger-side floor and a fleece-lined black jacket draped over the console. This will be the start of her journey, then. A new beginning. Armed with a little knowledge and protection from the elements, she can meet her past head-on.

Chapter 6

The *Block Island Times* offices are like everything else Blake has seen on the island besides White Hall and the interior of Martin's restaurant: weathered, tiny, and quaint. A black sign with gold lettering informs Blake she's in the right place. An American flag waves wetly in the wind. Blake parks, pockets the keys, and after a moment's hesitation, shrugs into the fleece-lined jacket. It's ill-fitting but better than nothing. She looks longingly at the umbrella, but it's a short distance to the front door, so she jumps out, darts up the ramp, and ducks inside.

The reception area is quiet and unlit. Blake is wondering what to do next when a door to her left opens, and the man she saw standing with Fiona in the back of Above the Rocks saunters into the room. He is even taller than she first thought—well over six feet—with dark, slightly bushy eyebrows. His hair, brushed back from his wide, smooth forehead, is thick and full. Blake guesses him to be about fifty. His cheekbones are high and his face is clean-shaven.

"Thanks again, Earl," Martin calls and shuts the door behind him. He checks his phone, slips it into his pocket, and looks up. His expression betrays no surprise at the sight of Blake.

"I'm Blake Bronson."

"I know who you are."

"I'm staying at White Hall and—"

"I know that too."

Blake is unsure what to say next. Martin sighs and gestures to the right-hand door. "Aileen told me you were on your way. Come inside."

His office is cozy and functional, devoid of the dark, ornate decor of his eponymous restaurant. "Thanks so much for seeing me," she says. "I'm not sure if Aileen told you *what* I wanted to see you about, but—"

"That, she didn't tell me."

Before she can lose her nerve, Blake blurts the whole thing out for the second time that day. She manages to keep her eyes dry and her emotions in check. When she's finished, she studies Martin's face. There is something familiar and—despite the aloofness about which Aileen warned her that is very much present—oddly comforting about him. Martin reaches for a stainless-steel water bottle and sips at length. When he places it back on the desk, his eyes seem a little softer, his mouth a little less pursed.

"What a thing, to have overheard you have a sister who wasn't given up," he says with quiet contemplation. "And after you've come all this way and shown such bravery."

In an instant, Blake's hackles are up; this is the kind of sarcastic comment an old-timer would make to a trust-fund baby who shows up at AA and whines about drinking away Daddy's booze money.

But then, Martin looks her in the eye and says, "I can relate to your dilemma more than you know. My own mother abandoned my family when I was a boy. She went for a coffee, got on the ferry, and we never saw her again. My father more than made up for her absence, teaching my brother and me how to be men, to make the most of what the Dempseys—architects and entrepreneurs—had built on this island over the last century.

"Some women don't understand the importance of family, of roots. That's one of the reasons I've always admired the Searles sisters so much, keeping up their ancestral home the way they have. Those women have grit, and that mansion above the bluffs? Heritage. True staying power. History."

Blake feels relief that she is not the butt of a joke, as well as a pang of sadness. Another AA euphemism: you can never tell someone's story by looking at them. She nods her head in solidarity.

"As owner of Above the Rocks, I've known Maureen a long time," Martin continues. "She's been employed there, believe it or not, for the past twenty-seven years, since right after my father transferred ownership of the restaurant to me."

This math doesn't require a feat of mental gymnastics to complete. "She was working at the restaurant when she had me? You must remember her being pregnant, then. Did she take a leave of absence? Did she tell anyone the details of the delivery? Do you know why she didn't keep me?"

"I'm sorry," Martin says, shaking his head. "But I don't know. I seem to remember Maureen taking a leave of absence, but I believe it was to go to the mainland to care for an ill relative."

"Is there anything about Thalia you could tell me?"

Martin hesitates, and Blake closes her eyes. She shouldn't be so pushy. She doesn't need this man—who, like Aileen, has expressed an inexplicable willingness to help her—thinking she's some kind of stalker. "I'm sorry," she says. "We just met. The last thing I want is to put you in an uncomfortable situation. If you don't want to give me Thalia's full name or where she lives, I understand."

"It's not that. It's just, again, I'm not sure. But I know someone who might have that information. How long are you staying for? Can you give me a day to reach out and try to get you Thalia's address?"

"Of course," Blake breathes. "Absolutely." If meeting her mother doesn't work out, getting her sister's address would make the trip at least somewhat worthwhile. She'll give Martin whatever he needs in repayment for his kindness, though she doesn't say so, fearing, again, what he might think of her.

"In the meantime, I have another idea." Martin checks his watch. "Would you care to take a drive?"

Chris would be furious if presented with a list of decisions Blake has made since leaving Boston, and it does occur to her, as she climbs into Martin's pickup truck—now with Aileen's umbrella in hand—that going to an undisclosed location with a man she just met isn't high on the list of great ideas. Still, he owns the most popular restaurant in town along with, what had Aileen said? A slew of other businesses and properties? She isn't sure why he's helping her—even taking their mutual abandonment issues into account—but murdering her seems unlikely. She needs only to silence Chris's voice in her head, stay vigilant, and go along for the ride.

Martin says nothing during the short drive, and the volume on the radio is muted. The rain beats insistent, probing patterns on the windshield. He pulls up in front of a white-pillared inn, the name—Graham's Resort—of which Blake is surprised to recognize. It's a popular spot for Bostonians who want to experience the thrill of an island vacation without having to leave New England.

"Sit tight," Martin says and goes around to open the passenger side. He gestures at the umbrella, she opens it, and they hustle for the door.

The bar is seasonal; that much is obvious. The shelves are empty of bottles and the floor clear of tables and stools. She trails Martin through a door at the back of the barroom and down a long, musty-smelling hallway. He ducks through another door, and they come out into the inn's lobby, everything done up in wicker and royal blue. Martin raps his hand on the wall and, belying the stillness of the building, a man's voice hollers back, "One second."

"Keep your enemies close," Martin whispers and grins. Blake is taken aback by the heretofore unseen charm that animates his face. "Graham's is the biggest source of competition for Above the Rocks," he explains, "so Timmy Graham and I have a real give-and-take kind of relationship."

A door behind the front desk opens, and a bearded man in green plaid flannel steps out. Expressions ripple over his face like the tide. Surprise is one of them; distaste might be another. The expression he settles on is a curious sort of amusement.

"Martin, buddy. It's been a while. What can I do you for?"

"Hey, Timmy. Sorry to bother you, but this young lady and I need to take a look at the guest book. You still keep it in the honeymoon suite with the other relics?"

Timmy swivels to a wall of keys behind a glass partition. He opens it, selects a key from the top left, and holds it out to Martin, but his mouth twists into an unexpected leer. "'Looking at the guest book,' huh? Is that what the kids are calling it these days?"

Blake stiffens. Is that what this looks like, a clandestine hookup? But no, Martin's already waving the resort owner off. "Watch yourself, Timothy Graham," he says.

Timmy shrugs indifferently. "You're right. Not my place to ask questions of New Shoreham's town selectman."

Martin leads Blake away from the desk and toward an elevator. "Thanks for being so accommodating," he calls back, and there's a finality in his tone. Timmy must take the hint because he doesn't say anything further.

Martin pushes the button for the third floor. "I told you," he says once the doors had closed, "Timmy and I have an interesting relationship." Blake is bursting with questions but senses Martin's already moved on from the interaction in the lobby to the task at hand. His demeanor is that of someone about to perform a trick or unveil a long-planned surprise.

The elevator spits them out into a carpeted vestibule, and Martin leads her to where the hallway curves sharply back toward the inn's center. They pass a half-moon window with a stunning view of the seal-gray ocean. Martin stops at a door just past the window and inserts the key into the lock.

For a second, Blake's earlier fear assails her. She's a fool to have followed Martin here. Years of substance abuse have rendered intuition and self-preservation nonexistent. But then Martin is holding open the door, and she's stepping into the room. Too late to turn back now.

Like the captain's quarters of a ship, the suite is all gleaming maple, porthole paintings, and shiny brass and copper. There are glass-encased shelves on the walls as if they've entered a museum. Maps of Montauk, Martha's Vineyard, and Nantucket are centered over the bed, dresser, and love seat, respectively. A copper diving helmet stares down from a stand like a sentinel.

"His old man used to have this stuff displayed in the lobby, but the first thing Timmy did when he took over was move everything up here to the honeymoon suite. Now tourists pay a bigger premium for the nicest room in the inn, and these documents and artifacts don't get trashed by every drunk frat boy hoping to win a bet." He points to a podium along the right wall. Set atop it is an enormous leather-bound book, the word *Guests* embossed in gold on the cover.

"It was sort of a joke when Timmy and I were college-aged," he says. "Guys would book a room for their dates and sign the guest book so everyone else could see who they, well, conquered." He looks at the floor. "Excuse my idiotic, early-twenties self, Miss Bronson."

Blake raises the hand not holding her umbrella as if to say, *No harm, no foul.* She's heard far worse at twelve-step meetings.

"The tradition spread," Martin continues. "What can I say? It's an island. There are only so many ways to get one's kicks. A lot of people have signed that book, and I thought . . ." He trails off, looking unsure of himself. "It's probably a dead end, but when you asked me if I remembered Maureen being pregnant, something sparked in my memory. At first, I couldn't figure what it was, but then I recalled one night at the restaurant when I was helping my dad close up. Timmy and another guy came in, completely hammered, saying they'd been drinking at Graham's. Maureen Mills had appeared in the lobby with a man they didn't recognize and was about to sign the infamous book."

Martin nods at the guest book when he says this, and a frisson of anticipation courses through Blake's body. This isn't what she expected, but she's not about to say no. Her feet remain rooted to the helm-and-anchor-patterned floor, despite her brain's orders for them to carry her across the carpet. Is she mere seconds away from seeing her mother's *and* her father's names etched into a decades-old book?

Finally, she drops the umbrella, lurches forward, and, once moving, careens toward the podium so fast she almost bowls it over. She steadies herself, inserts a finger between brittle pages, and wrestles the giant book open. 2005. 1997. 1984. She's flipped back too far. 1992. She backtracks, mere months away. Then weeks. Then days.

Nine months before she was born would have been around the end of July 1991. She goes backward through the month, not sure exactly what she's looking for. M. Mills? M.M.? She gets to the last day of June without seeing anything that resembles her mother's name. Despair, black as tar, fills her lungs. She can't breathe. Then, on her second scan, she spies it, two weeks into July.

The words are in a looping scrawl of thick blue ink. The same person wrote the entire entry, though there are two names listed: *Maureen Mills, a.k.a. the Mulberry Maiden, and her Doting, Dashing Lover.* Blake manages a shallow breath and grips the podium beneath the guest book. She will not cry. She will not black out.

"Did you find something?" Martin asks. He's cautious, hesitant to intrude on whatever Blake is experiencing.

Blake takes another breath. "Maureen Mills, a.k.a. the Mulberry Maiden," she reads aloud. "What does that mean? What's a Mulberry Maiden?"

Martin leans over to examine the entry, then straightens and rubs the side of his head. "I'm not sure," he admits, and Blake steps back, defeated. "Though, by now you probably know White Hall includes fifteen acres of mulberry trees," Martin continues. "It's been a functioning winery for as long as I can remember. I don't recall Maureen having any connection to the mansion or the Searles sisters. You said you told

Aileen that Maureen is your biological mother? Aileen Searles is a bit of a recluse, but she's also an open book; she would have told you if there'd been anything there to tell."

Blake stares at the white-capped ocean through the suite's bay window, then says, feeling like she's in a trance, "Her Doting, Dashing Lover. I wonder why she called him that."

Martin's shrug makes him look much younger and, for a moment, Blake sees him leading his own maiden through the doors of one of Graham's more tucked-away suites. He's old enough to be her father, but she can't deny he's handsome. She can see why Fiona's been with him for so many years.

Martin places a hand on her arm, and Blake yelps. "Sorry," Martin says and pulls back as if Blake's sweater has burned him. "It's just, do you have anywhere to be right now? I thought of somewhere else we could go that might give us some answers."

Blake lets out a soft chuff of laughter. *As the AA old-timers like to say, faith without works is dead. Right, Chris?* She pulls out her phone and snaps a photo of the Mulberry Maiden's entry, then smiles. Her earlier fear that Martin might harm her seems like the construction of an irrational child.

"Only wherever you're planning on taking me," she says.

Chapter 7

Martin drives them to a slope-roofed, gray-shingled building. The sign on it reads: ISLAND FREE LIBRARY. "Established in 1875," Martin says. He seems strangely elated, as if in possession of some unsaid punch line or long-held secret. "Ethel's the librarian, but she's also head of the historical society and runs a museum on the corner of Old Town Road and Ocean Avenue. If there's anyone who'll know who the Mulberry Maiden is, or what it refers to, it's Ethel Gilbert Brown."

Blake says nothing, for the day has taken on the whiplash quality of one of her runs. She could be in Boston right now, hustling for vodka or opiates, so frenzied is this bizarre scavenger hunt for information. Martin is too preoccupied to open her car door or remind her to take the umbrella. She scrambles to follow him up the mud-splattered walkway.

The library is as empty as the resort and newspaper offices were, but the tinkle of classical music drifts up from somewhere below them. The shelves are drab in the low light, and the large lobby, extending into what appears to be the fiction section, is drafty. Blake wonders if someone forgot to close a window and is grateful all over again for the fleece-lined jacket. She'll have to tell Aileen she borrowed it.

They start down a set of rubber-matted stairs. "Anyone down here?" Martin calls, and again Blake gets the sense that there's a joke she's not in on. His voice has the tiniest tinge of singsong quality to it.

The basement is home to what appear to be the library's oldest tomes, books that have aged, been stored and forgotten. A dusty card catalog sags on antique legs in one corner. Displaced reference volumes with broken bindings are strewn across a large oak table. The space is actually better lit than the first floor, away from the rain-splattered windows and illuminated with numerous overheads as it is. Seconds pass. The classical music clicks off. Shuffling footsteps replace the violins.

A bespectacled woman with a loosely pinned bun, burgundy leather flats, and a mustard-colored blouse tucked into an ankle-length skirt pokes her head out from between metal shelving units. Blake would laugh at how utterly this woman embodies *librarian* if she didn't look so frightened by their presence. One would think the woman had forgotten that the point of a library is for people to visit it.

"Hello, Ethel," Martin says, and places his hands on Blake's shoulders. This time, Blake manages not to flinch. "We have a newcomer to the island, and I'm doing my best to be star selectman, showing her around, helping her locate some information, that sort of thing. Are you busy?" He looks around and chuckles. "Either way, we won't take too much of your time."

Blake was expecting a woman bordering on elderly based on Martin's description, but the librarian looks to be in her midfifties. She smooths both her startled expression and the wisps of hair poking from her bun, but the smile she gives Blake is strained and unconvincing. "Hello," she says in a voice soft as a sea breeze. "How can I help you this evening?"

This evening? Blake looks at the clock above the staircase and is shocked to see it's almost six. The old Blake definitely wouldn't have made it this far on a steady stream of alcohol. The opiates, however, always gave her a burst of energy right after she took them. Somewhere within the ventral striatum region of her brain, a little light flickers at the idea—once, twice—and then stays on. It would be so much easier to deal with this—the uncertainty, the vulnerability, the feeling that the island, that White Hall, is stretching, expanding, like an orb weaver's web, to accommodate her presence here—if she could take the edge off. But, of course, she cannot. She needs to be strong.

The librarian is waiting for a response. "I don't actually know," Blake admits. When Martin still doesn't help her, she says, "Martin? Are we looking for a book like the one at Graham's Resort?"

"No, no, no," Martin says. "We're looking for something far more elusive than some old book." He gestures toward the oak table, entreating Ethel to sit. "What we're looking for can only be found in Ethel Brown's mind."

Ethel pales. Blake doesn't think she would have noticed if she isn't so used to seeing people at their worst in the meeting halls, people who sweat and cower and tremble. Ethel doesn't like Martin. Blake is sure of it. She also gets the sense, though she's not sure why, that were she not with him, Martin wouldn't have had the nerve to come here. But she must be wrong. Martin and Ethel *live* on the island. Why would Martin need her to make a move in some personal chess game?

Despite whatever negative emotions are simmering below the surface, Ethel walks to the table. Blake takes the seat across from her. Martin remains standing.

"What exactly do you want to know?" the librarian asks.

"You're friends with Maureen Mills, right?" Martin says. Blake whips her head around. Martin hadn't told her Ethel was a *friend* of Maureen's.

But Ethel's expression does not warm in a way that could be expected at the name of a friend. "I used to be. A long time ago."

"Did you have a falling-out?"

Ethel shakes her head. "Nothing like that. Maureen had a daughter, Thalia, in 1989. She was busy, juggling work and a toddler. We simply drifted apart."

"Do you have any memory of Maureen getting pregnant a second time? Of having another baby and giving that baby up for adoption?"

Ethel tilts her head as if to gauge the seriousness of Martin's question. "Maureen? Another baby?" Her voice has jumped an octave higher.

"Of course not. I would have remembered that. If it was anyone else, I'd say it was possible, that the stress of another pregnancy while waitressing seventy hours a week and juggling childcare would have led them to consider adoption. But Maureen wasn't that type of person. She would have done what it took to make things work. She took care of what was hers and loved too fiercely."

Blake's heart calcifies in her chest. She stays perfectly still, looking forward, refusing to blink. Are this woman's memories valid? Is this the closest Blake has come to peering into Maureen's head?

"I see," Martin says. "Thank you so much for your insight."

"Why are you asking these questions?" Small fires glint within Ethel's irises. Her fiery gaze flicks to Blake but doesn't stay there. If she has an inkling as to who Blake is, she doesn't seem to want to pursue it. "Maureen works for you," Ethel continues. "Why not ask her?"

Martin smiles, but it's not the charming one. It's one that makes him look like a shark. In fact, in this basement, with the librarian, Martin no longer strikes Blake as a comforting presence. He reminds her of the chairman of her AA home group who breaks his own rule not to tell war stories of drinking and drugging so as to avoid triggering others; it's an authoritarian air tempered by a glint of mischievousness, and it always puts her on edge.

"Thank you, Ethel. You've been incredibly cooperative."

"Is that everything?" Ethel asks.

Blake wonders again at the history between them. She imagines passions could run high on the island, and grudges deep. How could they not, when families lived here—and interacted with other families—for generations?

"Actually, no," Martin says. "I have one more question. The Mulberry Maiden. Have you heard of her?"

Ethel goes stone-still. Her pupils are as big and black as fish eyes. She swallows, and Blake can see she is trying very hard to keep her composure. "No," she says flatly. "Why do you ask?"

Impatient with Martin's beat-around-the-bush tactics and hoping to put Ethel at ease, Blake cuts in, "I'm planning on introducing myself to—"

"Blake," Martin says sharply. He turns back to Ethel and grins his shark grin. "We're just trying to find out who the Mulberry Maiden might be," he says lightly. "Blake here has a vested interest in the case."

"I'm afraid I can't help you." Despite the fear Blake still sees there, Ethel's voice is steel. She stands and nods at the clock. "It's time for me to close up. I'm sorry that's all I can offer. Blake, I hope you enjoy your stay. Now, please see yourselves out."

Martin drives back to the *Block Island Times* far more quickly than the weather warrants. The wiper blades squeak across the windshield, and Blake welcomes their mind-numbing cacophony. When he pulls into the spot behind Aileen's Jeep, light from an outdoor sconce above the office doorway refracts through the rain-slicked window, tattooing Martin's face with rippling waves.

"Why didn't you want Ethel to know who I was or that I'm here to meet my mother?" She tries for curiosity, but the question comes out sounding accusatory.

Martin levels his gaze at her, but his expression is serene. He's back to the helpful, concerned public official. Why had she ascribed less-than-benevolent motives onto him in the first place? She can't remember.

"Though she may not seem it," he says, "Ethel's one short step away from being the town crier. If we'd told her the truth, the whole island would know you were Maureen's daughter by the time the sun rose tomorrow."

Ethel doesn't seem the sort, Martin's right about that. Sure, there was something hard beneath the librarian's timidity, but Blake doesn't imagine that hardness is used to gossip about her neighbors. Still,

Martin has given hours of his day to help her, and she won't repay him by arguing. Telling Ethel who she was would have had no bearing on what the woman said.

Now that their outing is over, the inevitable return to White Hall slices into her like a razor. She wishes she could teleport to her apartment in Boston for the night, then return in the morning, shaken free from the chain of events she feels so wrapped up in. A part of her is grateful for Aileen and Martin's involvement, for the assistance of Timmy Graham and Ethel Gilbert Brown. But another part is confused as to how she became entangled with so many inhabitants of the island so quickly. Has she really made progress in getting closer to her mother, or has she only complicated things further?

"I understand," Blake says, because Martin is waiting for some sort of response. "And thank you so much for today. I don't know what I would have done without you. I'm not sure I learned enough to confront Maureen without risk, but I do feel like I know more about who she is, for whatever that's worth."

"I'll try to get your sister's address for you, like I said. And I'll rack my brain about the Mulberry Maiden. I would ask Maureen myself if I thought I'd be met with anything but suspicion. Until then, get yourself back to White Hall for a good night's rest."

"About White Hall," Blake says, then stops.

"Yes?"

"Never mind."

"No, go on. What about it?"

"Is there anywhere else to stay on the island?"

Martin's eyes narrow. "What's the matter?" His tone is dangerous. "Aileen's dinners not delicious enough for you? Has Fiona been slacking on updating the vintage decor and historic artwork? Are the views lacking? White Hall is the most beautiful—and successful—business on the island. I'd give up every property I own in New Shoreham if it meant possessing it. So, please, enlighten me."

She's upset him. Wonderful. Fiona Searles is his girlfriend, and here she is, turning up her nose at the Searles family's estate. A place where at least one of the proprietresses has gone above and beyond to help her, feeding her, connecting her to indispensable island resources, letting her use their car.

"That's not it at all," Blake stammers. The only way she can see to remedy this is to tell the truth. She cringes, shoulders slumping, head bowed. "I'll just have to get used to the way voices float there, I guess," she admits. "And how Mary Hopkins Searles's eyes follow me from her portrait above the stairs."

"Ahh," Martin says and, to Blake's great relief, chuckles. "A little case of the heebie-jeebies? I could see that. White Hall has enough history to support its fair share of ghosts." He looks out the windshield. "There are a few inns on the island, the nicest being closed for renovations at present. I should know; I own it." He looks back at her and grins. "Otherwise, you'd have to go with an Airbnb, but that'll cost you more than you're paying now, and for far worse accommodations."

Blake nods to hide her disappointment. "I figured. Like I said, I'll just have to deal with feeling like I'm at the mercy of some unseen writer's plot twists."

"You've lost me again," Martin says.

Blake sighs. "It's stupid, but, this whole trip, the rain, wanting to meet my birth mother, White Hall, my"—she searches for a way to describe her pending court case without losing Martin's sympathy—"sobriety issues," she finishes. "I grew up in foster care and harbored a rather obsessive affinity for gothic novels. You know, those stories in which the oft-fainting heroine is trapped in a crumbling castle set against a backdrop of perpetual rain, having returned to her ancestral village to get to the bottom of a long-buried secret?"

Martin laughs. Blake takes a breath and continues, "I can't help feeling like"—God, she can't believe she's saying this out loud—"like I'm *in* a gothic novel. It's nuts, I know. But, come on. Tell me there aren't at least a few similarities?"

"Oh, absolutely," Martin gushes, and she feels both relieved and patronized. "No, I totally get it," he insists. "And that must be overwhelming. But I assure you, you won't find a more welcoming establishment anywhere on the island. Aileen and Fiona are the best."

She nods. "I'll stay put, then. Thank you for everything." Despite feeling like she should give him a hug—or at least a handshake—Blake grabs the umbrella and slides out of his truck. She maneuvers Aileen's Jeep out onto the road, and even then, she feels his eyes on her vehicle like binoculars, or a second pair of headlights, until his pickup recedes in her rearview mirror.

For a moment, as she drives, she thinks the rain is finally stopping. The novel of which she's the reluctant heroine will not—cannot—continue under the warmth of the sun. This is not a request or a recommendation; it's a staple of the genre. The rule. Maybe, just maybe, Blake's story is shifting into the realm of a feel-good drama.

By the time Blake pulls into the circular drive at the front of White Hall, however, she sees she was wrong. The sky darkens from moonstone to hematite, hematite to obsidian. Clouds travel like race cars, trees bend like promises, and the rain comes down harder than ever.

Chapter 8

After a trip upstairs to change and jot a few notes in her journal, Blake makes her way to the dining room, where Aileen clucks and crows over her guest's return. Though her hostess doesn't bombard her with questions, Blake has a hard time concentrating on anything but the new information whirlpooling around her brain. She spoons haddock, lobster, and mussels into her mouth, and though the broth is thick and the spices plentiful, it might as well be a bowl of tepid water. She is as hollowed out as one of the clamshells.

"So," Aileen says, and when Blake looks up, she realizes Aileen is sipping from a veritable goblet of mulberry wine. She tenses, and a blaze of anger courses through her. She tries to douse it with a gulp of berry-infused sparkling water she poured from a nearby pitcher. Yes, she told Aileen she wasn't drinking, but Aileen has no obligation not to drink herself. The woman owns a vineyard. Of course she'd have a glass with dinner.

Blake doesn't catch the rest of what Aileen is saying. "Sorry?"

Aileen leans forward conspiratorially. "Fiona's out for the evening, so we can continue our conversation."

Blake blinks. "About my mother?"

"Nooo." Aileen drags the word out as if Blake is a child who has said something silly. "About how you saw the ghost of my great-great-grandaunt in your room last night."

"Oh." The disappearing shape from the night before has faded, literally and figuratively, into the woodwork, though the experience must have been contributing to her overall unease all day. Blake sets down her spoon. "Does White Hall really have a ghost?"

The instant she says the words, she wishes she could take them back. She has played right into the house's plan. Now Aileen will relay the background of White Hall's resident specter and, during the inevitable moment when she comes face-to-face with the ghost, she'll recall this conversation and know she set the whole thing in motion with her misguided curiosity.

"White Hall indeed has a ghost, but the story's not for the fainthearted." Blake wants to inform her she is solidly in this camp, but Aileen doesn't give her the chance. "It starts soon after Mary's father, Edward Searles, built White Hall and moved his family here from Massachusetts," Aileen continues. "Everyone on the island was enamored of the Searleses' reputation and tastes, and all the young men were enamored of Mary Searles. She was an unusual beauty, as is clear from her portrait. Large, wide-set eyes and cheeks like apples." Aileen pauses. "You know, she looked a lot like you."

Blake imagines Mary Hopkins Searles incarnate standing across the table. She sees her curtsying and smiling, glowering and pouting, doing all the things a rich twentysomething-year-old girl would do. Mary spins around the foyer, eyes on the chandelier, and runs on slippered feet up the light-dappled staircase. She tries on silk scarves and feathered hats in front of a full-length mirror framed with brass peacocks, brass anthuriums, brass ivy.

Blake feels Aileen watching her, wine in hand, but she cannot pull herself from her trance until she's put the finishing touches on the mental image she's conjured. The vision of Mary dissipates the moment Aileen places her glass back on the table, and Blake is enveloped by the tart, woodsy smell of alcohol.

"One young man in particular, Merritt Dempsey, took a liking to Mary," Aileen says, "and Mary took a liking to him in return. He courted her for the duration of one long, rainy winter, but when winter turned to spring, and he still hadn't proposed, Mary grew impatient.

"Mary's father was one of the richest men in America at the time, with a passion for backing huge architectural projects. The story goes that Edward Searles took his wife, second daughter, and young son on a short trip to Windham, New Hampshire, to research the site of an upcoming project. Twenty-four-year-old Mary stayed behind and took advantage of the time away from her family. Only Dream House's servants knew of Mary's plan to invite Mr. Dempsey over that evening. The kitchen staff served them dinner, after which Mary dismissed everyone but her lady's maid." Aileen takes another swallow of wine. Blake tries not to inhale. "Here is the point where the main account of events becomes contested.

"According to the staff who were dismissed, Mary must have confronted Merritt over what she saw as his reluctance to ask for her hand, and an argument ensued. Mary was heard sobbing. Glassware broke. More than one servant claimed to overhear Mary demand Merritt prove his commitment with an engagement. When Merritt refused, citing their youth and his need for more time, Mary became hysterical. She poured a bottle of arsenic from the cabinet into a glass of mulberry wine, drank the whole thing down, and penned a letter to her family while the poison did its work."

"Why was there arsenic in the dining room?"

Aileen winces. "Even now, White Hall occasionally suffers a rat-infested winter."

"And why was this story contested?"

"Because the only one besides Merritt and Mary who was in the room that evening—Helen, the lady's maid—was *not* in the room when the other servants forced the door open. She was never seen or heard from again."

Blake looks at the room's single entrance. "That's impossible."

Aileen shrugs. "Maybe so."

"Merritt *Dempsey*? Any relation to Martin?"

"His great-great-grandfather."

"When you first mentioned the ghost this morning, you said, 'Fiona calls this Arsenic Wing because it's where Great-Great-Grandaunt Mary tried to poison her lover with arsenic-spiked wine.'"

Aileen nods. "There's another version of the story. That Mary was clandestine in her retrieval of the arsenic and poured it in Merritt's glass first." Blake grimaces and Aileen chuckles. "Don't worry, Miss Bronson, the only undeniable fact is that Mary Hopkins Searles died in White Hall more than a century ago. What house this old hasn't had a few deaths within its walls? And, well, I guess there's something else that's undisputed."

"What's that?"

"Over the course of the ensuing century, there has been no shortage of people who claim to have seen Mary's ghost in White Hall."

Though she's physically and mentally exhausted—and finds Aileen's campfire-tale delivery to be more than a little annoying—Blake can't help but ask, "What exactly do they see?"

"Do you really want to know?"

Blake nods, but the annoyance shifts to something darker. Now she feels like a mouse on the trigger of a trap. Like she's run into a dealer offering her a free bag after a brief but crucial respite.

"Dark tears, darker than blood, drip from her eyes," Aileen says. "The skin of her cheeks has been sloughed away, as if the tears are poison. Her hands are full of what looks like entrails, but then you catch the tart scent of the mulberries. She wrings her hands, and bloodred juice drips from between clenched fingers like acid rain."

A fire burns in the hearth not far from where Blake sits, but the skin on her arms rises in gooseflesh anyway.

"Don't worry," Aileen says again. Her tone is reassuring. "The only ones who ever seem to encounter her are those going through some sort of major upheaval. Guests dealing with divorce, death, illness, et cetera. One young woman, a few years back? I feared for her sanity long before she ever reported seeing ghosts. Right after checking in, she said the island, that White Hall itself, was a spider's web, expanding to accommodate her presence here."

Upon hearing her own thoughts regurgitated back to her, Blake freezes, but Aileen misattributes her shock to her overall commentary. "I don't mean to say that's *your* situation. You have to understand, I don't actually think you saw her. It was a shadow, a trick of the moon shining through the windows along with all that rain."

"Right," Blake says and stands, whacking her hip on the table. Aileen's glass of wine wobbles precariously. "If you'll excuse me, Aileen, I have to be getting to bed."

Blake lurches through the dining room toward the exit. Aileen stands herself, concern etched into her wide, rugged features. "It's just a story. I didn't mean to upset you!"

Blake doesn't answer.

"Please, Miss Bronson! Don't run off before dessert. We both know there's no such thing as ghosts!"

Blake still doesn't answer. She pushes through the doorway.

"Sleep well," Aileen calls out after her.

Chapter 9

Blake turns the windshield wipers up. She has no idea what she's thinking, taking Aileen's Jeep out again, scanning the bars and restaurants for signs of life. She should have gone to bed, like she'd been planning to after dinner. But that was before the mustiness of the room overwhelmed her and the thought of sleep was like a nail being driven into her brain. She repeats the same thing she told herself twenty minutes earlier as she slunk down the stairs: *I'm not* planning *on drinking*. She needs some company, that's all. Another human to talk to besides Stephen King–wannabe Aileen.

Just when she's resigned herself to the reality that nothing is open at nine o'clock on a rain-soaked Wednesday in February, she drives past Martin's Above the Rocks. The tables are empty, but the lights are on at the very back of the restaurant, and Blake catches a glimpse of someone sitting at the bar.

Blake has parked and is out of the car before she can admit this is a bad idea. The door to the restaurant is locked, but she rattles it several times, peering through the window. A man slides off his barstool and crosses the room. When the door opens, Timmy Graham stands before her. Blake doesn't bother to hide her shock.

"Hey-hey!" Timmy looks her up and down. "Martin's friend, right? You out in search of a nightcap?"

"Is it open?"

"Technically, no." He gestures behind him. "But Eva helps a few of us out when we need a change of scenery." He turns, and something passes between him and the bartender. He spins back to Blake. "You coming in?"

Blake hesitates. If she accepts this after-hours invitation, she'll *have* to drink, won't she?

"Don't be shy." Timmy laughs. "Booze or companionship, it's the only place to find either at this hour, so now's your chance."

Dread roiling in her stomach, she follows Timmy across the restaurant.

The brass lanterns are dimmer than they were that morning but still tint everything with a hallucinatory glow. "What do we have here?" the bartender, Eva, asks. Her hair is a strange shade in the light, like phosphorescent ginger root.

"I'm Blake. I couldn't sleep."

Eva nods as if this is a perfectly reasonable explanation. "Okay, Blake-who-couldn't-sleep. What can I get you?"

Vodka cranberry. Vodka on the rocks. A shot! "Can I start with a soda water?"

Timmy turns to the other late-night patron, a middle-aged woman guzzling a maraschino-garnished manhattan. "You hear this? The girl finally finds a place to drink and orders seltzer."

"You said booze or companionship," Blake deadpans. "I'd like to see if one is worthwhile before embarking on the other." It's an old-Blake thing to say—full of both the confidence and testiness of her presober self—and it earns her a look of respect from Eva.

"You're a newcomer, aren'tcha?" the woman says to Blake as Eva places her soda water on the bar top. "I remember everyone I've ever met over the age of 'newborn,' and I don't recognize you." She chuckles, but Blake doesn't get the joke. "What brings you to our little island paradise?"

"I don't want to talk about it."

"That's fine," she says. She holds out her hand and Blake shakes it. "Corrine Daniels. I don't like to talk about what brought me to this shithole either."

Blake laughs despite herself.

"How do you know Martin?" Timmy pushes.

"I don't want to talk about that either."

"Ohhhhkay," he says. "Can you tell us where you're staying, then?"

"White Hall." *All these questions.* Blake breathes an internal sigh of relief that no one was here earlier to see her staring like some sort of stalker at her mother.

Corrine lets out a long, low whistle. "I didn't think anyone stayed in that behemoth during the off-season."

"You think Fi and her hermit sister would give up the prospect of extra money?" Eva asks.

"Fiona—and Martin—they're not here, are they?" Blake looks to where the pair was standing that morning, glowering at her from the hallway.

"Martin knows Eva entertains a couple of patrons after closing, but if he's not here, he can feign ignorance *and* make more money," Timmy says. He moves closer to Blake. She slides her stool in the opposite direction.

"How are you liking White Hall, dear?" Corrine asks. Her tone is kind, but the words all run together. It's obvious the manhattan she holds is not her first.

"It's okay."

Eva laughs. "Fiona—and Martin, for that matter—act like White Hall is a *castle*, but that place has been crumbling down around the Searles sisters' heads for years."

"That's what I was saying to Martin earlier," Blake exclaims. "I feel like I'm stuck between the pages of a gothic novel."

Corrine whistles again. "*Love* gothic novels. I used to read Phyllis A. Whitney constantly when I worked third shift at Rhode Island Hospital."

Blake straightens on her stool at the name of the hospital on her birth certificate. "Nurse?"

"Labor and delivery, thirty-six years."

Wild thoughts—*You must know Maureen Mills . . . Do you remember her being pregnant with a second child? Did you deliver her baby?*—fire in Blake's brain, but before she can voice them, Corrine hoots with laughter. "If I'd been doing a bit less of *this* since retiring"—she raises her glass—"maybe I'd remember key moments of my career *and* the plots of all those Phyllis Whitney novels!"

Self-loathing settles over Blake's shoulders like a shroud. What did she think, that on the one in a million chance she ran into the woman who delivered her, she'd stand out among thousands of babies brought into the world over thirty-six years? As if sensing her disappointment, Corrine nudges her. "I remember enough to know White Hall would be the perfect backdrop for one of those books." She throws back the last of the auburn liquid from her glass and lifts the fresh one Eva's provided. "But why do *you* feel like you're in a gothic novel?"

Blake feels Timmy's eyes crawl across her skin, waiting for her answer. "It's a long story," she says. "But trust me, I do."

"Well, if you *were*," Corrine says, "you'd just need to steer clear of men with marriage proposals on their lips." Noticing Timmy's leer, Corrine continues challengingly, "And lust in their eyes. Wish I'd known that one before I said 'yes' to ol' Montague." When Blake eyes her bare ring finger, Corrine says, "He's my ex."

Blake chuckles, happy to distract herself from the bottles winking at her from beneath the oval mirror. She wants a drink. God, does she want one. But she knows this relapse would go about as well as any of the others, and she can't afford to suffer the endless negative consequences at present. Plus, watching the former labor-and-delivery nurse admit to complete alcohol-induced memory loss after a three-decades-long career put a damper on her craving.

"You're right," she says to Corrine. "I need to observe the rules of gothic fiction to get through this."

"The rules!" Corrine says, holding up her drink again. "I like that. So if rule number one is *Be wary of opportunistic men*, rule number two is *Don't go into any dungeons!*"

"Or attics," Blake counters, stifling a giggle.

"Rule number three: *If a storm descends, remain in your bedroom!*"

"And keep the smelling salts handy."

"Rule four: *Don't have sex with anyone . . . he might be your long-lost brother!*"

Blake almost chokes on her drink. "Rule number five: *Stay away from family members in general to avoid the passing down of an ancestral curse!*"

"Six: *Take your nightmares seriously.*" Corrine tries to project solemnity but lets out a snort. "They might be visions."

"Or omens," Blake adds. "Oh, and number seven should be: *Beware of anyone with mental health issues. Madness equals murder.*"

"Lastly," Corrine says, wiping her eyes where tears have smudged her already-clumpy mascara, "rule number eight: *Treat anything seemingly supernatural with a healthy dose of skepticism.*"

Blake pushes back from the bar and puts her hands on her knees, struggling to catch her breath. Eva is looking at them with perplexed amusement. Timmy's mouth is agape. Corrine holds up one hand, and though Blake feels a little foolish, she returns the high-five. "You two are something," Eva says, wiping down the bar.

"I'll say." Irritation ripples through Timmy's voice. It's clear he's miffed that Blake's arrival at Above the Rocks hasn't resulted in a willing partner in flirtation. "You ready for that drink now?" He jerks his head at Eva while keeping his eyes on Blake.

"You know," Blake says, realizing only now that any lingering anticipation of having a drink dissipated during her back-and-forth with Corrine, "I don't think I will." She smiles at Corrine. "I need to keep my wits about me if I'm going to avoid breaking any of the rules."

"A fine plan," Corrine says.

"I agree." Eva tosses the rag in the sink and unties her apron. "Especially since it's about that time." Timmy groans, and Eva shoots him a look. "Go drink at your own bar, Timothy Graham." She walks through the swinging half door into the main portion of the restaurant.

Blake slides off her stool. "Thanks for the soda water," she says to Eva. She turns to Corrine. "And thank you for the conversation."

"Where's my thank-you?" Timmy asks. "I'm the one that got you in here."

Blake starts across the restaurant. "Martin told me how you two are always competing with one another," she calls over her shoulder. "So thanks for vouching for me on the nonexistent chance of screwing me because you think that's what Martin did."

"Didn't he?" Timmy shouts. When Blake doesn't answer, he adds, "Remember your own stupid rule! Watch out for opportunistic men. Martin's the most opportunistic of all!"

Is he, Blake thinks as she pushes through the door to the wet night outside, *or are you?*

Chapter 10

Blake wakes in the middle of the night with a gasp. The wind rattling the panes sounds like coyotes before a hunt, and the rain that pummels the mansion's peaks and gables somehow comes straight-on rather than from the swirling cauldron of a sky above. At this point, the weather in conjunction with the isolated setting should have been on the nose to the point of absurdity, but there's nothing funny about the creaking floorboards that roused her from sleep, or the low groan emanating from the part of the L-shaped room she cannot see.

Blake doesn't remember crawling to the wrought iron footboard, yet she's gripping the curved metal hard enough to leave painful indentations in her palms. Though she's been in this room the last two nights, its shadow-dense crooks are still unfamiliar. The intermittent flashes of lightning through gauzy gray curtains dizzies, rather than orients, her.

She waits. The groaning has stopped, replaced by the splatter of water, slow and rhythmic, on the floorboards. Is the sound really separate from the rain against the windows? It's too difficult to tell. Blake releases the footboard and crawls to the head of the bed. She is leaning over the nightstand where, on a whim after returning from the bar, she'd jotted down her and Corrine's "rules" of gothic fiction (number three, about remaining in your bedroom when a storm descends, seems particularly pertinent) when a floorboard creaks anew.

Her brain screams at her to freeze, to stay absolutely silent, but it's as if her hands are under someone else's control. They rifle through the sheets, fast and frenzied, and she can't help a sharp exhalation of relief when she registers the smooth, cold metal of her phone.

She swipes for the phone's flashlight, but the screen remains lifeless. Blake stares, wild and wide-eyed, into the dark. Every window in the spacious room is closed and double-latched, and yet the sound of water splatting onto the floor continues.

It returns to her then, as abrupt as lightning—the description of the ghost Aileen had spoken of at dinner, the ghost she claimed had been seen on more than one occasion in White Hall. Were those blood-dark tears falling to the floor—drip, drip, drip—or the juice of mulberries strangled to a pulp by the wraith's impatient hands?

Without lowering her gaze, Blake drops one foot to the floor beside the bed. She slides off the mattress, but has to steel herself against a wave of light-headedness. Her thoughts are like birds stunned into immobility, unable to take flight. There's a delay between when she blinks and when her vision reconfigures.

A wall of wind slams against the mansion, but when it retreats, the eerie groaning at the other side of the room continues. The corners of Blake's vision go black, and this time the vertigo doesn't pass. The armoire, the fireplace, the rocking chair, the chaise, they shudder like dinghies in a hurricane-ravaged sea.

Something shakes in her fingers. Blake yelps before realizing it's her phone. It's been off, not dead, and she inadvertently squeezed it to life in her white-knuckled fear. It takes her three swipes to activate the flashlight, and when she finally holds it up, it's met with a flash of silver-white lightning through the east-facing windows.

The figure caught in the beam of Blake's phone should not, *cannot*, be. She's a specter, a living shadow, an impossibility. A horror-movie phantom who's stepped off the screen. She emits a sound like something dragged up through layers of wet, worm-laden earth. Blake tries to draw in a breath, but her lungs have been rendered too weak to fuel a scream. The woman's outline flickers, as if she is contemplating abandoning this plane for another. Her maroon silk dress ripples like a silt-sheened pond disturbed by errant pebbles.

There are no mulberries in her hands, but the skin there is stained a dark purplish red. The tears, though. Aileen was right about the tears. They fall from the woman's glittering eyes like wine from a splintered bottle. Her pale white lips emit unnerving groans.

The groaning rises in volume and intensity until it becomes a creaky, keening wail. Blake steps back, but the baroque nightstand blocks her retreat. She needs to turn, to move, to call for help, to run. All she can do is stare as the awful, inhuman sound lengthens into a word:

"Gooo," the ghostly woman says, and Blake can see teeth stained as purple as her fingers. The woman is a wolf, Lamia, the heroine-turned-vampire in a black-and-white film who's gorged on the blood of her first victim.

"Goooooo," the woman—Mary Hopkins Searles, for who else could this be?—says. "GOOOOOOHHHHH!" The distorted command devolves back into a grating shriek.

Blake manages to sidestep along the nightstand to the door. She gropes for the knob, finds it, and turns. Above the sound of the rain and the slamming of her heart, she swears she makes out the rattling of the key inside the lock on the other side. *No way out!*

Mary steps forward, smearing dark liquid across the floor. She cocks her head, taking Blake in. With arms outstretched, she creeps closer. And closer. When she is mere inches from Blake, she leans forward, her eyes shocking in their wetness, and growls, "Go from here, while you still have the chance. Before a fate worse than mine, worse than death, befalls you."

Blake smells rotten fruit, and the sickly-sweet odor of something far more animalistic. Something decaying. Then the wine-stained fingers wrap themselves around her throat, and everything goes dark.

Chapter 11

The next morning, Blake rips the paper with the scribbled gothic "rules" out of her notebook, sticks it between the pages of *The Mysteries of Udolpho,* and shoves the book back into the nightstand drawer, not wanting to look at any of it. She is downstairs before Aileen has started making breakfast, a tartan scarf wrapped around her neck. The dizzying fear of the night before has left her feeling hungover, and though she's returned again and again to what happened, she can't make the pieces fit. She woke in her bed, tucked beneath the blankets as neatly as if she'd just fallen asleep, and though her neck is sore, there isn't a single bruise or scratch there.

"You're up early," Aileen says as she bustles in. "I was going to make eggs Benedict."

"Actually, Aileen, if it's all the same to you, I was hoping to grab a quick coffee to go. I've decided that today is the day I'm going to the restaurant to tell Maureen who I am. There's no sense in putting it off any longer. If she's willing to speak to me, great. If not, that's her choice. And if that's the case, I've got to get the hell off this island."

Aileen's face falls. "I'm sorry to hear that. Not sorry that you're going to speak with her. You should. That's what you came for. But I'm sorry you're finding Block Island not to your liking. Maybe you can come back in the summer. Block is a different place between June and September."

"I doubt that," Blake says curtly. Beneath the scarf, the tender muscles sting, and she fidgets.

"I'll get that coffee going," Aileen says, understanding, finally, that her guest is in no mood for pleasantries.

While Blake waits for the coffee to brew, her eyes dart around the kitchen. That it's raining again is hardly worth noting. Aileen, still going ahead with the eggs Benedict preparations, circles the counter several times, collecting English muffins from a drawer and eggs, lemons, butter, and Worcestershire sauce from the fridge. The marble island appears longer today than on the previous morning; Blake thought it was the same length as the stove range, but now it extends a few feet past it. Or, is it still the same length but no longer in the same location? Blake closes her eyes and shakes her head.

So Aileen is shifting the furniture around while Blake sleeps now? She's already decided that she's losing it, but could the complete mental collapse wait until after breakfast? Or better yet, tomorrow? She needs to keep it together for one more day. If Maureen rejects her, she can be on the ferry back to Point Judith by this evening. The thought brings her immense, full-body relief, much like that which she's experienced after making the conscious decision to throw sobriety out the window on a whim and drown her worries in cocaine. Or OxyContin. Or Valium. Or gin. Endless negative consequences be damned.

The coffeepot ejects a final spray of liquid, bringing Blake back to the present.

"I have a sleeve of those disposable coffee cups around here somewhere," Aileen says. She disappears into a walk-in pantry, rifles around, and reappears with what Blake is happy to see is an extralarge cup.

"Black, right?" Aileen fills it to the rim and secures the lid.

"Thanks." Blake feels guilty for being short with her, especially when she took the Jeep last night without asking and is about to inquire whether she can borrow it again. Before she can do so, the door swings open and Fiona breezes in. Remembering what Aileen said the day before, Blake swallows the question, inwardly cursing. She doesn't want to have to rely on taxis today.

"Where's the mail?" Fiona asks Aileen. She takes a bottle of Perrier from the cabinet and pours it into a glass without ice. "Didn't we just have a conversation about how the 'gorgeous old wooden letter organizer on the parlor wall' has held White Hall's outgoing mail since before Prohibition? So where is it?"

"I haven't made it to the parlor yet, dear sister," Aileen says. "It's in this drawer. Are you going to town straight away?"

Fiona sips from her glass. "I am. It's the first Thursday of the month. Town hall meeting. Why, is there something else that needs my attention?"

The door swings open again, and Martin strides in. He heads for the coffeepot, where he fills a to-go cup similar to Blake's, leaving room for cream and sugar. "I'm heading out," he says. He goes to Fiona and kisses her lightly on the mouth. "Glad you convinced me to go for that run. I'll never get the mud out of my sneakers, but you were right, it looks like the morning's going to be the driest—and I use that word loosely—part of the day."

He nods to Blake, the gesture devoid of any recognition. Aileen wipes egg whites from her hands and stops Martin before he gets to the door.

"Are you going to the restaurant? Blake here was going to call a taxi and head that way now. Catching a ride with you would save her time and money."

Fiona whips her head around and glares at Blake. Aileen takes Fiona's shoulders and pretends to shake her. "God forbid we go above and beyond in helping our guests make the most of their stay!"

Fiona pushes Aileen away. "You're impossible." She shoots Blake another irritated look, then turns her attention to her sister. "The description on our website says *nothing* about transportation services. If you provide one guest with additional perks, and they leave a review, the next guest is going to expect the same thing and end up disappointed. And what do disappointed guests do?"

"Disappointed guests ask for their money back," Aileen and Martin say in unison.

Fiona groans and throws up her hands.

"I won't leave a review," Blake says. What would she even write: *Food's great but the murderous ghost makes for a rough night's sleep?* Aileen, Fiona, and Martin look at her at the same time, and she feels herself shrinking. "Not because I'm disappointed or anything. I'm *not* disappointed, I'm just"—*I'm just an idiot*—"not the review-leaving type," she finishes lamely.

While Blake has wondered several times since arriving at White Hall when the floor would open with a great, screaming split of marble and plunge her into an abyss, she wouldn't mind if it happened at this very moment.

"Right," Fiona says with undisguised annoyance. She turns to Martin. "Hon, will you take Aileen's new pet to the restaurant with you? I'll be back this afternoon, once the meeting's over." Without waiting for a response, Fiona pours the rest of her sparkling water down the sink, throws Aileen a final, withering glare, and storms out.

Martin shrugs. "Ready when you are, Blake."

∞

Five minutes later, Blake sits in the front seat of Martin's pickup for the second time in as many days. He climbs in, starts the engine, and grumbles under his breath, but it's about the weather, not Fiona or Aileen.

"This is the worst stretch of rain I can remember." He maneuvers the truck through water half a foot deep. "You know, a taxi might not be able to get to White Hall in another couple of hours. If it goes on too long beyond that, you might need to consider an ark for your return trip."

Blake adjusts the seat belt so it's farther away from her neck. The muscles there still throb, and Fiona's attitude did nothing to improve her mood. Had she seemed perturbed by more than the possibility of giving future guests unreasonable expectations? Had she seemed jealous, perhaps? At the idea of Blake riding with Martin? Blake shakes off the ridiculous notion. "I'm hoping to be on my way home before it comes to that."

"Really?" Martin sounds genuinely surprised. "Shall I take it this is the big day, then? You're going to say something to Maureen?"

"I am," Blake says with far more confidence than she feels. "Come hell or"—she looks out the window—"higher water, I guess."

"All right." Martin nods as if to pump her up, but then a nervous wince takes over his features. "I should tell you, though . . ."

Her stomach drops. "Tell me what?"

Martin sucks in air through gritted teeth. "Today is Maureen's day off."

"Her day off? Meaning, she won't be at the restaurant."

"That's kind of what a day off means."

"Shit!" Blake shouts. As soon as the word is out, it's swallowed by the splatter of rain against the windshield. She wants to yell it again. And again. Until it eradicates everything with the completeness of a wrecking ball and blots out all sober, rational thought.

"I thought that might be your reaction," Martin says. "I was hoping you wanted a ride to the restaurant to do more recon. Because if you were hoping to talk to Maureen, that's not going to be the place."

Blake's chest grows tight. The last thing she wants to do is cry, but why does everything have to be so horrible? Why didn't she just stay in Boston and wait for her DUI sentencing? Continue the downward spiral she's been on since she realized a can of beer or a tablet of Xanax made her memories of orphanages and brutish foster mothers turn as sepia-toned and serene as the childhood photographs she never got to have?

"But," Martin continues, and Blake snaps her head in his direction so fast, she tweaks her injured neck. She bites her lip and repositions the scarf a third time. She's not sure why she's going to such lengths to hide the damage when there's nothing there to hide. And maybe that's it. She's hiding the *absence* of bruising from herself. To see the smooth, unblemished skin would drive home the reality of having imagined the whole incident.

"But?"

"If you're serious about talking to her today, I could take you to her house. I can't imagine she'd be anywhere but home on her one day off."

Blake turns this option over like an AA medallion, examining both sides of it. Would she knock on Maureen's door and tell her who she is right there on the stoop, or say just enough to get inside and reveal her identity . . . what, over a tray of lemonade and gingerbread like a reunion scene in a coming-of-age film? "Are you sure that's a good idea?" Blake asks, hoping he'll make the decision for her.

Martin shrugs. "I think it's a better plan than trying to talk to her at the restaurant."

This is probably true. And seeing where Maureen lives might give Blake more insight into where she came from. "Okay," Blake says. "Okay, yes. Let's do this."

Martin flips his left blinker. Five minutes later, he turns onto a long, tree-lined road. There's a sign advertising fresh eggs and horse-back-riding lessons, but it's near illegible, chipped of much of its paint. The houses aren't massive but boast things like wraparound porches, pond views, and numerous acres between neighbors. He stops fifty yards from the nearest driveway, reaches into the back seat, and hands her his umbrella. When he does, she realizes with a start that she forgot to leave both Aileen's umbrella and the fleece-lined jacket in the Jeep. They must be somewhere in the growing mess of her room.

"That's the one," he says, bringing her back to the present, nodding at a contemporary-style house beyond a white aluminum mailbox with gold-plated numbers on its side. There's no garage, but a navy Subaru is parked in the drive. "I don't think Maureen should see you getting out of my truck. It might start things off on a weird foot. I'll give you my number and have you jump out here."

Blake presses her phone into his hand. He punches in the number and hands it back. "I won't go far. Text me when you're ready. Or, if you end up having to leave, uh, abruptly, just start walking. I'll scoop you up at the end of the street."

Blake nods, and while this whole thing feels questionable, she supposes it's no weirder than the act of her coming to the island at all. "I guess the only thing left to do is go knock on the door," she says.

Martin's hand covers hers before she can reach for the door handle. He's staring at her with an intensity she wouldn't have expected. "I told you my own mother left," he says, more serious than she's ever heard him. "I'm not sure I'd have the courage to do what you're doing. To face her. I just wanted to say good luck, and no matter what happens, you're braver than Maureen herself has ever been." He squeezes her hand. "Good luck," he says again.

Blake squeezes back, closes her eyes for a beat, then pushes open the door. Under the cover of Martin's umbrella, she avoids the deepest of the puddles, but she does not move slowly.

She's been waiting for this moment her entire life. She runs.

Chapter 12

Martin pulls up five minutes after she texts him. Any confusion as to why she's so far from Maureen's house must dissipate upon seeing her appearance. The front of her white shirt is a Rorschach of black mascara and graphite eyeliner. Mud, gravel, and grass cake the knees of her jeans from where she landed after tripping over a pothole. She climbs into the truck, and Martin pulls away from the shoulder. He takes a left onto Center Road, then a right onto Beach Avenue. It's hard to get her bearings, but she knows where they're going. White Hall. Back to the mansion.

The landmarks beyond the rain-splattered windshield lengthen, straighten, into the wall-to-wall bookshelves in Maureen's living room. Blake remembers the pleasure she felt at the titles, which could have been a hand-picked curation of Blake's favorites from adolescence. Then, *The Old English Baron*, *The Turn of the Screw*, and *A Sicilian Romance* are replaced in her mind's eye by the shelves of her mother's medicine cabinet, glimpsed surreptitiously on a trip to the bathroom meant to help her get her bearings: Diazepam. Percocet. More diazepam. Ativan. OxyContin. Gabapentin. Clonazepam. Fluoxetine. Proof that her sole connection to another person is a mere link to her addiction.

Blake wants off this island, but the idea of packing her things, taking a taxi to the terminal, and boarding the ferry is as realistic as reaching the moon. She should ask Martin to stop at a liquor store now but doesn't want to deal with the potential pushback. Not a problem.

Aileen had said the entrance to the wine cellar was in the kitchen. She'll find it the moment Aileen is busy elsewhere in the mansion.

As they approach the stone-topped entry pillars, she feels Martin's eyes on her. "That bad, huh?" he asks. His voice is probing but gentle.

She lets out a bitter little laugh. "You have no idea."

"I can guess." He sounds regretful. "It wasn't my place to say so before, but Maureen Mills has been a coldhearted woman for as long as I've known her. I hoped she would show a different side to you, her own daughter, but I can't say that I'm surprised she didn't."

Blake doesn't have the energy to say that she didn't even tell Maureen who she really is. She'd pretended to be a reporter with the *Boston Globe*, and when that hadn't worked, she said she was a friend of Blake's, sent by Blake to see if Maureen was open to meeting. Blake shivers at the memory of Maureen's rage, her denial of a second daughter. Her eyes well again. In another moment, the pickup's tires are plunged into a stream of rushing water.

Martin grits his teeth and slows the truck. Water fountains up from the tires in thick, dirty sprays. They move toward the mansion at a crawl.

"Were you still hoping to be on the last ferry out of here?" Martin asks.

Blake responds with a miserable sigh.

"I'm sure it doesn't feel like it," Martin continues, "but it's for the best that you stay. It'd be too dangerous trying to get off the island tonight. I doubt the ferry is even running." He guns the engine, popping the wheels up off the washed-out drive and onto the comparatively dry cul-de-sac. "If you want a ride to the ferry tomorrow, I'd be happy to bring you."

Blake stares at the raindrops racing down the windshield.

"Hey," Martin says, and Blake finally looks at him. "I'm sorry things went so poorly today."

She refrains from saying that things have gone poorly every day of her life. She says goodbye and climbs out of the truck. At the front door, she turns, expecting to see him taking the other, smaller drive around back. Blake has no idea what kind of relationship Martin Dempsey and Fiona Searles have, but if there is ever a night to stay at White Hall, this is it. Martin, however, goes straight. He must have another destination in mind.

The foyer is still and silent. Blake considers making a go for the wine cellar now, but it would be stupid not to start with the bottle already in her room. Once that's gone, she'll be less wary in her pursuit of a second. Or a third. The thirty-two days of sobriety she's put together is a thirty-two-day reset button on her tolerance, and she has no idea what mulberry wine is like in terms of alcohol content.

She is beside the portrait of Mary Hopkins Searles when her phone vibrates. She slides it from her back pocket, sees her sponsor's name flashing across the screen. Blake hits the lock button twice to end the call and continues up the stairs.

Once in her room, however, the phone vibrates again. Chris has been texting her all day, but she couldn't muster the energy to read much less respond to them. Blake sits on the bed, wincing at the state of her clothes, finger hovering over the green button. She'll get this over with, then be free to inflict the maximum amount of damage onto her misguided recovery.

"Hi, Chris."

"Blake, Jesus. Where have you been? You've been treating me like a one-night stand who's been talking about how great it would be if we moved in together. You're a royal pain in the ass, you know that? Listen, your lawyer showed up at the Big Book meeting last night, looking for the sign-offs on your attendance."

Blake doesn't know if this is a good thing or a disaster. She attended one meeting a day for thirty days, right up until she bought a ticket for the ferry and sailed into this never-ending rain—and shit—storm. "What'd you tell her?"

"I gave her the sheet. Said you'd been coming faithfully and that, as your sponsor, I've been really impressed by your commitment. I said it'd been a long time since I'd seen someone who wanted to get—and stay—sober as much as you do. I also told her I knew exactly where you were, and that you'd cleared this little trip with me ahead of time."

"You did?"

"I did. So, I gotta ask, where the hell are you right now, Blake?"

Blake looks around. How to answer that? In a nightmare? A castle? Stuck between the pages of a gothic novel? "It's complicated," Blake says.

"Complicated because you're dealing with something sober? Or complicated because you're dealing with something after falling off the wagon?"

"I'm sober," Blake says. *For the moment.* "Chris? Why did you tell the public defender all that?"

"Because everything is true *except* that last part, and I wanted to give you the benefit of the doubt. Please tell me you're not about to make a fool of me. Because, here's the thing . . ." Chris trails off. Blake can hear someone ask where the coffee filters are. Metal chair legs scrape across a gritty linoleum floor. Her sponsor is in the basement of Saint Monica's, getting ready to recite the serenity prayer with forty-five other former degenerates. The woman has been sober thirty years and never misses a meeting. *The woman has been sober thirty years* because *she never misses a meeting*, the AA-indoctrinated part of her brain corrects her.

"Here's the thing," Chris repeats, "Lynch said someone in District C-6 told Wally Stevenson's legal team you'd joined AA. That the accident caused you to reevaluate your mess of a life, and you were committed to getting clean. Apparently, Wally Stevenson is an ACA—"

Blake is about to cut in before she remembers ACA stands for *Adult Child of an Alcoholic.*

"—and he's got it in his heart to forgive."

"Forgive?"

"Meaning, not to press charges. Or, not to have his lawyer push for felony charges, I should say."

"If it's a misdemeanor, that means no jail time?"

"Right. My guess is you'll have to continue attending AA and show clean drug screens once a month for up to three years."

It's a long time, but prison would be far longer—and a far greater nightmare—than any twelve-step meeting. Her eyes dart to the bottle on the dresser. It's dark as tar and threatens to paint her future far darker. Still, the look on her mother's face when she said she had just one daughter flashes in her mind. She longs for oblivion, misses being able to blot out feelings of being unloved and unwanted. What, then? Does she choose the disappointment and chaos of her past or the vulnerability and uncertainty of the future? Remain trapped in a decaying castle, or climb out of the rubble despite there not being a single shard of daylight to be seen?

"When are you coming back to Southie?" Chris asks. "Kim said you were going to Connecticut or something? To meet up with some family member?"

Good ol' Kim, resident AA gossip. Thankfully, years of drug use had rendered Kim's powers of recollection practically nonexistent. "Something like that. It turned into more of a recon mission than an actual reunion."

"So you're okay then?"

Blake suppresses a sigh. "I'm fine. Thank you for buying me a bit of time when it comes to my lawyer. I'll be back tomorrow. I'll probably make it to the Looney Nooney. If not, I'll definitely be at Saint Monica's for the meditation group at eight."

"I'm really glad to hear that. I'll be seeing you soon, then."

Blake hangs up and drops her head into her hands. She still wants to get annihilated, but the possibility of staying out of jail is more probable than she thought. Still, it's not like she's going to be able to stay sober forever. Next time, she might not just smash a poor father's leg into a dozen pieces and traumatize his child. She might kill someone. She might kill several someones.

Blake paces the room, pausing to glance up at the rain every few rotations until she catches her reflection in one of the water-streaked windows and turns away. She doesn't want to see the face her own mother didn't recognize.

Is it you? Maureen had spat the words at her when the reporter story had worn thin. *Is that why you're here? Are you the woman who* thinks *she's my daughter?* The questions had ricocheted against Blake's skull, leaving in their wake an echo like listening to a bell toll from inside the tower. Her thoughts had swirled with a mixture of recognition and confusion at her mother's reaction: both, *How is this happening?* and, *Ah, yes, but of course.*

If the weather would break for fifteen goddamn minutes, she could go for a walk to clear her head. But the clouds are as thick as ever. Giving the bottle a wide berth, she crosses the room to the farthest window. *Rule number three,* she thinks bitterly. *If a storm descends, do not venture outside. Remain in your bedroom, and keep the smelling salts handy.*

Acres of mulberry trees stretch to the east, parallel with the ocean. She can see the edge of the bluffs in the distance. The clay cliffs drop off at a ninety-degree angle. There's a fence, but it looks flimsy at best, rotted out from years of seafoam and salt spray at worst. She shivers, and it occurs to her that a bath in the luxurious clawfoot tub would warm her up. It would also keep her from having to make a decision about the wine for at least another hour. She turns toward the bathroom, but a flash of white draws her gaze back to the window.

Kitty-corner to the mansion stands a perfect replica of White Hall, everything from the rusticated wood to the entry pillars topped with twin stone globes. It's the same English Mannerist style and symmetrical sides separated by a central—albeit smaller—hall. A domed cupola glares down from the highest point of the structure, and beach roses, switchgrass, and arrowwood shrubs press through fence slats like skeletal arms.

Blake spins around. The mulberry wine is still there. She isn't experiencing some sort of wine-induced hallucination. "What the hell?" she whispers, then decides, rain or not, rule number three or not, she's getting the hell out of this room. She's getting that trapped feeling again, and the strange little replica looks inviting. At the very least, she can get wasted out there as easily as she can in here.

She dresses in her thickest leggings, corrals her hair into a bun, and pulls on her still-damp jacket. Her phone gets zipped into the front pocket of her backpack. The bottle is on the dresser. She could leave it, go out to the little replica of White Hall, or better yet, down to the cliffs. She could scream into the wind, drop to her knees, and pray, ask for her Higher Power's help. She could do any number of things that've been suggested to her by members of AA.

The problem is, when Chris explained the concept of a higher power, she told Blake it didn't have to do with any religious construct. She said it could be a fellow alcoholic, someone she looked up to, even a family member. Blake decided on her Higher Power immediately. She knew it was stupid to give the biological mother she'd never met that much control over her well-being. But she'd never been able to abandon the idea that her mother was a decent person, forced into giving her up through no fault of her own. Blake had concocted stories through the years, everything from a superhero mother needing to sever all connections with those she loved to the horrible—but justifiable—possibility that her mother had been assaulted, or otherwise coerced into a sexual relationship, and given Blake up to protect her.

It's silly now, but when she was a kid, shuffled through the doors of one foster home after another, these fantasies—along with her favorite novels—got her through the night. Blake wasn't certain Chris knew she'd chosen her mother as her Higher Power, but she thought her sponsor might suspect it. Chris never judged, or hinted that Blake should consider changing her mind, but now it seems like another reason her sobriety isn't meant to last.

Since Blake can decidedly *not* pray to Maureen Mills for the serenity to accept the things she cannot change, she slips the wine into the backpack, swings the bag onto her back, and heads for the stairs.

Chapter 13

Blake cuts across the circular drive toward a footpath that follows the sharp angles of the mansion. Prickly branches from nearby shrubs trail across the backs of her hands and neck. When she clears the west side, she's relieved to find the terrain switches from garden path to paved walkway. The stone extends into a vast, impressive courtyard that looks to be part of the mansion's very foundation.

To get to the replica, she'll have to find a way off the courtyard level and down to the grass, then out to the boardwalk that stretches from the lower level of White Hall's exterior to the north end of the beach. She knew the view from her room was deceiving, but now that she's traversing it, she is floored by how extensive the Searleses' property is.

After several minutes, she finds a ladder extending down the base of the courtyard, carved in the space between two covered arches that stretch to the ground. The grooves are shallow, but she's managing, until the nail of her left ring finger catches in a chink in the stone and rips. Blood oozes from the nail bed and cascades down her hand. She jumps off the final step and stares at the blood until a fat drop of rain snakes beneath the collar of her jacket. Blake sprints across the grass, bringing her finger up every few paces to suck at the sting.

Along the bottom portion of the courtyard are six arches in addition to the two she climbed down between. When she cuts right, there are eight more. The ornamentation is deceiving; each arch is a doorway that can be raised or lowered, leading to an area beneath the mansion. Perhaps the sisters use the space for storage.

At the mouth of the boardwalk, Blake eyes the slick, sand-coated wood. Up ahead, the mouth of the mulberry forest yawns. The thunderous crashing of waves displaces the whooshing wind and the patter of the rain. *Searles' Folly, indeed. Who else would build a castle on the edge of an island, inaccessible on one side by a mulberry forest and on the other by rocky cliffs and treacherous ocean?* She crosses the boardwalk toward the mini mansion with cautious steps.

The building is about the size of a small guesthouse and in serious disrepair. Where White Hall looks to have been maintained enough to preserve some of its former grandeur, the model is chipped and listing, moss-covered and faded. Its close proximity to the water likely contributed to this deterioration, but it instills in Blake a feeling of *wrongness*. If White Hall is an errant queen, this smaller structure is the discarded head of one of her victims. It seems unfinished rather than crumbling. Out of place and yet a perfect match to its prototype. It's an oxymoron. An enigma.

And Blake feels drawn to go inside it.

The middle of three forward-facing arches obscures a latch on its left. She starts forward, backpack bumping against her, the weight of it reminding her of what she carries. The rain blurs her vision, teasing the intoxication to come. She can almost taste the bitter juice of the berries.

The wood frame resists her efforts; it would make sense for the Searleses to keep the building locked. But then, Blake is falling forward as the door flies open. Words bloom in her brain like dandelions: *sepulcher, tomb, crypt.* It's silly; she's aboveground, and there are several small windows letting in drab, diffuse light. Still, when she pushes the door closed behind her, the crash of the ocean and the howl of the wind disappear as if into a vacuum.

There's an energy in the room. Or, rather, a lack of energy. The building is dry, deathly silent, and cool, but not cold. Blake shivers anyway, unnerved by the pulsing quiet and utter stillness. The sense of something waiting beneath the floorboards.

The hall splits into left and right wings, but unlike the actual mansion, these wings lead nowhere, ending in windowless, detail-less walls. It's the main foyer that stretches back into a darkened hallway. Blake starts down it. There's that sense of waiting again, that things are happening, or about to happen, outside her periphery.

This hall *does* split left and right at the end. The right door leads to an out-of-order restroom. The plumbing looks to be mid–twentieth century. Blake tries the door on the left. It opens onto a large, strange space, its architecture rife with compositional tension and visual trickery, listing columns, rust, and mildew. The room appears to have been employed as a bathhouse; there are changing stalls in one corner, and in another, a porcelain basin.

There's no chance this structure was ever included as a selling point for bed-and-breakfast guests; the place is a relic, a symbol of the gilded age of the mansion's opulent past. Why keep the replica at all? Or, if Aileen and Fiona didn't want to spend the money to raze the building, why not empty the room of the moldy and must-smelling furniture? Blake tugs the backpack off her shoulders and sinks into the leather chair.

Why keep it at all? The voice that asks this won't be silenced. *Because it's a distraction. A reminder that everything—rusticated wood, leather, flesh—is deteriorating.* This forgotten, ruined building was once part of a thriving island home. Treasured. Appreciated. Full of possibility. A lot like a newborn baby.

Treasured things lose their sheen. Everyone knows that. Blake unearths the bottle from her backpack. She tips and straightens it in the silvery light of the room's two small windows, imagining how the wine will balloon warmly in her stomach and iron out the knife-sharp corners of her vision.

You tell this Blake character that I have one daughter, her mother had said. *Whatever she thinks happened twenty-six years ago has nothing to do with me. Or my family. Say that you understand.*

"I understand," Blake says to the empty room, and laughs. The laugh turns to a strangled, hopeless sob. Even if she avoids going to jail for what she did to Walton Stevenson and his son, she won't be able to stay clean. The prescription bottles in Maureen's cabinet are proof of that.

No one knows she's on this island. She could stay, skip her court date, stop attending the endless, tedious AA meetings. Get a job waitressing—or better yet, as a seasonal worker at the Searleses' vineyard—and make enough to rent a crappy apartment and keep herself stocked in vodka. Hell, she could schedule an appointment with whichever island physician keeps Maureen up to her eyeballs in benzodiazepines, as long as the Massachusetts court system doesn't check out-of-state prescription-monitoring programs when searching for fugitives.

She's been fearful of her fate since arriving on Block Island, having sensed that walking through the door of White Hall set into motion actions that couldn't be undone. Blake places one hand around the neck of the bottle and the other on the cap. She twists, but it's sealed too tightly. "Come *on*." She tries again. The cap won't budge.

Blake drops to her knees. Her heels smack against the foot of the leather armchair, and it shoots back several inches. She tries the cap again. A frustrated scream escapes her lips. She tries again. A red welt appears in the palm of her hand. She raises the bottle above her head to smash it, thinks better of the idea and, after placing the wine down beside her, slams both hands against the floor in rage. Confusion. Hopelessness. She stays there, palms flat, forehead to the ground. It's the same position in which the police found her on the blood- and rain-slicked pavement after she struck Walton Stevenson.

Why did he have to be pulled over on the side of the highway? Why did she have to hit him? Why was his son in the car? Even if she could have forgiven Maureen for abandoning her, why is her mother so awful now? Why does Blake feel like everything—her circumstances, her actions, her addiction, this house—is a whirlpool pulling her down, and down, and down?

As she cries, her body hitches. Her arms shake and spasm. It takes a moment to realize that the floorboards echo hollowly. Wrongly. Blake wipes her face on her sleeve and moves the bottle out of the way. Placing both hands flat again, she shakes the floorboard. It shifts—about half an inch in either direction—beneath her. She presses her ear to the ground.

She hears nothing, but that doesn't mean there's not some sort of crawl space below her. Scanning the visible expanse of floor, she spots a set of hinges almost flush with the base of the counter. She skirts the area and slides the counter back from the hinges. The floor beneath it is light with discoloration.

Blake circles the hollow-sounding floorboards a second time and slides her fingers into a divot across from the latch. Her ruined nail bed catches on a sliver in the wood, and she hisses. The wood sticks in the frame for a beat, before the whole thing rises like a drawbridge. She lowers the trapdoor to the opposite floor.

The depths beyond the opening are too dark for the weak light to penetrate. Blake makes out a few cobweb-hung stairs and nothing else. She looks up at the room with its odd pillars and archways, its mismatched geometric designs. She looks at the waning daylight, the waiting bottle of mulberry wine. She looks back down into the hole.

She has placed one wet sneaker on the top step when, down the hallway, the bathhouse door creaks open.

Chapter 14

Blake leaps out of the hatch as if the floor is on fire. "Hello," she calls. "Is someone there?" Several steps into the hallway, she calls out again, "Hello? Aileen?" No one answers. *The wind,* she tells herself. *Just the wind.* She walks back, and is peering into the yawning hole in the floor when symphonic chimes burst shrilly from her backpack.

Blake gasps, jumping away from the hatch a second time, and scrambles for the phone. Martin's name glows across the screen. She swipes to accept the call.

"Martin? Are you there?"

"Blake." She can barely hear him. "—ake, it's Martin. I—for—"

"What was that? The service is terrible."

"—dress for your sister, Thalia."

"What? A dress?"

"No, I—can you hear me?—sent me the address for—ister."

"The address! Great. I can't believe you got it!"

"—at White Hall now." The rest is swallowed by static.

"Sorry?"

"I'm at White Hall now. Are you in your room?"

"I'm not." She glances at the windows. The rain has increased in intensity. It will take her longer to get back than it did to get out here. "Could you slip it under my door? And thanks so much. I appreciate you seeing this through." She doesn't add, *If I'm going to write to her at all.* That she's more likely to communicate with her drug dealer than her sister when she gets back to Boston is her business, not Martin's.

"—can't hear you. I'll come by now."

"No, Martin, I'm not there. Just stick it under the door!"

"—*wants* to talk to you, Blake!"

"What was that?" She moves to the window, puts the call on speaker, and holds the phone up as high as she can.

"I hope you're not mad"—his voice is clearer now, unbroken—"but I reached out to Thalia myself. She wants to speak with you. To tell you about Maureen, why she is the way she is. The sooner the better, is what she—"

The connection goes spotty again, then drops. "Shit!" But the small flame of excitement has already been lit. She needs to get to her room, to talk to Martin in person. To find out exactly what Thalia—what her *sister*—said.

She looks down. There's still a mysterious hatch at her feet. "Rule number two," she says decidedly, "don't descend into any dungeons." It's probably an old wine cellar anyway. If she's being honest—and she's been trying to be since discovering the nature of the connection between herself and her mother—she's not sure she would have gone farther than that top step. Aileen's admission that White Hall occasionally suffered a rat-infested winter had not been forgotten.

She lowers the door over the hatch, regards the wine for what feels like the hundredth time, then shoves the bottle into the mesh side pouch of her backpack. Getting drunk out here was probably a worse idea than descending into the underground lair of a coastal rat king. Flashes of lightning force themselves through the windows, and thunder responds with a similar warning.

The hall seems longer than when she traveled it earlier. The door is indeed latched, and she pushes it open. Rain pelts her cheeks with the force of hornets. Blake breaks into a run. Lightning flashes out over the ocean. She doesn't need to count the seconds between it and the thunder to know the storm is gaining on the island.

The sky opens, and the rain comes down in buckets. Her foot slips on the boardwalk, and she goes down. On hands and knees, she looks up to see White Hall looming before her like a haunted house. Like the cover of a horror novel, every detail perfectly rendered. The castle with peaks like teeth. The rain soaking through her inadequate clothing. The heroine crouching pathetically in the foreground, chased by what's behind her, cursed by what's before her. The skeletal trees and waning gibbous moon in the swirling, nickel-gray sky.

Somehow, she gets to her feet. Her nail is bleeding again, trailing pink-tinged water between her fingers. Wiping her hand futilely on her wet jeans, she fights her way to the top of the boardwalk. She's about to start across the grass, when she sees the figure. The woman stands before one of the courtyard arches, staring at Blake as if contemplating a painting, unbothered by the deluge. Blake would think her on a different plane from this one if her maroon silk dress hadn't darkened to black and the veil over her face wasn't slicked against her cheeks.

The specter from her room, the ghost of Mary Hopkins Searles, steps forward and brings up a hand. Lightning crackles across the sky. "Go!" Mary shouts, and thunder detonates. Blake yelps and runs in the opposite direction.

The edge of the cliff comes up fast. Blake catches herself on the fence and gasps for air. Did she really see Mary, or was it merely a mulberry tree, the wind echoing through branches raised like arms?

Another blast of thunder shakes her thoughts loose. She cannot stay on this island. She has to get away. If the mansion wants to consume her, to claim her as another of its ghosts, she won't make it that easy. Won't go down without a fight.

Blake grips the top slat and climbs over. From this height, with the rain coming from every direction and her emotions in a similar state of chaos, the dream she had the first night at White Hall, of facing a demonic sky and tempestuous sea in a bathtub, returns to her. "Rule number six," she screams into the rain. "Take your nightmares seriously!" The ocean is not a hazard but an out-and-out predator. Its waves will reach up and snatch her.

The bathtub. Why isn't she in the pristine, inviting bathtub back in her room right now? Why can't she ever do anything normal, like choose a soak in a tub over a jaunt in a hurricane with a vengeful ghost? If she makes it back to her room, back to the mainland, she'll choose the bathtub every time. But for now, she needs to do what she's going to do.

Blake inches forward, leans over the cliff . . .

. . . and tosses the bottle of mulberry wine over the edge.

She climbs between the slats rather than over them, and once back on the grass, she doesn't stop until she makes it to the bottom of the courtyard. The sky is hemorrhaging water. She can't see more than six inches in front of her. Climbing the stone ladder right now would be suicide. She squints at the arched doorways, chooses one, and tries to force it open. It doesn't budge. Neither does the next one, or the one after that. The first arch after she rounds the corner, however, pulls open so fast, she's lifted off her feet.

Blake releases the panel as it rolls up like a garage door. She ducks inside, and reaches for the bottom, but the torsion spring on which the panel operates has pulled the bottom portion out of her reach. She'll have to tell Aileen that she left it open, but the thought makes her tired. She retreats farther beneath the courtyard, searching for a way inside the mansion, telling herself that she won't see Mary, cheeks sloughed off and hands full of rotten berries, looming out of the shadows.

Perhaps the underground tunnel, or storage unit, or whatever this mazelike cave system is, connects to the wine cellar. If so, she could pop right up into the kitchen. Envisioning Aileen's little tray of teas and honey, Blake pats her pockets for her phone. She wraps wet fingers—finally free of blood from her torn nail—around the plastic case and swipes for the flashlight. The weak beam shines on Mary Hopkins Searles, directly in front of her.

Blake shrieks and almost drops the phone. Not Mary but a man. Bearded and disheveled and . . . familiar. The groundskeeper. He pulls the bottom of the arched panel down and stares at Blake. "I saw you running across the grass," he says. "I came to help you out of the storm."

"You scared me half to death. I thought . . ." She doesn't finish her sentence. The groundskeeper—Monty, Aileen said his name was—starts across the cavernous space. Blake has no choice but to follow.

"Storm's bad," he says. "And it's not safe beneath the courtyard. I've got to fix some loose stones." He jerks his chin at the rain. "There's another entrance around the side there. Come on."

Monty leads her past the stone steps she descended earlier. They make their way up a small incline, and the side entrance Monty spoke of appears. He follows her inside and closes the door. Blake turns to thank him.

But the groundskeeper is gone.

Blake spins in a circle. There's a door to the left of the one they just came through, but why disappear without saying goodbye? She sighs, squeezes water from her hair, and continues forward. Before she can reach the end of the hallway, a silhouette darkens the frosted window set into a thick wooden door ahead. The door swings open, and Blake steps into a small anteroom. The furniture is threadbare, and there's a strip of wallpaper peeling in one corner. She recognizes another frosted window that looks into the parlor. The door swings closed to reveal Aileen.

"I just took a shower myself," the proprietress says, fingering her wet hair. "But in the bathroom like a normal person." Blake flinches at the word *normal*. "What on earth were you doing out there?"

Blake's tired of questions. Questions from the lawyers, her sponsor, Martin, her mother, and now Aileen. "I wanted to go for a walk."

"A walk."

"Yeah, I . . ." Blake sighs again. "I needed to clear my head. And now I'm dripping all over your rug. Let me get upstairs. Actually, let me say good night. I've got to go to bed."

Aileen looks at the loudly ticking clock. "You'll come down for dinner? I'm making—"

"Please, don't bother. I'm sorry to be rude or ungrateful, but it's been a long day. I need to get some sleep. Tomorrow, I'll be out of your hair. No more meals, requests for rides, or baby-biological-mama-drama. No more bothering Martin. I'll call a taxi, the rain will stop, and before you know it, it'll be spring. White Hall will be full of vibrant, happy vacationers, and you'll forget all about me. My stay here will be little more than a bad dream."

"You're not bothering anyone," Aileen says. "In fact, Martin was looking for you. He left this with me to give to you."

Aileen holds out a piece of paper. Blake unfolds it and reads the neat words printed at its center.

"He had to run, but he said this was something you needed sooner rather than later."

"Thank you," Blake says, not entirely believing what she's been given. She reads the words a second time, and then a third: *Thalia Mills. 135 Clarendon Street, Boston, MA 02116.*

"You're welcome," Aileen says. "You know, Martin didn't say anything specific, but when I asked him how things went today, he made it sound pretty grim."

Please no more questions. I can't take any more questions.

"I'm just the B and B owner. I don't want to overstep my bounds, but if you were looking for something to do tonight, something to take your mind off things, you can't do any better than using that address as the catalyst to writing a letter."

Blake jerks her head up. "You know what this is?"

"Martin told me. He was hoping that having it might take the sting out of today."

Blake stares back down at the paper.

"And if you've still got that bottle of wine," Aileen says carefully, "I'd be happy to take it off your hands. So you don't, you know, make a decision you're going to regret."

Blake wants to be mad at Aileen's interference, but she *did* throw her wine—a thoughtful gift for the large portion of the population who aren't alcoholics—over a cliff despite Aileen having offered to take it back that first night *and* littered on the property in the process. "That's okay," Blake says. "Like I said, I'll give it to someone as a gift."

Thunder rolls in response. "It's supposed to clear tomorrow," Aileen says when the echo dies away. "High of fifty-two and sunny. But this weather's not going down without a fight."

Blake tries to imagine the sun shining on this dreary place. Will she stand in its warmth on the deck of the ferry as the ship surges toward the mainland? Will birds sing in elms, in oaks, in anything but mulberry trees, as she makes her way home, to another chance at a sober, worthwhile life?

"That'd be nice." Blake stands, wincing at the wet spot her clothes made on the ottoman. "Good night, Aileen. If I don't see you in the morning, I want to thank you for all you've done for me. You've been more than hospitable. You were a downright lifesaver. In fact . . ." She pauses. Aileen looks up.

Blake shakes her head and chuckles. "Maybe I'll leave a review, after all."

Aileen walks Blake to the foyer. "Good night, Miss Bronson, and good luck with whatever comes next."

Blake climbs the stairs, stopping to inspect Mary Searles's portrait. Aileen was right: large, wide-set eyes and cheeks like apples. Mary does look a little like her. She searches Mary's face. "Was that you I saw out in the rain?"

Mary doesn't answer. Blake stares into her unseeing brown eyes a moment longer before continuing up the stairs.

Chapter 15

The sound of water filling the tub is the antithesis to the rain. Blake undresses while it fills and steps into a chenille robe she found in a drawer. She sits on the bed, a towel wrapped around her hair.

She should relax in a scalding bath *before* she writes to Thalia. That, at least, was her plan. But staring at the blank page, she's overcome with the urge to snatch up the pen from the nightstand. If there's one thing the trauma of the day might be good for, it's transferring her thoughts from brain to paper. She leans back on the pillows, props the notepad on her knees, and writes.

She stops to turn the faucet off before the tub can run over, returns to the bed, and writes some more. She leaves nothing out, includes her reasons for coming to Block Island, for wanting to meet Maureen, and for wanting to reach out to Thalia. She includes her fears that she's tied to a fate borne of her upbringing. There's likely *too much* about the White Hall ghost and her paranoia, but when the letter is complete, she is a little awed by it, as if the great novelists of the past have guided her hand. So awed, in fact, she fears she'll lose her nerve if she waits to send it in the morning.

Blake addresses and stamps one of the sophisticated-looking light-brown envelopes from the nightstand drawer and slips the letter inside but pauses before she seals it. Who's to say Thalia won't simply throw the letter away, unconvinced of any of the admissions within it? The tangibility of the hard-won birth certificate in her backpack occurs to her. While the thought of relinquishing it is frightening, what good is it to her now, in the wake of Maureen's rejection? Before she can change her mind, Blake unzips the backpack, pulls the certificate from its inner pocket, and slips it in behind the letter before sealing the envelope.

She dashes on quiet feet down the hall, descends the stairs, and delivers the letter to Aileen's trusty wooden mail organizer on the parlor wall, pausing only to give the envelope a superstitious kiss. She's back in her room before the bathwater has lost too much of its heat.

She feels—strangely, unbelievably—good. Not great, but not as bad as she did this afternoon. Sure, Thalia might end up being as cold and dismissive as her mother, but maybe not. And maybe that's what this feeling is: hope. A slice of optimism that her future doesn't have to be a jail cell or some dilapidated apartment with empty pill bottles and shot glasses for company. Maybe Thalia left Maureen behind because she was following the rules of surviving a gothic horror novel herself; maybe she wanted to minimize the prospect of inheriting the family curse.

Blake smiles at the thought of having a real relationship with Thalia, something elevated above the connections orchestrated by the inherent fellowship of AA, which is all Blake knows. Maybe they could truly be sisters. Maybe they could be friends.

As she shrugs out of the robe, she notices the umbrella from Aileen's Jeep, the fleece-lined jacket hanging by its tag from the umbrella's point in a corner. She'll have to bring them downstairs in the morning. Aileen never goes anywhere and hadn't wanted Blake to drive the car when Fiona was around; the Jeep is probably *Fiona's*. The last thing she needs is Fiona Searles thinking she stole from her.

Though, now that she's looking at the jacket—really looking at it, free from the urgency of bad weather that forced her to borrow it in the first place, to ignore its tapered cut and roomy sleeves—she realizes she *recognizes it*. It's the black jacket she first saw Martin in, when he stared at her from beside Fiona at the back of Above the Rocks. Why hadn't he said anything when she'd marched into the *Times'* offices wearing it? *He probably didn't want to embarrass you.* She sighs. Tomorrow, it won't matter. This island—and everyone on it—will be nothing but a memory.

Blake walks to the bathroom, the memory of ice-cold rain sluicing down her exposed skin making her shiver. Soon, bathwater warm as a cocoon will cover her limbs, her stomach, her chest, her still-sore neck, caressing her like silk. She lights a candle from the dresser and flicks off the bathroom light. The mirror is fogged over, and the towel on the floor is plush and perfectly white. The marble, the walls, the sink, the tub—everything's white. The lack of color equates to silence. It's sooth-ing. Like a sober, static-free brain without the ensuing anxiety. She steps in and lets out a groan of pleasure.

Every once in a while, something comes close to the euphoria of a Percocet tablet, the flush of a fifth of gin. The water is everything. Warm. Safe. Like a mother's embrace. She lies back, kicks a bar of lav-ender soap off a small dish, and lets the water go milky. She closes her eyes. Wishes, still, there had been a ferry off the island this evening, but will settle for being gentle with herself. For once.

The first creak of the floorboards she chalks up to the wind. The storm, which seemed to have tired itself out over the last hour, has returned for another go at the island. The second creak comes between rumbles of thunder. Separate from the storm. Distinctly human.

Or, distinctly once-human.

Blake doesn't call out. Aileen has not come into the room to give her more soap or towels. She knows no one will answer. The water is, quite suddenly, not as warm as when she slipped into it. She sits up slowly, preparing to crawl out of the tub. Better to meet whatever is creeping across the floorboards without the risk of slipping on the por-celain enamel coating. She thinks, for the second time tonight, about the tub in her dream that became her coffin. Why hadn't she taken rule number six seriously?

She is leaning on the lip of the tub and pulling her feet beneath her when a conglomeration of black crepe and maroon silk rushes through the door like a tempest. Blake is thrown back hard, skull thumping against the side, shriek muffled by a black-gloved hand. She blinks, but everything's fuzzy. Then what she can see of the world is blocked by an impossibly black cloud of swirling lace and muslin.

This time, she manages an actual scream, and scrambles for purchase on the tub's slick bottom. Damn that lavender soap. The black glove catches her wrist, and sharp, bright pain ignites there, a sting akin to any of the dozens of times she pressed a needle to the crook of her arm. She feels the same warmth of release in her veins. There's a resultant shift in her brain that is not the euphoric rush of an opioid, but a sort of opposite; not in terms of the euphoria—there's no outright pain—but in the closing of a dam, the sucking up of serotonin. Before she can fully process it, the same sting and release occurs along her left wrist. The bathwater is mulberry wine. Then, the mulberry wine reddens to the color of blood. Blood splatters the marble. The walls. The sink.

Blake is still in the bathtub, but the bathtub has been transported to the sea. She grabs for something, anything, but there's nothing but more water, and more water, and more water. Her head swims, her vision swims, the tub swims, drifts, rocks away. There's a flash of lightning from outside her room. Or else the lightning is in her head. There's a sensation that she's sinking, but it goes on far longer than the depth of the bathtub would deem possible.

She wants to laugh. She wants to cry. Because for all her self-hatred and misery and dissociation and depression, she wants, very much, to live. To get sober. To make amends. It's why she came to this godforsaken island rather than ending it in Boston. To entertain the hope that, in meeting her mother, she'd discover some fundamental element at the core of her being that connected her to someone, to one other person in the world. She found that connection, but it bred more disappointment. In the end, however, there was—confoundedly, unexpectedly—hope.

Everything goes black. This is it. But then there's breath on her neck and bombazine, like the wisp of a butterfly wing, against her cheek.

"You stayed when you should have gone," the voice says. "You did not listen. You will learn the identity of the Mulberry Maiden, after all."

The last thought that crosses Blake's mind before she dies is one of irony: she has succumbed to the plot of her gothic horror novel. She tried to follow the rules, but the restless ghost haunting her halls and derailing her objective proved too worthy a foe for her fragile disposition. Though, if she's about to suffer an untimely and mysterious death, does this mean she *wasn't* in a gothic horror novel . . .

. . . or does it just mean she wasn't the heroine?

The world becomes water. Sound is reduced to the rocking of waves, the pattering of the rain. The rain slows.

Then stops.

Silence. And more silence. And more silence.

PART II

Chapter 16

Thalia Mills opens her umbrella as she steps off the ferry, but rain still slicks her bare arms and dampens the cuffs of her jeans. The terminal is flooded, each undulating puddle a smaller version of the rough and endless ocean she's just crossed. It's only twelve miles from Point Judith to Block Island, but the squalls caused the journey to take on an Odyssean quality. She scans the lot for Sarah Liang's taxi, focusing on her hunger and desire to get out of the rain. Anything to avoid what she's actually feeling, which is heavy, nauseating dread.

Her phone vibrates in her purse. She fishes it out, swipes a wet finger across the screen, and squints at the I'm staring right at you text. Thalia looks up and still sees nothing, then remembers there's another lot to the right. Two steps in that direction reveal Sarah in her idling taxi, arms raised to indicate her excitement.

She's not prepared for how thoroughly the sight of her oldest friend levels her. In the space of an instant, she's transported back to the small brick schoolhouse that—to this day—supports Block's entire student population, to the playground where Sarah smacked Nancy Bliven off the climbing dome with her lacrosse stick after Nancy made fun of Thalia for kissing her fifth-grade crush, Emily Griffin. Sarah was the only Asian student at Block Island School, so in the minority herself—but a giant when it came to standing up for what she believed in. No one had given Thalia trouble for kissing a girl—or going to homecoming with a girl, or later, dating Emily Griffin seriously—again.

Despite wanting, as a teenager, to get as far away from the island as possible, it suddenly strikes Thalia as inconceivable that she'd collected her high school diploma, packed for college, and simply said goodbye to Sarah. Sure, she's seen her on a handful of occasions over the last ten years—always on the mainland—but how many times had Thalia rejected Sarah's requests to get together, citing plans with Laura or being buried with work? They hadn't just been best friends, once; they'd been as close as sisters. And as she drags her suitcase across the tarmac, wincing as her leather boots plunge into puddle after puddle, a new feeling displaces her hunger and dread: guilt.

Sarah opens the car door as she approaches, but Thalia waves her back inside. "No sense in both of us getting wet!" The wind steals the words, but Sarah gets the idea, and retreats. The trunk holds accoutrements from every season of island life: a quilted jacket atop a down one, a pair of Scottie dog–printed galoshes, and enough colorful beach pails to entertain a small army of children. Sarah must use the taxi as her personal vehicle in the off-season, though with the minuscule number of tourists in the winter, Thalia can't exactly blame her.

She hoists her suitcase on top of a pile of reusable shopping bags, closes her umbrella, and tosses that in too. By the time she's opening the passenger door and sliding into the warm, dry seat, her lilac silk blouse has darkened to eggplant, and mascara runs down her cheeks.

She lowers the visor and rubs the worst of the makeup away with her fingers. There's a balled-up scarf in her purse, and she wraps it around her shoulders. When she finally turns, Sarah is looking at her with a mixture of amusement and annoyance.

"I'm soaked," Thalia says unnecessarily, "so don't worry about hugging me. Saving me from this downpour is the only gesture of affection I—"

Before she can finish, Sarah grabs her over the middle console and wraps her in a rough embrace. Thalia feels any awkwardness or friction between them melt away.

When Sarah releases her, and Thalia has caught her breath, she nods at the rain pelting the windows. "Should I have expected anything less for my joyous return?"

Sarah shrugs. "Don't feel too special. It's been raining for a month straight. Honestly . . ." She trails off. "Never mind."

"No, what?"

"Well"—Sarah puts the taxi in reverse and backs out of the lot— "it's been raining since the beginning of February." She glances at Thalia, then back to the road. "Since right before that poor girl's murder."

That poor girl. Thalia refuses to tense up, though she swears she hears Blake's birth certificate beating like a telltale heart from her purse. She knew Sarah would want to discuss the murder, but hadn't expected it to be this soon. "Yeah," she breathes, forcing an outsider's incredulity into her voice. "We haven't talked about what happened. It's absolutely crazy."

"Right?" Sarah says, then sips from a bottle of iced tea she plucked from the floor of the taxi. "I mean, Fiona Searles *murdering* a random mainlander visiting the island? Slashing her wrists in a big clawfoot tub in that creepy old mansion? It's like something out of a Lifetime movie."

"Or a horror novel," Thalia mutters.

"Huh?"

"Nothing." *Couldn't we have caught up on each other's lives before delving into why Fiona Searles killed my sister?* Not wanting to tell Sarah who Blake was exacerbates her guilt at retreating from her friend's life for all these years. "So is that what happened?" she says, forcing casual interest into her tone. "Fiona killed her in a tub?"

Sarah is maneuvering onto Corn Neck Road, but pulls her eyes from the rain-slicked pavement long enough to shoot Thalia a look. "Don't tell me you haven't been following every detail of this from

Boston. I know you haven't lived here in forever, but come on! When was the last time there was a murder on Block Island? The eighties? The sixties? Longer? Not within our lifetimes, that's for sure."

"I've been following the stories, I guess," Thalia says. She pulls the scarf tighter, unable to get warm. "I didn't know Fiona Searles well. Of course I have vague recollections of seeing her at Above the Rocks a few times when I was a kid. Fiona was always 'Martin Dempsey's girl' before she was anything else, and while getting along with the boss's girlfriend was a problem for some of the waitresses, Mom liked her well enough. She and Fiona were about the same age."

The rain, which has been pummeling the windshield since they left the terminal, lets up slightly, and Sarah relaxes the speed of the wipers. "I have the same sort of memories," Sarah admits. "You'd think I'd have different ones, newer ones, having lived in the same town with her a decade longer than you, but she's always so private and nondescript. Just another person making a living—albeit a big one. Making a life. When I was younger, I thought she was so sophisticated, much more so than the other women on the island. She gave me a Clearly Canadian from the walk-in fridge once. Fixed me with this little half smile and told me not to tell your mom or Martin."

Rain-battered hills and soggy farmland whiz by outside the windows, and a long-forgotten truth occurs to Thalia: the island in February is not the same as the one that exists in June, July, and August. When tourist season is in full swing, Block Island is all cloudless skies and the coconutty smell of suntan lotion, 109 square miles of pristine beaches, speeding mopeds, and bustling shops. September and October are temperate, weather-wise, but the number of people on the island decreases by half. And from November to May, the island is as hospitable as the dark side of the moon.

I hate it here.

Winter in Boston could be long and unpleasant, but the throngs of people hurrying down sidewalks and pouring into subway cars never let up. It was one of the reasons why she left Block Island to move to the city.

One of the reasons, but not the only one.

"Thalia?"

"Hmm?" She shakes off the past, realizing Sarah was still speaking. "Sorry, what did you say?"

"That when you called to see if I would pick you up at the terminal, I said to Patrick, 'Why is Thalia coming home for the first time in a decade right after some poor girl was murdered here?' Then I thought, *It's a coincidence, obviously.* I mean, I'm giving you a hard time for not following the story, but the whole world isn't clamoring for an explanation as to how Fiona Searles could have murdered someone, even if that someone was having an affair with Martin Dempsey."

"Right," Thalia says, and swallows the ball of irritation rising in her throat. There it is again, the nameless victim: *that poor girl . . .* how Fiona Searles could have murdered *someone*. No longer cold, she pulls the scarf from her neck and stuffs it back into her purse. *Blake,* she wants to say, to see her friend's eyes widen in surprise that she does, in fact, know it. *That poor girl's* name is—was—Blake Bronson.

Instead, she changes the subject with the same dexterity that's earned her the respect of senior partners at her firm. "Where did you say Hilda and Willow are this weekend? With Patrick's mother?" Thalia met Sarah's daughters once, two years ago, at a play Hilda was acting in on the mainland. They're sweet kids and very smart, as sarcastic and quick-witted as their mother. Most daughters *are* like their mothers. Thalia squirms, wanting to keep her thoughts far away from her latest argument with Laura, from her unwillingness to explain to her partner why she didn't—now or ever—want to adopt a child or research sperm donation and IVF. That apple might not fall far from her tree, and wasn't Thalia's tree born of an apple that hadn't fallen far from her own mother's?

Sarah groans. "Pat's brother. Pat was supposed to be off until Monday, but the boat came up with a broken propeller. He dropped the girls so they could have a sleepover with their cousins. They'll be back tomorrow afternoon."

"I hope I get the chance to see them," Thalia says, and means it.

"What about your mom? I've been dying to hear what she said when you told her you were coming."

The dread that enveloped her when she stepped off the ferry swells into a dark, shifting mass, a murmuration of starlings rising from the surface of a once-glassy sea. "She hasn't said anything," Thalia replies, "because I haven't told her."

Sarah's eyes go wide and her mouth drops open. "Are you nuts? Maureen wouldn't have taken kindly to a surprise visit *before* you decided to stay away from the island for ten goddamn years. How could you have thought this was a good idea?"

Thalia shakes her head. "I didn't think it was a good idea at all. But if I told her I was coming, she would have just picked up extra shifts to minimize the amount of time she had to see me."

"Still," Sarah says, and her knuckles are white around the steering wheel. "I'm glad I won't be there when you walk in unannounced. That's all I'm going to say."

Thalia takes a deep breath, though she fears the more island air that circulates through her lungs, the greater the danger she's in of returning to the old Thalia—that less rational, more emotional girl who used to reside on this island. "You're right," she admits. "I should have called her. I should have called *you* earlier than I did. I'm lucky you dropped everything to pick me up, to *put* me up."

At this, Sarah goes quiet. Her gaze doesn't stray from the road. Thalia studies her friend's profile, the dark skin under her eyes, the thinness of her face, and feels guilty all over again for having no idea what's going on in Sarah's life. Goddamn Maureen and her totalitarianism, driving Thalia away from the island so thoroughly, she'd abandoned her dearest friend.

Not to mention obliterating any possibility of knowing her sister.

"Sorry?" Thalia asks. She's missed what Sarah said again.

"You must be hungry. Pat and I didn't eat yet either. I'll order pizzas when we get to the house."

Thalia nods and leans back in the seat. Sarah turns up the radio. The rain picks up again, and Sarah increases the wipers. The sky darkens from graphite to slate, slate to lead, and Thalia lets the film reel of her memories go dark as well.

Chapter 17

They arrive at Sarah's modest gray-shingled house ten minutes later. There's a Toyota Tacoma in the driveway next to a shrink-wrapped Boston Whaler. "Broken propeller boat?" Thalia asks.

"Nope. 'Nonfishing, fun-only boat,' according to Patrick."

"Speaking of Patrick, did you end up taking his name at some point and forget to tell me?"

Sarah scrunches her face. "No, why?"

Thalia nods to where *The Shermans* is spelled out in blocky decals across the mailbox.

The wrinkles in Sarah's forehead smooth. "It makes the neighbors more comfortable. You know islanders. They still can't wrap their heads around a Taiwanese-born taxi driver in their midst, let alone one who refused to take her white, local fisherman-husband's last name. It'd be different if my parents had stayed, but I'm the only one, now, whose face doesn't look like theirs." Her tone changes to one of exaggerated reverence: "When they call me *Mrs. Sherman*, I like to think they're paying me a compliment, bestowing upon me the name of one of their own, rather than actively erasing my heritage." She guffaws and gives Thalia a light punch in the arm, then pulls the taxi into the garage.

Patrick appears in the doorway like an attentive valet. "Thalia!" he crows. "It's been way too long! I can't wait to catch up." He hugs her before hoisting her suitcase up the steps and disappearing down the hall.

"I made up the guest bedroom for you," Sarah says, gesturing for Thalia to follow. "Towels are in the bathroom closet. Blow dryer is in the bottom drawer." Patrick emerges from the room a moment later, sans suitcase, and Thalia thanks them both. She is stripping off her wet clothes before the sound of their footsteps dies away.

It takes a scalding shower, dry hair, and thick Boston University sweats—the only practical thing she packed, she's now realizing—before Thalia begins to feel warm. She finds Sarah in the kitchen, wearing her own heavy sweatshirt. "Dinner should be here in ten," she says.

Thalia sits beside her at the island. The Formica is stained in several places and chipped at the corners. Seeing her eye it, Sarah says, "We're thinking of redoing the kitchen this summer."

"The kitchen's great," Thalia says. "The whole house is"—she looks around, gesturing vaguely—"homey."

Patrick strides up to the island and drums his hands on the counter. "Enough about the kitchen." He raises his eyebrows, and in a conspiratorial whisper, says, "I want to hear Thalia's theories on the Fiona Searles murder."

Of course the conversation has gone here again. For everyone on the island, it's been the top news story—the only news story—for weeks. The murder has risen beyond mere gossip to become the most sensational of stories. She longs to tell them of her connection to Blake, but it doesn't feel right. Not yet. So she swallows and says, "Sarah and I talked about it on the way here. I feel awful for the victim's family." Thalia pauses. She's not ready to tell them, but she also can't say things now that could be construed as lies when she comes clean later. "Sorry to disappoint, but I haven't a single theory." At least that's the truth. "What are the police saying?"

"That the girl was here for several days before she was murdered," Patrick says. "But they don't know what she was doing on the island." Sarah nods along to Patrick's words. They've clearly discussed all this before.

"At first they thought it was suicide," Patrick says. "There was no reason to suspect otherwise. Her wrists were slit. And thousands of guests have stayed at White Hall over the years without so much as a stolen wallet. But then they found Fiona's fingerprints on the knife and determined the wounds in the girl's wrists were not self-inflicted. They were made by someone standing *in front of her*. She was *definitely* murdered." Patrick's tone is that of a man being interviewed for a true-crime podcast, and Thalia suppresses a rush of anger. She reminds herself that, like Sarah, Patrick has no idea Blake was her sister.

"The more they questioned the people she crossed paths with," Sarah cuts in, "the more they realized there was one name that came up more than any other. 'Martin,' everyone said. 'We saw her with Martin Dempsey.'"

"They met at Martin's Above the Rocks on her second day in New Shoreham," Patrick continues. "Annie Minor, one of the waitresses there, remembers the girl coming into the restaurant and being cagey, acting like she had an in to talk to Martin."

"An 'in'?" Thalia asks. "What does that even mean?"

Patrick shrugs. "Something about saying hi to one of the other waitresses there, acting like she had connections. I don't know the details. Annie just remembers her behaving as if she had a secret. And over the next few days, Martin and the girl were seen together all over the island. She was in his truck outside the library and at his office at the *Block Island Times*. Timmy Graham said they went up to the honeymoon suite of his resort together, and Martin was at White Hall even more than usual while she was staying there."

Thalia had heard these details before, having consumed every article about the murder she could find after receiving Blake's letter. "The library?" Thalia says, infusing her tone with as much skepticism as possible, hoping her friends will see beyond rumors. "And doesn't Martin own the *Block Island Times* now? Those hardly seem like the activities of two people having an affair. Maybe she was researching something—she could have been a journalist—and Martin was showing her around."

If Blake *had* been a journalist, this detail would have made it into the papers; Thalia knows she sounds ridiculous, but she can't understand how anyone could think Blake had been involved with Martin.

"I knew you were following the case more closely than you let on!" Sarah exclaims.

"I'm not," Thalia says. She looks at Patrick, as if convincing him will make it true. "I'm not," she repeats. "I saw something about it in line at the bodega."

"Whatever you saw," he says, matter-of-fact, "I'm sure the article didn't include this. Justin Taft is a buddy of mine on the force, and he told me himself."

"Justin Taft," Thalia sighs. "It sounds like he enjoys gossiping as much now as he did when we were in high school. So, what did Justin Taft tell you?"

"That the victim had some of Martin's things in her room after she was found. Martin's jacket. Martin's umbrella. Belongings that Fiona— going in for housekeeping or turndown services—would have noticed and that caused her to see red. The girl had recently been arrested for a DUI and was supposed to stay sober for the charges to be dropped. But Aileen Searles reported the complimentary bottle of wine given to all B and B guests was missing from the room. If she'd been drunk when Fiona accosted her in the bathtub, she would have been an easier target."

"Oh, come *on!*" Thalia half shouts, and Sarah raises her eyebrows as if this outburst proves Thalia shares their morbid fascination with the case. "She could have thrown the bottle away if she was trying to stay sober. And a jacket and an umbrella are, like, the number one and two items someone—*anyone*—would let you borrow during a weeklong rainstorm."

Patrick shrugs. "I agree. I don't think Martin was sleeping with her." He looks at his wife. "Sarah, on the other hand, thinks Blake was sad and lonely, desperate to make a connection with someone while on vacation, and Martin was that guy. Regardless, Fiona obviously took the jacket and the umbrella—along with reports of Blake being spotted all over the island with Martin—as evidence of an affair."

There. Someone has finally said Blake's name. But Thalia doesn't want to hear any more of this, not without them knowing what she does. It is helpful, however, to have been proven right in what she suspected all along: no one knows Maureen was Blake's birth mother and that Blake was on Block Island to meet her. "Okay," she says, holding up her hands in mock surrender and closing her eyes. "That's all the drama I can take on an empty stomach."

A knock cuts through the mournful wail of the wind. "How's that for timing?" Patrick laughs. When Thalia stands, he puts a hand on her arm. "I'll get it. Sarah, hon, can you grab some plates?"

Thalia is holding in a breath while counting to ten the way she does before walking into the courtroom when Patrick's confused "Hey, Thalia?" comes from the doorway. Sarah and Thalia both turn to him at the same time.

Rather than pizza boxes, Patrick holds a bottle in one hand, and a light-brown envelope in the other. The envelope is darkened in several places where it was spattered with rain. "It's got your name on it," he says. Thalia walks over. Indeed, *Ms. Thalia Mills, Esq.* is scrawled across the front of the envelope. The bottle is unlabeled but sealed, the liquid inside so dark it appears almost black.

"Whoever left it was already gone," Patrick says, and walks to a drawer at the end of the counter. He riffles through it and pulls out a corkscrew. While Patrick goes to work opening the bottle, Thalia slides a finger under the envelope's seal.

"What does it say?" Sarah asks when Thalia has unfolded and read the single piece of cream-colored paper from inside it.

Thalia looks up. "With sympathy," she says. "That's it. No signature. No note." She glances at Patrick, who, after sniffing the contents of the bottle—and to Thalia's mild amusement—actually scratches his head.

Sarah verbalizes what Thalia's thinking: "You're like the human version of a golden retriever, you know that? Tell us what's in it already."

"Wine." He pauses. "With sympathy for what?"

"I don't know," Thalia says, though she's pretty sure she does.

Sarah frowns. "Weird."

"They probably just delivered it to the wrong house." Patrick walks over to Thalia, and thrusts the bottle into her hand. "Our gain. Wine goes great with pizza. It smells expensive too."

Thalia gives a tentative sniff. It can't be a coincidence, this mysterious drop-off the first night she's in town. A sympathy card from an unknown benefactor, sent for an unnamed loss. Thalia slides off the stool, meaning to carry the wine over to the sink, to get as far away from it as possible. Someone *did* know what Blake was doing on Block Island. That's the only thing this could mean. Thalia bristles at the thought of a poncho-draped intruder creeping around outside Sarah's house, propping the envelope against the door, and disappearing beneath a veil of rain.

She shakes her head, pushing her thoughts past paranoia and exhaustion. She hasn't made junior partner at her firm after only six years by being illogical and high-strung. Until she knows more, she'll have to believe it's what Patrick said: the result of a hastily scribbled address.

"Thal, you okay?" Sarah's voice comes from very far off.

Thalia whirls around, meaning to say, yes, she's fine, but the pounding on the door comes before she can do so. She gasps, and her fingers lose their grip on the bottle. The silence after the explosion of glass on the tile is complete. Even the knocking on the door has subsided. "Oh God," Thalia says. "Sar, I'm so sorry."

Sarah's already at the stove, pulling a dish towel from its handle. "Don't worry, really. But are you okay? Man, that was loud. You looked like you saw a ghost."

Thalia doesn't answer. She grabs a handful of paper towels and helps Sarah mop up the dark liquid. The wine is tart-smelling and thick, and in an instant, their fingers are stained a deep, bruise-like purple, the stains bisected by the ridges and furrows of their skin.

Thalia apologizes again over the pizza that was, of course, the reason for the knocking. Sarah and Patrick wave her off, and don't mention the sympathy card—or Blake—for the rest of the meal. Thalia insists on cleaning up; Sarah acquiesces and follows Patrick down the hall. Ten minutes later, Thalia turns off the kitchen light. The sounds of muffled conversation and running water have ceased from the master bedroom, and she pads to the guest room.

Now she lies beneath a too-thin comforter, still in her sweats, listening to the hypnotic pinging of the rain. Her thoughts aren't on Fiona Searles in jail, or her best friend up the hall, but on her mother, no longer separated from her by a stretch of Atlantic Ocean and two states, but a few short miles down the road.

How will Maureen react when she opens her door to find Thalia standing there? Will she hide behind her usual wall of cigarette smoke and exhaustion, or has she changed? Thalia considers—yet again—the logistics of what her mother has done, of having a second baby before her first daughter was old enough to remember it, putting that baby up for adoption, and never mentioning her again. She's been reeling since she saw Blake's birth certificate, trying to reconcile the fact of her mother's name printed there with her own understanding of the past. Tears smart in her eyes, and she blinks them away.

She'd often wondered whether there was more to Maureen's sternness and rigidity; she knew personally how stoicism could be used to conceal suffering, but there was never anything to hint that Maureen's aloofness stemmed from some past trauma. Eventually, Thalia had been forced to face the truth: Maureen was an uncompromising and private person, a woman for whom even motherhood did not allow intimacy or permissiveness.

Or, maybe it had. Here, the familiar script unfurled in Thalia's head: the rationalizations and justifications, the reminder that Maureen was not only *not* a bad mother, but an undeniably loving one. Thalia remembers the endless hours her mother spent reading to her when she was little, the extra shifts she worked if Thalia had to travel to the mainland for a field trip, or needed new lacrosse cleats. And though Maureen feared the cruelty of other children (prior to Sarah using the school bully as a lacrosse ball), she was understanding and supportive of Thalia's sexuality. That's what made her inflexible nature—even her occasional coldness—so inexplicable.

She tosses on the mattress. Whether her mother is the same, or has loosened up in the last decade, Thalia would prefer to confront her with more than a handful of hours of sleep. But there's an antidote to her restlessness. The letter from Blake. From her sister. Postmarked the morning after her death and calling to her like a siren in the mist.

It's not like she hasn't read it a dozen times since receiving it, hasn't searched every line for hidden clues as if she were analyzing a case. It's different from the other piece of paper contained within the envelope: The birth certificate is concrete. Objective. The kind of currency Thalia understands. The letter is abstract. Slippery. As objectively helpful as an image glimpsed within wisps of smoke curling up from a campfire. Certainly now, after learning the entire island believed her sister had been an *active* alcoholic, and that the basis for Fiona's motive was the relationship between Blake and Martin, she has new reason to return to the words her sister wrote.

She flips on the bedside light and plucks the letter from between the pages of a volume on litigation she brought for the ferry ride. She hesitates, knowing that if she starts dissecting the letter now, she'll never fall asleep. As she stares at the envelope, the uniqueness of the light-brown envelope strikes her anew. It's expensive-looking and soft, like something she'd receive at the firm. Like something she'd receive containing a note of sympathy.

Thalia reaches for the envelope on the edge of the nightstand that accompanied the now-shattered wine bottle. The soft, expensive-looking, light-brown envelope. She holds the envelopes side by side. They are identical in size, color, and texture. It would be a surprise if they *weren't* from the same batch.

She studies the note from the envelope, turning Patrick's explanation for the delivery over in her head. Eventually, she places the note, along with Blake's letter—she'll try for sleep, after all—back between the pages of the litigation book.

How likely is it that Blake—who'd been living in a decrepit Southie apartment with three other recovering addicts when she died—had owned a set of fancy envelopes? And if she had, what are the odds that she'd arranged for one containing an anonymous sympathy card to be sent to Thalia after her unexpected death?

Thalia has to stop. The best way to figure out what happened to Blake is to determine what happened between her and their mother, both two and a half weeks and twenty-six years ago. She can only hope that tomorrow, Maureen has not only changed but feels like talking.

Like opening up about the past.

Chapter 18

When Thalia walks into the kitchen the next morning, Sarah is dressed in jeans and a thick wool sweater, a steaming coffee in hand. "If you want me to drop you at Maureen's, we need to go early," Sarah says. "I have a couple of rides booked this morning."

Thalia nods and pours a cup of coffee, murmurs good morning to Patrick, and turns to find Sarah staring at her thin, off-the-shoulder frock and the same leather ankle boots from the night before.

"You know it's still pouring, right?" Sarah asks, her tone better suited to asking if Thalia's aware she's a moron.

Thalia gulps a swallow of coffee and bites her lip. "The other outfits in my suitcase are more of the same."

"Outfits," Sarah repeats. "There's your problem. You can wear 'outfits' in Boston, and 'outfits' here in the summer, but the only thing you can get away with on Block in the winter is boots." She looks at Thalia's shoes again. "Actual boots," she adds, raising an eyebrow.

Thalia opens her mouth, but Sarah continues, "It's me, Thalia. I know how you are. You're using those clothes as a shield."

"Sar, leave Thalia alone," Patrick says, buttering a bagel.

"I'm not trying to be a jerk. I'm just making sure she's aware." She pauses, drains her coffee, and places the cup in the sink. "She's going to freeze trying to prove to *herself* that she doesn't belong here."

"I'm not proving anything to anyone. This is just how I dress." Although, hadn't she purposefully packed her newest, nicest things?

She's not even that fashionable, not by Boston's standards, but something about coming back to the island made her feel vulnerable and in need of a . . .

Shield? Goddammit.

Some shield, anyway. Held up against the rain, her newest, nicest things are like stitched-together tracing paper.

"There's no way you can go out in that today. By the time you turn up on Maureen's front porch, you'll look like one of the water rats from under the pier."

"Sarah!" Patrick gives his wife a chastising look. "Thalia can wear whatever she wants."

"No, she's right," Thalia says. "If it's raining as hard as it was yesterday, these boots don't stand a chance." She turns to Sarah, feeling like the thirteen-year-old girl she used to be, asking to borrow Sarah's letter jacket to wear to the Misquamicut Spring Festival because Maureen wouldn't buy her one. "Do you have anything that would fit?"

Fifteen minutes later, Thalia is climbing into Sarah's taxi, toes tight against the tops of the same Scottie dog–printed galoshes she saw in the trunk the night before. She's zipped into a chunky, handknit sweater, boyfriend-style, with cowl collar and rib trim. It's wool with fleece lining—the two brown envelopes tucked into an interior pocket—and she has to admit that she's cozier and more comfortable than she was in her frilly top. But she's also more the Thalia from ten years ago, as if the sweater, in buttressing her against the wind, has stripped her of her city veneer.

The rain is a cool, steady shower, but the sky is clearer, the clouds lit from behind by a stubborn sun. Against a backdrop of beating wipers, Thalia listens to snatches of Sarah's conversation with her daughters. She marvels at how patient and attentive a mother Sarah is. A sense of home, a sense of safety, radiates from the very timbre of Sarah's voice. Hilda and Willow don't know how lucky they are.

But Thalia does.

They pass the farm that marks the entrance to her childhood street. The sign declaring fresh eggs and horseback-riding lessons is near-indecipherable with age. She fidgets, wishing Sarah would get off the phone. She doesn't want to be alone right now, needs to feel like her best friend—regardless of Sarah's lingering annoyance—is with her as they near Maureen's driveway. She wants Sarah to distract her from the worry gnawing at her stomach like so many water rats under the pier.

"All right, honey-bunny," Sarah is finally saying. Thalia smiles in her direction, as if she's been focused on their sweet good-morning conversation and not the fireworks display soon to take place on Maureen's doorstep. "See you tonight. And yes, you'll see Thalia then too."

Sarah disconnects the call as she pulls farther down the road, and Thalia breathes in while counting to ten. She watches the houses pass—not mansions but undoubtedly the homes of the upper middle class. For the first time in her life, Thalia wonders how her mother afforded to live in this neighborhood on a waitressing salary. The taxi slows beside a white aluminum mailbox with a gold-plated *1054* on its side. Sarah nods at the contemporary-style house and navy Subaru parked in the driveway. "You ready?" she asks.

Thalia grimaces.

"Don't dillydally. The last thing you want is for her to see you sitting in the driveway. Get in there. And, good luck."

Thalia pushes the door open. Under the cover of Sarah's umbrella, she avoids the deepest of the puddles. Her mother's eccentric little house with its squat porch and surprisingly verdant winter landscaping looks as it did when Thalia left. She climbs the steps and props the umbrella against the house. Her mother always hated it when she left an umbrella dripping on the floor. The veil between the past and the present feels thinner than ever.

She raises her hand to knock, then stops. Before she can think about what she's doing, she's in the front garden, unearthing a hide-a-key rock from beneath a holly bush. She's traveled too great a distance; she's not going to give Maureen the opportunity to refuse to open the door. Thalia jogs back up the steps, slips the key into the lock, and lets herself into her mother's house—her old house—unannounced.

Through the low-lit hallway, past the sign with a quote from *The Secret Garden* Maureen uncharacteristically cross-stitched one Christmas ("Where you tend a rose, a thistle cannot grow"), and into the horrid, dated kitchen Thalia always despised. The Tiffany-style pendant fixture still hangs above the cherrywood table, and the large glass ashtray and piles of women's magazines elicit in Thalia such a strong sense of déjà vu that, for a moment, she thinks she's stepped back into 2008.

Her mother's laptop is asleep, but when Thalia bats at the mouse, the screen illuminates, displaying the contents of Maureen's Amazon cart. At the sight of the silicone spatula, tea biscuits, and cotton pajama set, Thalia turns away, embarrassed. Yes, Maureen is her mother. Yes, Thalia feels she is owed answers to innumerable questions, but it feels wrong to have broken into her house.

Thalia drags a finger across the magazines. The layer of dust is an inch thick. What other unpleasantries await her here? She peers into the living room, but only a three-foot-tall glass cheetah statue stares back. The cheetah sits beside an unsightly red leather couch and a bookcase sagging at the center. Thalia turns away from the books, the past threatening to leap out from them and engulf her.

She backtracks through the kitchen and turns left, away from the foyer. Her mother's room is at the end of another hallway, this one barren of even out-of-place cross-stitch quotations. Orangey light seeps from the crack under the door. Thalia squares her shoulders and exhales on a count of ten, but her stomach still does a little flip.

Why does her mother make her feel like this, ten years later? Maureen's love for Thalia never could overcome her impulse to control her, to keep her from making her own decisions, living her own life, and that reality still guts her. Thalia goes to straighten the hem of her blouse before remembering she's wearing the ridiculous chunky sweater and dog-print galoshes. She wishes she looked like herself right now, the person she's become *despite* Maureen Mills. She wishes she didn't care what she looked like at all.

Thalia pushes the door open as quietly as possible. It doesn't matter. Maureen is asleep. There's a prescription bottle on the nightstand. No, there are *seven* prescription bottles on the nightstand. The room is a disaster far beyond the horrible, mismatched decor. Lipstick-stained water glasses and coffee cups litter the dressers. The white down comforter is yellowed with age. In one corner, laundry is piled as high as Thalia's waist. In another, folded stacks of black shirts and dress pants teeter atop a chair meant for the vanity across the room.

Thalia creeps toward her mother, who is snoring softly but deeply. The sound comes from the depths of her throat rather than her nose. Thalia recognizes the snore as one induced by Valium. The snore of a woman who will not be easily roused.

But rouse her she must, and so, with fear very much like that which she felt before telling Maureen she'd bought a one-way ticket for the ferry to Point Judith a decade prior, Thalia reaches down and shakes her mother's arm. The shake becomes a yank, and then she's gripping her mother's shoulders and applying pressure, hoping to both wake her and minimize the vampire-springing-up-from-the-coffin motion that is inevitable.

"Uhh!" Maureen grunts and indeed sits up like the waking dead. Thalia says nothing, praying the initial disorientation wears off quickly. She has no idea when the anger will come, but it's coming. Anger at being woken from a drug-induced coma and at Thalia's brazen presence.

Maureen's eyes roll over Thalia half a dozen times before they fix on her, and even then, it's clear Maureen doesn't recognize her daughter. Thalia won't capitulate to having to tell her who she is. Even before she knew the word for it, Thalia refused to enable her mother.

Admittedly, Maureen's control issues were the dominating force in Thalia's childhood, not her substance abuse. Her proclivity for antianxiety medications progressed to active addiction slowly but surely, like a storm system that gains ferocity after hurtling over the warm currents of a tropical ocean. By the time Thalia realized how bad things were, her acceptance letter to Boston University had already arrived.

"Thalia?" Maureen finally says and, to Thalia's surprise, it's not anger that narrows her mother's eyes. It's muddy calculations and confusion. "Why are you here? Did someone die?" The moment the question is out of her mouth, Maureen puts the pieces together; Thalia can see it. "It's that girl, isn't it? The one who was murdered. You're here because of her."

Chapter 19

"Why would I be here because of Blake Bronson, Mom?" Thalia asks. "You tell me? Why would I return to this wet, awful place after *a decade* because a woman I've never met, a woman with reportedly no connections to the island, came here a few weeks ago and wound up dead?"

Maureen pushes herself up against the pillow. It's so much like her mother, to be visibly incapacitated and yet worry that Thalia might use that incapacitation to gain the upper hand. Thalia's never had the upper hand, not once, not ever. She's going to do everything she can to get it now.

"Tell me about Blake," Thalia insists. "Did she come to see you? Did you know she was here before she died? Or did you only find out after the fact, like me? Did you get a letter too?"

Maureen's eyes are cloudy from what is clearly more than the indicated dosage of her prescriptions, but there's still something desperately alert about them, as if she believes something terrible might happen if she lets her guard down. "I don't know what you're talking about," she says. "If you came all the way from Boston to ask me this, it was a wasted trip, because I won't say a word about it."

"You know exactly what I'm talking about," Thalia says, but what she's thinking is, *How dare you deny this when I finally know the truth?* "For once, can you just stop lying?"

"I'm not—"

"She sent me a letter, Mom. I want to know if you got one too."
When Maureen continues to stare past her, Thalia raises her voice.
"Did you hear me? Blake Bronson mailed me a letter, written the
night she died. *She sent her birth certificate with it.* I didn't get it until
after Fiona was arrested for her murder. Blake *was* your daughter. She
was born almost three years after I was. I would have been just young
enough to have no recollection of you being pregnant or bringing a
baby home." Thalia pauses. "If you brought her home at all. But I don't
think you did."

Slowly, Maureen pulls her gaze away from the chaotic room beyond
Thalia. When she looks into her eyes, there is more anger there than
Thalia can ever recall seeing. That anger paralyzes her. "Please, Mom,"
she manages, softening her tone. "You have to tell me—"

"I don't have to tell you anything," Maureen whispers. "I won't."

"Blake had a horrible life," Thalia says. "She grew up in foster
care." She looks pointedly at the bottles on her mother's nightstand.
"She struggled with substance abuse and had been clean for thirty days
when she came to Block. In the letter, she . . ." Thalia pauses, deciding
how to best word this. "She didn't seem entirely well. She was staying at
White Hall. At the Searleses' bed-and-breakfast. She said a few things
that were . . ." Thalia pauses a second time and then says, "Troubling.
Things that didn't make sense."

"She sounds unstable," Maureen says. "And I don't know what type
of document she sent you, but I can assure you it was forgery. That
woman was not my daughter. No one came to see me, and—"

"Jesus, Mom!" Thalia explodes. "There were things in the letter
that made it clear she was in your house! She referenced *The Secret
Garden* cross-stitch by the door, the countless Valium prescriptions.
What are you, utilizing an off-island doctor to get even more scripts
than before?" Thalia waves her hand. "If you want to tell me you gave
Blake up because you didn't like being a mother, that's fine! It would
explain *a lot* about my childhood. But I want the truth. No more shut-
ting me out."

Maureen stares at her hands. Her fingernails are short, unpainted. She reaches over, picks up a prescription bottle, and examines its label. She sets it down, picks up another, and moves this one closer to the bed. She picks up a third bottle, makes a little sound of disgust at the back of her throat, and pushes it farther away. Thalia is losing her patience.

"You've been looking for answers inside those bottles for years," she says quietly. "And you haven't found them yet."

Maureen abandons her inventory reconciliation and returns her attention to Thalia. Tears glisten in her cloudy eyes. She suddenly resembles not just a Valium-addicted career waitress on her day off but a Valium-addicted career waitress too old and ill to make it through another shift. Maureen blinks and the tears fall. She closes her eyes. A flash of hope—and fear—shoots through Thalia. *Please, just tell me what happened. I can handle it, no matter how inexplicable—or awful—it is.*

"For a long time, I thought I could do what I needed to protect you," Maureen says, her voice hoarse, "without becoming a horrible mother. But then I realized—probably when you were about six—that the lengths I needed to go to protect you were inconducive to a happy childhood. All mothers struggle to protect their children. But this was different. I *knew* beyond a shadow of a doubt—not just feared—there was a hungry wolf in the woods, ready to attack the moment you strayed from the path."

Thalia tries to cut in, but Maureen holds up a shaking hand. "So I kept you from venturing out, from truly living, and prayed that, despite my inability to explain myself, you would understand. And it worked. At least until now. You grew up and got off the island. I hoped you would never come back."

"I had one friend my whole childhood," Thalia says. She can feel the loneliness as she speaks, a literal tightening in her chest. "You never let me do a single activity unless it was something you could oversee. That's why you liked lacrosse, because the practice schedule didn't conflict with your shifts. You pushed me away, despite loving me. Because I know you love me. And now, I find out you did the same thing with another daughter, only worse. You *gave her up for adoption.* Cut her off from the only real family she had, and from the place she was born."

"Stop," Maureen whispers.

"Your explanation isn't good enough," Thalia says.

"Stop," Maureen says more loudly. There's not just anger in her voice but fear. Her mother's hands tremble as they grip the bedclothes. She is frightened. Maybe even terrified. *But why?*

Thalia will not stop. She can't. *Explain to me why I am the way I am. Why the thought of ever having my own daughter brings me to my knees.* "Tell me what you're so afraid of!" Thalia demands.

"Get off this island," Maureen barks. "Go home to Boston, and don't come back here." Maureen's face is blotchy, and she's breathing fast. She leans forward and pounds her fists on the mattress. "If there's ever been an instruction I want you to listen to, it's this one. Go! We're done here."

"Mom," Thalia tries.

"No." The word is a dropped gavel. "I don't want to see you," Maureen continues. "I don't want to see you anywhere, ever again."

The room swims. Thalia swallows. *I don't have a mother anymore. No, I've never had a mother. I've been an orphan all along, just like Blake. I'm worse off than Blake because I never knew just how alone I really was.* She feels guilty as soon as she thinks it, because of course she's not worse off than Blake; Maureen's disowning of Thalia hadn't gotten Thalia killed.

"You don't want to see me again? Fine," Thalia says. She makes a fluttering motion with her hand. "Your wish is my command."

It's a stupid, childish thing to say, but Maureen has made Thalia feel stupid and childish. She whirls from the bed and runs for the door. Behind her comes the sound of a dozen small white pills rattling against an upended prescription bottle.

Chapter 20

Sarah is scrolling on her phone when Thalia throws open the door of the taxi and dives inside. She yanks the seat belt out, but the locking mechanism engages after only a few inches. Thalia pulls at it again and again, knowing her anger is so far misplaced as to be almost comical. And while hysterical laughter does threaten to erupt from her throat, it's the tears that win. She drops her head into her lap and cries, suppressing the urge to scream. *I wanted to leave my mother behind, but I've been carrying her with me every day, every step since I left this island.*

"Jesus, Thalia, what happened?"

Thalia cannot answer. What could she say? *I may not have a substance abuse problem, but I'm just as messed up as my mother and my sister?* She feels Sarah's hand on her back and accepts the comfort another moment before lifting her head. Sarah reaches across her for a pack of tissues from the glove box. Thalia takes one and dabs at her eyes. She's not going to wallow like this. It's not her. Maybe she *has* been lugging around the weight of her childhood, her mother's issues, since she was eighteen, but doesn't this prove her *strength*, not her instability? Look what she's accomplished despite all that emotional baggage.

Realizing the truth of this, Thalia decides to face something else that's weighing on her. "I haven't been honest with you," she says to Sarah. She looks at her friend head-on, still feeling the decade-old guilt but refusing to let it control her. "I haven't been honest about a lot.

Starting with the fact I haven't just been 'following' the Blake Bronson case. I've been living it. Blake Bronson is—was—my sister."

"What?" Sarah's face twists in shock and confusion. She puts the car in reverse, but doesn't take her foot off the brake. "What do you mean she was your sister? What are you talking about?"

"Drive," Thalia says. "Back to your place. And I'll tell you everything."

Sarah drives.

Thalia talks.

∞

They're still sitting in Sarah's driveway when Thalia finishes. Rain beats against the roof, and the car's grown chilly in the hour that's passed since Sarah turned off the engine. Sarah's come to the end of Blake's letter for the third time. She folds it up and hands it back to Thalia, then stares out the foggy windshield, shaking her head. "The mansion replica? Mary Searles's restless ghost? I haven't heard those old stories since we were kids. This is crazy."

"I know," Thalia agrees.

"And Maureen wouldn't admit to anything, wouldn't give you any information."

"Nothing."

"What are you going to do now?"

"I need to go inside and repack my stuff. Tell Hilda and Willow I'm sorry, but I'm not going to be able to see them tonight. Will you bring me to Mansion Beach?"

At Sarah's bewildered expression, Thalia says, "I think the sympathy card that showed up at your house last night came from Fiona and Aileen Searles's B and B. I'm going to rent a room there."

"You're going to rent a room there," Sarah repeats slowly.

"Yes."

"At White Hall."

"At White Hall."

Sarah's about to say something else when Thalia's phone rings. The screen informs her that the call is coming from Block Island Medical Center. Thalia hurries to accept it, her stomach lurching.

"Is this Thalia Mills?" an official-sounding voice asks.

"Yes."

"Ms. Mills, I'm very sorry to have to tell you this, but Maureen Mills was brought in by ambulance about twenty minutes ago for a suspected drug overdose. She's in a coma. You're listed as her emergency contact, but it says you live in Boston. I wanted to call as soon as possible in case you needed to manage the ferry schedule."

Thalia's thoughts fire, lines connecting between the bottles on her mother's nightstand and the words coming over the phone's speaker. She blurts out, "I'm here. I'm already on the island. I can be there in less than ten minutes."

She hangs up and sits in silent shock, but Sarah has already started reversing the taxi. "Where are we going?" she asks.

Thalia swallows and takes a breath. "BIMC."

Block Island Medical Center is barely larger than the island schoolhouse, and Thalia can hear the doctor conferring with two nervous-looking nurses from the waiting area. Sarah is standing by an empty fish tank, folding and unfolding her hands.

You did not cause this, Thalia tells herself repeatedly, and though she knows it's true in an objective sense—*If Maureen took extra pills after you left the house, that's on her. That was her decision*—she can't help but think this never would have happened if she hadn't gone to see her. She has an overwhelming urge to tell someone from her old, sane life on the mainland what has happened—and she does send Laura a quick text update—but to call her girlfriend means telling a story she doesn't completely understand.

A story. That's what—in her letter—Blake said she felt like she was trapped in. A horror story of castles and secrecy and supernatural occurrences. Has Thalia unwittingly become another character? *Nonsense. I'm a lawyer, on track to make senior partner in my firm after six years because they value my levelheadedness.* Still, when things happen over which one has no control, it's convenient, almost comforting, to feel as if you're a cog in a narrative in medias res. Thalia sighs and wishes she had a coffee spiked with a couple of shots of espresso to help her think straight. But she needs to stay focused. Be her usual, rational self.

Her mother's condition is stable, the doctor has at least told them that. *And if it hadn't been? If she'd been close to death because I broke into her house and selfishly pushed her to the brink?* She chastises herself for the thought; wanting the truth after twenty-nine years was hardly selfish. An elderly neighbor who regularly went over for tea and a game of pitch on Maureen's day off had found Maureen unconscious in her bed sometime after Thalia left. As for when—or if—Maureen might wake up, the doctor was unsure.

Thalia shifts in the metal chair. The antiseptic smell of the place makes her nauseous. The doctor finishes speaking with the nurses and walks over. Dr. Maddox has been a staple in the island's medical community—no, perhaps the *entirety* of the island's medical community—since Thalia was a little girl. He doesn't look much older than he did when she was in high school, though his hair has grayed a little at the temples. She stands as he nears them. Sarah remains in the vicinity of the fish tank, but Thalia feels her perk up, as anxious for news as she is.

"I'm sorry for the wait," Dr. Maddox says. "I wanted to get more information on your mother's vitals. She's still stable, but I'd like to narrow down how long she might have been with minimal oxygen. Tabitha Green said she went over at ten thirty. The EMTs got there about eight minutes after that." Behind thick glasses, the doctor's eyes dart rapidly, studying Thalia's face. "About what time did you leave your mother alone?"

"Ten twelve," Sarah cuts in. "I sent my husband a text message when Thalia got back to the car, and that was at ten fifteen."

Dr. Maddox raises the clipboard from his side and makes a note. "Okay. That's good. Thank you, Mrs. Sherman." He looks at Thalia again. "And was she showing any signs of overdose before you left? Bluish skin. Abnormal breathing. Anything like that?"

Frustration swells in Thalia's chest. If her mother had been having trouble breathing while she'd been there, she would have called 911 herself. "I mean, she didn't look great. She looked like she'd chased her antianxiety medication with half a dozen mimosas."

Dr. Maddox nods. "Thank you, Ms. Mills. I know this is hard."

"When can I see her?"

"That was the other thing I wanted to tell you. I don't allow family members to visit a comatose patient until at least twenty-four hours have passed. Your mother's lungs have been compromised, even if it was less than thirty minutes or so of decreased oxygen. I need to keep the risk of infection, of pneumonia, to a minimum. In the meantime, I'm going to have one of the nurses give you her personal effects."

"Personal effects?"

"We removed her bathrobe to get her into a hospital gown, and the pockets were pretty full. There was at least one prescription bottle in addition to several other odds and ends." He pauses and looks back and forth between her and Sarah. "I can't imagine what you're going through, coming back to the island after all this time only to be met with this. If you'd like to leave for a bit, have Mrs. Sherman take you to wherever you're staying, we'll call you the second anything changes."

Thalia bites her lip and nods. A nurse appears and hands Thalia a reusable shopping bag. One fuzzy fleece arm of her mother's bathrobe hangs out. She thanks Dr. Maddox and tells him yes, please, call her with any changes in her mother's condition. When he leaves, she sits back down on the edge of her chair.

Together, she and Sarah empty the contents of Maureen's bathrobe pockets. In one, there's a crumpled-up receipt from Above the

Rocks, three hair elastics, a tube of lip balm, and a little screwdriver to repair eyeglasses. The other holds the prescription bottle Dr. Maddox mentioned—Valium—and a folded-up light-brown envelope. She unfolds it. Aside from *Maureen* on the front, it's unaddressed.

"Is that another light-brown envelope?" Sarah asks. "Like the one that was left at my house?"

"Yup." Thalia can hardly believe it. A cream piece of paper pokes up from behind the broken seal. Thalia slips the paper out. As they read it, the blame Thalia felt over her mother's condition changes. It's still there, but it feels alive now. Helpful rather than debilitating. It's morphed into motivation to solve the ever-expanding mystery of what the hell is going on here.

The *With Sympathy* appears the same as it did on the card Thalia received. Again, she traces the loops of the large, slanted *S*. There's more, here, however, than those two simple words:

> With Sympathy.
>   Is it harder to love something you have lost, or to
> lose something you never had?

Thalia reads the words again, her mind reeling. When she received the card at Sarah's, she was pretty sure someone else on the island knew who Blake was to Thalia and Maureen. This second card solidifies that belief. But why send it anonymously and with no return address?

"Someone else has to know," Sarah says, echoing Thalia's thoughts. "Did they leave it unsigned out of respect for you and your mother's privacy? The sender could be acknowledging that neither you nor Maureen have publicly claimed a connection to Blake."

"But Fiona Searles is going to be tried for *Blake's murder*. If someone knew Blake was Maureen's daughter and had come to the island, why would they keep that to themselves?"

Sarah is quiet. "Come on," she says after a moment. "We're not going to figure out the answer here. Like Dr. Maddox said, there's no sense sitting around. It could be—" she cuts herself off, an uncomfortable expression on her face.

"You can say it," Thalia says. "I know. It could be weeks before she comes out of it. It could be never." Thalia stuffs her mother's personal items back into the robe's pockets and shoves the cigarette-reeking garment into the bag. The Valium—it sounds like there's less than a handful—and the letter she puts carefully into the bottom of her purse. She follows Sarah out of the waiting room, through the automatic doors, and toward the taxi. They climb in and shut the doors in unison.

"Am I still taking you to White Hall?" Sarah asks.

Thalia stares at her hands, suddenly on the verge of crying again. The thought of her mother in a coma makes her head hurt. But the thought of her mother in a coma two and a half weeks after her sister was murdered makes her head *spin*. And now, a third light-brown envelope has surfaced. One too many to be a coincidence.

Thalia lifts her head. "Yes. You're still taking me to White Hall."

Chapter 21

The last time Thalia was at White Hall was for a field trip in the seventh grade, when Mrs. Burke's class had gone for a tour of the Searleses' wine-making facilities. She remembers Aileen's awkward attempts to be funny as she explained things like bottlenecked fermenting chambers and wholesaler supplies costs, the kids snickering at her lumbering mannerisms and coughing the word *dyke* behind her back. Thalia, acutely aware of her own sexuality even at twelve, felt bad for the woman, though she was pretty sure Aileen wasn't a lesbian. She also remembers, thanks to her penchant for facts and numbers, that each batch of mulberry wine took at least a year to process before the racking and cask aging, and was thus much slower to produce than a wine using regular grapes.

As for the Searleses' recent history, those are details of which Thalia isn't as knowledgeable. On the way to the bluffs, she asks Sarah what, if anything, the Searleses have been up to during the ten years she's been in Boston.

"Honestly," Sarah says, "the only thing anyone ever says about the Searleses is that it's crazy Fiona and Martin had been together as long as they have without getting married. And that Aileen, despite managing the logistical operations for the B and B *and* the winery, relies on Fiona for all aspects of the business that would require leaving White Hall or interacting with members of the community."

Sarah pauses. "I just thought of something else," she says a moment later. They are almost to Corn Neck Road. "Rhode Island is one of the few states that recognizes common-law marriage. Fiona and Martin have been together a long time. Does that mean they're legally married?"

"Common law isn't the result of a couple being together for a specific duration of time. The two parties have to not only act as if they are married and demonstrate intent to behave as husband and wife, they have to actually file for common-law marriage."

Sarah raises an eyebrow. "That's a lawyerly answer if I ever heard one."

Thalia shrugs. Sarah pulls her eyes from the muddy road long enough to shoot her a look of pride. "Seriously, Thal," she says. "I think it's really cool you're doing so well with your career."

"How do you know I'm doing well?"

"Because, before I made you change into something you weren't going to catch hypothermia in, the blouse you were wearing probably cost as much as I spend on clothes for Patrick, the girls, and myself in an entire year."

"I doubt that." Thalia laughs. "But thanks. I've worked really hard, so that's kind of you to say. And yeah, unless Fiona and Martin applied for common-law status, they're no more married than Laura and I are. As for how they engage with one another, you tell me. Do they act like they're married? Or, did they, before Fiona was charged with my half sister's murder and arrested?"

"Not really, no," Sarah admits. "Martin proposes to Fiona once every couple of years, and she always says no. She loves him, at least that's what people say, but she's loath to muddy the waters between their two sets of assets, Martin's restaurant, the newspaper and other properties, her B and B and winery. But Martin doesn't give up." Sarah nods out the windshield at White Hall. "Is it like you remember it? Or weirder?"

They pull down a driveway marked by two brick entry pillars. The mansion looks different—bigger, somehow—from the last time Thalia saw it. The beach grass and evergreen shrubs are as wild and impenetrable as a hedge of thorns. The structure itself is a study in contrasts. Light, almost ethereal stonework. Upright corners holding darkness within. Neat edges and sloping arches. The two halves—bisected down the center by what could be a mirror, the similarities are so exact—glower at one another like conjoined twins.

Blake called the mansion Otranto, the haunted castle of Horace Walpole's 1764 novel, and described it as "claustrophobia and tragedy and decay." When Thalia found out that the sister from whom she'd just received her first correspondence had committed suicide on Block Island exactly fourteen days prior—*the night before* sending the letter—it wasn't as big of a surprise as it might have been. Blake's letter was disturbing. It did more than hint at long-standing pain and disappointment. Her talk of ghosts and being trapped in a horror novel unnerved Thalia to her core.

But after reading additional articles and seeing that Fiona had been charged with Blake's murder, Thalia wondered if her sister's letter was actually the frightened ramblings of a stressed-out young woman trying to navigate life newly sober. Fragility and raw emotions were hardly a precursor to suicide. And now that she is seeing White Hall for the first time in almost two decades—and wishing she were back home in Boston—she is even less convinced; who wouldn't see ghosts and suspect supernatural occurrences while staying in this place?

"It's rusticated wood," Sarah says, startling Thalia from her reverie. "Not stone like people think. I told your sister the same thing when I drove her here that first night."

"Wait, what? You drove Blake here?" Thalia's voice is shrill with incredulity.

Sarah winces. "I'm sorry. I didn't think to mention it last night. I was too overwhelmed, I guess, with seeing you after so long. I tried to cut in when you were explaining things earlier. After that, everything with Maureen happened, and I guess I forgot to say something until now. But yeah, I picked her up from the terminal and dropped her at White Hall." Sarah stops, still looking sheepish.

"So you met my sister," Thalia says. "Something I'll never get to do."

"I'm so sorry, Thal. God, I wish I'd somehow known everything when I picked her up. I wish I'd never driven her to this place." She looks up at the monstrosity before them. They've pulled into a circular drive that curves past the looming front door.

Thalia follows Sarah's gaze, shuddering despite the heat blasting from the taxi's vents. "I wish you'd never driven her here either," she says.

"What's your plan?" Sarah asks. "How are you going to figure out if those envelopes came from here?"

"For starters, I'm going to check in."

"Then?"

"Then, I'm going to . . . I don't know. Talk to Aileen? I doubt she'll know who I am, so I'll use an alias. Maybe I'll tell her I'm a journalist."

"She'll be on high alert for reporters looking for details on the murder. She might not let you stay."

"Then I'll tell her I'm a travel writer. Writing a—what do they call those lighthearted pieces—a human interest story?"

Sarah shrugs. "It could work," she says.

"After that, I'm going to do whatever I can to figure out what happened to my sister. To see if she was really having an affair with Martin and if that's why Fiona killed her."

Sarah sighs and looks up at the mansion again. "This is bonkers. I haven't seen you since Hilda's play in Providence two years, ago and now we're part of a regular old murder mystery. Are you sure you don't want me to stay here with you? Patrick can handle the girls for a couple of nights."

"I'll be fine," Thalia replies. "As much as I'd love the moral support, the second Aileen sees you, my out-of-towner cover is blown."

Sarah nods. "All right. But text me constantly. I mean, I want minute-by-minute updates."

Thalia grins and leans over to put her head on Sarah's shoulder. "Of course. And Sar? Thanks for jumping right back into it with me."

"What do you mean?"

"Don't tell me it hasn't been easier here without me. You and I were best friends, but having to put up with Maureen and her, let's say idiosyncrasies, made your life almost as hellish as mine."

Sarah purses her lips. "We *are* best friends. And that's not true. I'd give anything to have you around again. And I'm worried to death about your mother. But if I know Maureen, she's going to pull through. She'll be up and giving them heck at BIMC before we know it. Dr. Maddox will be ripping his hair out dealing with her."

Thalia doesn't laugh. She can't. It's true, she can't imagine anything besting Maureen, but she also can't forget the way her mother looked as she screamed at Thalia to get off the island and not come back. Maureen wasn't simply resolute in her directives, she was frightened. And Thalia's going to find out why. Starting with this creepy mansion.

Thalia gives Sarah's arm one last squeeze and collects her bags. Sarah rolls the window down. "I mean it," she says. "Text me."

Thalia nods and turns toward the door. Sarah's taxi pulls away. She is dragging her suitcase across the cobblestones and examining the imposing facade when movement draws her attention to the left. A bearded man in a thick brown jacket stares at Thalia from under a dogwood. His gaze is intense, almost knowing. He doesn't wave. He doesn't smile, but his overall demeanor isn't distressing, only off-putting. She thinks he lets out a grunt of acknowledgment but can't be sure over the rain and the distant whoosh of breaking waves.

"Hello?" she says, and though she's looking right at him, the man steps back into the brush and vanishes. She watches the trees another moment, but he doesn't reappear. "Ohhhkay," Thalia whispers and walks the last few feet to the door, galoshes squeaking with every step.

With a sigh, she stops, sets her bags down, and searches the tote for her leather ankle boots. She pulls them on quickly, grateful the overhang provides decent shelter from the rain, and shoves the Scottie dog galoshes into the bag, then strips off Sarah's chunky sweater and stuffs that in too. It's disconcerting, how vulnerable she feels without it. The island is attempting to reclaim her, to turn her into the helpless person she used to be while living here. But in the off-the-shoulder frock purchased from a trendy boutique on Newbury Street, Thalia feels enough like the version of herself for whom this desolate landscape is foreign territory.

Like the out-of-towner she needs to embody.

Chapter 22

"Anyone here?" Thalia calls after she's pushed open the door and stepped inside. The echo dissolves up the massive staircase. "Hello? I'm looking for a room."

No one appears, and she considers googling the number of the B and B and telling whoever answers that she's standing in their foyer. A moment later, there are footsteps to her left, and Aileen Searles comes bustling over the threshold. Her expression is hard to read, but Thalia doesn't think it's recognition. She'll go with the travel writer angle, then.

"Hello," Thalia says again. "Sorry to show up like this, but I've just arrived on the island and was hoping to rent a room?"

"Rent a room?" The proprietress's confusion is palpable.

"You take guests in the off-season, correct?" Thalia keeps her tone light, as if it's no matter whether Aileen rents the room to her or not, she'll just head down the road to the next lodging establishment.

"We do, yes," Aileen says. "Sorry, you took me by surprise. Guests usually reserve in advance. I haven't had any requests for reservations come through today."

"I didn't submit one. The taxi driver dropped me off here when I asked for somewhere nice to stay."

Aileen is studying her. Does the woman know she's Maureen's daughter? And if so, does this mean Aileen is the one who sent sympathy cards to Thalia and her mother? If Aileen knows Blake was Thalia's sister, and that Thalia has come to White Hall in search of answers, playing dumb might still be her best option, at least until she learns more. Though she's decided to play the part of travel writer, Thalia adopts the professional air she uses in the courtroom; it's the fastest way she knows to convey that she's friendly but not to be trifled with. "I'm on assignment with a Boston paper," she says briskly. "It's a human-interest piece about Block Island life in the winter."

"How wonderful." If Aileen knows Thalia's lying, she does nothing to indicate it. "And I'd be happy to provide you with a room. There's no one else checked in at the moment."

"What about the man I saw outside?"

"That would be Monty Daniels. Our groundskeeper."

"Oh?" *Blake had written about an "enigmatic groundskeeper" in her letter.* But Aileen says nothing else and gestures toward the stairs.

"The Barrel Room is already made up, if you'd be happy with accommodations on the east side of the mansion. I have to be frank, though, Ms.—?"

"Mrs. Reiser." Laura's last name rolls off her tongue.

"Mrs. Reiser," Aileen finishes. "I usually don't take same-day reservations. It doesn't give me enough time to prepare a menu. We—I— usually serve breakfast and dinner at the mansion. Tonight, I'm afraid I wouldn't be able to do any better than a basic pasta primavera."

Thalia is going to say this won't be necessary before realizing she needs to take every opportunity to spend time with Blake's murderer's sister. "I'm vegetarian, so pasta primavera sounds wonderful."

"Great!" Aileen exclaims, though the cheeriness sounds forced. Thalia has definitely caught the woman off guard. She fixes her with her winningest courtroom smile and follows Aileen up the stairs.

A life-size portrait confronts them from the first landing. "Former mistress of the manor?" Thalia asks, though expressing curiosity about the house isn't keeping with her plan to exude breezy professionalism.

Aileen merely nods and continues climbing.

The hallway on the third floor is as long as a football field. The balls of her feet sting against the soles of her ankle boots. She's usually distracted from the unpleasantness of the four-inch heels by urgent legal briefs or vodka sodas and laughing friends at the bar after work. She can hear Sarah in her head, chastising her for being so shallow as to think her appearance has any bearing on how people treat her, but she can't help it. To her, shedding the L.L.Bean wardrobe and adopting a sleeker appearance is the physical manifestation of renouncing Block Island.

Aileen stops in front of a room, and Thalia suppresses a sigh of relief.

"Here we are," she says and unlocks the door. "In addition to fresh towels—and the barrel nightstand for which the room is named—you'll find a bottle of mulberry wine on the dresser."

Thalia walks into the room and places her bag on the bed. The bottle sits harmlessly on the polished wood, nearly identical to the one left on Sarah and Patrick's doorstep, though this one boasts a White Hall Vineyards label. Thalia remembers the line from Blake's letter: *I refuse to surrender the thirty days of sobriety I patched together, holding on to this medallion as if it's a life raft.*

What would it have felt like for her sister to be confronted with a bottle like this? Would she have refused it? Said nothing? "Do you offer these bottles to every guest who stays at White Hall?" Thalia asks.

"I do."

"What about those in recovery for substance abuse?"

Aileen's dark eyes narrow. She's a formidable woman, and when she places a hand on one hip, she gives the impression of a defense lawyer about to counterattack. "It's a lot of extra work on my end to ask ahead for the minuscule percentage of people who wouldn't appreciate a complimentary bottle of wine."

"I see."

"I can take it back to the storeroom if there's a problem."

Thalia picks up the wine. She's a long way from finding out what happened to Blake, but it couldn't have been pleasant for her sister to discover this bottle the moment she entered what would have otherwise been a sanctuary during the difficult journey ahead.

"There's no problem," Thalia says. "I'll have a glass with dinner." She places the wine back on the dresser. "This mansion," she says, changing the subject, "is beautiful, but it must take some getting used to in the winter. It reminds me of the novels I read when I was younger. *Rebecca* was my favorite. Have you read it? I can't be the first guest to feel like the second Mrs. de Winter, spirited up to Manderley's highest chamber and at the mercy of the sinister Mrs. Danvers." This is a terrible idea, but Thalia wants to see Aileen's reaction. She fiddles with an earring while keeping her gaze aimed at the woman's round, expressionless face.

A pensive smile widens Aileen's lips. Again, the cutthroat energy of an opposing lawyer springs to Thalia's mind. "You know . . ." Aileen trails off, seeming to revel in the suspense she's creating. "You are the first to say anything of the sort. That's interesting, though. *Rebecca*. I'll have to give it a try." She steps back and gives an awkward little bow. "But I should let you rest before dinner. I hope you enjoy your time here, Mrs. Reiser. And remember, dinner is at seven thirty."

Thalia opens her mouth to say thank you, but Aileen has turned and is walking down the hallway. She's surprisingly agile for a woman of her stature. Thalia hurries to the door and peeks around its frame.

At the end of the hall, Aileen disappears. Thalia darts out of the room and follows until she hears Aileen's footsteps on the staircase. When she's sure Aileen is on the first floor, Thalia turns and—as best as she can in the troublesome boots—jogs back down the hallway. Inside the room, she enables the flimsy hook-and-eye latch and stands there, frozen. She rests her forehead on the cool, carved wood of the door.

"Okay," she says out loud. "I'm here. What the hell do I do now?"

Whether there are ghosts in White Hall or not, no one answers.

Chapter 23

During the six days when Blake's death was still being treated as a suicide, the *Block Island Times*' articles about the tragedy had been open for online comments. An officer with the New Shoreham police force—*not* Justin Taft, for once—had responded to one that he wouldn't be able to get the image of the blood-filled clawfoot tub out of his mind for years. Once Fiona was arrested and the tragedy had become a murder investigation, the officer's comment was deleted, but not before a number of national outlets had discovered the detail and run with it.

Blake's letter had not included much by way of a description of her room, but she had referenced the playhouse-size replica of the grand mansion. Thalia hasn't thought of that strange structure since her childhood field trip to White Hall, but if she's going to determine which room Blake died in, she needs to find a bathroom with a clawfoot tub and a view of the replica. While Aileen is preparing dinner, Thalia plans to see whether any of the other bedrooms are unlocked.

Before she heads out, Thalia inspects the bathroom in her own room. There's a tub, but it's not a clawfoot. Thirty seconds later, she's in the hallway, approaching the door beyond hers. Aileen said the Barrel Room *specifically* was already made up. If the other rooms needed attention and the B and B proprietress wasn't expecting guests, maybe these rooms would be unlocked. Thalia places her hand on the cool brass knob and turns it.

The door opens into a walk-in closet. Thalia stares at shelf upon shelf of linens, paper products, and individually wrapped bars of soap. She shuts the door and moves down the hallway. The next door opens as well. It's some sort of conference room; there's a fireplace, a long table with eight ornately upholstered chairs, and numerous mirrors and Victorian-era paintings.

The next room *is* a bedroom. Mary Searles stares from a different portrait on the wall. The curtains are open, and Thalia goes to the window. Through the rain and dwindling light, the vegetation-enveloped driveway leading away from the mansion is visible. Thalia realizes that none of the rooms on this side of the hall are going to have a view of a structure overlooking Mansion Beach. She recrosses the room.

She's reaching for the knob when a noise comes from somewhere down the hallway. Thalia holds her breath and pulls the door closed as silently as she can. Dropping to the floor, she presses her cheek to the carpet but hears no footsteps and sees no shadows. Thalia gives it another minute, then opens the door and peers out.

Nothing. No Aileen. No one else. She's alone.

Thalia crosses the hall and gets lucky yet again; this door, too, swings open. Instantly, she's struck by a feeling of anticipation, a sense that the room is holding its breath. It's the air, she decides. It's not stuffy in here, like the other rooms. It feels lived in, breezed through, flayed, or, *filleted*. Its secrets ripe and ready for the picking. This could be the room in which Blake was murdered. Thalia can't be certain until she sees the bathroom, but it feels right. She shuts the door behind her and engages the hook-and-eye latch on the back of it. Aileen said they were the only two people in the mansion and should be cutting up vegetables for dinner at present, but Thalia isn't taking any chances.

She moves through the room as if inspecting evidence, examining each piece of furniture and adornment as if it will come up later in a jury deliberation. *But what am I looking for? Bloodstains? Signs of a struggle? Two and a half weeks after Blake's death and after dozens, if not hundreds, of law enforcement and forensic personnel have already inspected the crime scene, what do I expect to find?*

She goes to the window, pushes gauzy gray curtains aside, and there it is. A strange little ghost of a miniature mansion, floating in the mist above the sea. She has a vague recollection from her seventh-grade field trip that the replica was originally used as a bathhouse. Did Blake go out to it? If so, did she go inside? Thalia wants to ask Aileen about the White Hall replica at dinner, but she'll need to word her inquiry carefully; an ancient bathhouse has little to do with life on Block Island in the winter.

To her left, a pair of candelabra sit on a rolltop desk. To her right is a lowboy topped with a lace doily. Thalia looks back to the door through which she came, to the ornate nightstand by the bed. Its surface is clear of everything but a stained-glass lamp, the pattern of which resembles dangling cobwebs. Last night, Patrick had told Thalia that Aileen informed the police of Blake's missing complimentary bottle of wine. Had Blake drunk it? Or had it been removed by someone else? Aileen? Fiona? There's no way to know. Thalia's a civil litigator, not a criminal one. And she's starting to feel a little like Scooby Doo.

No. You're making progress. You might've even found the right room already. She looks away from the window, toward the bathroom door. It's open slightly, the darkness beyond beckoning her, daring her to come closer.

The bathroom is empty and uncompromised, Blake wrote in her letter, a bathroom in which Blake would be murdered that very same evening. It upsets Thalia beyond measure to think that her sister wrote the only words they'd ever exchange perhaps mere minutes before her wrists had been slashed.

Blake described following a veiled and shadowy specter into the bathroom the first night she stayed at White Hall, finding only four smooth walls of eggshell white and neither windows nor doors besides the one she'd come through. She'd been able to see every nook from floor to ceiling without turning her head, as Thalia can now. There's not even a cabinet in which someone could hide. Whatever black, shifty shape Blake saw—or imagined—disappeared like a cormorant in the fog.

What is still here, however, is the massive slab of enamel-coated cast iron: the clawfoot tub that became her sister's coffin.

Thalia is, unexpectedly, struck breathless. She walks into the room as if walking into a church. She runs her hand over the lip of the tub, tears springing to her eyes. *We never met, but I am so sad and angry and horrified over what happened to you. And if what the police and the islanders and my—our—mother say happened isn't what actually happened, if Fiona didn't kill you over an alleged affair after you'd relapsed, I'll be damned if I'm going to let your life—and your death—be overshadowed by lies.*

Thalia drops to her knees. She wants to say a prayer for her poor, departed sister. Or, not a prayer, but a promise. A promise she'll see to it that things are set right. Thalia's never been religious, so what spills from her mouth sounds like the closing remarks of a case rather than gospel. It doesn't matter. She means every word:

"I'm sorry, Blake. I'm so sorry. But one thing I am *not* is scared. I will confirm, or disprove, every last statement that's been made against you. I'll get to the bottom of our mother's fears. I'll figure out if something was really going on between you and Martin. I know you were dealing with a lot, both on this godforsaken island and back home in Boston. I know you felt like you didn't have anyone on your side. It's too late, but hopefully not too little, for me to be on your side now, in death. If the ghost of Mary Hopkins Searles can make herself known in White Hall, well, then, so can you. Through me."

She bows her head and squeezes the lip of the tub. She's imagining her sister's blood dripping over the smooth porcelain and onto the tile, letting the image stoke the fires of her anger. She breathes out and—in the silence after the exhalation—hears something in the room behind her. Thalia freezes. She can't call out, ask who's there. She isn't supposed to be in this room in the first place.

Turning as quietly as possible, she presses her back against the tub. She pushes up slowly, thighs burning, and slides to a stand. She creeps to the wall behind the door, listening hard for further sound. She sees her own wide eyes and pale skin in the gilded baroque mirror.

Nothing more comes. She must have imagined it. Sneaking around within an hour of checking in, of course she's going to be paranoid. But no, there it is again. A muffled click, maybe halfway between the bathroom and the door, around the location of the fireplace. Thalia's blood cools like the surface of the ocean after sunset. She takes a breath as if she's preparing to approach a judge and leans forward to peer into the room. It's imprecise and shadowy and far spookier than the sum of its parts.

As Thalia stares, a shape in the corner by the rolltop desk morphs into the silhouette of a woman. Or, is there not a desk in that corner at all, but a larger piece of furniture that would explain the upright figure? Thalia can't quite see the exact layout of the room from this angle. If it *is* a woman, she appears to be wearing long, full skirts and perhaps a veil to obscure her features. Thalia stares so hard the image gets blurrier rather than sharper. Just when she decides she's allowed herself to become frightened over nothing, the silhouette glides back to where the room cuts into an L and out of Thalia's sight. The fear that flooded her limbs and lungs turns, suddenly, to anger.

So what if she's not supposed to be in here? Aileen said there were no other guests, and Fiona is in jail. Who is Aileen to sneak in after her, trying to scare her? Thalia pushes the door open with a bang, stomps into the room, and claps her hands.

"All right, we're both caught, then," she declares. It's not a shout but close. She marches forward, cuts over to where the room shifts right, and throws her arms out to either side.

The room is empty. Silent. And, after Thalia spins in a complete circle, feeling like she's stage-side for a magician's trick, she sees the third detail in the you're-definitely-alone trifecta: the hook is still inserted into the eye closure at the back of the door.

"There *was* someone in here," she whispers.

She unlatches the lock and is about to slip from the room when she spots the nightstand. Not a wine barrel, like hers, but a piece of Baroque Revival or Second Empire furniture. She shuts the door again, curls her fingers around the nightstand drawer handle, and pulls it open.

Nestled at the center, next to an ancient-looking Bible, is a stack of cream stationery and light-brown envelopes, and beyond that, a thick paperback novel, the pages weathered and yellow. She's about to shut the drawer when she sees the novel's title: *The Mysteries of Udolpho*. Thalia lifts the book from the drawer and opens the front cover. Written in smudged pencil on the title page are two words: Blake Bronson.

Something clicks behind her, and Thalia turns, but it's just the room. Settling. Or, not settling. Waiting. Persisting in its energy.

And angry she's discovered one of its secrets.

Chapter 24

Thalia sits in the mansion's extravagant dining room, pushing forkfuls of pasta around her plate. Aileen served her a heaping helping before returning to the kitchen, and Thalia decides to text Laura while she eats. It's been way too long since she contacted her, the last time being before Dr. Maddox spoke with her at the hospital.

The cell service at White Hall is poor, the bars fluctuating from one room to another, but for now, it's enough to send a few short messages to her girlfriend. No, there's no news on her mother—though Thalia plans to call the hospital after dinner—and no, she didn't get into a fight with Sarah; she'd explain why she was staying at a B and B later, when they could speak by phone. Thalia tries to concentrate on Laura's own updates—contractors installed their new kitchen countertops without issue; their across-the-hall neighbors adopted a goldendoodle puppy that is beyond adorable—but she can't get the shadowy figure from Blake's room out of her mind, nor the list of "rules" scrawled on the piece of paper she found tucked into *The Mysteries of Udolpho* once she returned to her own room.

Had Blake really believed that chronicling everything from being wary of opportunistic men to taking her nightmares seriously was key to her survival? And had the figure been something legitimate, or an overreaction to White Hall's gloom? Thalia hadn't turned on any lights when she entered, and the room's layout was different from her own (she'd confirmed this upon returning to it). She could have mistaken the rolltop desk for the hunched figure of a woman, the rain on the roof for the sound of someone in the room with her. Either way, Thalia is annoyed with herself, her lack of discernment. From this point forward, she has to treat her investigation into Blake's death as the most difficult—and important—case she's ever worked on. No detail is too small to be overlooked, no moment too uneventful to let down her guard.

Voices come from the direction of the kitchen. Thalia places her fork on the table and, for a moment, just listens. The voices are muffled, but the speakers sound animated. When the volume of the conversation increases, Thalia stands and glides silently to the door Aileen disappeared through five minutes earlier. There *is* someone else in the mansion, then. Perhaps this is the figure Thalia saw in Blake's room. Thalia examines the frame of the door, finds that it swings in both directions. There's no way to open it even the narrowest of margins without alerting the speakers to her presence. There is, however, a small oval window at the top, slightly opaque, but perhaps clear enough for her to see through. At five feet three, Thalia is a few inches too short for the window to be eye level.

Don't waste this opportunity, she thinks, and runs back to the table. She returns with a dining room chair, high-backed and a bit too antique—that is, wobbly—for her liking. She climbs up anyway, wincing as her ankle boots sink into the upholstery. She holds the doorframe with one hand to keep from accidentally grabbing the door and sending it swinging. Looking through the frosted window is like trying to see to the bottom of a murky swimming pool. Still, the crack between door and frame is wider at the top, and it's easier to hear the individuals conversing. She cranes her head even higher and breathes as quietly as possible.

"What was I supposed to do?" Aileen says. "Push her back outside and slap a sign on the door that reads, *No Vacancy*? She walked right in and said she wanted a room."

"Just remember," the other voice says. It's male and disconcertingly familiar. "The last thing you want is for Fiona's actions to cost you

White Hall. You can't have family members of the deceased—*or* reporters, when actual reporters do turn up—getting ahold of information that will turn this place into a legend trippers' paradise. You want to continue operating an exclusive B and B and sought-after winery, not the next Lizzie Borden House.

"Whether she knew the girl or not, Thalia Mills—for we both know that's who's sitting in there—is obviously upset, or curious, enough to have come here. So you cook her meals, answer her questions, but do not speculate *at all*. We don't know any more than the police—or anyone else on Block Island, for that matter—about why Fiona did what she did."

So much for ten years off the island providing me with a much-needed disguise.

Aileen says something Thalia doesn't catch. The male voice responds with, "The cops know I wasn't having an affair with her. It's crazy to me how anyone could have thought that, most of all Fiona, but everything's cleared up now. I told the police the same thing you did, which is the truth: I helped the Bronson girl with her search for her biological mother—though, I didn't say who that biological mother was. Fiona taking shaky appearances and the word of island gossips over asking me for the truth was horrible, but it should have never progressed to something so tragic."

Martin, Thalia thinks. *Martin Dempsey, here to speak with the sister of his longtime girlfriend after she supposedly murdered a woman she thought he was sleeping with. But he said the words himself! He and Blake hadn't had an affair!*

Thalia's shoulder cramps from the awkward angle at which she is clutching the doorframe. She won't be able to balance on the spongy seat forever, but she's loath to miss anything. Now that she knows Aileen is aware of her identity and Martin's interest in Blake had not been romantic, what other information might she come by if she can perch here just a little longer?

Thalia takes a breath and rolls both feet to the sides of the loose leather boots so that her soles are flat against the chair's uneven center.

She's lost a bit of her height, but if she leans forward carefully, she can touch her ear to the crack in the door without applying pressure to it.

"I still can't believe it," Aileen says. She sounds close to tears. "I never would have thought Fiona capable of such a thing. Not in a hundred, no, not in a thousand, years."

"I know," Martin says, and he, too, sounds emotional. "I know. The only person more shocked than you is me. But we can't think about that now. It'll only make us more upset."

There's a pause. Thalia can't be certain, but Martin might be hugging, or otherwise trying to comfort, Aileen. Then he says, "Let's just keep doing what we're doing: managing the press, helping the police when they need it. But I should get out of here while the rain's still light and head to the restaurant. Maureen's hospitalization has left me short-staffed." Another pause, as if he's shaking his head. "Though I feel far worse for her daughter in there than for my scheduling manager."

A moment later, he continues, "You should talk to her. See if you can figure out if she's here because of her half sister and why she's trying to keep her own identity a secret. Like I wouldn't recognize Maureen Mills's daughter, even after ten years. Explain to her that Blake trusted you—and by extension, me—with why she was here, with Maureen's secret. As long as Thalia's not helping some journalist write a big exposé on the 'White Hall Bathtub Murder,' or whatever, you shouldn't have to worry about the future of your business."

There's yet another lull in the conversation. Has Martin left? She can only see a single figure. No, wait a minute. Are they embracing? If she could get a little closer, she might be able to see through the glass. She tries to get back up onto the heels of her boots without reaching down and using her fingers.

The chair shoots out from under her, and Thalia crashes to the floor. The only tiny bit of luck the universe affords her is that her trajectory is straight down. Somehow, the door doesn't swing even an inch on its hinges. Thalia ignores the pain in her knees and wrists to jump, catlike, to her feet. She runs the chair back to the table without breathing. Then, she careens into her own chair and—mindful not to make any additional noise—turns the bottle of mulberry wine onto its side. Its contents, dark as oxygenated blood, glug out over the table, soaking the linen and stretching out like the skeletal limbs of a listing tree toward her plate.

When Aileen bustles in a moment later, Thalia is mopping at the spill with a stained napkin. "I'm so sorry," she says. "I'm never this clumsy. I've ruined your tablecloth."

"Don't worry about it," Aileen responds. "I'll get this cleaned up in a jiffy, and grab another bottle."

"That won't be necessary," Thalia says. "I was pretty much finished." She gestures at her plate, grateful she made a solid dent in the pasta before embarking on her plot to eavesdrop.

"Are you sure? Mulberry wine goes great with dessert, and despite my lack of preparedness, I did whip up a flourless chocolate cake with raspberry sauce."

No detail too small to be overlooked. This is the discovery stage of the case; she needs to gather as much evidence as possible from the opposing party. "Okay, sure. That sounds great."

Aileen starts toward the kitchen, but Thalia slips into the I'm-leveling-with-you form of her courtroom persona and stops her with an earnest-sounding, "Ms. Searles?" Aileen turns, one eyebrow raised.

"I have to come clean with you about something. I'm not a reporter working on a story for a Boston paper. I *do* live in Boston, but I'm from here on the island originally. My name is Thalia Mills. I'm Maureen Mills's daughter. Blake Bronson was my sister. I lied because I wasn't sure what sort of reception I'd get if you knew who I really was, and for that, I'm sorry. But I also understand—from a personal correspondence—that Blake told only you and Martin Dempsey who her mother was, and what she was doing here, and for whatever reason, you and Martin have not disseminated this information to the rest of the island."

A range of emotions compete for space on Aileen's face. Before she can speak to any one of them, Thalia continues, "I didn't even know

I had a sister until after Blake was killed. I came here hoping I could learn a little bit about who she was. And if that isn't going to work for you because of *your* sister, then I understand."

When enough time has gone by for Thalia to feel like she's made a mistake by being honest, Aileen says, "Neither Martin nor I shared Blake's maternal parentage because Maureen denied it when Blake confronted her. That, and because Blake herself said she wished the matter to remain private. It's hard to have secrets on the island, so I wanted to extend that small measure of respect. Martin, too, said he thought that was important. I also said nothing because I'm truly sorry for what happened to your sister, for what Fiona allegedly did. That's why I sent sympathy cards to you and your mother."

"*You* sent those sympathy cards?" Thalia asks. "They were so . . ."

"Anonymous?" Aileen offers.

"Sinister," Thalia clarifies.

Aileen blushes. "Fiona always said I was too brusque to be in hospitality. I didn't mean to come off that way. Really, I wanted nothing but to express my condolences. Blake was a nice girl, though I didn't know her well, of course, or long. I don't want to talk about Fiona's part in things, because I don't understand it myself. But I'd be happy to answer whatever questions you have about Blake's time here, if I can."

No anger at her lie *and* an admission of sending the letters? This is a far better reaction than Thalia expected. "Thank you. I appreciate you saying that. But how did you know to send the card and wine to Sarah Liang's? I had only just arrived there."

"Martin was at White Hall when your ferry came in," Aileen says. "When Officer Taft's on duty in the winter, he gets a report from the captain as to the number of passengers arriving on the island. Apparently, the captain recognized you from high school. You know how these islanders are. They can't help commenting on a familiar face. I heard your name on Martin's scanner."

"Ah. I see." Justin Taft again. He really was an incorrigible gossip. "Wait, why does Martin have a scanner?"

"He's town selectman." Aileen shrugs. "Why wouldn't he have one? And anyway, it's probably left over from his father's time as police chief." Aileen continues to stand at the center of the dining room as if unsure if she should return to the table or fetch dessert as originally planned.

"If you're up for talking more over wine and cake," Thalia pushes, "then so am I."

Aileen's shoulders drop several inches and she smiles. "Okay, got it. I'll be right back."

When Thalia's alone, she takes out her phone and drafts a text to Sarah:

Everything's fine, but I'm getting the same creepy vibes that Blake was. It's like someone pulled this mansion—and these people—straight from the pages of Matthew Lewis.

A second later, Sarah texts her back:

Who?

Thalia sighs.

Author of *The Monk*? Most messed up novel ever, about . . . you know what? Never mind. Can you just call the hospital and ask for an update on Maureen?

Three dots, then:

Of course.

Thalia slips the phone into her pocket.
And waits.

Chapter 25

Thalia opens her eyes the next morning to more mist and rain. She knows where she is, but for a moment, she forgets the conversation with Aileen over dessert the previous evening. She remembers with bitter disappointment how the B and B proprietress told her nothing Thalia didn't already know, and nothing that seemed all that monumental for *Aileen* to be aware of.

Yes, Blake seemed troubled, Aileen said. No, Aileen didn't know anything about her pending court case. Yes, it had been Aileen's idea for Blake to tell Martin who she was.

"For what reason?" Thalia asked.

"He helped Blake collect some information about your mother before she went out to the house on Cooneymus Road to meet her."

"What about after Blake was killed?" Thalia asked. "You didn't think it wise to tell the police what she was doing here?"

"I thought I did." Aileen's tone was guileless. Thalia made it a practice to suss out guile in clients and casual acquaintances alike. "If not, then Martin certainly did. The police know Martin was helping Miss Bronson, and that's why Fiona thought Martin and Blake were . . ." Here, Aileen not only trailed off but clammed up.

"Does Martin ever come by?" Thalia asked, trying another tactic to get Aileen to speak more freely about her imprisoned sister's boyfriend. "Maybe I could ask him where he and Blake went."

"I haven't seen Martin much lately." The lie was obvious even if Thalia hadn't hidden behind the kitchen door. Aileen puckered her lips, shrugged, and looked everywhere but at Thalia. This told Thalia that Aileen wouldn't be owning up to Martin's earlier visit, but it also made her believe that everything Aileen had said prior to this was the truth. At least, the truth as much as the proprietress understood it.

If Aileen's plan is to keep Martin from Thalia, fine. She'll catch up with her mother's employer eventually. Until then, she has other islanders with whom she wants to converse. Starting with Timmy Graham, of the notorious Graham's Resort, vacationers' paradise and site of 97 percent of Block's drunk-and-disorderlies. Patrick had claimed Timmy was being more than vocal about Blake and Martin's trip to the honeymoon suite.

Sarah is waiting in the taxi when Thalia exits the mansion. She'd texted an hour earlier asking to be picked up, to which Sarah responded:

FINALLY!

"So Graham's Resort?" Sarah asks.

"That's what I'm thinking. Are you sure you don't mind driving me around all day?"

Sarah snorts. "Riiight, because you're keeping me from all the other people clamoring for a cab ride. Shut it, Mills, and get in. I *do* have to stop and get gas. After that, my cab is your chariot."

When Sarah stops at M&C's station, Thalia calls the hospital. She listens to the nurse's report while the tank fills and Sarah runs in for twin coffees.

"No change with Maureen," Thalia says when Sarah gets back in the car.

Sarah nods. "That's what they told me last night too. We'll head to Graham's now, but if you want to go to the hospital right after, we can."

Thalia grunts. She wants to see her mother, but awake, not hooked up to a feeding tube and unresponsive.

"Want me to come into the resort with you?" Sarah asks.

"Timmy's still a creep, right? He'll probably show his true colors more easily if he's not confronted with another islander."

"You're an islander, too, Thal."

"If you say so. But you know I'm right about Timmy."

They drive in silence the rest of the way. When Sarah stops in front of Graham's, Thalia grabs her umbrella. "Is it ever not raining on this damnable island?"

Sarah eyes Thalia's vermilion top, its intricately embroidered collar designed to resemble the petals of a flower, and rolls her eyes. "I keep telling you not to dress like a bohemian-obsessed college student at Coachella," she says.

"I do not—*grr*, never mind. We'll continue this later." Before Sarah can say anything further, Thalia's out of the car and running for the door. It's locked, but she rattles it back and forth, hoping the noise will alert Timmy to her presence. Sarah said Timmy still lives in one of the off-season rooms, so he has to be here.

A minute passes. No one comes. Thalia googles the resort number and calls it. A man's groggy voice answers on the seventh ring.

"It's Thalia Mills," she says, though whether Timmy has a single memory of her is anyone's guess. "I'm outside the resort right now. I need to talk to you."

Timmy swears under his breath. She hears rustling, as if he's pulling a shirt on while still holding the phone. "Thalia, you said?" he asks.

"Thalia Mills." She hesitates, then says, "I'm a lawyer from Boston. I used to live on the island." Let him think she's come on behalf of some drunk tourist who got hurt at the resort over the summer and wants to sue him. She'll set him straight soon enough, but in the interim, maybe he'll hustle down the stairs a little faster.

"Be right there," he says, and the call disconnects. Thalia turns back toward the taxi and gives Sarah a thumbs-up. It's raining too hard to see if Sarah returns the gesture, but a moment later, the door is opening. Her being a lawyer did get Timmy to move.

"Come on," he says, looking down with dismay at the droplets darkening his gray T-shirt. The rain does seem to be coming down sideways. She steps inside, her footsteps echoing in the mostly empty barroom.

Timmy looks her up and down, visibly attempting to put bits and pieces of memories together. A moment later he says, "Thalia *Mills*, right. I recognize you. Maureen's daughter. I heard she's in the hospital for an overdose. Was it intentional? Gee, I sure hope not."

Thalia resists the urge to groan at Timmy's take on her mother's hospitalization. Instead, she says, "She's in a coma, but stable."

"Too bad," he says, then glances at her again. He looks terrible. His eyes are red-rimmed, and his skin is pallid. She'd have known he was hungover even if the next thing that came out of his mouth wasn't "Can we talk at the bar? I need a little hair of the dog."

"That's fine."

"Care for one yourself?"

The thought makes her queasy, but the less attention she brings to Timmy's drinking problem, the more at ease he'll be with her. "Why not?" she replies, and Timmy pours two vodkas over ice and tops them off with Bloody Mary mix from the fridge. The resort is cleaned out for the winter of everything except what its owner needs.

Thalia takes the drink and ventures a minuscule sip. The mix must be homemade and long-perfected, because—mercifully—she cannot taste the booze. She sets the glass down and leans on the bar, but it's awkward without stools. That's probably another reason Timmy wanted the drink: holding a glass is like donning a suit of armor for an alcoholic.

She thinks of Maureen with her pills, of Blake, seemingly severed from New Shoreham, yet bound with an invisible wire to its culture of addiction; and even of Aileen with her mulberry wine. It's a cliché that folks who grow up on an island drink to excess, but Thalia sees the truth of this now, coming back as an adult. It's sad and sobering. She pushes away a bizarre mental image of the alcohol in Timmy's bloodstream insulating him like blubber on a whale, and takes another tiny sip.

"You're a lawyer, you said?" Timmy asks. "What kind?" He takes three long pulls of his drink and smiles the kind of blatantly sleazy smile Laura would call a lesbian-maker.

"It doesn't matter," Thalia says. She has to assume that Timmy, like everyone else, has no idea Maureen was Blake's mother. "I'm here because my former client, Blake Bronson, was at your resort with Martin Dempsey the day before she died. I'm hoping you can tell me a little about their visit—specifically, why they came here."

Timmy laughs, then sucks at his straw again. The Bloody Mary is almost gone. "Freakin' Martin. Serves him right to be getting some pushback for what he was up to with that girl."

"What were they up to?"

"They were banging. That's why Martin's old lady up and offed the poor little idiot. I gotta hand it to Fiona Searles, I always thought she was as cold as a January ocean. Killing someone on account of her man? That's some white-hot passion if I ever heard it."

He shakes his head and laughs again. "What a psycho," he continues. "I would have never thought she had it in her. Though, the girl, she denied there was anything going on with Martin."

Thalia's breath catches. "Blake told you that?"

"Hinted as much. Acted like she was too good for anybody, to be honest."

"When?"

"When what?"

"*When* did she act like she was too good to sleep with Martin?"

"She came into Above the Rocks a couple of nights before . . ." Here, Timmy stops and mimes the slashing of a knife against one wrist then the other. "It was after closing, but me and the bartender, Eva, go way back. I convinced her to let Blake in."

"Did Blake drink?"

Timmy's expression turns thoughtful. "She didn't. How did you know?"

Thalia ignores him. "If Blake wouldn't admit to the affair, was it Martin who told you they were sleeping together?"

"No way. Martin hates me. No more than I hate him. That asshole came here with the girl and asked for a room. He had that look in his eyes. I didn't ask questions, just handed him the key."

"You hate each other, yet you gave him the key to one of your rooms?"

"Yep. For free, even."

"Why would you do that?"

He sighs. "Martin and I have a long history, girlie. You wouldn't understand."

"Try me."

He sighs again, finishes his drink, and makes another. Thalia suppresses a grimace and takes a couple of swallows from her glass.

"Martin owns the newspaper," he says finally, after popping a few green olives into his mouth. "And the M&C gas station. He owns Dempsey Realty—along with half a dozen residential properties—and Martin's Above the Rocks. He's the town selectman. Before *he* owned all those things—with the exception of the gas station, which he bought a few years back—his father owned them. Before Martin's father owned them, his grandfather did, and so on and so on, back more than a hundred years.

"Martin told me once—though he was drunk off his ass when he said it—that his great-great-grandfather originally owned the land that's now White Hall. Or, maybe it was that his great-great-grandfather came up with the *design* for White Hall? I can't remember which. But I do know that before this resort you're standing in was Graham's, it was, wait for it"—he pauses, tapping his fingers on the bar in a drumroll—"Dempsey's. Martin's father, Michael, sold it to mine to help him out of debt. Martin and I grew up with the mindset, promoted by our fathers, of 'keep your enemies closer.' We've had to take advantage of that adage a lot over the last twenty-plus years."

Though Thalia remembers some of this shared history between the Dempseys and the Grahams from when she was younger, she needs to confirm what she suspects are the implications of this symbiotic relationship.

"So you hit a tree on Skipper's Island Road coming back from a tourist's Airbnb one night and get a DUI," she says. "Martin's paper doesn't report it. You're in hot water for sleeping with a young, drunk coed. The town selectman steers the victim's family toward a quiet resolution. In exchange for his discretion and influence, you give Martin a room at the inn when he needs it." She glances up, at where the rooms in question must be. "For whatever he needs it for." *And you have no proof of his affair with Blake other than an instance of Martin cashing in on this arrangement.*

She's presented the scenarios as hypotheticals, not accusations. Thanks to her litigation skills, she's perfected the art of speaking without judgment. The tactic works. Rather than indignation—or anger—Timmy is matter-of-fact; impressed, even, that she's put all this together. "That's a good way to describe it." Forgoing his straw, he lifts his glass and downs half of the new Bloody Mary.

"Can I see the room?"

The question catches him off guard. "The room they banged in?"

She winces, but he's taking another sip and doesn't notice. "I'm putting together Miss Bronson's closing documents, and need to be able to dot my i's and cross my t's."

It's a ludicrous statement that means nothing, but Timmy, drunk idiot that he is, falls for it. "Yeah. I mean, sure. If you need to. For closure and all."

She stares at him.

"You mean like right now?"

"Yes."

He guzzles the last of the drink and comes out from behind the bar. "Suit yourself."

She follows him down a long, musty-smelling hallway, and they come out into the inn's lobby. The wicker and royal blue give the room a dated feel. Timmy swivels to a wall of keys behind a glass partition. He opens it, selects a key from the top left, and holds it out to Thalia.

She takes it, careful not to touch his fingers. Her distaste for Timmy Graham has grown exponentially since she got here. "Thanks," she says, forcing a smile. She turns, spots the elevator. "Which floor?"

"I'll take you up."

"That won't be necessary."

"I insist."

He hurries out from behind the front desk, but she holds up her hand. "Really, Mr. Graham—"

"Mr. Graham was my father." Timmy chuckles. His eyes are wild. Thalia swallows her repulsion and places a hand on his arm. *I'm not going any further with this drunk POS than I have to.*

"To be honest, that Bloody Mary was a little weak for me. Let me run up, check the room, and when I come down, we'll have another drink together. Yeah?"

Bingo. "Yeah," he laughs. "I knew any daughter of Maureen Mills was going to know how to drink."

Thalia winces, trying not to think of Blake. Judging from his air of self-satisfaction, he's mistaken her disgust for excitement. The guy really is a pig. "Like I said, I'll just be a minute."

"Third floor, take a right, and follow the hallway around a sharp curve. You'll pass a half-moon window. It's just past that on the right."

"Thanks." She starts for the elevator.

"He's such a dumbass," Timmy says suddenly.

She turns back. "Who, Martin? Why?"

"He and I both knew he was here to bang that girl silly. But he was playing it cool when they walked in, acting like I didn't know what he was all about. He fed me a load of bull, like, 'Hey Timmy, this young lady and I need to take a look at the guest book. You still keep it with the other stuff in the honeymoon suite?' Sure, bro, like I really think you're taking that doe-eyed nine up to the best suite in the inn to look at the freakin' guest book."

"Ha," Thalia says, heart pounding at this revelation. "That is a lame excuse."

"Right? Okay, then. You know where to find me when you're done."

Hopefully at the bottom of the ocean. "See you in a few."

Chapter 26

Thalia stands outside the room, having followed Timmy's instructions. She unlocks the door and steps inside. The room's aesthetic assails her city senses, but more than that, its remoteness fills her with unease. Blake had, according to her letter, been an addict for years. Had she set her survival instincts aside to come here with a man she'd just met? Did she wonder whether anyone would hear her if she cried out for help? If Timmy were Thalia's only chance for rescue should something go wrong, she would be too paralyzed with anxiety to go on.

Thalia scans the suite. The gleaming maple, the porthole paintings, the shiny brass and copper—the place is a ship captain's wet dream. Though, Michael Dempsey had owned the resort before Timmy's father, so the decor could have been his idea, and hadn't his real estate signs once declared him *The Captain of Block Island*?

What kind of worldview might one adopt after holding such power and wealth for so long? If Timmy was right, then Martin had navigated life on Block Island without fear of repercussion since the moment he was born. Martin seems harmless, sure, but it was a rare man of influence and privilege who remained immune to corruption. Thalia walks past glass-encased shelves and framed paintings—as impressive as those in any museum—wondering what sort of maps and artwork would be on the walls in the museum of Martin's mind.

There's a podium along the right wall, atop which is an enormous leather-bound book, the word *Guests* embossed in gold on the cover.

Why bring Blake here? Aileen said Martin was helping her locate information about her mother. What connection might there be between Maureen and Graham's Resort?

Thalia stares at the guest book, reaches out, and inserts a finger between brittle pages. The book creaks as she wrestles it open. She flips through, quickly at first, then slowly, paying attention to the dates on the pages: 2013. 2002. 1992.

Blake's birth certificate listed her date of birth as April 22, 1992. Nine months before that would have been July 1991. Thalia would have been three. So Maureen was leaving Thalia home alone, or else spending hard-earned waitressing money on a babysitter, in order to gallivant around Graham's Resort with the likes of men like . . . Timmy Graham?

She's about to close the book. This is stupid. Then she considers that a full-term pregnancy is forty weeks, not nine months, and flips back further, into July. Thalia stares at the entry as if it might change before her eyes: *Maureen Mills, a.k.a. the Mulberry Maiden, and her Doting, Dashing Lover.*

This is why Martin took Blake here. But why? Did he know what they'd find? And why had he allowed Timmy Graham to believe he'd brought Blake here to have sex with her? *He had that look in his eyes,* Timmy said. Thalia shakes her head and wishes, not for the first time, that Blake had gotten ahold of her phone number that night. That she'd called her instead of writing a letter, though, admittedly, she has no idea how Blake even got her address. She didn't know her sister. One letter constitutes nothing. Maybe she did have sex with Martin. Why is Thalia so convinced that everything in the letter is the truth, or that, at the very least, Blake didn't lie by omission?

For a moment, Thalia sees Martin leading Blake—an eager maiden, smiling and tossing her hair—through the door of this isolated suite. Martin is handsome. He was when Thalia was younger and he still is now. It's not out of the question that Blake could have fallen for him, especially in the fragile state she was in. But it *feels* wrong, and though

Thalia never lets intuition overshadow facts, she can't stomach the idea that the affair really happened.

And if the affair didn't happen, how is it possible a woman as shrewd as Fiona Searles believed it did to the point of murder?

She pulls out her phone, snaps a photo of the Mulberry Maiden's entry, and shuts the guest book. "Where are you going to take me next, Blake?" she whispers to the empty room.

∞

Having retrieved Sarah's umbrella from the front desk, Thalia means to exit the resort from the lobby rather than going back through the bar. Let Timmy drown in Bloody Marys while he waits for her to reappear. She's within arm's reach of the door, her mind on her mother's decades-old handwriting preserved in the guest book, when she feels a hand on her lower back.

"Where you runnin' off to?" The words all run together. Timmy is far drunker than when she left him.

"I have to get back to my B and B." Her words are curt, but Timmy is undeterred.

"Is that an invitation?"

"No."

Timmy pushes the door closed before she can open it more than a few inches. Slowly, she raises her gaze and fixes Timmy with a withering glare. "Are you going to make me tase you?"

"I ask again, is that an invitation?"

Thalia growls in disgust and reaches for the pocket in which there is decidedly no Taser, but Timmy—probably no stranger to woman deploying their self-defense weapons on him—falls for it.

"Okay, okay, relax," he says. "It's just that it'd be pretty sick to bang both mother and daughter."

Some cross between denial and revulsion pierces Thalia's chest. "What are you talking about?"

Timmy leers. There's a pepper kernel from the Bloody Mary mixture between his teeth. "I'm talking about Maureen Mills. I meant what I said about it being too bad she's in the hospital. Maureen's a hot ticket, even at her age. You, though. Taking you upstairs would be like stepping into a time machine. Like being with Maureen all over again."

"I don't believe you."

"What, that banging you would be like banging your mother?"

Thalia winces. "I don't believe you were with my mother at all."

Timmy goes to lean against a wooden beam, but he's farther away than he thought and stumbles. Would he be this horrible, this crass, if he were sober? Thalia thinks he would be. For Timmy, alcohol only amplified an already lecherous personality.

He shrugs off the stumble, or maybe, Thalia's incredulity. "No skin off my back. I've got memories to keep me warm at night."

"I doubt you can remember what happened yesterday, let alone something that took place, you tell me, how many years ago?"

Timmy appears to be counting in his head. "Twenty-five? Before I took over running this place for my old man."

Thalia pushes down a frisson of panic at the timeline. "Did you make a note of this conquest in your little guest book?" *No way Timmy Graham could ever be called doting or dashing.*

"Nah, I didn't take her here. It was some party a guy we knew back in high school threw at his parents' beach house."

Is that the truth? Is any of it? "I've got to go," Thalia says and pulls the door open. Timmy shuts it harder than before and grabs her by the shoulders.

"Come upstairs. You won't regret it. Your mother didn't."

"Get your hands off me." Thalia shoves him backward, but he grabs her again. Sarah's umbrella is balanced against the doorframe. She reaches for it, wraps her hand around the metal ribs, and jabs it forward. Its point catches Timmy in the center of his stomach.

He lets out a groaning *whoosh* of air and falls backward, his own hands curled around the body of the umbrella.

"Let that memory keep you warm at night," she growls and exits the suffocating darkness of the lobby where, for once, the rain—cool and cleansing—is a welcome sight.

∞

"Where's my umbrella?" Sarah asks as Thalia jumps into the taxi.

"Hopefully embedded in Timmy Graham's liver." Thalia relays her and Timmy's parting exchange while Sarah pulls away from the resort.

"God, that guy's a grade-A creep and sexual predator. Do you really think he and Maureen . . . ?" Sarah trails off.

"I don't know what to think. He believes Martin and Blake were sleeping together, but then he said something about seeing Blake out in New Shoreham one night and that she denied it. Aside from Blake's own letter, that's the first piece of evidence against the affair we've had. Timmy also made a comment about Martin coming to the resort to see an old guest book. He thought it was a cover, but I think it was the real reason Martin and Blake were there."

Sarah glances away from the windshield to look at the photo Thalia's holding up for her. "It's my mother's handwriting."

"Maureen Mills, a.k.a. the Mulberry Maiden? Why would she refer to herself like that? And who do you think the doting . . ."

"Dashing lover," Thalia finishes for her.

"Right, who do you think the doting, dashing lover is?"

"I have no idea, but it certainly seems like it could be Blake's father." Thalia looks down at the image of the guest book page again, reading the words anew. The lover couldn't have been that doting if he abandoned Maureen with two children. Thalia turns the phone facedown in her lap and lets out a groan. "Regardless of anything else," she says, "I think it's safe to say Martin took Blake to the resort to see the guest book, *not* to have sex with her."

"Fiona Searles was no idiot," Sarah says. "If there wasn't actually an affair, why would she have thought there was, to the point where she'd be driven to murder?"

"Exactly!" Thalia exclaims. She smacks her hands on the glove compartment. "That's the *exact* thought I had." They are at the crossroads between Water and Spring Streets. Thalia bites her lip and glances out the window, then back at Sarah, her jaw set.

"I know that look," Sarah says. "We're not going to the hospital, are we? All right, new plan. What is it?"

"When's the next ferry off the island?" Thalia asks.

Chapter 27

Like Dorothy stepping from black and white into Technicolor, the rain ceases as they approach Point Judith. There are only four other passengers aboard, but Thalia still drags Sarah to the gangplank; they have no time to waste if they're going to make it to the prison before it becomes too late in the day to request a visit.

Sarah found the Rhode Island Department of Corrections' policy online and discovered that, if not a relative or friend, a prospective visitor must be a "prior acquaintance" of the inmate. Those inmates not on restricted status were granted three visiting periods a week, but the duration of their visit—if permitted—would be up to the warden.

"Oh no!" Sarah had exclaimed when they were halfway across the twelve-mile stretch of the Atlantic. "It says you'll need to have passed a background check by one of two different national criminal database trackers." She looked stricken. "This whole trip is a waste."

"What if I told you I already submitted to the background check?" Thalia replied. At Sarah's bewilderment, Thalia continued, "I'm a lawyer, remember, and an annoyingly conscientious one at that. The day after I received Blake's letter and saw that Fiona had been arrested, I submitted the background check and asked one of the administrators at my firm to expedite it. It'll be tight, but the first day they could have it on file would be today."

Sarah's bewildered expression finally cracked into one of disbelief. "'Annoyingly conscientious,' huh?" she said. "Is that what your colleagues call it?"

Thalia shrugged. "I knew I'd want to speak with her in general," Thalia said, "because of what she's accused of but also—now that I've seen Blake's list—because of rule number seven, madness equals murder."

"Huh?"

"I found a book of Blake's in White Hall. Inside was a list of 'rules' she'd made up for surviving a gothic horror novel."

"Whoa. Heavy."

"Tell me about it," Thalia responded. "But it makes me want to determine all the more if Fiona really was insane."

It's a forty-minute drive from the terminal to the prison, but their Uber arrives quickly. When they pull into the parking lot, Thalia can only stare. She was expecting flat, featureless steel, not peaks and stone worthy of a novel slipcase.

"Whoa," Sarah says again. "This is . . ."

"Creepy?" Thalia finishes.

"You said it."

"Come on."

The process for entering the building and requesting a visit goes more smoothly than Thalia would have expected. Rhode Island state prisons operate differently from those in Massachusetts in that they run both a pretrial and sentence facility, so Fiona is being held in the intake portion of the women's division. While they wait, Thalia studies the photo she took of the Mulberry Maiden entry in the Graham's Resort guest book.

"Thal?"

She hears the note of seriousness in Sarah's voice but doesn't look up. "*Mmm?* Yeah?"

"Have you considered that your father and Blake's could be the same person?"

Thalia pries her gaze from the phone. Sarah is studying her with an intensity that reminds her of lying on their backs on the roof of her mother's house, sharing cigarettes—and their secrets. "Of course I've thought that," she admits. "You know Maureen's story about who my father was isn't exactly rife with details, just that he had been a tourist from the mainland who'd said he'd return to see her, but once she told him she was pregnant, never did."

Sarah nods; she knows. Thalia had analyzed the possibilities with her at various points throughout their friendship, whenever a new identity crisis or adolescent milestone hit. "It's just that she kept everything so hidden from you," Sarah says, "from everyone, and now she's doing the same with the identity of Blake's father. Maybe because the situations were the same." Sarah pauses and makes a face. "Or, maybe Blake's father really is Timmy Graham."

Thalia makes a gagging sound, but she's interrupted by the whoosh of a nearby door. She sits up as a corrections officer walks in. "Thalia Mills?"

"Yes?"

"Your request to visit inmate two-five-eight-seven has been granted. Please ready your cell phone and other belongings to be left in a secure area, and follow me."

Thalia stands, suddenly panicked. Even with expediting the background check, she hadn't really thought this would work.

"Go on," Sarah urges. "I'll wait here." She glances at the airlock doors. "Obviously."

"Right," Thalia whispers back. "See you soon."

Thalia follows the officer through a metal detector and down a long corridor. Here, the unexpectedly Gothic architecture makes a reappearance in the stone floor and the ogival arch of the ceiling. *Focus,* Thalia thinks. *Don't let what were Blake's preoccupations distract you.* They enter—and pass through—one room, then another. Finally, they reach a second metal detector. Thalia hands over her personal effects.

She follows the officer through a final anteroom, and that's when she sees her. Fiona Searles, regal despite the orange jumpsuit, sitting at a small table in an otherwise empty room. Thalia takes a deep breath.

"No handshakes, and stay on your side of the table," the officer advises. He goes to stand in the opposite corner of the room.

Thalia sits, her eyes on Fiona's, which are startlingly similar to Aileen's if not in color, than in their shape and set in her face. "Thank you for seeing me."

"Maureen Mills's daughter, right? Why are you here?" Fiona's face is gaunt, as if she hasn't eaten a thing since she was incarcerated two weeks prior. Her blonde hair is loose around her shoulders.

"Blake Bronson was my half sister. I want to know why you killed her." She wasn't planning on such a blunt approach and senses rather than sees the officer stand up a little straighter across the room. Fiona, however, answers her just as bluntly.

"I didn't."

"Why were your fingerprints on the knife?"

Fiona shrugs despairingly. "It was a knife from our kitchen. I used it a hundred times over the course of owning it."

"But the police found Martin's things in Blake's room, started investigating further, and discovered that you believed the two of them were having an affair."

Fiona sighs. "Yes, the police thought that *I* thought they were having an affair. And that was enough to change the whole direction of their investigation," she says. "Not to mention the orientation of the wounds in her wrists." There's hopelessness in her voice.

Thalia opens her mouth to ask her next question, but Fiona isn't finished. "I'm sorry about your half sister. But I'm happy you've come here. You want answers, and that's *why* I'm happy. *Because I can't give you any.*" Fiona's eyes light up, and she smiles as if she's said something profound.

Thalia can't help the thought that flickers through her brain: *She is mad.* She inhales on an abbreviated count of three and keeps her voice steady when she says, "I don't understand."

"I honestly thought she committed suicide. Like I said, the police think I killed her because they determined the knife wounds weren't self-inflicted and because I thought she and Martin were having an affair. I *did* consider that they were sleeping together—I knew he had taken an unhealthy interest in her and was driving her all over the island. But Martin's never cheated on me before, and I wouldn't *murder* someone even if she *was* sleeping with my boyfriend."

"His umbrella and jacket were in her room."

"I didn't know that until *after* I was arrested. Once she checked in, I never went into that room."

"So if she didn't commit suicide and you didn't kill her, who did?"

"That's what I'm trying to tell you. I have no idea! I didn't even know she was related to you, and I certainly didn't know she was Maureen Mills's daughter." Fiona's eyes light up again. "In fact, I'll be sure to tell my lawyer that. Maybe your mother killed her. She's crazy enough."

"My mother's sick," Thalia says, "but she's no killer."

"Neither am I."

Thalia wants to believe her. Like Sarah, she, too, remembers Fiona as the picture of sophistication when they were younger. Hell, she used to want to be Fiona, all pinned-up hair and plum-colored lipstick. Likely, Thalia modeled her own idea of what a career woman looked like on Fiona Searles. But Fiona's defense is nothing more than her word, and why should Thalia take her at that? She sighs. "Is there anything else you can tell me? Anything that might help me direct my search?"

"Besides your mother?"

Thalia shoots her an angry look. "Besides my mother."

Fiona looks down at the scuffed linoleum floor, clearly desperate for something, anything, to say. Thalia suddenly feels the claustrophobia of this place, the weight of the walls pressing in on them, tightening, squeezing, the resultant anxiety manifesting as the dull throb of an impending headache.

No. She pushes back against the walls, mentally thrusting the foolish fear away. *Something needs to come out of this visit,* she thinks. *And it's not going to be a stupid, self-induced headache.*

"What about Aileen?" Thalia asks. "Could she have had anything to do with this?"

Fiona scoffs. "Aileen has as much capacity for murder as a lamb."

"And Martin? He's the only other person who's regularly at White Hall."

"Martin's the most successful business owner on Block Island. His family's lived there for over a century. Why on earth would he murder a young woman he'd never met before?"

"Does Timmy Graham ever come to White Hall?"

Fiona's face wrinkles with distaste. "Timmy Graham? No, never."

"Do you know who the Mulberry Maiden is?"

Fiona frowns. "I have no idea. Is it a Twitter handle or something?"

"Think more along the lines of an alter ego of one of the islanders. Something connected to the history of the place." Thalia's making things up as she goes, anything to spark something in Fiona's mind, her memories.

"If it has something to do with the island's past, the person to ask is Ethel Gilbert Brown."

Of course! Why hadn't she thought of Ethel before?

"Five more minutes," the guard interjects.

Thalia's mind races. *Aileen. Martin. Timmy. The Mulberry Maiden. There's no one else. There's no one else.* The guard moves again, and it's a flash of dark clothing on her left. Dark . . . clothing . . . at the outer edge of her periphery . . .

"What about Monty?" she asks.

"The groundskeeper?" Fiona tilts her head. "I mean, he's been employed at White Hall since 1991. I only know that because we hired him right after Hurricane Bob. There was too much cleanup around the property to handle ourselves."

"Could your groundskeeper have murdered Blake?"

"I don't think—"

"*Could* he have murdered her?" Thalia presses. "Did he have access to the mansion and know Blake was staying there?" She's in full-on lawyer mode now.

"I guess. I mean, yes. Yes to both of those questions. But I still don't think—"

"Time's up," the officer says. "Inmate, cross the room and face the wall."

Fiona does as she's told, but her eyes remain on Thalia. "Please," she says as the officer places her wrists in handcuffs. "If you want justice for your sister, you have to keep looking."

Thalia watches as Fiona's led away. The door behind Thalia opens, and another guard appears to escort her to the lobby.

"It wasn't me," Fiona calls, her voice full of a desperate, final pleading. "I swear to you, Thalia Mills, I did not do this!"

Chapter 28

Thalia's unwilling to speak in front of their Uber driver, so they ride back to Point Judith in silence. On the ferry, Sarah can't get her questions out fast enough.

"So that's what's next on the agenda?" she says after making Thalia repeat every instant of her exchange with Fiona. "You're going to talk to this Monty guy?"

"I'm going to find out more about Monty," Thalia clarifies. "I don't think it's a good idea to approach him. Not yet. I think we should follow up on Fiona's suggestion to talk to Ethel Gilbert Brown."

"Ethel?" Sarah considers this. "Makes sense. Though, we never even figured out what happened between her and Maureen all those years ago."

"We didn't," Thalia admits. "All I know is that they used to be friends but stopped speaking when I was really young. It's not like they hated each other. Maureen still let us go to the library all the time, remember? It was like she was upset with Ethel but still trusted her to keep an eye on us. Regardless, I think it's our best bet for new information."

It's late when they disembark and retrieve Sarah's taxi. "Are you sure you don't want to come back to my place?" Sarah asks.

"I need to be at White Hall. To think. But thank you." By the time Sarah pulls up to the mansion, however, Thalia's motivated more by the prospect of sleeping than thinking.

"The library opens at ten tomorrow," Sarah says. "I'll pick you up at nine and we'll go for coffee?"

"Perfect," Thalia says. Sarah must be just as exhausted as she is, because she wastes no time pulling onto the drive and heading back toward the globe-topped pillars marking the mansion's exit. Thalia scans the trees, her eyes lingering on the dogwood tree under which she observed Monty. There's nothing there now but a few lingering berries and scale-like bark glistening with droplets of water.

Thalia sighs. Of course it won't be that easy. He's not going to come to her. She turns for the door. When she's ready, she'll have to go looking for this Monty character herself.

∞

Sarah picks her up at nine as planned, but she already has the coffees. They park at Great Salt Pond and talk about Sarah's daughters, Thalia's job, everything but the craziness of the last two days. Finally, Thalia eyes the dashboard clock, and they exchange a look. Sarah finishes her coffee, starts the engine, and pulls back onto the road.

It's been more than ten years since Thalia has seen the Island Free Library, but unlike the resort or White Hall, she remembers every detail of the building. This was one of the few places Maureen would allow her to come spontaneously and without stipulation. If she was at the library, she didn't have to be home until it closed, and didn't have to be accompanied by Maureen on one of her few-and-far-between days off.

"Remember, Ethel might be trustworthy, but she's also a loner—and painfully quiet," Sarah says, peering at the library through the pumping wipers.

"Maybe she'll feel like talking today." Thalia reaches in the back for the umbrella before remembering its fate. "Timmy's probably using it to stir his Bloody Marys," she mutters.

"What?"

"Nothing. Let's go."

Sarah rubs her hands together. "Right. Let's go talk to the weirdo antisocial librarian." She turns to scan the back seat. "Crap. That's what you were talking about. Timmy's probably using *my umbrella* to stir his Bloody Marys. You're buying me a new one when this is over."

"Fine," Thalia says.

"If it's ever over," Sarah adds. "I'm starting to think the more people we talk to, the more complicated things will get."

"I'm not leaving this island until I find out what happened to Blake," Thalia says.

"Understood."

"Good. I'm glad we're in agreement over that point."

They stare at each other. Thalia feels thirteen again. "Well, come *on*, then," she finally says.

The library door is dark and heavy-looking, and the windows reflect light like they're keeping secrets. Sarah's right, talking to Ethel will be difficult, so Thalia tells herself she's anthropomorphizing the slope-roofed, gray-shingled building to take on the same tight-lipped qualities of its keeper.

"This library's been here since 1875," Sarah says. "I'm pretty sure Ethel's been the librarian for that same amount of time."

Thalia suppresses a giggle. "Stop it, Sarah. Ethel's fine. Even if she did always dress like a grandmother and act like she ran a historical society."

"She *does* run the historical society," Sarah says. "And a museum, on the corner of Old Town Road."

"There you have it," Thalia says, whispering now. They're at the door. "That's good. If there's anyone who'll know what the Mulberry Maiden refers to, it's her."

She ducks through the door, and Sarah scrambles in behind her. Thalia's amazed by how little has changed. The fiction shelves still spread in every direction beyond the drafty lobby. Labeled displays—*Local Authors, Women-Penned Classics, Middle-Grade Fantasy Featuring LGBTQ Characters*—break up the path between the checkout desk and a café. Classical music drifts up from below them. She catches Sarah's eye, and gestures toward the stairs.

At the top, Thalia has the sudden, childish desire to take her friend's hand. *You're being ridiculous. Ethel is hardly an imposing figure. And far less so than Timmy Graham, or Aileen Searles, for that matter.* They creep down together.

"Hello," Thalia calls. "Ethel, are you down here?"

The basement has changed as little as the first floor. It's still home to the island's oldest documents, books, and newspaper archives. *Before Martin owned the island's only newspaper,* Thalia thinks. Sarah sweeps her hand over a dusty pile of books on an oak table. Seconds pass. The volume of the classical music is lowered. Ethel emerges from the stacks, her hair swept into a bun, her loafers scuffed and flat. She wears a pencil skirt and a cardigan. The cardigan is missing a button and stained with ink.

A teenaged Thalia would have snickered, but something occurs to her that never has before: Ethel's style might be less a choice than a necessity, as much a suit of armor as the island's alcoholics' perpetual beverages. Despite the bun and the cardigan and the dowdy shoes, Ethel is a beautiful woman. Her eyes are a vibrant green and catlike. Her skin is smooth and unblemished. The wisps of hair that escape the bun curl into ringlets that frame her heart-shaped face. Ethel wears no makeup, no jewelry. Her eyeglasses are so outdated they've almost come back into fashion. It's like Ethel has gone out of her way to appear unattractive but hasn't really succeeded.

"Hello," Sarah says, and Thalia silently thanks her for speaking first. She closes her eyes and imagines herself in a courtroom. *Concentrate. You have one opportunity to pull information from this woman. Make it count.*

But Ethel doesn't give her the chance. "You need to leave," she says. The words are thick with some emotion Thalia can't identify, but whatever it is, it has Ethel visibly shaking. She turns to Sarah. "I have no issue with you, Sarah Liang, but I won't speak with *her*. I refuse."

"Why?" Thalia says, and leans forward, trying to force the older woman to meet her gaze. "Is it the same reason my mother won't tell me anything? Is it because you're afraid?"

Ethel's eyes flash in Thalia's direction. A less experienced attorney might mistake Ethel's stance, those eyes, for that of a deer, but Thalia knows better. Ethel isn't a deer in line with a hunter's crossbow, but a cornered coyote. Thalia's seen the predatory canines since living off the island, knows that behind the raised fur and pricked ears, there is no fear. Just power and cunning and, when they appear to be trapped, a keen mind calculating their best chance for escape.

"Please, Ethel. We need to know what's going on. Blake Bronson came to see you, right? With Martin Dempsey?"

"Stay away from Martin," Ethel says. Whispers, really. It's cautionary, but the words also hang with the weight of knowledge. Ethel isn't repeating some vague warning. She has her reasons for wanting them to stay away from New Shoreham's selectman.

Sarah takes a seat at the book-strewn table as if this will have some effect, as if Ethel will change her mind about speaking to them because Sarah's made herself at home. "Why do we need to stay away from Martin?"

"You're right," Ethel says to Thalia, ignoring Sarah, "something's going on. And I don't have a clue what it is. But I know that if a Dempsey is involved, you need to stay out of it. Yes, Martin came here with that girl, and I told him enough to appease him, to keep him from getting angry. But I can't say any more. I won't." She's still looking at

Thalia, her green eyes shimmering like emeralds. "I won't involve you. I bet before Maureen ended up in the hospital, she told you to get on the first ferry off the island, didn't she? I bet she warned you. Like, once, a long time ago, I should have warned her."

Thalia leans toward Ethel. "Does this have something to do with why you and my mother are no longer friends?"

Ethel only stares.

"Please, tell me what you're warning me about!" Thalia says, her voice approaching a shout. The emotion is part tactic to elicit Ethel's cooperation, and part truth, a manifestation of her growing frustration. "All I know is, by the time I received a letter from the sister I never knew I had, she was dead. The official report is that she was murdered by Fiona Searles for initiating a relationship with Martin Dempsey, but Fiona insists she's innocent, and Blake's letter didn't even hint at an affair. The police don't know about the letter, and I don't want to give it to them until I know for myself what's going on."

Ethel takes a small, staggering step backward. "Blake Bronson was your sister." It's not a question. "Maureen Mills's daughter." The words are barely audible. "I wanted to believe Martin had no idea what he was talking about."

Thalia is torn between comforting Ethel—who looks horrified by her own naivete—and using that horror to push for more information. She compromises, taking two steps toward Ethel with her hands raised, as if poised to calm her, while saying, "If you don't tell me what's going on, I'm not sure there's anyone who can. Please. Can you at least tell me who the Mulberry Maiden is?"

Despite her paleness, Ethel's eyes flash again, with panic, frustration, and—unexpectedly—sadness. "Oh, Thalia. You're going to keep digging, aren't you? You're not going to let this go?"

"She's not," Sarah says. "I can tell you that for a fact."

"I don't know anything," Ethel says weakly. "Not really. I don't know what happened to Maureen—why she had another baby, who the father might have been. I don't know why Martin took an interest in helping your"—Ethel closes her eyes, as if she can't bear to say it—"your sister. What I do know is a story from the past. About a young woman who was broken by a brutal, powerful man." She looks up, and there are tears in her eyes. "Do you want to hear it?"

"We don't want to hear it," Thalia says. "We need to."

"Fine," Ethel says. "Though I still think this is a bad idea." She sinks into the chair across from Sarah, tucks a wisp of hair behind her ear, and shakes her head wearily. "It starts, of course, with the island."

Chapter 29

"Once upon a time," Ethel says, and Thalia pulls out a chair beside Sarah, "there was a young woman looking to start a new life. She moved to Block Island, a place where her great-great-great-grandmother had lived one hundred years earlier, and set herself up in a little cottage. This was at the end of 1989, and property was much more affordable."

1989, Thalia thinks. *The year I was born.*

"She had a degree in library science." Ethel smooths her skirt with shaking fingers. "And procured a job at the island's library. It was as a circulation associate, but the girl was ecstatic for the opportunity.

"She settled into a nice routine. Working, walking the beach, filling her cottage with meat and milk from the market and vegetables from her garden. Occasionally, she'd go to White Hall and buy vines of mulberries and eat them until her fingers and lips turned purple. She'd even made a friend, a nice woman who had just started working at the local restaurant. Aside from that friend, she kept to herself, but she wasn't lonely.

"Then she met Michael. He was sweet, soft-spoken, caring. He courted her for months before she agreed to go on a date with him. After that, the girl fell quickly. She and Michael were inseparable, though they spent most of their time at her cottage. He was from a powerful family, and he'd asked her to keep their relationship quiet. The girl didn't mind. Her friend had gotten pregnant by a vacationer to the island who'd left her, and she didn't want to rub her relationship in her friend's face, especially when Michael started talking marriage. She'd yet to give herself to him, to anyone, but she felt certain he loved her, they'd be married, and they'd live happily ever after.

"One afternoon in May of '91, Michael picked the girl up from her shift and told her he'd made a reservation at White Hall B and B. 'We'll walk the beach at sunset,' he told her, 'and have a delicious dinner. Think of it as a dress rehearsal for our honeymoon. It's early in the season, and there'll be hardly any other guests there. It will be so romantic.' The girl wasn't sure this was a good idea, but what reason did she have to doubt him? She was also cheered by the prospect of their relationship being out in the open. He picked her up around three on a gorgeous spring afternoon, the kind of weather that ends up on a postcard."

Ethel pauses. The concrete walls of the library basement have drifted away for Thalia, and she imagines they have for Ethel too. She can almost hear the sounds of summer—birdsong and ice cream truck jingles—as opposed to the muffled thrum of rain.

"They arrived at White Hall," Ethel says, "and the girl was keen to head down to the beach, but Michael wanted to catch up with the proprietor and request that they be brought their meal in their suite. The girl was growing increasingly worried. Mrs. Searles—that would be Fiona and Aileen's mother—brought up the food, and the girl had the wild thought that she should ask Mrs. Searles to help her leave the mansion and get home. She didn't. But she was right. She should have said something. By the time the proprietress adjusted the vase of mulberry blossoms on their tray and was heading for the door— and Michael made it clear he wished for them to be left alone—it was already too late.

"Michael never planned to go down to the beach. There would be no sunset, no sea breeze, no smell of salt on their skin. He raped her, and when she tried to get away, when she fought him like she would a shark, he bludgeoned her with a candlestick. He left her to the floor, to her shock and broken bones, her blood patterning the hardwood like the pulp of an oyster dropped to the bluffs by an unforgiving gull—but far more quietly. The only noise the girl remembers at all was Michael calling her his Mulberry Maiden. He said that she would serve him until her berries ran dry.

"Afterward, he ate, got in bed, and went to sleep. When the girl tried to creep from the room in the middle of the night, he caught her, beat her, and raped her again."

"Jesus," Sarah whispers. Ethel doesn't seem to hear her. She isn't in the library, but in White Hall on a warm spring night, terrified and hopeless and, perhaps worst of all, wondering how she could have been so wrong about her fiancé.

"How did the girl get away?" Thalia asks.

"She didn't," Ethel said. "She had to stay with him until he brought her home. Michael made sure she never had a moment alone with Mr. or Mrs. Searles or their daughters. After that, well, where could the girl go? She had her job, yes, but not much money. Not enough to get herself off the island. And she couldn't go back home. Those bridges weren't just burned; they sat at the bottom of the ocean, current-worn and bacteria-eaten. So Michael continued to act like nothing had changed, only now marriage was off the table and satiating his lust was on it.

"As for her injuries, the island doctor came to treat her, but Michael told him she'd fallen down the library stairs. Why didn't she go to the police? Because Michael's family was as established in New Shoreham as the hawkweed that invades every field and roadside on the island. Michael's father was Michael Dempsey Sr., chief of police."

"Oh my God," Sarah says. Thalia can't even manage that.

"A report against Michael Dempsey Jr. would have gone nowhere. There was one person I did tell, however."

I. Thalia and Sarah exchange a glance. Interesting to hear at what point in her narrative Ethel switched from third person to first.

"Who?" Sarah asks softly.

"My only friend on the island." Ethel looks at Thalia. "Your mother. Maureen Mills."

Thalia's heartbeat quickens.

"When I'd been out of work for a week, Maureen came to check on me. I told her how I'd kept my relationship with Michael hidden and what he'd done to me. For some time—whole, endless minutes while I sat there shaking on my little floral couch—Maureen was speechless. When she finally did speak, it wasn't what I was expecting: 'I've got to do something.'

"I told her I didn't want her to get involved. She said she wanted to confront Michael, and I asked if she was crazy. She conceded, then reminded me she worked at Michael's brother's restaurant. Michael Sr. had recently made Martin's position as owner of Above the Rocks official, coinciding with his being sworn in as police chief. Maureen said Martin was a kind boss and a patient listener, and she couldn't imagine him not being appalled by his brother's actions. She left my house angry but determined. Three days passed, and I did not hear from her. On the fourth day, I handled the pain of my injuries long enough to show up at Maureen's apartment."

"Apartment?" Thalia couldn't help but interrupt. Her mother had always lived in the house Thalia grew up in, hadn't she?

"Before Maureen lived on Cooneymus, you two lived in a one-bedroom apartment on High Street."

"I must have forgotten," Thalia says. "Please, continue, Ethel."

"Maureen ignored the buzzer and only let me in when I started yelling. I asked her what had happened, but she only stared at me, wild-eyed, like she thought I was hiding a recording device. 'What did Martin say when you told him?' I begged her, and she sent an ashtray flying off an end table. It shattered against the wall. 'I didn't talk to Martin,' she shouted. 'I didn't talk to anyone. I'm sorry about what happened, but you have to let it go if you want to keep living on this island.' Just then, you started crying from the bedroom."

Thalia's brain stutters at this mention of her presence in the story.

"Maureen wouldn't say another word," Ethel says. "She held open the front door until I left."

All three women are quiet for several long seconds. When Ethel speaks, there's a tremor in her voice. "I was in a bad state after that. Out of work. In pain. Alone except for my abuser. Sometimes, I wonder where I'd be now. How long the nightmare would have gone on for. If it weren't for Michael's cockiness and Bob's sense of timing." She lifts her gaze. "Hurricane Bob, that is. The Great Hurricane of '91."

"I remember when Michael Dempsey was police chief," Sarah says, "and I remember hearing what happened to Michael Jr. during that hurricane too. He went out to try to save his father's yacht. Stations on the island recorded gusts of one-hundred-and-five miles per hour. He got swept out to sea."

"It was like God himself came down and whisked him away from me," Ethel says.

"To this day, there are some who insist he didn't die," Sarah adds, "but used the storm to escape to the mainland. That he'd gotten into some kind of trouble with gambling debts and bad business deals."

"He's dead," Ethel says. "If he wasn't, I would never have been free of him."

"Did Maureen talk to Martin?" Thalia asks. "Do you think she told him what Michael did?"

Ethel shakes her head. "I know she didn't. Maureen went back to work for Martin right after I went to see her. Twenty-seven years later, she still works for him, and by all accounts, they have a solid relationship." She pauses. "She was terrified that day in her apartment. I think she feared for her life." She looks at Thalia. "And for yours." Ethel closes her eyes. "Despite me telling her not to, I think she went to see Michael."

Thalia grips her chair. "You think my mother confronted your rapist . . ." She pauses, triple-checking her math. "In July of 1991?"

"Thalia," Sarah says from beside her. "Remember Timmy Graham's little confession? We don't know for sure that Michael Demp—"

Thalia holds up a hand, and Sarah goes quiet.

"You think," Thalia says again to Ethel, "that my mother confronted Michael Dempsey nine months before my half sister was born?"

Ethel still hasn't opened her eyes. "I was so scared," Ethel whispers. "I had no one. Maureen was from here. I thought she might be able to help. To talk to Martin. I never knew about the baby she put up for adoption. She hid the pregnancy from everyone. I don't even think Martin knew. That's why he came here asking questions."

"What kind of questions?" Thalia asks.

"If I knew who the Mulberry Maiden was, for one thing. I don't believe Maureen spoke with Martin back then, but that doesn't mean Michael didn't tell his brother himself."

"I'm so sorry for everything you went through," Thalia says. Sarah murmurs an agreement.

"I didn't tell you this to make you sorry. I told you so maybe you would understand." She leans forward, and her eyes burn with the fire of a cornered coyote again. "Stay away from Martin. By virtue of his being a Dempsey, you cannot trust him. I knew that my great-great-great-grandmother Helen had gone missing on the island—it was one of the reasons I came here, so that I might discover some clue of what had happened to her—but I only found out after I became head of New Shoreham's Historical Society that she disappeared in the presence of a Dempsey."

Thalia pushes her chair back, wanting to go somewhere where she can breathe and *think*, goddamn it, think, for five minutes away from the patter of the rain. "You came to the island looking to find something, and to escape your past. Blake came here for the same reasons. You turned to my mother when Michael ensnared you. Blake had no one. She should have had a mother. She should have had a sister. She should have had a friend."

Thalia stands. Sarah looks up, startled, but stands too. "Thank you for telling us this," Thalia says. "I know it must have been devastatingly hard. But staying away from Martin is not a promise I can make. I'm going to hound him—and everyone else on this island—until I get answers. I'm going to make him tell me everything he knows. And when Maureen wakes from her coma, I'm going to get answers from her too. Blake deserved answers." She holds Ethel's gaze for another moment, hoping the woman will feel both her gratitude and her determination. "You need answers, too, and you deserve them, even—or especially—after all these years."

Thalia walks toward the staircase. Sarah follows. Ethel doesn't try to stop them. Their boots squeak on the rubber mats covering the stairs.

"You tried talking to Maureen already," Sarah whispers as they climb. "If you do get another chance to ask her about Blake, do you really think she'll tell you anything?"

"No," Thalia says. "I don't." She strides across the fiction section. "But she's still in the hospital, isn't she?"

"Yeah, and?"

"And," Thalia says, stopping at the exit to stare hard at Sarah, "for the moment, there's no one in her house."

Chapter 30

"This is a terrible idea," Sarah hisses as they stand on the porch of Maureen's house. "What if the neighbor who found Maureen has tasked herself with keeping an eye on the place?"

"I'm not a little girl anymore, Sar," Thalia replies, and unlocks the front door. She'd been too upset after that first conversation with Maureen to remember to return the key to the rock in the front garden. "I'm not afraid of my mother."

"You might not be afraid of her," Sarah mutters. "But I sure don't want to be on Maureen Mills's bad side when she regains consciousness. And for *breaking into her house*, no less."

Thalia spins to face Sarah. "I remember those rumors too. That Michael Dempsey wasn't really dead, just running from a boatload of problems. If Michael is Blake's father and he's still alive and somehow found out who she was and that she was on the island, what do you think he would have done?"

Understanding clouds Sarah's features. "Holy crap," she whispers.

"Exactly," Thalia says. "If you hurry up, we could be finished before any potential nosy neighbors know we're here. I already let you talk me into parking the taxi on a different street." Thalia shuts the door behind them and hurries down the hall.

"What are we looking for, anyway?" Sarah asks, taking in the messy kitchen. "A journal with an entry from halfway through July 1991 that states: 'Today was a good day. I woke up. Made breakfast. Had sex with

John H. Doe—or Timmy Graham, or, God forbid, was attacked by Michael Dempsey—and conceived his child'?"

"Of course not," Thalia says. "Though, that would be convenient." She walks into the living room. "You start here. I'll take the bedroom."

Sarah sighs, steps onto the garishly patterned carpet, and looks around at open cabinets full of trinkets, the teeming desk drawers and overstuffed magazine racks. "You've seen the glass partition in my taxi," she says irritably. "I don't like touching other people's stuff."

"You'll be fine," Thalia says, then sees the rows of novels parading across the bookshelves. Suddenly, she smells her mother's perfume—a hint of citrus, a wealth of flowers—feels the scratchiness of the cheap down comforter in sharp contrast to the surprisingly honeyed tone of Maureen's voice as she reads from *Northanger Abbey*, those nights when Thalia felt like she had a real mother.

No. She needs to focus. Thalia reaches for Sarah's hand and squeezes it. "I—"

"I know, I know, 'thank you so much, I wouldn't be able to do this without you, Sarah,'" Sarah says, smiling. "Get going. If your mother's bedroom is anything like it was when we were kids, I'm going to have to join you in there to make anything like a dent."

Thalia cuts back through the kitchen and down the opposite hall from the one to the foyer. At her mother's bedroom door, she stops, scanning the room with fresh eyes now that Maureen's robed form is absent from the bed.

What *is* she looking for, anyway? Her mother was never one to keep a journal. And despite Maureen's rigidity and restrictions, she and Sarah had been typical kids, snooping through Maureen's things on occasion. But at twelve, Thalia didn't know she had a secret sister. Maybe there was something hinting at Blake's conception that had been right under Thalia's nose the whole time.

The smells inside the room are less than ideal. Cigarette ash and stale drinks, a trace of acrid vomit. Thalia goes to the bed and kneels beside it. There's nothing beneath it but three or four pairs of waitressing shoes, their soles thick and dirty, the black leather scuffed. She goes to the dresser and starts opening drawers. Underwear. Bras. Socks. Sleep shirts. Sweatpants. More socks. Sarah's right. This is stupid. There's nothing to find here. Thalia resigned herself long ago to the fact of Maureen's enigmatic personality; why does she think she'll find some clue to her mother's identity, her decisions, now?

A cabinet shuts in the living room. Sarah, likely nearing the end of her search. Thalia starts for the door, then thinks, *I'm here, might as well check the closet.*

The door slides open on creaky tracks. Thalia takes a step back. The closet is far fuller than she remembers it being as a fifteen-year-old, hoping to borrow her mother's beat-up jean jacket or one of her scarves. Maureen added a closet organizer system at some point over the last ten years; belts hang like snakes, waitressing aprons form precarious mountains on particle board shelves, and bins of T-shirts and leggings spill their contents as if, somewhere farther back, a dam has been breached.

Thalia sweeps great hangerfuls of clothing to one side and feels along the back wall. She stretches up to the top shelf and searches for something other than old purses and bunched-up sweaters. Her fingers close on something sharp-edged, but further inspection reveals a shoebox. She drops to her knees and gropes through throngs of shoes, sputtering as Maureen's long sweaters brush up against her face and shoulders like leafy hanging vines.

She crawls back farther, trying not to gag on the smell of old cigarette smoke. She feels like a firefighter riffling through singed debris. Again, what does she expect? She can't even pinpoint a hypothetical jackpot: A photo album? Another copy of Blake's birth certificate? A . . . *Jesus Christ, is that a safe?*

The safe is smooth, cool metal, compact and solidly constructed, with reinforced steel walls of indeterminate thickness. It slides forward easily on the carpet, out from under the wool and cotton and rayon. Thalia examines it from every side. The shallow recesses around the door and the digital keypad are the compact safe's only features. She curls her fingers under the bottom and lifts. The safe weighs about as much as she suspects it would when empty. Could there be photos or birth and adoption documents inside?

I can carry this out of here, no problem. Figure out how to get into it before Maureen wakes up, returns home, and finds it gone. I can— Her rapid-fire thoughts are interrupted by footsteps coming down the hall.

Sarah bursts into the room. "Thalia!" The word is a high-pitched whisper, pressurized. "Someone just opened the front door. They're in the house!"

"What? Who?"

"I don't know!" Sarah narrows her eyes at Thalia half-buried in Maureen's closet. "What are you doing? Is that a safe?"

Thalia looks down, seeing not the safe but her childhood home as if from above, the rooms and entrances drawn out like a map. If someone has entered through the front door, there's no way she and Sarah can get out without being seen. Sarah had insisted they park the taxi on Peckham Farm Road, so if they move quickly—and hide smartly—this new intruder might remain oblivious as to the presence of the first two interlopers prowling around Maureen Mills's house.

Moving quickly won't be an issue; adrenaline has already turned Thalia's muscles to springs. It's hiding smartly, or at all, that's the problem. "Shit," Thalia whispers, and pushes the safe back into the closet. She grabs Sarah's hand and pulls her farther into the bedroom. "Get down," she commands, and pushes her friend to the floor. Together, they slither under the bed, folding limbs and bodies around shoes and pushing dust bunnies away from their faces. To sneeze now would be akin to setting off a fire alarm.

Footsteps sound in the hallway before Thalia has straightened her body into any sort of tolerable position. She breathes out slowly, willing herself not to make a sound. She can't turn her head, but she leans left enough to see into Sarah's eyes. They're watery and frozen and wide with panic. Sarah brings a hand up to cover her mouth. She must know—as

Thalia does—through some mechanism of survival or intuition, that it's no elderly neighbor about to enter the bedroom.

Someone steps onto the faded carpet. Thalia has enough of a vantage point from beneath the bed to see the buttery brown men's Oxfords, darkened by rain, sink into the beige loop pile, and the cuffs of chinos, also water-stained. Sarah tenses beside her, a slight but obvious tightening of her shoulders. The man takes two steps forward and stops. Thalia guesses he's taking stock of the bedroom. He seems neither winded nor nervous, for she doesn't hear him take a breath. Could it be a case worker from the hospital doing some sort of home visit? Perhaps Maureen has regained consciousness and they need to determine whether she has a safe place to which she can be discharged.

Thalia knows this is far-fetched even before the man goes to the dresser and starts opening drawers. A second later, balled-up socks, camisoles, and underwear fall to the floor like rain. More drawers open. In a matter of minutes, every one of Maureen's drawers has been ransacked. *He's doing what we were doing. He's looking for something. And he may very well check under the bed next.*

Sarah must have come to the same conclusion. Her chin juts and lines form at the center of her forehead, her eyes welling with the strain of trying to communicate silently. Thalia knows what she's saying. *We're screwed.* Thalia's brain goes into trial mode, ticking off their options: *Can one of these shoes be used as a weapon? Can the two of us take him together? If we jump out from under the bed before he finds us, will he be surprised into inaction, giving us the chance to run?*

Thalia presses her fingers into the carpet, preparing to push herself out from beneath the bed. Just as the bed skirt touches the backs of her heels, Sarah reaches out and grabs her arm. Her grip is so hard, Thalia has to bite her tongue to keep from crying out. With her other hand, Sarah curls three fingers; Thalia follows the direction of her point. The man has abandoned the dressers, but rather than kneel before the bed, he is on his tiptoes, running his hands along the top shelf of the closet.

Hangers slide along the closet rod, then grate, one by one, as if the man is picking out something to wear. *What is he looking for?* The hangers slide in unison again, to the opposite side. Thalia strains forward, cranes her neck, and sees the moment he drops to his knees. He is mere inches from the safe Thalia was lucky enough to have found, and stupid enough to have left where it is. She knows he's going to find it—knows, now, that he came here looking for it—before she hears the slap of his palms against steel. She also knows he will leave with it, and quickly, and that if she doesn't see who he is, all the progress they made today will have been for naught.

Thalia touches Sarah's shoulder. Sarah widens her eyes: *What?*

Move over, Thalia mouths. *That way.* She jerks her head to the right.

Are you crazy? Sarah mouths back.

Do it, Thalia mouths, and Sarah's eyes, somehow, widen further, though this time in exasperation rather than fear. Sarah inches to the right. *More,* Thalia mouths, and Sarah inches over a little more. Thalia nods once, and starts spinning the orientation of her body, slowly and using just the balls of her feet. When she's turned as far as she can without her shoes poking out from the side of the bed, she inches up so that the bed skirt brushes her cheek. It's as soft as butterfly wings, but Thalia knows she's being incredibly reckless. Again, the last thing she needs to do is sneeze.

The man gets one foot under him. He is holding his prize; Thalia feels it. In another half a second, he'll be all the way on his feet. With every nerve in her neck pinching, Thalia lifts the bed skirt with her cheek. The man's chest dips slightly as he climbs to a stand. She can see his smart navy sweater, the hint of a white T-shirt beneath it. She lifts her head higher, face poking completely out of the bed skirt. If he looks over even slightly, he'll see her. If he perceives movement in his periphery, they are caught.

He doesn't look down, or over. He doesn't see her. But she sees him. She tries to pull her head back under the bed skirt, but she doesn't have any traction. To push herself back, she'd need to stick one arm out in front of her, and there's no way he wouldn't see that. Just as she's about to panic, to yelp and claw her way out to face him before he can catch her vulnerable on the ground, Sarah grabs her by the ponytail and yanks her backward. The bed skirt drops over her face like a curtain, like she's just performed in the world's most stressful Shakespearean play.

The intruder walks out of the bedroom. On his way out, he turns off the light. They listen to his footsteps. Down the hall. Through the kitchen. Into the foyer. A moment later, the front door slams. Still, Thalia holds her breath.

A minute passes. She hears nothing, not an engine start, not the whoosh of a car taking off from Maureen Mills's driveway toward some unknown destination. Maybe, like them, the intruder parked away from the house. They wait three more minutes without speaking. Then, Thalia first, they creep out from under the bed.

"Let's go," Sarah whispers. "Out the back. We'll cut past the pond to get to the car."

"He took the safe." Thalia doesn't bother to whisper. The man's gone. "The safe I found in Maureen's closet. I shoved it back inside right before we hid. And he took it."

"Did you see who it was?" Sarah asks. "You better have, with that crazy stunt you pulled, sticking your head out from under the bed skirt."

"I saw him," Thalia says. "And Sarah? I think Ethel was right."

"She was?" Sarah still looks too worked up from their near-disaster to fully grasp what Thalia is saying.

"Yes. We cannot, under any circumstances, trust Martin Dempsey." She looks back at the closet, from where the potential for additional answers was snatched away. "It was him. Martin broke into Maureen's house and stole her safe."

Chapter 31

They drive to White Hall in silence. There are innumerable questions, but neither woman has any of the answers. As Sarah pulls into the circular drive, her phone rings.

Thalia zones out while Sarah talks to Patrick. She half expects the taxi's overhead light to flicker and the voice of Rod Serling to pronounce her having entered the fifth dimension. Out of all the questions circulating in her head, two pop up most often: Why would the man who'd employed her mother for twenty-plus years steal a safe from her closet? And was it Thalia's imagination, or did he seem like he expected to find it there?

"Okay," Sarah is saying. "No, I promise everything's all right, things have just been"—she looks at Thalia and her eyebrows crinkle—"weird. I'll be there soon. Tell the girls I'll tuck them in." She hangs up and tosses the phone in the cupholder. Thalia continues to stare out the windshield.

"Should we call the police?" Sarah asks. "And tell them Martin stole Maureen's safe?"

"Right," Thalia says, hating how dismissive she sounds. It's not like she hasn't had this exact thought. "And when they ask how we know this, we tell them it's because we saw him while hiding under my mother's bed. And then when they ask *why* we were hiding under her bed, we tell them the sister I didn't know I had is dead, my mother is desperate to keep me from finding out why she had her, I'm trying to get info from the local B and B, but the resident ghost is making things difficult, and their most respected citizen—and town selectman—broke into my mother's house, all after the island librarian told us to stay away from him and the island drunk insisted he was screwing the heretofore unknown, now dead, sister?"

"I see your point," Sarah says. "Well, what are our options?"

"*Your* only option is to go home. You need to see your girls. I'm going to hang around here, I guess." Thalia sighs and shakes her head. "I can't figure why Martin would break into her house and steal that safe. If Michael really was Blake's father, Martin could be trying to keep what Michael did to my mother from getting out. But if Michael's been dead for almost three decades, what would it matter?"

"Unless he's not dead," Sarah reiterates.

"Now we're really in the Twilight Zone, unable to operate under the assumption that someone with a death certificate and a headstone is off the suspect list."

"That means the Mansion Ghost shouldn't get a pass either."

"Focus, Sarah!"

"Sorry, you're right. Yes, it's weird Martin took the safe now, after you showed up on the island."

"It has to have something to do with Blake, right? The safe can't be new; what would she be hiding in it, pharmacy receipts? It's just . . ." Thalia trails off and shakes her head again. "The whole thing is making me crazy."

Sarah puts a hand on her arm. "Remember, Thal, yes, we're trying to figure out the—extremely messy, utterly bizarre, and possibly conflicting—circumstances surrounding Blake's death, but regardless of how those circumstances clear up, Fiona Searles was charged with Blake's murder based on the physical evidence."

"Fingerprints on a knife that she used on a daily basis?"

Sarah sighs. "All right, it's not much. But can you cool it with the detective stuff for tonight? Avoid grilling Aileen over dinner or skulking about the mansion, looking for whatever secret passageways the White Hall ghost uses to get around?"

"Rule number two, don't go into any dungeons," Thalia says and purses her lips.

"I mean it. Who warned you someone was in Maureen's house? How well do you think you would have fared if you'd gone inside alone?"

"I'll tell you one thing, there would have been a lot more room under that damn bed."

Sarah socks her in the arm, and Thalia doubles over in exaggerated pain. She realizes she's starving but says nothing. If Sarah thinks she's going to partake in one of Aileen's White Hall dinners, she'll know Thalia won't be keeping her promise to forgo mystery-solving for the evening. She thanks her friend and starts to open the taxi door, but Sarah grabs her arm before she can climb all the way out.

"Text updates, like last night. After today, I'm more adamant about that than ever, even if I don't want you searching for clues without me."

"Of course."

"And Thalia? Order a pizza. BI Pizza Pie Company will deliver to White Hall. I know you. If you take Aileen up on dinner, you're going to get into what happened today, start asking questions about Martin, about Ethel and the Mulberry Maiden. Leave it alone for tonight. Relax. Take a ba—"

Sarah shuts her mouth so hard that Thalia hears her teeth clack.

"Ugh, sorry," Sarah says. "That was a terrible thing to say. Do *not* take a bath. Don't even *think* about taking a bath, clawfoot tub or not. But, oh, I don't know, put your headphones on and listen to a podcast, or whatever you Bostonians do to unwind while still being hip and well informed."

Thalia laughs. "Get out of here before you miss bedtime with the girls and break your promise to Patrick."

Sarah gives her a little salute. Thalia shuts the car door and walks toward the mansion. She will not take a bath, that much is certain. But ordering a pizza doesn't sound like the worst idea. She pushes open the door and walks into the foyer. She's a third of the way up the stairs and nearing the portrait of Mary Hopkins Searles when a voice comes from the foyer below her.

"Thalia Mills," Martin says. "Long time no see. I'm glad I caught you."

Thalia pauses, one foot raised above the next stair. "Oh?" she says, trying to sound curious as opposed to completely caught off guard. Is the *Long time no see* in earnest, as in, *I haven't seen you in a decade?* Or is he telling her he knows she was just at Maureen's house? She won't meet his caginess with anything other than confidence, won't concede to his commanding the upper hand. She waits for his response.

Martin smiles. It reminds Thalia of a shark.

"I think you and I need to talk," he says.

Chapter 32

The grand table in the dining room is set for two. A bottle of mulberry wine glints from the center under the light of the chandelier. Aileen is bustling in and out, depositing large silver spoons, Parmesan cheese, and crushed red pepper. A massive bowl of seafood cioppino already steams on the table.

"All right, then," Aileen says. "That's everything." She turns for the door.

"You won't be joining us?" Thalia asks.

Aileen's response is directed at Martin. "Oh, no, I ate, thank you. You two enjoy. I'll be in the kitchen if you need anything."

Then the proprietress is gone, and Thalia is left staring at Martin. She goes to a chair, sits, and spoons pasta onto her plate. She's thankful she's as hungry as she is, otherwise it would be hard to eat, sitting across from this man whom, even without Ethel's warning, she's now realizing she trusts as much as an opposing client's counsel.

Martin waits for Thalia to set the spoon down, then takes a small scoop himself. "When you've owned a restaurant as long as I have," he says, seeing Thalia notice the minuscule portion, "it becomes hard to muster much excitement for food."

Thalia shrugs. Martin opens the wine and pours them each a glass. "So," Thalia says, pausing to take a sip. "What did you want to speak with me about?"

"I'm worried about your mother," he says, and his voice is thick with concern. So much concern, in fact, that Thalia can't help but believe he's merely displaying what he thinks an employer should show for his longtime employee. "I heard what happened, of course. Have there been any updates on her condition?"

"No," Thalia says, and takes another small sip from her glass. It's too pungent for her liking. "And while I appreciate your concern, I have to say, I didn't realize you two were so close."

"There's a lot you don't realize," Martin says, and takes a swig from his own glass, "being away from the island, from your mother, for so long."

"It didn't take being away from the island to not be close to Maureen," Thalia shoots back. "She wasn't the warmest or most open of mothers."

Martin chuckles. He hasn't touched his pasta. "You were right, though."

"Sorry?"

"You were right. Maureen and I aren't close. Not in the normal sense of the word. She keeps people at arm's length, though perhaps even that's being generous. With me, she only relays certain things. And another thing about your mother, she doesn't always behave in a manner that makes sense."

"What do you mean?" she asks. A little alarm goes off in her brain. *Careful. He's taking control. Don't let him lead you where you don't want to go.*

"Do you talk to your mother often? Do you really know what's going on with her? How she's been doing since you left?"

"We talk once a month," Thalia says. "She tells me enough."

"Interesting word. So she's told you of her mental health struggles? That she's been diagnosed with borderline personality disorder?"

"Diagnosed by who?" *What is happening?* Thalia hates to be caught off guard, and that's exactly what he's done here. Also, damn Maureen if this is true and she hasn't told her.

"By a psychiatrist I helped her procure."

"That seems far beyond the responsibilities of a normal employer."

"Who else does she have?" Martin asks. When Thalia bristles, he continues, "It's fallen to me many times over the years to ensure she didn't become a danger to herself. This last suicide attempt has not been her only one."

"I don't think we can call it a suicide attempt while Maureen herself is still unconscious. If that is, indeed, what it was, she should be the one to say so."

Martin shrugs. "If you insist. But she's admitted as much on the previous attempts."

You're falling into trap after trap. "I—"

Martin doesn't let her finish. "Was your mother pleased you traveled to the island?"

"No."

"She was upset?"

"Yes," Thalia admits.

"That seems irrational to me. She talked about you favorably enough while you were away. Though, that's what I'm trying to tell you. Rationality's never been Maureen's strong suit. This was only the latest in a long line of questionable behaviors."

Thalia narrows her eyes, angered by his description of her mother and brought to suspicion by the memory of the librarian's story. Had Michael attacked Maureen when she confronted him about Ethel, and Martin knew? Was Martin trying to protect his dead brother's reputation by making Maureen out to be mentally unstable? "Did you tell any of this to Blake when she asked you for help?" Thalia asks.

"Your sister didn't ask me for help," Martin responds. "Aileen told me what Blake had come here to do and thought it would be wise if I assisted her. Aileen's heard enough of the fallout of Maureen's diagnosis over the years from Fiona. At least, she did, before Fiona herself went mad. I tried to warn Blake without making it seem like I was against her mission. Maureen was her mother. It was her right to meet her. I didn't want to stand in her way. I just wanted her to know that Maureen was unlikely to react favorably to her showing up here. And, well, I was right."

She's formulating a cutting response when something occurs to her. What if Timmy Graham really had spent the night with Maureen at some house party and—in a completely separate turn of events—Maureen had been frightened into keeping quiet about Michael? What if Martin is telling the truth? He's seen Maureen almost every day for the last ten years, and Thalia has not seen her at all. She *does* only speak to her mother the third Tuesday of every month, at Thalia's request. It's easier that way, having a schedule. Knowing they can talk about the same shallow topics for fifteen minutes before Thalia feels justified in hanging up: Thalia's kitchen renovations, Maureen's garden, the pitch games she plays with her neighbor.

Maureen occasionally mentioned her work schedule when she'd picked up more or less than the usual number of shifts. If Maureen had been diagnosed with a personality disorder, of course she wouldn't tell her daughter. They've never had a relationship based on honesty. What if Martin's been taking care of her all these years, giving her a place to work, helping her with her medication? What if Martin took the safe out of Maureen's closet as a way to protect her?

Martin sighs, interrupting Thalia's thoughts. Some of the pasta is gone from his plate. He sets down his fork, dabs his mouth with a napkin, and lays the cloth back over his lap. "All I'm saying is that Maureen has not been well for a long time. She's good at her job; if anything, her occasional lack of boundaries leads to stronger connections with the patrons, and I'm glad I've been able to help all these years by keeping her employed. As far as reliability . . ." He smiles the shark grin she's coming to know well, though this version is tinged with sadness. Thalia finds herself wondering yet again if she's misjudged him. "Maureen Mills is the quintessential madwoman in the attic, and I occasionally have to help her down."

Thalia balances her own fork on the edge of her plate. Though she's eaten far less than she anticipated, she's no longer hungry. "I didn't know any of this. I apologize. And I appreciate everything you've done for my mother. I'm curious, however, how a psychiatrist in good standing could prescribe her enough Valium each month to tranquilize a small elephant."

"You know as well as I do that your mother has taken benzodiazepines since you were little."

Thalia nods. There's no denying this. She holds her glass of wine so tightly she's afraid the stem will crack. She gulps the too-sweet contents, feeling it coat her throat and curdle in her stomach, a sickening whirlpool of mulberries, lobster claws, and clam bellies.

"With all due respect, *why* are you telling me this?" Thalia asks. She feels like she does when she's lost a case, and has to remind herself again that Martin might, in fact, be helping.

"Because I think it's time to increase your mother's level of care. I think an admission to an inpatient facility is long overdue. When she comes out of this coma, I've arranged for her to be seen at Butler Hospital in Providence. Maureen's taken advantage of Above the Rock's subsidized health insurance since I first offered it, but there might be unforeseen costs. I don't want to act without Maureen's family on board."

This is so far from the conversation she expected to be having, Thalia struggles to formulate a response. "I still think Maureen's overdose was accidental," she says stubbornly. "Things have been stressful on the island. You know that as well as anyone. But Maureen's substance abuse alone has warranted inpatient treatment for years, so I'm not against it. Still, I feel like this is a conversation I should have with my mother. When she wakes, I'll discuss treatment options with her, and if Butler is the best fit, I'll pay for whatever her insurance doesn't cover. That's all I feel comfortable committing to right now in terms of a plan."

Martin sees that she's starting to stand and pushes his chair back too. As if she'd sensed the culmination of their meal, Aileen appears in the doorway. "Thank you for dinner," Thalia says. "And Martin, again, thank you for what you've done for my mother. But if you'll excuse me, I've had a long day and would like to go to my room."

"Of course," Martin says. "Oh, and Thalia, a warning. I'm not sure how long you plan on staying, but there's a storm expected, which will likely culminate in a weather advisory tomorrow evening. If you were planning to head back to the city to await news of your mother's condition, tomorrow *morning* is the time to do it."

Thalia looks back and forth from Aileen to Martin. "It's strange," she says. "This rain, so similar to when Blake was here. I spoke to my mother a few days before I saw the news about a murder on the island, and she mentioned the rain had been biblical. I know winters on the island can be wet. But Blake must have felt like even the weather was conspiring against her."

"She did!" Aileen bursts out. Thalia and Martin look at her, startled. "She told me she did. That was the first time she mentioned she felt like she was trapped in a gothic novel."

"Blake told you she felt that way?" Thalia asks.

"Yes." Aileen turns to Martin. "Remember, when I first called to tell you what she was here for? To see if you could help her with Maureen? I said, 'The poor girl has built this trip up so much, even the weather has her seeing ghosts.' Although, after Fiona"—she stops, comes at the thought from a different angle—"after I realized the bottle of wine from Blake's room was gone, I thought her talk of specters and scary books was because she'd relapsed and—"

"I remember," Martin says sharply. "But you heard Thalia. She'd like to be getting to her room."

"Of course," Aileen says. "I just thought—"

"Aileen," Martin says sharply. "Thalia's just heard all about how ill her mother is. I'm sure she doesn't want to be told things that will make her suspect her sister possessed a similar constitution."

Aileen lowers her eyes. "You're right. Forgive me, Ms. Mills."

"It's fine," Thalia says, though she remembers how, upon first arriving, Aileen feigned ignorance at Thalia's comparison of White Hall to a Gothic castle. She wants to hear more about what Blake told this cloistered B and B proprietress—and what may have been passed from Aileen to Blake's murderer's lover—but she knows the time to do so is *after* Martin departs. "Besides, Blake told me a little about how she was feeling in her letter."

"Letter?" Martin asks. Thalia feels that, for the first time this evening, she's caught *him* off guard.

"Yes. Blake wrote me a letter the night she died. I assumed she put it into some sort of outgoing mailbox, because it was sent out the next morning rather than entered into evidence."

Martin is looking at Aileen as if he, too, is wondering how a letter was sent from White Hall without their knowledge. Either he's not the one who provided Blake with Thalia's address or—for whatever reason—he didn't anticipate there being enough time for any letter Blake penned to be sent.

"Have you thought about giving it to the police?" he asks.

"I was going to," Thalia says, "when everyone thought Blake had killed herself. I thought she'd intended it to be her suicide note. But once Fiona was charged, I knew there was no point."

Aileen and Martin both start talking at once, but Thalia continues, "There's nothing in it, really. Nothing that's of any interest to anyone but me, her long-lost sister." She smiles. Let Martin stew on this until she figures out the reason he took her mother's safe.

"Good night," Thalia says and makes her way toward the dining room exit. It's so quiet in the high-ceilinged room that Thalia swears she can hear the ocean out beyond the courtyard—constant, remote, and restless—smashing with ungovernable power against the bluffs.

Chapter 33

It's close to midnight, but Thalia can't calm down. She's being driven mad by her conversation with Martin at dinner, by her lack of understanding of some core facet of this whole situation. She paces the room. She sneaks across the hall to what was Blake's room and looks out to where the White Hall replica glows in the milky moonlight. She returns to her room, pours another glass of wine, then dumps it down the sink. She washes her face and changes into comfortable clothes, but still, she can't unburden her mind.

Thalia flops onto the bed and pulls her purse up from where it leans against the nightstand. It takes a bit of digging before she's able to unearth Blake's letter. She slips it out of the litigation manual—leaving the birth certificate safely in place—and unfolds it, careful not to tear the cream-colored paper. Martin and Aileen were uneasy over the letter's existence, and she wants to know why. She runs her thumb over the chaotic, angular letters, and begins to read:

> *Dear Thalia,*
> *They say that truth is stranger than fiction, and while I'd never been inclined to believe this before, I'm afraid that, now, I'd have to agree. I'm writing to you from Block Island, a place I understand you no longer visit, and I'm not finding it hard to see why. This place is a dark and dismal one. It's full of secretive coves and more*

secretive people. The locals, the wildlife, the architecture, the weather . . . I've met junkies and jailbirds and prostitutes and dealers who are less enigmatic than the things that inhabit this island.

But I'm getting ahead of myself. My name is Blake Bronson and I am . . . (deep breath) . . . your sister. I managed to get ahold of an actual copy of my sealed birth certificate (don't ask) and I (foolishly, I can add in hindsight) booked my trip to Block Island soon after.

I tried to introduce myself to Maureen. To say it didn't go well would be an understatement. She is desperate to preserve the illusion that there is no connection between me and your family. You're her rose, I imagine, and I'm the thistle she plucked out like a weed. Normally, I'd take that disappointment, stuff it down with all the others, and go back to what I've done for years, which is drink and drug to obliterate every last scrap of anything resembling an emotion. If Maureen's medicine cabinet is any indication, she copes in the very same way.

But I didn't go back to drinking and drugging. Something about this island changed me. In addition to feeling like I had to come here to meet Maureen, to catch even the briefest glimpse of anything that could connect me to a person or a place other than the countless foster homes or families I endured from infancy to eighteen, I realized upon stepping off the ferry and into the shadow of White Hall, that there's been something calling me here for a long, long time.

When I was in those foster homes, I took solace in the work of Ann Radcliffe, Charlotte and Emily Brontë, Mary Shelley, Anne Rice, Shirley Jackson, and Toni Morrison. I saw myself as Jane Eyre, Eleanor Vance, or, at my darkest, Frankenstein's monster. I felt like my life *only moved forward on the arcs of these novels, that it only had meaning when I was lost in their pages, away from the realities of being abandoned and alone. When I got older, and ran away from most of my foster parents, I sought that escapism in alcohol and opiates instead of stories of terror and the sublime. But when I walked through the door of Edward Searles's Dream House, my dream of connecting with my biological mother became a nightmare.*

White Hall is Otranto. Manderley. It is claustrophobia and tragedy and decay. Something—whether Mary Searles's ghost (I'm not sure I'll ever get Aileen's description of her out of my head), Maureen's stubbornness and anger, or White Hall itself, its trajectory in a never-ending time loop of destruction and despair—forced me into a story I was incapable of changing. I'm a fly who's placed one thin leg onto a strand of spiderweb, and the house, the weaver, felt the vibrations, heard my thoughts. Even my own past, my history of addiction, and a terrible accident I caused before finding out about Maureen pushed me forward, impervious to deliberate decisions or attempts to change my fate.

The wheel is careening toward its inevitable climax, and yet I remain here. I refuse to surrender the thirty days of sobriety I patched together, holding on to this medallion as if it's a life raft. I bow to a God not of my understanding, but of my imagination, as insufficient a replacement as the playhouse-size replica of a grand mansion. I refuse to crack the seal on the "gift" given to me by the endlessly helpful proprietress of this B and B (though I stupidly did not surrender it upon settling here). I refuse to let the footsteps of Mary's ghost— or the mansion's enigmatic groundskeeper—haunt me right over the edge of the clay cliffs (and I assure you the ghost is real . . . I followed her into the bathroom, to no avail, empty and uncompromised as it was, and the night after Martin took me around the island to learn about my mother, that maroon-clad, berry-stained ghoul attacked me).

Likely, you'll see this letter as the ramblings of a mad-woman, the confession of an addict, the climax of one of the more melodramatic of gothic novels. But on the chance that your reaction to my existence is different from that of Maureen's, I'm writing to you. I'm appealing to you. I'm slipping you a candle as we pass one another in an abbey basement; I'm on my way to confession; you're on your way back outside, aboveground, into the light.

My court date for the accident is next week. Maybe we can get together following it. I don't know what you do for work, or if you know the courthouse in the South Boston Division, but I'll be there February 8, at nine a.m., as long as the judge doesn't go against the plaintiff's desire not to press charges and throw me in jail. There are too many specters with their hands on my hems. I don't expect to make it there, let alone to see you. And if I don't make it, it very well might be because I didn't follow the "rules." But in the spirit of the heroine who refuses to give up, I'm putting this letter into the post.

And letting the ghosts of White Hall take it wherever they want it to go.

Sincerely,

—Your sister, Blake Bronson

Thalia places the letter beside her on the mattress and stares at the ceiling. There are *more* mysteries now than when she arrived on the island, hoping to coax her mother into relaying the details of

Blake's conception and erasure, and to determine whether Fiona had been correct in her assumption of Blake's affair with Martin Dempsey. Though, at least now, after finding the list tucked inside Blake's copy of *The Mysteries of Udolpho*, Thalia's confusion over why the word "rules" had been in quotations is sated. But the entry in the guest book, the stolen safe, Martin's unexpected presence at White Hall and insight into her mother's mental health issues, the feeling of being watched her first night at the mansion mirroring Blake's experience of seeing Mary Searles's ghost; these details swirl around Thalia's brain like puzzle pieces.

Thalia groans and rolls onto her side. If she was working on an actual puzzle, this would be the part where she threw it across the room. She reaches for her phone and sees it's a few minutes before midnight. Too late to text Sarah now.

She lays her head back on the pillow, but it's useless. Sleep is hours away. She sneaks across the hall, returns to the window, and studies the jagged peaks of the White Hall replica in the distance. *I bow to a God not of my understanding, but of my imagination, as insufficient a replacement as the playhouse-size replica of a grand mansion.* Did those words mean Blake had been out to the replica?

Thalia contemplates as much of the route from mansion to model as she can before the path winds out of sight. It had rained as much, if not more, during Blake's time on Block Island, as it had the last two days. It would have been an incredibly muddy walk. Muddy, but not impossible.

"Screw it," Thalia whispers. She runs back to her room and grabs her jacket. She isn't being rational, but neither was Blake. Wishing she had an actual flashlight with an easier-to-wield handle, she stuffs her phone in her pocket. She eases open the door and heads for the stairs.

Past Mary Searles's portrait, through the foyer, and out the front door, Thalia creeps on quiet feet. The rain is irritating, but light, and she should be able to reach the replica without getting soaked. Across the circular drive and around the side of the mansion, Thalia navigates the muddy ground beneath both deciduous and evergreen shrubs, wishing the Searleses' groundskeeper had thought to lay a little mulch. She clears the west side to find that the mansion sits on a platform of elaborate stonework.

Thalia crosses the courtyard—mercifully outfitted with several floodlights—to a set of steps carved in the space between two covered arches stretching to the ground. The grooves are shallow, but she makes her way down, passes six additional arches along the bottom portion of the courtyard, cuts right, and passes eight more.

Thalia could run straight ahead, to the cliff, or veer right, to where the boardwalk begins. The descent to the beach appears to be more gradual than the drop to the bluffs. *Searles' Folly*, Sarah had said. That's what some of the islanders call this monstrosity above the cliffs. At the sight of the boardwalk, its slick wood made hardly more passable by a coating of sand, Thalia can see why. She can also see how Blake found a castle on the edge of an island—surrounded by a mulberry forest, rocky cliffs, and a treacherous ocean—to be infused with doom and gloom.

The boardwalk levels and eventually splits. Though she came out here to explore the replica, Thalia turns instead for the cliff. It comes up fast, the edge of it, the blind, vertigo-inducing drop. The waves crash with deafening intensity below. Thalia tests the fence, but it's sturdier than it looks, and she steadies herself against it.

Had Blake really come out here before she died? Did she scream into the wind after the trauma of meeting their mother? Her letter had seemed so final when Thalia thought Blake had committed suicide, but now each one of her sister's words seem shot through with fear and energy and possibility. Without thinking, Thalia grips the top slat and climbs over. A film of mold leaves her fingers feeling slick. From this height, with the rain coming from every direction and her regret over what happened to Blake swirling just as chaotically, the crest and fall of the waves is hypnotizing. Or anesthetizing.

Was Blake tempted to let those waves reach up and snatch her, to carry her out to sea? Did she really come out here with a bottle and a plan to relapse? What did she see when she looked over the edge? Water so much more unforgiving than that which she'd die in, mere hours later.

Thalia inches forward over the cliff . . .

. . . and sees a bottle of mulberry wine stuck in a wedge of mud just over the edge.

Chapter 34

"What the hell?" Thalia's words are lost beneath the churning tide. She tries to lean over farther, but while the fence isn't actively shifting beneath her weight, she doesn't trust the depth or constitution of its posts.

This is a winery. Some tourist bought a bottle and proceeded to drop it over the cliff after partaking too enthusiastically in an afternoon tasting. This is the obvious explanation. But tourist season was seven months ago. The wine wouldn't still be here, clinging to an ever-eroding slope. *A little less than three weeks* later, however, the bottle Blake received upon checking in could have feasibly avoided plunging into the ocean after it'd been thrown there. And the label still looks to be intact. If she can get it, can somehow determine it was Blake's, it would mean Blake hadn't relapsed before she died.

Before she can talk herself out of it, Thalia lets go of the fence, shrugs out of her jacket, and loops it over the rail. She turns and drops to her stomach on the cliff. Holding on to the jacket's sleeves, she inches her feet toward the bottle, steeling herself for the moment in which she'll take the neck between her feet before clawing and heel-toeing back up to the fence. It's not her best idea, but it's the only option she's got. She feels the bottle's neck against the sole of her shoe, but she's about four inches too high. Relaxing her shoulders, tightening her grip, Thalia drops a little lower, wincing as her blouse slides along the mud and moisture seeps into the knees of her jeans.

Her foot hits the glass again, and she feels the dip where the neck extends into the wider portion of the bottle. She lifts her right foot around to the other side of the neck, squeezes the bottle between her feet, and pulls herself up using the arms of her jacket. Her hands are wet, and the jacket's material is slick. If she manages to make her way back to the other side of the fence, she'll thank Ken, her Back Bay yoga instructor, for the endless iterations of crow pose. But she could be doing much better at present with her mindful breathing.

She clears the lip of the overhang enough to lie flat on her stomach. Reaching down with one hand, she brings the bottle up and props it up against the fence. She lies there, panting for a minute, then rolls over and crab walks under the fence. Struggling to a stand, she grabs the bottle and turns away from the cliff. She's had enough of that particular view of the ocean to last a lifetime.

Back on the boardwalk, Thalia grips the rail. Now that she's avoided plunging to her death, the last thing she needs is to slip and break her leg. She looks back to see White Hall looming behind her like a haunted house. Like a nightmare. Like the cover of a horror novel. It bares its teeth, beckons her through the rain and the gloom beyond the skeletal branches of the waiting mulberry forest—for it's after midnight, and the previously bright moon has pulled a cloud over itself like a blanket. The black boughs stand out as if they've been embossed against the eddying, whale-gray sky.

Slowly, Thalia makes her way down the right-hand path to the mini mansion, ignoring the eerie sense of déjà vu, of feeling the way she had after her mother dismissed her and she decided to tell Sarah everything, when Sarah's taxi crept closer to White Hall, and Thalia had the strange, but distinct, sense of wanting to go home.

The replica is larger than it looked from the third-floor window of the room across the hall, about the size of a small guesthouse. It's chipped and listing, moss-covered and faded, and instills in Thalia a feeling of *wrongness*. If White Hall is a pair of disgruntled twins, this smaller structure is one of their discarded playthings. It seems incomplete rather than deteriorating. Incongruous, and yet, a perfect match to its prototype. It's a paradox. An enigma.

And Thalia doesn't want to go inside it.

Despite hinges that shriek like the damned, the door opens without trouble. The light is dim. Thalia hurries to employ her phone's flashlight. When she pulls the door closed, the crash of the ocean and gusts of wind disappear as if she's entered a courtroom the moment after a verdict has been delivered.

Thalia shivers. Years ago, she visited Pompeii—she and a girlfriend for whom she was trying to muster up feelings despite their glaringly incompatible personalities. They'd walked, awestruck, through the once thriving-city, now buried under meters of ash and pumice. Thalia feels the same sense of preservation in the replica. Of something waiting for her beneath the floorboards.

She creeps down the hall and to the door on the left. It opens into a large room rife with uneven angles and corners that don't match up, as if the design was pulled from the blueprints of Sarah Winchester's Mystery House, that architectural anomaly known for crooked staircases and doors that lead nowhere.

She leans against a tufted leather armchair that's held up better than the moldy bench seats, her phone's flashlight illuminating cloudy sconces, baroque paneled wall art, and half-wood pillar accents. She's covered with slick red clay from the cliff, but pulls the hem of her shirt out to dry the bottle of wine with the underside of it. It takes several minutes to work the worst of the mud and grime away. When she's finished, she stares at the words on the label with a combination of horror and awe: *To Miss Bronson. Welcome to White Hall. Sincerely, The Searleses.*

Aileen said she feared Blake was going to relapse that final night, that Blake acted like this tragic conclusion was unavoidable. A fly who'd placed one thin leg onto a strand of spiderweb and the house, the weaver, felt the vibrations in the curve of its tarsal claws. The trap, cleverly set, had been sprung.

Thalia places both hands around the bottle, wishing she still stood atop the cliff so she could hurl it into the ocean. She wouldn't, of course; the bottle is evidence. Of what, she's still not sure. But at the very least, evidence that Blake hadn't drunk the most easily accessible alcohol in her vicinity at White Hall. Thalia's angry—angry that Blake had been suspected of relapsing on so little—and convinced this inaccurate portrayal is the key to something larger. Anger fading to frustration, Thalia looks up . . .

. . . and sees a discoloration of the floor at the foot of a counter across from her, as if the counter used to be positioned forward several inches. In front of the discoloration is a set of hinges.

Thalia sets the bottle aside, goes to the hinges, and uses the counter to angle her phone's flashlight. She drops to her knees and feels around, searching for a groove in the floorboards. When she finds it, she follows the groove until her fingers slide into a larger divot across from the latch. She lifts, and the wood sticks for a beat, but then it rises. Thalia straddles the growing hole to push the hatch all the way open, then lowers the trapdoor to the floor.

The depths beyond the opening are very dark, but Thalia is able to make out a stone staircase. She looks back up at the room with its odd pillars and archways, its dizzyingly incompatible designs. She looks at lightless windows and at Blake's recovered bottle of mulberry wine. She looks back into the hole.

"Goddamn it," Thalia whispers. What had Sarah said when they'd parted? Not to go skulking about the mansion in the middle of the night, looking for whatever secret passageways the White Hall ghost used to get around? And then there was rule number two. But sometimes the heroine *had* to explore the dungeon while she had the chance, before the villain could use her ignorance of it against her. "Goddamn it," she whispers again and grabs her phone.

She places one wet sneaker at the top of the stairs. No alarm bells ring out, no angry proprietress rushes from a hidden room screaming for Thalia not to go any farther. Thalia places another sneaker on the same step, grabs the side of the trapdoor and—on the off chance someone followed her out here—slowly lowers it over her head. Then, she takes a deep breath and starts down.

Chapter 35

The flashlight on Thalia's phone only allows her to see about ten feet in front of her, so she tests the dusty, crumbling rock with each new step. At the bottom, she shakes off a ripple of claustrophobia; the arched ceiling, at its highest point, is no more than a foot above her head, and the walls are close enough for her to reach out and touch on either side. She checks the battery on her phone: 43 percent. Not terrible, but not great either. "What am I doing?" she whispers into the darkness.

The tunnel appears to have been excavated from the inside—with the overlying material left in place—and then lined with stones to support the adjacent ground. She expected it to be damp, close to the shore like it is, but the air inside the passageway is cool and dry.

She walks quickly, heart pounding, sneakers crunching over gravel, red clay, and rocks of varying sizes. After about a minute, the tunnel forks to either side. The main passage appears to stay straight, and so Thalia does too. She walks, and just as she's wondering if she's going to end up in a root cellar beneath the mulberry tree forest or in the basement of the mansion, she comes to a four-way split.

It doesn't matter which direction she goes; she'll be equally lost down any passage. She takes the route second from left, stopping to shoot herself a text detailing this decision, the technological equivalent of bread crumbs in the forest. There's no cell service, but she takes a screenshot of the message with a little red exclamation mark next to it. Two hundred feet or so in, she comes to a crumbled pile of rocks as high as the ceiling. She backtracks, chooses the passageway second from the right, sends another text, takes another screenshot. If she had to guess, she is under the courtyard off the back of the mansion. This corridor, though narrower than any she's traversed thus far, leads her to a set of stairs. If her "under the courtyard" theory is correct, she's about to transition from underground tunnels to passages that wind around the many floors of the mansion.

At the top, Thalia stops. The rational, lawyerly part of her brain tells her not to go any farther. Thalia rarely, if ever, goes against that voice. The tunnels here are far tighter than any that have come previously. There are six, each tall enough in which to stand, but narrow enough so that, if someone were coming from the other direction, neither the fellow explorer nor Thalia would be able to pass. A bark of ironic laughter escapes her. If she comes across someone else in these tunnels, continued passage through them will be the least of her worries. She's about to check her battery level again, when she spots something in the stone, a groove that functions as a shelf. There's a flashlight and a set of keys on top of it.

She reaches for them, then stops. What if she can't find her way back to this spot? Does she want to indicate to anyone who might use this tunnel system that she's been here? She pulls her hand back, then reaches up again, and snatches both items. If she ends up needing them but doesn't have them, it'll be worse than if she takes them and gets caught. It's not like she signed a consent form when she checked in: *I will not access the underground cave system without explicit permission.*

She steps into the narrow tunnel. It twists in so many different, seemingly back-and-forth directions, that within a minute, she's disoriented, out of breath, and a little panicked. There are multiple sets of stairs, but she loses track of how many she ascends. The flashlight is doing more harm than good; the beam reflects off the shiny surfaces of the stone and blinds her. She switches it off, but the darkness is worse, so she switches it back on and brings a hand to her eyes. Just when she's decided to turn back, the passageway widens. The walls stop twisting and become sharp turns and precise right angles. She calms her breathing, realizing only now how close she was to losing it in the narrowest portion of the tunnel.

The passageway makes another sharp turn, and Thalia finds herself face-to-face with a door. Or, not a door, but a partition, a sliding wall of some sort. She shines the light along the four sides. In the center of the left-hand side, there's a divot in the wood. She traces the indentation, presses lightly against it, and leans forward to press her ear to the wall. There's a sense of solidity to the partition. Whatever it opens onto, it's far too thick to hear anything through.

She presses her thumb into the indentation. Nothing. She presses harder, and something clicks. Thalia keeps her thumb in place, not daring to move. Whatever's on the other side of this wall, she's only a breath from confronting it. When she relinquishes some of the pressure beneath her thumb, the board spins from a horizontal orientation to a vertical one. The movement is entirely silent, which surprises her more—given the primeval feel of the tunnels—than the fact that it's opened at all.

At first, she thinks she's been dreaming and has finally woken up. She's staring into her bedroom at White Hall. The gauzy gray curtains are open. Rain slides silently down the dark panes. A rolltop desk hulks in one corner. But then she sees the portrait of Mary Hopkins Searles. So not her room but the first bedroom she snuck into the night she arrived at the mansion and made a promise to her dead half sister on the floor before a bathtub. Ducking through the opening, she steps forward onto the antique throw rug, turns, and inspects the space from which she's exited. When in place, the ingress to the underground tunnels is one of two dozen rectangular panels making up an ornate late-Victorian-era wall. Thalia envisions the walls of her own chamber, but this rectangular pattern is absent from them. The entrance to the tunnels from the room she's inhabited the past two nights must be hidden somewhere else.

And there *will* be an entrance to her room. From the way the tunnels split into six different routes, then split further into right-angle turns that Thalia now understands follow the layout of the house, she is pretty certain there will be an entrance to *every* room. She'd thought she'd seen a woman that first night when she'd peered out of the bathroom, a woman in long, full skirts, a veil obscuring her features. The silhouette had then glided back to where the room cut into an L and out of Thalia's sight. She'd convinced herself it had been a trick of the rain and the shadows, a phantom born of her worry that she'd been caught sneaking around. She pictures someone sneaking into the room to listen to her whispered words before disappearing back into the tunnels, and the rush of anger returns.

Here is the solution to the mystery at the heart of Blake's horror novel. The real-world explanation for seemingly supernatural events. The justification for rule number eight. Here, too, is likely how someone snuck up on Blake as she lay in the tub, the unfortunate fate she'd been trying to avoid since setting foot on the island creeping toward her even as she contemplated it.

Thalia ducks through the space in the wall and into the passage. She spins the partition back to vertical. *Left,* she thinks, conjuring the layout of rooms off the hallway. She has to go left if she's going to find the entrance to Blake's room . . . or the entrance to hers.

She's walked a minute back in the direction of the last fork when she stops. There's a sound. Something very much like a boot scraping against the gritty floor. Thalia clicks the flashlight off and freezes. Breathing as quietly as possible, she strains to listen. It's only now she realizes she can hear the faint groans of wind and rustle of rain. Another ripple of claustrophobia assails her; she's inside the mansion's *walls.* Like a spider. Or a rat.

Her finger moves over the flashlight's button, but she doesn't click it. She stands against the wall, listening another moment. When no additional scraping comes, she switches the flashlight on again and continues forward.

She needs to find the entrance to her own room so that she can block it off. Thalia isn't sure how much longer she'll be staying at White Hall, but she won't be able to sleep another moment in the Searleses' Nightmare House if she thinks the passage to her room could be accessed at any moment. After a few twists and turns, she comes upon another partition, but it opens into the same linen closet she found on her first night in the mansion. Further support for her theory that there are hidden ingresses into each and every room.

She's getting closer, though. It's two a.m. Two hours since she set out for the replica. Thalia moves faster through the tunnels, not wanting to be cutting across the grass to the courtyard in the glow of a morning sunrise, visible to Aileen in the kitchen as she prepares breakfast for her only guest.

The next partition lacks a divot in the wood like the previous two she's encountered. This one is flush against the wall, though she can see its outline clearly. She runs her fingers around its lines, frustration growing. Just as she's starting to accept there's no way to unlock this partition, something clangs to the ground by her left foot. She reaches down and comes up with a tool like a putty knife. It must have fallen from a crevice in the stone somewhere above her. She angles it into the tiny crack between the wood and lifts, as if opening a can of paint. The partition pops open on a thin wooden hinge, and Thalia yelps, then claps a hand over her mouth. She listens, but no sounds come from inside her room.

And it is *her* room the strange spring-loaded partition has opened onto; her bed, her bathroom, her pile of clothes in the corner. The partition is *almost* as soundless as the others but for a muffled click. The same muffled click that prefaced the uncanny feeling of no longer being alone in a room with a single locked door.

Thalia ducks beneath the partition. There's only about two feet of space between the hinges and the opening. Once inside, she examines the ingress. It's not any of the locations she had in mind for the possible hidden door; rather than a panel of woodwork, the full-length mirror, or the back of the wardrobe, the unknown entrance has deposited her into the tiny fireplace along the right-hand wall. She's standing upright in the stone column, though when she raises her gaze, the "chimney" goes only a foot higher than her head. The hearth itself is a ruse. She wonders if there's ever been a visitor to White Hall B and B who's asked one of the Searles sisters to light a fire.

She steps into the room and looks around, but everything's as she left it, and she still needs to replace the key ring and flashlight, back-track through the tunnels, and shut the trapdoor in the replica before she can return here through the normal entrance. She already feels herself swimming through a whirlpool of delirium, that deep state of exhaustion she usually only reaches when pulling an all-nighter after being asked to cover a last-minute trial.

Thalia scrutinizes the fireplace, staring at it until she knows she's being ridiculous, as if the stonework, wood, and marble are going to vaporize and she'll be able to see the partition straight through the wall. She's trying to determine whether she should've known she's been sleeping beside the hidden entrance to a maze of underground tunnels for the past two nights. But no matter how hard she looks, no hints present themselves.

She guesses it's the same in every room, at the entry point to every passage. If the ingresses are so well hidden, have the tunnels been a secret to everyone but the Searleses since the mansion's conception 130 years ago? She's careful not to inadvertently trigger the partition behind her, certain there's no way to open it from the inside. The invisible entrances are too sophisticated.

If Fiona had killed Blake—and Thalia's more unconvinced than ever—she would have accessed her room through these passageways. But Blake had written that she was first attacked by the Mansion Ghost the night after meeting Martin. Would Fiona have suspected Blake of sleeping with Martin after a single afternoon, and snuck into her room dressed in Victorian clothing in an attempt to frighten her away? It's possible but not very likely.

Aileen, on the other hand, was the one who told Blake the story of Mary Hopkins Searles, and who's been quick to attribute Blake's talk of ghosts and gothic novels to her supposed relapse. And yet Thalia now has the very bottle of mulberry wine Blake was to have relapsed with. Did Aileen try to frighten Blake into leaving White Hall? And if so, why? Thalia starts to sit on the end of her bed, then remembers she's not really "back" in her room. Expelling a frustrated exhalation, she ducks back into the firebox and maneuvers through the opening.

Though as physically taxed as she is mentally drained, Thalia cuts through the tunnels in less time than it took her to go through them initially. She stumbles out of the mouth of one passage and into the location of the six-way split, across from the stone shelf cut into the wall. She sets the keys and flashlight upon it and reaches into her back pocket for her cell phone. As she's swiping the screen for the phone's light, she hears something coming up the main tunnel from the direction of the replica.

Footsteps. And they are coming fast.

Thalia presses the side button on her phone to douse the screen light and retreats into the tunnel she'd just exited. She reconsiders, darts forward, and moves one tunnel over. Backing into the shadows, she keeps her eyes on the main passage, thankful the tunnel she's chosen cuts back in one of the sharp angles she encountered closer to the mansion's upstairs bedrooms.

A flashlight beam bobs up and down over the stone. Thalia inhales slowly and holds her breath. The footsteps grow closer. And closer.

Then stop.

Chapter 36

Martin Dempsey stands in the space where the tunnels converge, his face above the glow of his flashlight as wan and eerie as a Halloween mask. For one horrible moment, Thalia thinks he must have found the open trapdoor, that he's down here *looking for her,* but then she realizes his demeanor is too calm, his expression too unaffected. That he's in the passageway is pure coincidence.

One hand goes to the shelf, where he places his flashlight next to the one Thalia replaced mere moments before. The beam now illuminates the wall across from the shelf. Under the opposite arm, he's carrying the safe from Maureen's closet. Thalia exhales through an open mouth and tries to suck in breath without sound. The blood whooshing through her temples is as loud as a hurricane gale.

Martin takes the set of keys and walks to the opposite wall. In the beam of the flashlight, he places his arms about a foot apart on the stone, and presses. Nothing happens, and he moves his left arm down about an inch. This time, when he presses, the wall opens like a regular old door, swinging on hinges perfectly obscured by jaggedly cut blocks of stone. Inside is not another tunnel, but a small room, about the size of an average coat closet. There are three shelves, piled with what appear to be dusty journals or ledgers, safe-deposit boxes, and another, larger safe. Martin opens this safe with a key from the ring, places Maureen's safe inside it, and shuts the door.

For a moment, he stands, looking at the contents of the stone closet. He has the stance and expression of a man taking in his newborn child. Martin even reaches out and trails a hand down a stack of journals before sighing and closing the door. Every trace of the room's rectangular outline disappears with the dull click of stone meeting stone.

Martin turns toward the place where the passage splits, and Thalia shrinks back. She presses a hand over her mouth, sure there's no way to hide the sound of her breathing. She has the horrible certainty that her phone—somehow—now has service and isn't on silent, that Sarah will choose this moment to wake up, see Thalia hasn't texted her since she dropped her off, and send her a message. Martin continues to stare, as if contemplating which passage to take. The seconds drag on. Thalia's heart beats wildly, and she feels nauseous. She can't really explain her terror, just knows that, should Martin find her after accessing his hidden cache, his reaction will not be favorable.

Finally, Martin replaces the keys, retrieves his flashlight, and hurries into the tunnel on the far right. Thalia is stuck by terror anew. For how long will Martin be in these passages with her? If she reenters the tunnel that leads to the replica, will he eventually double back and catch up with her, or was his entry point into this hellish maze off another of the underground tunnels? There are as many possible answers to the question "Which way will Martin go?" as there are tunnels themselves, and Thalia doesn't have time to contemplate any of them. She holds in a breath while counting to ten, exhales slowly, then takes off running, making sure to stay on the balls of her feet so as to proceed as quietly as possible.

Long before law school taught her that the antidote to her upbringing with Maureen was calm and rational thinking, Thalia enjoyed running for similar lessons in discipline and delay of gratification. Her runs had decreased from training for half marathons to jogging two to three times per week, but it's enough to sustain her pace from Martin's secret safe to the staircase beneath the replica.

She sprints up the staircase as well, and wastes no time in closing the trapdoor. She gives the room the quickest of once-overs to ensure everything's as she found it. The horrible, crazy, and potentially useful knowledge of what exists beneath the surface of White Hall bounces around her head like poisonous pills in a prescription bottle. *The bottle!* She turns, searching the floor, the countertop, scanning the surfaces of the armchair and the bench seats, but it's no use.

Blake's bottle of mulberry wine is gone.

Thalia resists the urge to shout in frustration and instead sprints up the hall, looking for signs—besides the missing bottle—that Martin passed this way before her. She reaches the replica door, pushes it open, and runs up the boardwalk and across the grass. For a second, as she passes the archways at the base of the courtyard, she thinks she sees something: a woman next to a tall mulberry tree, the branches of which are blowing in the wind. The woman stares at Thalia as if contemplating a sunset, unaffected by the weather. Then, Thalia blinks rainwater from her eyes, and the figure is gone.

She makes it back to her room without further incident and peels off wet, mud-encrusted clothes, eyeing the fireplace the whole time. Martin, Aileen, anyone coming out of the partition and into the bedroom won't be able to do so unseen unless Thalia is in the bathroom. Or asleep. She wishes it wasn't so late. Or so early. She'd call Sarah to come get her. She doesn't know how she'll ever sleep in this room again. But—and this is far more important than restful repose—as far as Thalia can tell, neither Martin nor anyone else knows that Thalia has discovered the mansion's secret. The replica's trapdoor, the tunnels, Martin's safe—all of it continues to exist in the shadow of Dream House, in the locked rooms of Martin's and Aileen's minds.

Now you sound like Ann Radcliffe, spinning spooky yarns. She has to get some sleep, secret entrance to the room or not. She checks the fireplace again, then drags the heavy wooden desk chair over and props it in front of the partition. Feeling slightly safer than before, she sinks onto the bed. She's still in shock that she found—and then lost—Blake's bottle of wine. She's back to her sister's letter being the only physical thing she has.

At least for now.

Tomorrow, she will find some way to get Aileen out of the house and ensure Martin stays away from White Hall long enough to slip back underground. She'll bring her suitcase and emerge with the journals and ledgers, the safe-deposit boxes, the stolen safe of her mother's—everything she can carry—and she'll bring it all to Sarah's. If they can break into Maureen's safe, maybe Thalia will be closer to figuring out what happened to her sister, and where Martin fits into the whole mess. Because while she still has little more than leads and guesses, false starts and dead ends, she knows one thing for certain.

Martin Dempsey is definitely involved.

Chapter 37

The morning dawns too quickly, and though Thalia is dehydrated and groggy from too little sleep, she forces herself out of bed and into the shower as soon as she wakes. There's mud on her skin and under her nails, and she scrubs with abandon, breathing in the scent of lilacs, allowing herself to focus only on this task of getting clean before stepping onto the tile floor and back into the present.

While she dresses, she realizes she needs to text Laura. She can't explain what's going on, since she has no idea herself, but a few quick lines to let her know she's all right will have to be sufficient. After she's sent them, and Laura responds back to be careful and that she's thinking about her, Thalia navigates to her text conversation with Sarah.

Can you pick me up? Don't be mad, but I didn't exactly take your advice to "order a pizza and get a good night's sleep." Kind of the opposite, actually. I'll fill you in on everything, and then I need your help to stage a diversion.

Sarah responds within seconds:

What are you, nuts? But yeah, okay, be there in thirty minutes.

What kind of diversion? Do I need a pantyhose mask? A flamethrower?

Thalia, who is examining the jacket she wore the night before and wincing as dried mud crumbles off the fabric and onto the floor, shakes her head.

Jesus. No. No mask. And do you really have a flamethrower? Don't answer that. Just bring me a jacket. Preferably something without Scottie dogs on it, okay?

When Sarah pulls up—right at nine thirty, as promised, and in Patrick's Toyota instead of her taxi—Thalia is standing in the foyer sipping from a to-go cup. The kitchen was empty, but there was coffee, and Thalia wasn't keen on sticking around long enough to find out if it was Aileen who brewed it, or if Martin's presence at White Hall had been extended.

She instructs Sarah to drive to Great Salt Pond so she can tell her everything that occurred at dinner as well as in the lightless corridors of the mansion's bowels. Sarah sips her own coffee, occasionally breaking the silence to ask if Thalia is "freakin' kidding" or to demand additional details of hidden partitions or camouflaged safes. But when Thalia is done, the only additional question Sarah asks is, "So how are we going to get you back down there?"

Thalia sighs. "There's no way to access the tunnels from my room unless the partition is already open from inside the passage, so I need to get back out to the replica without anyone seeing me. Aileen was MIA this morning, but that doesn't mean she won't be there when I return. I don't think she ever leaves the mansion. And I have a feeling that—after making his 'official' appearance at dinner last evening—Martin's going to be around a lot more often, most likely whenever he's not at the restaurant."

"Good news there," Sarah says. "I just drove past Above the Rocks, and Martin's car is parked next to a big delivery truck in the loading area. I could keep an eye on him from across the street, but you'll have to move fast. If he leaves, and you're already in the tunnels, I'm guessing you won't be able to get a text from me."

"I can probably get from the trapdoor to the safe and back in the time it takes Martin to drive up Corn Neck Road, if it comes to that."

"But that still doesn't solve the problem of Aileen."

Thalia gestures impatiently at the gearshift. "Let's head back. Martin's the one I'm really worried about, and if he's busy now, I need to take advantage of that. I'll come up with something to get past Aileen." She pauses and groans. "I almost forgot. There's a set of keys for the large one, but I need to figure out how to break into Maureen's safe once I get it aboveground again."

"Patrick broke into his brother's safe once when Jared forgot the combination. Something about using a wire hanger to hit the interior reset button. As a last resort, we can go old school and drill."

Thalia nods, satisfied, and gulps the last of her coffee. "Maybe I can convince Aileen to break into a bottle of wine over brunch, culminating in her need for a nap. Though she's no fragile flower. I'd probably need a barrel of mulberry wine to fell that tree." Sarah doesn't laugh, just nods grimly and continues maneuvering the Toyota toward Mansion Road.

White Hall appears too quickly. Thalia wishes the drive were longer, that she could get another coffee with her friend and sit somewhere watching the ocean instead of having to pursue this wild conspiracy. It's not raining for the first time since Thalia's been in New Shoreham, but the island is saturated and drooping and dismal, and the road leading to White Hall is flooded in parts, though Sarah gets through it more easily than she would have in the taxi.

She pulls around the circular driveway and shoots Thalia a look. "Text me if your plan's not working."

"I don't have a plan, remember?"

"Right. Well, then, there's no way for it to fail."

"*You* don't forget to text me the second it looks like Martin might be making a move. Hopefully I'll get it. Oh, and does Patrick have a flashlight?"

Sarah leans over, opens the glove compartment, and holds out one with a hefty LED bulb. They hold each other's gaze; then Thalia springs from the car and jogs toward the mansion, shoving the flashlight into the waistband of her jeans. As she walks into the foyer, Aileen is crossing into the parlor. *Looks like the time for the nonplan is now.*

"Morning," Thalia calls with a cheeriness that—thankfully—doesn't sound forced. "I was wondering if I could trouble you for some"—she looks down at her phone and sees the time—"brunch? Sarah and I were going out to eat, but she got a call from someone needing a taxi. Rather than sit somewhere alone, I figured I'd come back here."

Aileen, caught off guard, recovers quickly. "Yes, of course. I can whip something up. How does a hearty egg sandwich on a bagel sound?"

Thalia's glad she has the last of her pristine tailored blouses on, and she dons her courtroom persona like an extra cardigan. "I hate to be picky," she says in a tone that exudes pickiness, "but I was hoping for something a little more exciting. Maybe it's the weather or everything going on with my mother, but I feel like I need to let loose, even if it's just with my taste buds."

"Oh." Again, Aileen appears slightly shaken before she squares her shoulders and rises to Thalia's challenge. "Mulberry sauce crepes, then? With honey whipped cream? It's a White Hall specialty. I can do scrambled eggs and hash on the side as well."

Thalia smiles. "That sounds perfect. I'm starving."

"Great," Aileen says, and starts for the kitchen. When Thalia follows, Aileen turns. "It'll take me a few minutes to get everything ready and heat the griddle."

"That's fine," Thalia replies. "I'll keep you company."

"Okay, then," Aileen says.

Thalia gets halfway across the foyer, then stops. "Shoot. I forgot to take my pills. You know, birth control, vitamins, all that. I'm going to run up to my room. Be there in a sec."

When Thalia does arrive in the kitchen, the big bowl of fruit is in its usual place on the marble island. While Aileen collects ingredients,

Thalia slides a cutting board over, selects a ripe Anjou pear, and holds it up. "Okay if I make a little fruit salad as well?"

"Suit yourself."

Thalia chops the pear, an apple, an orange, and half a box of strawberries from the refrigerator. The next time Aileen passes, Thalia pretends to notice the rack of mulberry wine across the room. "I know *actual* sangria is supposed to chill for a couple of hours," Thalia says thoughtfully, "but I could throw this fruit in a pitcher with some mulberry wine and pour the whole thing over ice. You're the cook, but it'd make for a nice pairing with pancakes and eggs."

Aileen eyes her over the skillet where chopped potatoes and spices are browning. "They're crepes," she says evenly. "Not pancakes. But whatever you'd like. You're the guest."

Relieved, Thalia fetches a bottle and starts toward the cabinets.

"Bottom row, on the left," Aileen instructs. The crepes, sauce, and potatoes are finished right as Thalia is stirring the wine.

"I'll man the scramble," Thalia says quickly, hoping Aileen will bring the other dishes out to the table.

"I'm supposed to be serving you."

"And only me," Thalia points out. "It can't be cost effective to cook such nice meals for a party of one." She takes the utensil from Aileen and nods toward the door. "Really. I insist."

Aileen loads the stack of crepes and boat of sauce on a tray and carries it along with the potatoes into the dining room. Quick as a diving gull, Thalia plunges her hand into her pocket and comes out with Maureen's prescription bottle of pills. She dumps the diazepam—crushed into a fine powder while she was upstairs—into the bottom of a champagne flute, fills it with sangria, and garnishes the glass with a lemon.

According to Google, forty milligrams should be enough to knock Aileen out without risk of her ending up in the hospital with Maureen. Thalia fills a second champagne flute and garnishes this one with a lime.

She is turning off the stove and fluffing the finished scramble when Aileen returns.

Thalia separates the eggs onto two plates while Aileen loads the tray with utensils, seasoning salt, napkins, and crushed red pepper. Thalia picks the plates up and starts for the dining room. "Can you fit the champagne flutes on your tray as well?"

Aileen eyes the twin glasses. "Oh, I don't think I'll be having any—"

"Oh, come on, Aileen. You're not going to make me drink alone, are you?" She pouts and shakes her head, as if the thought is too depressing to bear. Aileen purses her lips. "Come on," Thalia says again. "Just one. I'm sure I'm not the only person Martin stressed out last night with his talk of mental health struggles and handing letters over to the police."

The Martin comment is a gamble, but it pays off. Aileen sighs, then breaks into a small smile. "All right." She picks up the glasses and arranges them on her tray.

In the dining room, Thalia's observations of Aileen's daily personal tea preparation do not go unrewarded. The proprietress takes the glass with the lemon. It's the kind of informed risk the senior partners at the firm love her for. With how strongly Thalia pushed the wine on Aileen in the first place, she couldn't afford to go so far as to put the drink directly in front of her and have the proprietress grow suspicious.

Thalia wasn't kidding about being starving and doesn't want to get shaky or light-headed in the tunnels. She manages an entire crepe with mulberry sauce and a few bites of potato before Aileen—who's talking about the upcoming tourist season—starts to slur.

Thalia puts down her fork. She didn't get a chance to try the scramble, but the bottom burned while she was mixing Aileen's drink, so no great loss. She realizes she's thinking nonsense thoughts in her nervousness. *Focus. Aileen's about to pass out. Ask her something before she does; maybe the drugs will make something slip.*

"Aileen?"

"Yesshh?"

"Do you know what really happened to my sister?"

Aileen's left eye twitches, and the woman flinches as if a mosquito has buzzed by her ear. "I . . ." She stops, looking dazed.

"What happened to Blake when she stayed in this house?"

Aileen pushes back in her chair as if to stand, then flops forward again, but catches herself with her elbows on the table. She murmurs something incomprehensible, and her left eye twitches again. *This is it.* Thalia gets ready to push back from the table herself. Aileen shudders, focuses her gaze on Thalia, and says, "I'm sorry. But it's the ghost. Mary Hopkins Searles. The Mulberry Maiden."

"What did you just say?"

Aileen opens her mouth a final time. Her lips quiver with some silent word, and Thalia leans in, trying to catch it. But then the woman is falling forward, forward, forward, onto her plate. Her cheek comes to rest on top of the mulberry sauce–topped crepes. A long exhalation escapes her parted lips.

Thalia jumps up, crosses the room, and stares down at the proprietress. For one terrible moment, she thinks Aileen has stopped breathing, but then she sees the puddle of mulberry sauce atop the pancakes quake beneath her breath.

"I'm sorry, Aileen," she whispers and checks her phone. No new messages from Sarah. She leaves the kitchen, collects her jacket and suitcase from the foyer, brought down after her trip to her room for the diazepam, and slips out the front door. She has a sudden, intense longing to be with Laura, snuggled up in their comfortable apartment, but shakes the thought away.

As if in response to the awful thing she's just done, it starts to rain.

Chapter 38

Even dragging the empty suitcase, Thalia makes it past the courtyard, across the lawn, and down the boardwalk so quickly that the guilt she feels over drugging Aileen intensifies. *Someone accessed Blake's—and probably your—room through secret tunnels,* she reminds herself. If it's Aileen, or Aileen knows who's doing it, and she spotted Thalia running toward the replica, it wouldn't take much for her to guess the trapdoor was no longer a secret.

Thalia rushes through the replica door, down the hall, and across the bathhouse, the suitcase's spinning wheels feeding her anxiety. She wrestles the trapdoor open, clicks on Patrick's flashlight, and checks her phone one last time. Nothing from Sarah. Thalia slips the phone into her pocket, lowers the trapdoor behind her, and hurries down the stairs. Visualizing the stone safe hidden in the wall, she runs.

She expects to reach the six-way split in under five minutes, so when she's been in the tunnels closer to ten, tendrils of panic flutter against her ribs. She doesn't remember passing a fork, but hadn't she texted herself instructions yesterday prior to reaching the split?

She must have been running too fast to notice the tunnel branching in another direction. She'll backtrack going perfectly straight until she reaches the staircase, then start out again paying more attention. When she reaches a fork, she'll refer to the screenshot with the directions from yesterday. The problem is, Thalia walks and walks, looking for where she might have missed a turn, but the staircase doesn't appear.

She turns around. Walks. No fork. No staircase. She turns again. Walks. And again. The color of the stone looks different from the dusty, crumbling rock at the tunnel's opening. She seems to have stumbled into something older than that which extends between White Hall and the replica. The rocks resemble the red clay of the bluffs, and when she reaches out to touch one, it feels damp and very much *alive* beneath her fingers.

Thalia drags the suitcase forward. Has the shade and consistency of the stone changed again? Is she moving back in the direction of the staircase? Up ahead, there's a clearing, a widening of the tunnels. It culminates in an alcove of sorts, an elevated extension of the tunnel. Before coming to this clearing, Thalia sensed she was moving down a passage parallel to the one she'd traversed yesterday. Maybe this alcove is a shortcut to the six-way split.

She drags the suitcase to the mouth of the alcove, releases its handle, and flexes her fingers. The bottom lip of the stone-trimmed recess is level with her chest. Thalia places her flashlight on the lip, flips the suitcase, and climbs on top of it. Right away, she sees the recess does not extend into another tunnel. It goes back only about ten feet, and stretches a few feet to either side of the trim. It looks as if the alcove was the site of a minor cave collapse. The recess's floor is a jumbled mess of crushed granite and other organic debris. Thalia shines the flashlight into every corner of the space. Definitely no shortcut. She sighs and is preparing to step down when the flashlight illuminates something besides the cracked masonry and fragmented stone.

It's a long, thin object, wider at each end than in the middle. As yellowed and dusty as everything else in the alcove but distinct. Familiar. It looks very much like a bone.

A human bone.

Thalia doesn't want to look. Doesn't want to know. She feels the weight of her phone in her pocket. Useless until she gets out of these tunnels. Sarah could be trying to text her right now. There's no time to slither on her belly into wreckage so jumbled, so fresh-looking, she fears the ceiling above her isn't stable. But she's a lawyer with a love of sifting through layers, and so a moment later, slithering on her belly is exactly what she's doing.

Once over the lip of the recess, she climbs to her feet and moves several stones with the head of the flashlight. It doesn't take much. Fully uncovered, the object is unequivocally a human tibia. It's too old, too bleached, to inspire revulsion, but Thalia feels a glut of horror lodge in her throat anyway. She drops the flashlight beam down and kneels in the dark, thinking. When she raises the light again, she steels herself for what she must do.

She moves forward, her illuminated phone in one hand while using Patrick's flashlight to till the rubble with the other. A minute passes. She finds a series of smaller bones—fingers, or maybe wrist. Another few minutes pass, and Thalia finds the wide, flat bones of a vertebral column. She forces herself to keep looking, but when her flashlight knocks against a rectangular chunk of stone to reveal an expanse of smooth, curved, indistinguishable bone, Thalia falters. "No. No, no, no."

She brushes a few chunks of stone away from the side of the skull. When she lifts it, the skull's blank, black eyes stare into her own. Thalia drops the skull, stumbles through the rubble, and jumps from the alcove. She only remembers to grab the suitcase because she knocks it over on the way down.

Then, she runs.

She runs not because she believes in ghosts and thinks that whoever's skeleton has been abandoned in this tomb is going to chase her. She runs not because she fears she's wasted too much time, and Aileen or Martin is coming. Thalia runs because now, more than ever, she needs to know what is going on in this mansion. She runs because the only potential place for answers is down here.

And she is going to find it.

She keeps the flashlight beam wide and ever-moving, and just when her breathing grows ragged, she spots a fork that she missed the first time she attempted to retrace her steps. This fork leads to another, and when she spills into a wider tunnel, she turns left rather than right, no longer needing to return to the replica staircase to get her bearings. She reaches the six-way split in under five minutes.

Thalia places the flashlight on the small stone shelf to illuminate the opposite wall and removes the key ring. She unzips the suitcase, lays it flat on the floor before the safe, and takes a deep breath. Martin had placed his arms about three feet apart, a little lower than shoulder height, but he has at least a foot on her. Thalia lifts her arms slightly above her shoulders. Bracing herself with one foot behind her, she takes another deep breath, and pushes.

Nothing.

She readjusts her arms. Pushes. Nothing again. She suppresses the urge to take out her phone and check for a message from Sarah. There won't be any service, and if Martin is on the way to the mansion, doing *anything* other than getting into this hidden closet is a bad idea. Thalia adjusts her arms again. Pushes. Nothing. Adjust. Push. Nothing. Adjust. Push.

Swing.

The door opens with as little fanfare as if she were walking into a grocery store. She inspects the lock on the safe and examines the keys in her hand. There's only one that could fit. The safe pops open, and Thalia takes Maureen's smaller safe from it, along with a pile of ledgers, and places everything in the suitcase. The journals go in next, two piles of five and another pile of seven. She refuses to leave so much as a receipt behind. She moves three safe-deposit boxes from shelf to suitcase, a stack of what looks like medical records, and several small containers that could be jewelry boxes.

Finally, there is nothing left but a whole lot of cave dust. Thalia pushes the stone door shut, zips the suitcase, and tests its weight. It's heavy. Too heavy, in fact, to make heading all the way back to the replica a feasible option. The partition to her room is much closer. Thalia throws the keys onto the shelf and grabs her flashlight.

The tunnel from the split up to the entrances to the third-floor rooms is steeper than she remembers. As the spring-loaded partition releases with its muffled click, she's met with an unfortunate realization: the suitcase won't fit through the opening.

Thalia kneels, opens the suitcase, and unloads it as quickly as she can. She feeds each stack, box, and journal through the partition, dropping them onto the fireplace floor. She steps through after them, almost tripping on a toppled journal, pushes everything farther into the room, then slides the entirety of the contents of Martin's safe under the bed.

She's sweating now, from fear and exertion. Even after extricating herself from the tomb, emptying Martin's safe took far longer than expected. *Service,* she thinks, and checks her phone. There are two text messages from Sarah:

Thalia!!!

and:

Are you there? Text me as soon as you're out!

Thalia texts with shaking fingers:

Did Martin leave???

There's no time to give Sarah details about her current location. In fact, there's no time to wait for Sarah's reply. In order to shut the partition fully, to maintain the illusion that she's oblivious to the existence of the passageways, she needs to get back through the tunnels with the suitcase, shut the trapdoor, and return to the mansion *aboveground*. She gives her phone a final, desperate look but doesn't even see three dots to indicate Sarah's typing. "Can't wait," she says out loud. "Got to go."

She crawls through, shuts the partition, grabs the suitcase, and runs. Past the now-empty stone closet, back into the main tunnel, thinking, in an offhanded kind of way, that while she didn't anticipate not being able to fit the suitcase through the partition, going to her room first was the right idea; it's still easier to return through the tunnels dragging an *empty* piece of luggage as opposed to one stuffed with Martin's secrets.

Thalia is gasping for breath by the time she gets to the replica's stairs; good exercise habits can only account for so much sprinting while panicked. When she's calmed her breathing enough to listen for signs of someone prowling around the bathhouse, she creeps upward, holding the suitcase under one arm so it can't bang against the stairs. With an appeal to Blake she didn't know she was going to make until she whispers it—"If you're here, and watching out for me, I'd love for there to be no one in the bathhouse"—she inches the trapdoor open.

She's alone among the rotted-out bench seats and baroque paneled wall art. "Thank you," Thalia whispers, then lowers the trapdoor and checks her messages. Nothing. It'll take a minute for her phone to locate the nearest tower. She darts down the hall and peeks out the replica's door. No sign of a drugged-up Aileen zombie-walking across the courtyard or a furious Martin sprinting at her down the boardwalk. She adjusts her grip on the suitcase and shuts the door. She's almost there. She's almost safe.

Approaching the boardwalk, Thalia can't help but feel the mulberry forest to her left, the spaces between the trees like dark, elongated eyes. She's just placed one foot on the wood when her phone chimes in rapid succession. One text, two texts, three, four, five, six.

Each sentence is a separate message, cascading down the screen:

Martin's still here.

You're still fine.

He just came out of the back entrance!

He's pacing around the back deck, talking on the phone.

He's getting in his car!

HE'S GOING IN THE DIRECTION OF THE MANSION.

Thalia's about to respond when a shadow falls over the boardwalk. "What are you doing with that suitcase?" a low voice asks.

Her fingers freeze on the phone. Thalia looks up. At first, she thinks Martin is standing before her, the resemblance is so uncanny. The beard and thick olive-green shirt allow Thalia's brain to recalibrate. It's the groundskeeper, Monty, who blocks her path to the mansion. Monty, who looks so much like Martin. Monty, who, according to Fiona, started working at White Hall right after the hurricane. The hurricane in which Michael Dempsey disappeared. The moving parts of her theory solidify. *How could I have missed it? Monty is Michael.*

"It's mine," Thalia says of the suitcase, struggling to focus. Not a lie, just not the whole truth. She can't get over his resemblance to Martin, is shocked she didn't see it that first day she caught him peering at her from under the dogwood. "I'm Thalia," she says, despite this seeming like the very opposite of a casual introduction. "And you are?"

"Doesn't matter," he says. "You need to leave here. Get off this island while you have the chance."

Thalia is so caught off guard by the warning—or the threat—that she almost drops the suitcase. If she's right, and this truly is Michael Dempsey, escaping his transgressions by hiding in plain sight for the past twenty-five years, that means Aileen—and Fiona—were complicit in his deception. Had they allowed Michael to live on the property and call himself Monty Daniels? "What's happening at this mansion?" she asks. "Why do I need to leave?"

The groundskeeper takes a step forward. Thalia steps back. Like Martin, he's tall, but broader through the shoulders, and his hands look like they could break one of the mulberry trees in half.

"I have no power here," Monty says. "I'm at the mercy of others. Aileen. Martin. Fiona. Still, if you listen to me, you'll be safe. I should have told your sister the same thing. But I didn't get the chance."

He knows Blake's her sister. Is he at the mercy of those in power because he relies on them to keep his presence secret? Relies on *his brother* to keep his sins buried in the locked safes and buried tunnels of the past? Did Monty—*no*, Michael—kill Blake because she was close to learning the truth, and Martin covered for him by allowing Fiona to take the blame?

"Let me through, please." Thalia's voice is low but firm.

Michael doesn't move.

"I said let me through."

When he still doesn't move, Thalia reaches down and lifts the suitcase. She sighs and starts to turn, as if she's resigned herself to returning to the replica to put the suitcase's contents back, then lifts the suitcase higher and throws it as hard as she can at Michael's head. It's not enough to knock him over—he's a veritable tree trunk—but it's more than enough to stun him. He grunts and turns away from the impact.

Thalia's already moving, darting by him while reaching out to hook her hand through the suitcase's handle. If he chases her, she'll have to drop it, but she thinks she's fast enough to outrun him unencumbered. And he doesn't chase her. She looks back to see him watching her from the boardwalk, as silent and expressionless as a ghost who's lost the ability to haunt the living.

Up the boardwalk. Across the grass. She takes the long way to the courtyard, though knowing Michael's still somewhere behind her—and that Martin could be somewhere ahead—fills her with dread. Along the circular drive, up to the front door, and then she's inside. She's started up the stairs, is right in front of the looming portrait of Mary Hopkins Searles, when the phone vibrates in her hand.

She yelps and almost drops it but manages to answer Sarah's call.

"I'm out!" Thalia says. "And I'm pretty much certain that Monty is really Michael Dempsey. He tried to stop me, but I got everything I needed. I'm going to load up the suitcase again—don't ask—and get a cab to your place."

"Great. That's great. But Thalia"—Sarah sounds excited—"the hospital just called. Your mother is out of her coma. We need to get to BIMC as soon as possible."

Chapter 39

When Thalia bursts into Sarah and Paul's house with suitcase in hand, Sarah's husband is waiting with a wire hanger, drill, flashlight, saw, and blowtorch.

"I told you he'd be up for the challenge," Sarah says. "Are you sure you don't want to go to the hospital first?"

Thalia shakes her head. "I called Dr. Maddox on the way over. They're running a few tests. If we go to BIMC now, we'll wait an hour or more anyway. I'd rather use that time to get into this safe."

She unzips the suitcase and pulls the safe out. "Nice," Patrick says, examining it. "Digital will be easier to open than a dial."

"Really?"

He pushes the saw, drill, and blowtorch aside and pats the counter. Thalia places the safe on top. "With a dial, we'd definitely have to use brute force. With digital, we should be able to avoid having to crack this puppy open."

"Bring the suitcase," Sarah says, gesturing toward the couch. "We can go through everything while Patrick plays James Bond."

Thalia drags the suitcase over, and Sarah hoists it onto the coffee table. She removes piles of journals, but Thalia can only slump onto the couch. Sarah sits and opens the first journal, but looks up when Thalia says, "There were bones, Sar."

"What do you mean, bones? In Martin's safe?"

"I got lost and ended up in some alcove. It looked like there had been a rockfall. There were human bones in the rubble. A tibia. Hand bones. A skull."

"Jesus."

Thalia wipes her brow and tries to clear her head. There's too much happening at once. She's ecstatic that her mother is out of her coma, but what if Maureen is as resistant to talking to her as she was before her hospitalization? If Thalia can discover what her mother's been hiding, maybe she can convince Maureen to fill in the blanks. She can't forget what Martin told her, too, about her mother's mental health diagnosis. Maybe Maureen will be lucid—and scared, after the overdose—enough to come clean before Thalia finds any more skeletons or secret closets.

"Thalia?" Sarah looks concerned. "Are you okay? Do you think we should call the police?"

"I do think that. But not until I figure out what my mother is hiding. Especially if what *Aileen and Martin* are hiding is Michael." She lifts out a pile of ledgers. Sarah reaches for a safe-deposit box. They get to work, reading, sifting, searching.

After forty-five minutes, Thalia wonders if she drugged Aileen without cause and fabricated the entire plot between Martin and Michael. Every box Sarah opens contains little more than rings of rusty keys, yellowed paperwork, brittle bank slips, and old receipts. The journals Thalia flips through seem better suited to the basement of Ethel's library: newspaper articles detailing marriages, births, and deaths, all from the early 1900s and stapled or glued to the journal pages, along with a smattering of interviews, profiles, and summaries of real estate changing hands, none of which includes any recognizable names or locations.

The sounds of Patrick in the kitchen—breathing through his teeth as he tries to keep his hand steady enough to hit the reset button on the safe's interior keypad through the corresponding bolt opening—set Thalia on edge. She feels the way she does upon taking a case for which litigation has already begun: there's too much information, some of which *might* be relevant, if only she had the time to read it *all*. She doesn't know what to pursue and what to discard. Thalia reaches for another journal, wondering if she should give up and head to the hospital. And that's when Sarah says, "Oh my God."

"What?"

Sarah's holding a particularly weathered journal. "This. You've *got* to read this. And here." Sarah extends her arm. She's holding a small brown box.

It appears to be a worthless, wooden thing, but when Thalia takes it, she sees it's immensely old, not crudely constructed, dust and grit concealing the delicate carvings of an antique cedar jewelry box. Sarah's already opened the front clasp, so Thalia has only to lift the lid to see what's nestled on the wine-colored velvet: A cameo pendant, a delicate gold locket, and a pair of aquamarine drop earrings in yellow gold. There's another locket set with a large black-banded agate cabochon; the gold is decorated with black enamel ivy leaves. Thanks to a case she'd litigated in which an elderly woman was plotted against for her impressive collection of Victorian brooches, Thalia recognizes it as a popular mourning jewelry motif from the 1800s.

Thalia shrugs. "Probably a great-grandmother's or something."

"That's what I thought," Sarah says. "Until I opened this one." She holds out a Black Forest jewelry box, about a half inch deep. There's another set of jewelry inside, though from a different, more modern era, including a necklace with pearls as large as hazelnuts. "And this one." Sarah holds out a plain black lockbox. A ruby ring and matching bracelet, white gold and surrounded with diamonds, lie inside it. "And this one." Sarah holds out yet another box. Thalia looks at her, eyes wide.

"Maybe Martin used the hidden shelves behind the stone wall to hide Maureen's safe, but everything else inside it belongs to the Searleses," Thalia says. "It makes sense, when you think about it. It is their house."

Sarah shakes her head. "I don't think so." She picks up the journal she'd been reading and hands it to Thalia. "Like I said, you have to read this." Thalia takes it, handling the brittle binding carefully, and sinks back against the couch. She is opening the worn cover, eyes navigating to the swooping, black-ink handwriting at the top of the yellowed page, when Patrick shouts from the kitchen, "Eureka! I got it!"

Sarah jumps up from the couch and runs over. "You delightful, diabolical man."

Thalia drops the journal on the cushion beside her and follows Sarah, heart thumping in her ears.

Patrick smiles and steps back, gesturing toward the safe almost reverently. It would seem silly, if Thalia didn't have the same deferential, anticipatory feeling herself. Within seconds, she is pulling envelopes and folded stacks of papers from the safe, making sure to keep everything in order. There's more crammed onto the two narrow shelves than she realized.

When the contents are on the counter, she reaches for a thick fold of paper, then changes her mind, and moves to an envelope atop the second pile. Her hands are shaking. Panic and exhilaration, like she's about to step off the side of a cliff with a hang glider on her back, whirl through her gut in equal measure.

She feels certain that inside this envelope will be answers to the mystery that began when she opened a different light-brown envelope, addressed to her and signed *Your sister*. The envelope isn't sealed. She pulls the contents out slowly, unfolds the documents, and reads. Her eyes jump down the page, turning the mind-boggling words into a horrible, heinous story.

It's an intake form from Rhode Island Hospital in Providence describing, in the dry, distanced way of medical reports, the rape and assault of Maureen Mills on July 17, in a room at Graham's Resort in New Shoreham, Block Island. Halfway down the page, a field reads, *Has a police report been filed?* and beside it, a small box is checked *NO*. Beside that, in parentheses, someone wrote, *Victim does not wish to identify her attacker.*

Thalia looks up. Her body is a building, and a bomb has detonated at her feet. She'd guessed this horrible truth after hearing Ethel's story, but it's different now, seeing the confirmation of it, the nightmarish words in black and white. She feels the aftershock. Feels her bones, the foundation, crack and splinter. The pillars begin to fall.

Sarah rushes forward and steadies her. She and Patrick help her into a chair at the counter. Sarah doesn't ask questions, just takes the paper from Thalia and reads it herself. Then, she takes the next bundle of papers and reads those too. Patrick reaches for the second stack, but Sarah puts a hand on his and shakes her head. He goes to the sink and pours Thalia a glass of water.

A few minutes later, Thalia picks up what Sarah's gone through. There's another hospital intake form, this one for Maureen to be administered a pregnancy test, which, of course, comes out positive. There are obstetric nursing notes—most signed by a woman named Corrine Daniels—and write-ups from trauma counselors, all conducted on the mainland. Then, the medical records stop, and the next thing Thalia holds in her hands is the document that started everything: Blake's birth certificate, though this one's the original.

After the birth certificate is the letter to an adoption agency, also in Providence. Thalia lowers the letter and stares unseeingly over Sarah's kitchen counter. Blake was a healthy baby girl—a healthy *newborn* baby—but Thalia knows she grew up in foster care, so why hadn't the adoption gone through? What went wrong? Thalia scans notes written by social workers, but can find nothing to indicate what happened after Maureen relinquished the baby.

She's about to fold everything back up and return the documents to the safe when she sees something she missed on one of the letters from the adoption agency. It's a handwritten note in the margins, no more than a scribble: *When pressed for information on baby's father, bio mother states bio father is deceased. Killed by a rising sea swell during Hurricane Bob last year.*

The kitchen grows fuzzy, then sharp. So sharp, Thalia feels she's been dropped into a virtual-reality simulation where the colors and angles are *everything*, and she is a meaningless avatar. She raises her head to find Patrick staring at her, his face clouded with concern. Sarah had returned to the journal she found with Martin's papers, brow furrowed in concentration, but she looks up when Patrick clears his throat.

"What is it?" Sarah asks, coming over.

"It was Michael. Michael Dempsey. Just like we thought after talking to Ethel. That's why Martin's hiding him at White Hall."

At Thalia's shocked, monotone delivery, Sarah goes into mom mode. "Patrick, use the Toyota to pick up the girls. I'll take the taxi. Thalia's going to need to get to the hospital to talk to Maureen right away." She takes Thalia gently by the shoulders. "I know you're reeling, but while I grab our coats, I need you to read one more thing. Can you do that?"

Thalia blinks, shakes herself, and nods. *If Sarah says it's important, I need to focus.*

Sarah hands her the journal she'd given Thalia right before Patrick broke into the safe. "You thought it was strange Martin was hanging around White Hall after Fiona was arrested. I'm not sure this explains his connection to the mansion completely, why he chose it as the place—and the Searles sisters as the people—to help him hide Michael, but it might be a start."

Sarah's eyes are on Thalia, but Thalia isn't moving. Sarah hugs her, then leads her gently toward the living room. "You're processing a lot right now," she says. "I get it. But you *have* to read this. And when you're done, put that journal somewhere safe. We're going to need it when we go to the police with what you found in the tunnels today."

Sarah turns for the garage, and Thalia goes to the couch. She feels a hundred years old as she collapses among the worn journals and boxes of jewelry. She's desperate to get to the hospital, but she's also exhausted. She feels as if she's swum across the Atlantic through great white shark breeding grounds and vicious rip currents, over jagged, barnacle-laden rocks, and now lies, gasping for breath, on the shore. She wishes she could unlearn everything she's learned. She wishes she understood more. Regardless, she has to read this. Sarah wouldn't be insisting if it wasn't important. She sits back and opens the journal.

Suddenly, she *does* feel like she's swimming. No, not swimming, thrashing, and is about to be pulled under. She closes her eyes, but the images continue to assail her. Images of her mother as a younger woman, beaten and terrified on a hospital gurney, and of her sister's bloody, bloated body hanging over the lip of a bathtub. Her sister as a baby being handed back from prospective adoptive parents, as alone as if she'd been put in a lifeboat and pushed out to sea.

Why had these horrible, heinous things happened to the women in her family? Thalia takes this question and fans its small, flickering flame until it becomes a full-blown blaze. She presses her feet into the floor and flexes her fingers, allowing the anger to fuel her, to spark her curiosity in the journal, her hope that answers may exist within its pages. Then, she envisions the stark, sleek conference desk in her Government Center law office—where she does her best work in preparation for her toughest cases—and she reads.

Chapter 40

November 4, 1890

Dear Dream House,

We've been on Block Island two whole months, and I love you, Dream House, I do. I love your towering stair-case, your starlight-starbright chandeliers, and your oddly patterned hardwood floors, which look like long-petaled flowers when I turn my head just so. Living here, with the secret passages and the mulberry trees and the vast, sometimes-black-sometimes-blue ocean, is like living in an enchanted forest.

I must confess that in addition to loving you, I may have fallen for another. Someone with whom I can converse and spend time with and not grow bored. He's been a little fast in vocalizing his affections, though he's only been calling on me several months, since his father, Merritt Dempsey Sr., signed off on the completion of Father's Block Island mansion, officially christened White Hall. Yes, I have feelings for Merritt Michael Dempsey II, son of the architect Father entrusted with his latest—and most glorious—project since Kellogg Terrace, though to be frank, I'm not sure I'm in love with him. The elder Mr. Dempsey has expressed his approval of our union to Father, which is frustrating. It seems a matter for his son to concern himself with, and no business of the father's.

Mother, Susanne, and Timothy will accompany Father at the end of next month on his trip to Windham. He's researching the site of an upcoming project there, after hearing that taxes in New Hampshire are far less onerous. I worry Father will become enamored of yet another untapped New England paradise. Me, I'd prefer to stay at Dream House 'til death do us part. And perhaps even longer than that.

Until then,
Mary F. S. Hopkins

December 10, 1890

Dear Searles' Folly,

That's what Merritt has called you! Searles' Folly. We've been cross with one another, for he's had the indecency to ask Father for my hand after I told him I wasn't ready. I don't see what the rush is, don't see why we shouldn't be allowed to court one another for longer than a single turn of the seasons. I could tell my reaction made Merritt angry, though he tried very hard to hide it. My lady's maid, Helen, believes his anger is a symptom of his love for me, but his short temper makes me fear for what things could be like if I were to bind myself to him in marriage. Still, in all other regards, Merritt is a kind and caring person. I will give him the benefit of the doubt while I push off a possible engagement.

Father won't travel to Windham until next month in order to be at White Hall for the holidays. It's hard to let Merritt's antics upset me when I'm spending evenings reading hearthside while the ocean pounds the cliffs below and a twelve-foot tree sparkles with great glass ornaments in the foyer.

Yours, even in folly,
—Mary

January 19, 1891

Merritt and I have rekindled the respect and friendship of our initial bond. He's backed off from speaking of marriage, and is content to spend our time together doing any number of pleasant and leisurely activities. We bundle up in our warmest frock coats and talk of spring and the wine production Father wishes to undertake.

Merritt also asks innumerable questions about the secret passageways my father had his father incorporate into White Hall's design, dissatisfied by the explanation that Father loves anything that makes a building unique. Things like "Do the partitions only open from the tunnels or can they be accessed from individual rooms?" (Answer: only the partition in the dining room opens both ways) and "Are the tunnels soundproof?" (Answer: What a silly question! I have no idea.).

I've warned Merritt to save his inquiries for when we are alone, for none of the servants are privy to the tunnels' existence. Part of Father's deal with the elder Mr.

Dempsey was that the tunnels were to remain a secret to anyone other than he, the architect, and the off-island builders. By right, Merritt should be as ignorant as the servants. Not even Helen knows of them.

Speaking of Helen, when my family leaves for Windham in a week and a half, I've enlisted her to help the kitchen staff whip up the grandest of suppers for Mr. Dempsey. We'll pretend we're lord and lady of White Hall (no, I don't want to rush into marriage, but that doesn't mean I can't have a little fun working through my reservations). We'll sit by the fire and read aloud to one another from John William Polidori or, if I'm feeling brave, this wholly terrifying novella that came out just last summer in Lippincott's Monthly, The Picture of Dorian Gray by Oscar Wilde. I love a creepy tale of gothic horror, as long as there's a bit of company about.

And though I've meant for dinner to be a surprise, I couldn't help myself, and have already alluded to the evening's festivities. Merritt was tickled when I told him. "We'll have the whole house to ourselves?" he demanded. I told him not to get too excited; the servants will be present in full force, and Helen is not one to leave my side, even when Merritt is around, to his full and utter dismay. Going to speak to Martha now about a seafood cioppino dish I know Merritt will relish!

In joy and haste,
MFSH

January 27, 1891

The dining room is set, the wine has been brought up from the cellar, and the kitchen is a bustle of activity. Father and the rest of the family departed at noon, so I've had several hours to prepare. I've chosen a maroon silk dress with chenille fringe, beads like black rutilated quartz, and carbon-colored lace. Helen has adjusted the boned bodice, fluffed the ruffles of my train, and smoothed the fringe-trimmed sleeves. "The Maiden of the Manor," she gushed as I twirled around. "The Mulberry Maiden," said I.

I've asked Helen if she will leave us once dinner is served, but she insists on being present. "I must ensure not a single impropriety occurs." She can suit herself, I suppose. I can't imagine what she thinks might happen. Merritt has seen the error of his ways and no longer pursues an early engagement. He knows he has to wait, and so wait he will. Alas, my waiting is no more! I hear him knocking. I'll receive him in the parlor.

Thank you, my Dream House, for being the perfect setting for what is sure to be a night to remember for this Mulberry Maiden and her doting, dashing lover. More tomorrow, for I fear I may be too giddy with wine later to provide anything like an accurate report!

-M

January 27 or 28, 1891—time unknown

Oh, to whoever fishes this journal out of the dungeon in which I find myself, please know how hard I tried to get free. I'm not sure how long after the fall I was unconscious, but my screams have gone unanswered. Or perhaps, the mansion walls are too thick to penetrate with mere sound. Alas, if I want my poor charge's journal to *be a record of what's happened, I have to get it down as coherently as possible. I'll start where dear Mary left off. My heart hurts at how differently this evening turned out from what she expected.*

Merritt Dempsey arrived, and he and Mary spent some time in the parlor, after which I informed them supper was ready. They took their seats in the dining room, the food was served, and Merritt dismissed all the servants, including me, from the room. "I'll be staying right here with Miss Mary," I told him, and he was about to protest, but Mary, good girl that she is, nodded her head. Merritt glowered at me and returned to his seat. No sooner had Mary buttered a slice of bread than Merritt started in about his love for her and his hope for their future.

"I thought we were past this," Mary muttered, and poured herself a glass of wine. "In fact," she said, "I find this topic quite boring. Can we change the subject?"

He sprang at her so fast, Mary was at a loss. She tried to stand, but he shoved her down by the shoulders. "I've had enough of your games," he growled. "You love me. Why the hell won't you marry me?" Mary, bless her heart, set her jaw, though she must have been terrified. "Whatever slight chance there was of me marrying you dissipated the moment you put your hands on me."

Merritt yanked her back by the hair, and Mary yelped. "You don't understand," he said. "My family will take possession of White Hall. My father showed your father a design for a project he wished to build, and your father stole it. If you don't marry me, I'll kill you. Then, when your family returns, I'll marry your sister."

She started to retort, and he yanked her head back again. "The only word I will hear from you now is 'yes.'"

"Never," she spat. He released her hair and slapped her. She did not make a sound, and Lord forgive me, neither did I.

"Here," he said, and shoved this journal at her. He'd taken it from the parlor sideboard and stashed it in his waistband. "If you refuse, then you write your own suicide note." She started to protest again, and he put his face not half an inch from hers. "If you don't, I won't court your sister. I'll kill her too."

Silent tears streamed down Mary's face, and I knew we were done for. Mary loves Susanne too much to risk her being hurt. "Write that you told me you were ready, that you begged me to marry you, and I changed my mind," Merritt said. He went to the cabinet. The cursed rats had been terrible all winter, so the bottles of arsenic were plenty. He poured the poison into Mary's wine. "Then you will drink this. Or I will make Susanne wish she'd never been born."

Mary scribbled several sentences. I didn't see them. Merritt tore the page from this book and placed it under her glass. He threw the journal aside, and I snatched it up, along with a bread knife, believing, foolishly, that the opportunity to wield a weapon might present itself. Of course, no opportunity came. I cannot, will not, detail the horror of Mary's death. Mary was a kind and beautiful soul. She did not deserve to suffer as she did.

When she lay still, Merritt came to where I cowered in the corner. "What to do with you?" He walked to the fireplace, knelt hearthside, and pushed against the back wall. I thought he'd lost his mind, but a second later, the wall opened into a yawning partition. Beyond was a black pit. I screamed, but he forced me through.

My fall was broken by packed dirt and unyielding stone. Mary's journal was splayed on the ground beside me. I had a small candle in my apron pocket and a book of matches. I'm writing by the light of the candle now, but its flame grows weaker with every word.

Before it goes out, I must find somewhere to hide this journal. Merritt Dempsey will come for me. Of that, I have no doubt. I can only pray he takes my body from this labyrinth of endless night to a proper resting place, even if it's unknown to anyone but him. I also pray sweet Susanne escapes this monster's clutches and that every Searles woman from now until the day White Hall—God willing—burns to the ground or falls into the ocean sees the Dempseys' wine for the noxious poison it is.

The candle's almost out, but I've found a place behind the wall. A hidden spot, too small to harbor me but perfect for a journal.

Farewell, pages, farewell, pen. Farewell, light, giving way to endless midnight. Hello, footsteps.

Hello, Mary, dearest friend.
—Helen Gilbert Brown

Chapter 41

Sarah drives the taxi with such recklessness, Thalia should be shouting at her to slow down, but her thoughts are in the dark with Helen Gilbert Brown in 1891, and in the hospital with Maureen in 1992. All her lawyerly tricks for staying focused, for allowing only the essential details through a funnel of intellectual discernment, fall flat. This is the most mind-bending case she's ever been involved with, and it's her life.

"Are you okay?" Sarah asks. "Sorry, don't answer that. I don't know what else to say."

"Me either." Thalia shifts in her seat to look at her friend. "You're sure when you left Above the Rocks, Martin was heading in the direction of the mansion? There's no chance we're going to walk into the hospital right now and Martin's going to be there, waiting to vindicate his brother's reputation?"

"Yes, he was heading toward the mansion. Well, I'm pretty sure he was. I mean, I don't know. I think so."

"Okay. Well, great," Thalia says, and somehow they both laugh.

"You know," Sarah says and turns left onto Pilot Hill Road, "Blake's letter doesn't seem so strange anymore."

"It doesn't," Thalia says. "But there are still some things I can't figure out. Like, if Martin found out Michael sexually assaulted two women and subsequently helped him hide out at White Hall, what did he tell Fiona and Aileen? It couldn't have been the truth, otherwise, Fiona would have pointed the police toward Michael as a possible suspect rather than going down for murder. So what do the sisters know? And if Fiona wasn't using the tunnels to 'haunt' Blake, who was the woman Blake saw? Also . . ."

"Also, what?"

"Also, I can't help but wonder, with all these horrible things coming to light, did my mother really overdose? Or did someone force her to swallow those pills?"

Sarah doesn't answer, and the questions hang over them as they screech into a parking space and jog through the hospital's automatic doors. The nurse in ICU smiles in greeting, but the smile drops when her gaze lands on Thalia.

"Ms. Mills? I'm so sorry, but you'll have to wait a little longer before going in to see your mother. I know we told the secondary contact listed—nice to see you, Mrs. Sherman—that Maureen was awake, but Dr. Maddox needs to conduct a few more procedures. Your mother's digestive system shut down while she was unconscious, and she's still very weak. I said the same thing to Martin Dempsey when he tried to see her an hour ago."

Sarah starts to speak, but Thalia grabs her arm. "Thank you"—she peers at the woman's badge—"Nurse Meeks. Not a problem. Could you do me a favor? I'd like to speak with my mother alone before anyone else is permitted to see her. If Martin returns while we're with her, could you see to it that he's made aware of my request for privacy?"

The nurse nods. "Of course, Ms. Mills. Mr. Dempsey did mention he'd be back. I didn't say anything to him because, well, he's pretty much the busiest and most important man in town, but I thought it was a little much for Maureen to see her boss's face upon waking up from a four-day coma."

Thalia thanks the nurse and moves to the waiting area. Fifteen minutes pass before Dr. Maddox appears. There's an air of hopefulness about him that was absent at their last meeting, and Thalia can't help but feel buoyed by this.

"We moved her to a room at the end of the hall," he says. "She's still got a long way to go." Dr. Maddox lowers his voice. "I wouldn't go bringing much more to her right now than love and well-wishes."

Thalia cocks her head. "What do you mean?"

"I know you're probably concerned for your mother's mental health, but now's not the time to go digging into the circumstances of why she overdosed."

"But she's stable?" Thalia asks. Guilt is already settling into her gut as she considers what she *is* about to bring to her mother. But she has the distinct feeling that upsetting Maureen now will have less dire consequences than saying nothing until her mother is better.

"She's stable." He gives her a final warning look that says, *But things can change.* "Take a left at the end of the hall. It's the last door on the right, by the staircase."

Thalia thanks him and starts down the corridor. She looks back to find Sarah isn't following. "What are you doing? Come on."

"I'll wait here and keep an eye out for our town selectman."

Thalia grabs Sarah's arm and pulls her forward. "Don't be ridiculous. I need you in there. We've come this far. Don't abandon me now."

Sarah relents. They take a left. The door to the stairwell up ahead is just closing. The distance between the left-hand turn and the last pair of rooms is short, and they reach Room 215 in a matter of seconds. With the documents from Maureen's safe tucked securely under Thalia's arm, she turns the doorknob and steps inside.

The room is warm and quiet. Too quiet. No hum of machines or rustling of bedclothes. For a moment, she thinks Maureen is asleep, or . . . *No! Please no! Has she slipped back into a coma?* Thalia walks forward on quaking legs, reaches out, and pulls down the sheets.

There's nothing on the mattress but a heap of pillows and a crimson splotch of blood. A second later, the bedside monitor emits a high-pitched tone that sends a chill down Thalia's spine. A shout comes from down the hall. It's answered by another, louder voice. There's a sound like a crash cart slamming into a wall.

The crash cart won't matter. Doctors and nurses can do nothing. Maureen Mills has vanished into thin air. A smudge of red on the bed tray catches Thalia's eye. She slides a plastic pitcher of water over. Two letters are written in blood on the shiny surface:

W H

Thalia looks at Sarah. Her best friend's face is grim, eyes wide. Thalia cannot move. She cannot speak. Cannot conceptualize how someone has beat them here, taken Maureen. Thalia is too late. Twenty-six years too late when it comes to the information in her purse. Perhaps only twenty-six seconds too late to keep her mother safe from whatever waits for her at White Hall.

Thalia opens her mouth, but Sarah is already holding out the keys to the taxi. "Go," she says. "I'll stay here and deal with the hospital staff. See if they can pull the security footage. Text me, tell me everything that's going on, so I'll know when to call the police. I'll call the department on the mainland. Bypass Martin's stranglehold on the island."

Thalia goes to hug her, but Sarah pushes her away. "Get out of here before you're asked a million questions you don't know the answers to!"

Thalia darts from the room and into the stairwell. Less than half-way down each flight, she jumps to the next landing. Her hand slides over the rail like a fish skimming the surface of the ocean. The sound of her feet slamming into the landing is a harbor cannon punctuating the sunset.

Chapter 42

Upon pulling up to White Hall, Thalia sees that the front door is hanging open. She rips the key from the taxi's ignition, shoves the ring into her pocket, and creeps toward the mansion. It's raining, and though she should be used to the patter of it on the roof, the windows, the concrete, the grass, her skin, the island, it's driving her crazy. It's a distraction, an infuriating buzz of endless white noise that makes parsing separate, more dangerous sounds—like footsteps and exhalations—all but impossible.

Thalia slinks over the threshold, but her stealth doesn't matter. The foyer is empty, and when she checks the parlor, she finds it empty too. The guilt she felt at the hospital sinks lower in her stomach, becomes a brick of dread, and as she creeps toward the kitchen, she wonders if it's possible for Aileen to lie there still, in a heap of mulberry crepes. Taking a deep breath, she pushes open the door.

The plate of pancakes *is* on the table, but there's no sign of Aileen. A sweep of the entire first floor, including several rooms she's never been in, turns up neither the proprietress nor her mother. Thalia returns to the foyer, looking warily at the looming staircase. Mary Hopkins Searles stares at Thalia from the prison of her portrait, and Thalia considers how deeply the rot of the ruinous Dempsey family penetrates, how much White Hall has functioned as the veritable spiderweb Blake saw it to be.

Two floors up, in a clawfoot tub of an otherwise unremarkable room, is her sister's deathbed. Somewhere in this haunted house, her mother, dragging every hurtful thing Thalia ever said in response to her overbearing overprotectiveness, wanders, dazed and in need of further medical attention. So much death and horror and mystery and misery can be traced back to this house. Helen had written that she prayed every Searles woman would see the Dempseys' wine for the poison it was from now until the day White Hall burns to the ground or falls into the ocean. Thalia wouldn't mind seeing either of those endings come to pass.

At the top of the staircase, she goes left, but a noise comes from behind her. She turns, eyes darting between the two doors on either side of the hallway. The noise comes again, a moan from the room on the left. She moves forward and turns the knob before she can lose her nerve. The door opens with a terrible squeaking of hinges.

Aileen Searles lies on the bed, her face a mess of purple bruises. She holds her left arm across her body in a way that suggests she's in immense pain. Her feet are bare and the toes of her left foot are black, crooked, and bleeding, as if the bones were crushed by an incredible weight. She rocks ever so slightly, as if trying to distract herself from the pain. She murmurs to herself, but the murmur rises in volume to another moan. Despite the squeaking hinges, Thalia's entrance seems, somehow, to have gone unnoticed. A moment later, however, the proprietress looks up.

"Nooo," Aileen cries with surprising force, then hisses in pain. "Get away from me. Don't come any closer."

Thalia gapes. "Aileen, what's going on? Who did this to you? Let me help you."

Aileen lets out a bark of ironic laughter, miserable and crazed. "Now you offer to help after you drugged and beat me senseless. Martin was right. You're as crazy as your mother." She sneers through her pain. "As crazy as your addict sister. Just because I found that bottle of wine I gave her out in the replica doesn't mean she wasn't a drunk."

Even ignoring this last part, it takes a moment for Thalia's mouth to catch up to her brain. "*I* did this to you? Are you insane? I wouldn't . . .

how could you think—" She pauses, collecting herself so that she can speak coherently. "Aileen, you are mistaken. I absolutely did not do this," she says.

Aileen laughs again, doubles over, then screams through gritted teeth and backs off her injured arm. "I was eating breakfast with *you*," she says. "A meal you returned to White Hall *specifically* to ask me to make. You insisted I have wine with you. You put something in my drink."

Thalia is so shocked by the woman's allegations of violence that it takes her a moment to remember she *had* drugged her sangria. "Okay," she says, "I need you to listen to me, because this is going to sound crazy, but I swear to you it's the truth. I did put something in your drink. An antianxiety medication. You obviously knew about White Hall's secret passageways. I needed to get to them unimpeded. I wasn't sure what your part has been in everything that's gone on here, so I needed to ensure I'd be left alone for the duration of my mission."

It does sound crazy, and like a bogus lie, and now that she's face-to-face with the inadvertent result of her hasty decision, she feels nothing but shame and horror. "I'm so sorry this happened to you. I thought it would be safer for both of us if you didn't know what I was doing."

Aileen says nothing, so Thalia continues, "Aileen, where's Martin? Why has he been in and out of White Hall since I checked in? Is he here now, with my mother?" She pauses, then says, "I think Maureen only overdosed because she was *forced* to swallow that many pills, and I think I know who might have done this to you." She approaches the bed cautiously, hands raised, needing Aileen to trust her. "How well do you really know Monty?" she asks.

As much as it can, Aileen's swollen face twists with confusion. "Monty? What does he have to do with any of this?"

"I think Monty is really Michael Dempsey, Martin's brother. I think Martin's been hiding him since right after Hurricane Bob, hoping to shield him from the repercussions of gambling debts and bad business deals—which I think you and Fiona knew about—and of raping two women—which I'm guessing you didn't."

"That's absurd," Aileen says, and her disbelief seems genuine. "Michael Dempsey died trying to keep his father's yacht from sinking in the storm."

"And if he hadn't? It couldn't have taken much to persuade Martin's girlfriend and her sister to help out the Dempseys—powerful family that they are—by giving Michael a job, a fake name, and a place to live here."

Aileen is shaking her head. "That never happened. You're crazy."

Thalia can't tell if Aileen's stubbornness is to maintain a lie more than two decades in the making or because she truly doesn't believe the Dempsey brothers capable of such a thing. "How well do you really even know Martin?" Thalia pushes.

Unexpectedly, Aileen smiles. "How well do I know him? Let me see. I know it might surprise someone like you, a slim, pretty, intelligent lawyer from the city, someone just like my sister in her business-woman condescension and snootiness, but Martin is my fiancé. We're going to be married as soon as my sister is sentenced."

"Fiancé," Thalia echoes. Shock crests and crashes like whitecaps. "So," she says when she's found her voice, "Martin would become part owner of White Hall?" *Just like Merritt wanted in 1891.*

Aileen stares at her, defiant.

"Would you sign some sort of prenuptial agreement?"

The question seems superfluous; if Martin owned White Hall, he wouldn't need to manipulate anyone to keep his brother's crimes—or his great-great-grandfather's, for that matter—hidden. No wonder he wanted Thalia—with her relentless pursuit of information—out of the picture.

Aileen scoffs. "We don't need a prenup. Martin had been growing apart from Fiona long before she did what she did. He confessed his feelings for me when she was arrested. I had always felt the same. Fiona never appreciated him. He tried to win her over for close to thirty years, and she dragged him along with no plans to ever marry him."

Fiona's words from the jailhouse—*Aileen has as much capacity for murder as a lamb*—come back to Thalia. The thing about lambs is, they're easily led.

"Rule number one, Aileen," Thalia whispers.

"Huh?"

"It's rule number one. For surviving a gothic novel. Be wary of opportunistic men." Something else occurs to Thalia. "Fiona didn't sneak into Blake's room and 'haunt' her, did she?"

Through her pain, Aileen looks pleased. "Blake only came to Block Island to cause trouble. That's what Martin told me. That she and Maureen cooked this whole thing up to get their hands on some Dempsey money. My job was to scare her away."

Dempsey money. Does this prove Martin knew his brother was Blake's father and that he told Aileen as much? "And when it didn't work?" Thalia asks. "When Blake remained on the island, did Martin ask you to kill her too?"

Anger flashes in Aileen's swollen eyes. "Of course not," she says. "That's ridiculous. Fiona killed her. How were Martin and I supposed to know Fiona was going to misconstrue Martin's interest in the girl as sexual impropriety? Fiona's jealousy was one more symptom of her unhealthy relationship with Martin. She didn't want him, but she didn't want anyone else to have him either."

Thalia sees unmitigated conviction on Aileen's face. The B and B proprietress was manipulated by Martin just as methodically as Blake, Maureen, and Fiona were. Fiona didn't kill Blake Bronson. Monty—no, she has to stop calling him that, *Michael*—did. Framing Fiona for Blake's murder got both women out of the way.

"Aileen, where is Martin now?"

"When I came to after you drugged and beat me," she spits, "Martin was helping me into bed. He said your Valium-addicted gold digger of a mother had just shown up, and he needed to deal with her."

"You saw Maureen?"

"No," Aileen admits. "And if I had to guess, I'd say she's gone already. Martin probably called the police so they could arrest her on charges of extortion. He needs to get them back here so they can get you for assault and battery next!"

"Okay, Aileen." Thalia's losing her patience. "But if Maureen came to White Hall, where was she while Martin was helping you?"

Aileen inserts her good hand beneath her injured one so that her arms are folded across her chest. "In the tunnels of course. Where else was he going to put her so she couldn't run off?"

Thalia doesn't wait for Aileen to elaborate. She sprints from the room and into the hallway. *Think, goddammit, think.* From which rooms does she know how to access the tunnels? Besides the trapdoor in the replica, there's her room, Blake's, and the linen closet. She starts toward her room. If she can't force the partition in the fireplace open, she will smash through it with the pewter candelabra. Once she enters the tunnels, how long will it take to find her mother? And what if Martin is down there with Maureen? What will she do then?

"Looking for me?" Martin growls from right behind her.

Chapter 43

Thalia lunges past Martin, hoping to lock him out of her room long enough to get to the partition. He catches her at the door and shoves her forward. Thalia collides with the metal footboard. She grits her teeth, refusing to give him the satisfaction of crying out.

"You're as nosy as your sister was," he says.

Thalia scrambles to her feet. "And you are as sociopathic as your brother. And your father. And your great-great-grandfather, Merritt."

Martin laughs. "I saw that you ransacked my safe, so I figured I'd had company during my last trip to the tunnels from the dining room hearth. Did you know that's the only partition that opens both ways? I also know the only place you could have brought the safe's contents to is the Liang-Sherman residence. Patrick Sherman—that sad sap of a man and even poorer excuse for a fisherman—will be more than willing to hand everything over if I pay him a visit while his little daughters are home. And if it's Ms. Liang I encounter, well"—he laughs again—"I can't imagine I'll get much of a fight from our resident taxi driver."

"That's what the men in your family do, isn't it?" Thalia asks. "Go after little girls and vulnerable women. Does it make you feel good? To hurt those so much less powerful than you?"

Martin groans. "I'm not a lawyer in one of your courtrooms. I'm not interested in discussing any of this. I get it, you know everything. You've figured everything out. And now, I have to deal with you accordingly."

"Still," Thalia says, ignoring the fear that climbs like ivy up her throat, "there are a few things it wouldn't hurt to tell me. Like how did Blake get my address?"

Martin rolls his eyes. He wasn't kidding; he is bored with her. "I gave it to her, of course," he says. "Everything I did was to expedite the moment in which she would disappear. First, I hoped she'd just leave the island, so I showed her what a miserable loon your Maureen is. When that didn't work, I tried to get her back inside White Hall from her idiotic trek out to the replica. A little white lie about speaking to you and dangling your address in front of her nose—which was easy enough to find—seemed as good a ploy as any."

"You wanted her back inside so Monty could kill her."

The surprise on Martin's face is too genuine. The second she sees it, Thalia knows she is wrong. Michael, Monty—whatever his name really is—didn't kill Blake. Martin did. To keep her from exposing his brother.

"You killed Blake," Thalia says incredulously. "It was you."

"Yes," Martin says. "I killed her. You thought . . . ? Oh, that's rich." He actually laughs. "My only regret is I didn't do it before she wrote you that letter."

No excuses. No more pinning it on poor Fiona, a woman with whom he spent close to three decades.

"I even dressed in black and put Aileen's silly little veil over my face," he continues. "Aileen was good enough at sneaking into your sister's room to see if there was anything we could use against her, but I had to coach her quite a bit before she was able to pull off the 'Victorian ghost' ensemble. Aileen told me about the nonsense Blake wrote in her journal, that White Hall was like a spiderweb. That she thought she was the heroine of some stupid book. I played into Blake's little haunted-house fantasy until the last."

Thalia is sickened, but she needs to keep him talking. "And Maureen's safe?" she asks. "If there was such valuable information in it, why did you let her have it at all? Why did you keep her *alive* at all?"

He smiles the toothy, jagged shark smile. "Because letting Maureen think she was keeping her secrets, that she had some semblance of control, meant she made no trouble for me. It allowed her to believe she had the ability to keep *you*, her precious daughter, safe. Why kill her when I could keep her docile?"

Martin actually appears to be stifling a yawn, and just as a voice in Thalia's head yells at her to watch out, to not be lulled into the false belief that he's going to continue engaging with her, he crosses the room in two long strides and grabs her—one hand on the back of her neck, squeezing so hard her vision goes black, the other tangled in her hair. Martin drags her toward the fireplace. The partition is already open. He knew she was coming. Probably heard her entire conversation with Aileen while he lurked in the hallway like a spider.

He tosses her through, and her bones knock against the sides of the partition like the limbs of a doll forced through the opening of a gift box. The skin along her lower back scrapes against splintered wood, and grit embeds itself in her elbows, but still, Thalia doesn't make a sound.

The second she hits the floor, she turns and scrabbles her hands up the wall, trying to insert her fingers between the partition and the wall, anything to keep it from closing behind her. She's too late. And not only that, but she hears the low scrape of a piece of furniture being dragged into the firebox and pushed against the partition. When she tries to turn the spring mechanism, nothing happens. The wood doesn't have the space it needs to rotate. This is no longer a possible way out. But there are others in the tunnel system. At least, for now.

She sprints down the passage—her phone's light bobbing wildly—and cuts right at the first fork. At the tunnel's end, however, the partition into the conference room will not budge. Thalia thinks of Martin's words just a few moments ago, thinks of the lady's maid, Helen: *Only the partition in the dining room opens both ways.* Merritt threw Helen into the passage after forcing Mary to drink arsenic, and Helen was never heard from again. A fluttery burst of panic explodes in her chest. There are dozens of trapdoors and swinging partitions into the mansion;

there's no way Martin could have blocked them all. Then again, if this is the closest a Dempsey has gotten to possessing White Hall in one-and-a-quarter centuries, Martin wouldn't want to take any chances.

She has to find Maureen and make it to the bathhouse. She has to believe there's at least one exit to the outside world still available to them. As she makes her way toward the six-way split, she checks her phone, but there are no messages. No bars. Not even a flicker of service as the strobe bounces over the tunnel walls. Walls she prays don't become those of her and her mother's tomb.

She is maybe two minutes from Martin's stone safe when her sneakers catch in something—a drop cloth or some other inexplicable length of fabric—spread across the ground. She stumbles, trying to remain upright, but whatever she's run into has wrapped around her ankles, and she loses her balance. Thalia goes down hard onto her hands and knees. Her cell phone skids away from her, stopping at the base of the wall. She reaches out for it, and as she does, the pile of dark fabric beside her groans.

Her fingers wrap around the phone, and she lifts it, illuminating the faded pattern of a hospital gown, then her mother's pinched, pale face. "Mom," Thalia says, crawling forward. "Mom, are you okay? Can you hear me?"

Maureen tries to sit up, but groans again. Her chin bobs with the chatter of her teeth.

"Mom, I'm going to help you sit up, okay?" Thalia puts an arm under Maureen's shoulder and helps her into a more comfortable position.

"Is he down here?" Maureen asks.

"No. But we have to get out before he blocks the exits. Can you walk?"

Maureen makes no effort to get up. She groans again, not in pain or discomfort but frustration. "Why did you come back here?" she asks. "He would have left you alone if you'd just stopped digging. Now that Blake's gone, and he's realized Aileen's the sister who's going to give him what he wants, I was the only thing standing in his way. As soon as he threw me down here, you would have been safe."

"We can still expose him. Together. We just have to get out of here first."

Her mother shakes her head. "We're not going to get out." Her voice is the creak of a wire-and-wood gate across a sandy boardwalk. Thalia feels the fluttery, nauseating burst of panic again, settling deeper, dropping below her stomach, into her lower back and legs.

"Please, Mom, get up. There are lots of ways out, we just have to move quickly."

"It's pointless," Maureen says. In the flashlight's glow, her face is pale, the circles beneath her eyes as black as oceans. But Thalia can still see it. Her mother is no longer terrified, not like she was when Thalia spoke to her that first day back on the island. She's resigned now. She's given up.

"I'm so sorry," Thalia says. "I never dreamed my coming here would lead to all this, but I've learned things. Things beyond who Blake was, how she came to—"

"I didn't end up in a coma because you came here."

"Mom, please, for once in your life, just listen! I found your safe down in these tunnels. Well, first I found it in your closet, but Martin stole it, then I found it again, but the point is, I read about what happened. How Blake was conceived." She takes her mother's hands in hers. "I know everything, Mom. And I'm not scared. I'm not going to run away again."

Maureen's face changes. Thalia sees it. Sees that Maureen still hadn't believed Thalia knew what happened at Graham's Resort twenty-seven years prior, despite things having progressed to their being thrown into a secret tunnel system beneath a murder mansion. Thalia puts a hand on her mother's arm. "I *know*," she says. "I know Michael Dempsey was Blake's father. I know he's the one who assaulted you, who raped you, when you confronted him about Ethel." It's torture, saying the words, but there can be no more hiding. A hundred feet beneath the earth, it's time to expose the Mills family's secrets to the light.

But her mother's face is wrong, somehow. Thalia expected fear and hurt and sadness. What she did not expect was the expression of pity that twists Maureen's features.

"My sweet," Maureen says. "My Thalia. My love. I love you so, so much. And I'm so sorry. But you are wrong." She pauses. "How to say this. I don't *want* to say this. But if we die down here—"

"We're not going to die," Thalia interrupts. "Please, just tell me."

Maureen expels a shuddering sigh, reaches out, and takes Thalia's face between her hands. "In July of 1991, I finished a shift at Above the Rocks," she says. "I told Martin Dempsey I needed to speak with him about something, and he suggested we go to Graham's Resort. He forced me to drink some mulberry wine with him, acted like he needed to steel himself for whatever I was going to say. It didn't matter. I never got the chance to tell him what Michael did.

"Martin raped me. We were in a room so close to the beach, I could hear the waves against the shore. I've been in a prison cell ever since, the bars of which are those deceptively benign lapping waves. I hear them constantly, rain or shine, though in the rain, they're much, much worse. I hear them whether awake or asleep. I hear them now. Occasionally, they go away, if I take enough Valium. No, my sweet. My love. I told the nurse at the hospital the baby's father perished in the hurricane to protect us. *Martin* is Blake's father. But Michael Dempsey did assault me. Two years before he made Ethel's life a living hell. That's why he wanted their relationship to remain secret once he realized she and I were friends. Michael Dempsey raped me in 1989. The details—where, why, how—don't really matter. What matters is that Michael Dempsey was your father."

Chapter 44

The tunnels have become a tomb, after all, for a part of Thalia has died. She feels neither hard ground beneath her nor Maureen's soft touch. She feels no horror or pain or shock. She feels only the dissolution of hope—like fog under the glare of a midday sun—that someday a kind-faced, slightly familiar-looking stranger might reach out to her on AncestryDNA and say, *Thalia, let me explain . . .* It's the discovery of that hope having existed at all—buried somewhere in her psyche like bones in a hidden alcove—that threatens to obliterate her in this moment.

Thalia watches tears stream down Maureen's face and soak the collar of her hospital gown. She reaches up to take Maureen's hands and, in doing so, comes back to herself.

"You must have been so scared." She wipes her mother's face with her sleeve. "Having to live on the island with Martin and Michael all these years."

Maureen's brow crinkles. "Michael?"

"Michael didn't die in that hurricane," Thalia says. "Martin convinced Fiona to let him hide out here under an assumed name."

Maureen shakes her head. "That's impossible. I snuck into the morgue myself. I needed to know at least one of my monsters was gone. I saw his body."

Thalia stares. "But the groundskeeper, Monty . . ."

"Couldn't be Michael," Maureen finishes for her.

"Then who is he? How does he know that Blake was my sister?" Thalia asks.

The questions hang in the stagnant air. Suddenly, Maureen sniffles and says, "Martin made me put our names in that guest book to mock me. *Maureen Mills, a.k.a. the Mulberry Maiden, and her Doting, Dashing Lover.* He called me that that night, though never since. Afterward, he said as long as I acted like it never happened, like Blake never happened, he would leave you—the child he believed was the product of some faceless tourist—alone. Everything I did, I did to protect you. My baby. The baby I already had. That I loved more than I loved myself. You were the only thing I cared about, so Martin knew threatening your safety would keep me quiet. And it worked. I did keep quiet, and it kept you safe."

"That's why you worked at the restaurant," Thalia says. "He made you. So he could keep an eye on you. That's why he made sure you got addicted to your medication, so he could keep you under his thumb."

Maureen nods. "And why he paid me enough to afford the house on Cooneymus Road. Not everything Martin does makes sense. But it always makes sense to Martin. He plays by his own rules in a world entirely of his making." Her head jerks up, and she grabs Thalia's wrist. "I didn't overdose," she says vehemently. "Martin came to the house right after you left that morning. He meant to kill me, and he failed. He won't fail again. I don't know exactly what happened to Blake, but I know she's dead because Martin needed to keep her identity a secret. He's worked too hard to become the most powerful man on Block Island to let my illegitimate daughter expose him for the rapist he is."

"I know what happened to Blake," Thalia says quietly. "Martin tricked Aileen Searles into believing he loves her. They're going to be married. A Dempsey will finally own White Hall, and a Dempsey will finally have control over ensuring the bodies buried within these tunnels *stay* buried. Martin manipulated Aileen and, in turn, tricked Fiona into believing he and Blake were having an affair." She'd put it together when Aileen was talking about Fiona misconstruing Martin's interest in Blake, and when Aileen had insisted on not needing a prenup, but Thalia still feels light-headed from the wallop of finally arranging the puzzle pieces into a coherent picture.

"Martin killed Blake," she continues, gaining confidence in her understanding of things, in the solidification of the story. "Then he laid everything out as perfectly as if he were plotting a novel, and all the clues—his jacket and umbrella in her room, being seen together all over the island, the fingerprints on the knife—pointed to Fiona having murdered Blake. Once Fiona was arrested, Blake was dead, and you were silenced, he was free to marry Aileen."

"He staged an affair with his own daughter?"

"Yes, but neither Fiona nor Aileen knew that he staged it. Aileen believes Fiona misconstrued Martin's interest in Blake. When I went to see Fiona, she thought *you* might have killed her. No one knows the truth but Martin, me, and you. Well, and Sarah." Thalia prays Sarah doesn't come to White Hall. That she calls the police on the mainland and stays far, far away. She already lost her biological sister. She can't lose the person who's *acted* as her sister too.

"It's all my fault," Maureen says. "I should have told Blake the truth. I thought I was helping her by refusing to let her connection to me come to light."

"This is *not* your fault. Martin did what he did because there's a sickness in that family. He's just like"—Thalia forces herself to say her father's name—"Michael, and like Merritt."

"Who's Merritt?"

"His great-great-grandfather a hundred years earlier. Martin wanted you—to hurt you, to possess you—twenty-seven years ago, but he was with Fiona, and because he's a monster, he took you anyway. Merritt, Michael, and every other Dempsey man in between has failed to gain possession of White Hall. If Fiona had found out what Martin did to you, there would have been no chance she would have married him." Thalia takes Maureen's hands. "Don't you see? We *have* to get out of here. If we don't, no one will even find our bodies. Blake will have died for nothing. Fiona will go to prison. And as soon as the dust settles, Martin will kill Aileen too."

Maureen makes no move to get up. The fluttery panic inside Thalia grows. Thalia pushes it away. *I won't leave her behind like I did ten years ago. I won't leave her like she left Blake.*

Thalia stands, and in doing so, lifts her mother to her feet. Maureen sucks in a breath and holds one hand to her rib cage. Dr. Maddox said her mother's digestive tract had shut down. She needs to get Maureen back to the hospital as soon as possible. She needs something to push aside the skull-vibrating chant—Michael Dempsey was your father, Michael Dempsey *was your father*—and get them moving.

"Remember *Northanger Abbey*?" Thalia asks. Maureen looks puzzled, but when she responds in the affirmative, Thalia ducks under her mother's arm, grabs her around the waist, and propels them forward slightly. As they walk, Thalia rambles out details of the novel's plot. It's difficult, keeping up the constant chatter while bearing a good deal of Maureen's weight, but she manages.

"You know," Thalia says eventually. She's breathing hard but refuses to slow. "Martin makes General Tilney look like the most milquetoast of antagonists. I don't care what Jane Austen thought she was doing." Her mother makes a sound that very well might be a laugh.

They pass the split down which is the tomb Thalia now knows to belong to Helen Gilbert Brown. She thinks of Ethel, of the possibility that the librarian will soon know of her great-great-great-grandmother's fate. They're close now. Thalia concentrates on not letting the prospect of daylight excite her into making a mistake.

Finally, she sees the staircase that will carry them up to the bathhouse. She leans Maureen against the wall and puts a finger to her lips. "Even if this door is unlocked, it's a long way to where I parked Sarah's taxi, and we can't be sure Martin hasn't moved it somewhere or slashed the tires. We need to stay one step ahead of him until I can get enough service to call for help."

Maureen slumps against the crumbling archway. Thalia climbs the stairs slowly, hoping to mitigate the sound of grit against stone. At the top, she lifts her hands. *Please, please, let it open.* She places her palms flat against the underside of the trapdoor and pushes.

Chapter 45

For a moment, it sticks. Thalia's heart drops. Then the sea-swollen wood releases, and the trapdoor opens. Thalia expels a breath like a crashing wave and crawls out.

The sight of their escape route must give Maureen the strength she needs to move forward, because she climbs the stairs on her own. Thalia helps her mother over the lip of the trapdoor and lowers the wood. "Come on," she says and grabs a handful of her mother's hospital gown, pulling her forward. They make their way down the hall.

"What is this place?" Maureen asks.

Thalia shakes her head. There's no time to explain. She was so intent on making it out of the tunnels, she only realizes the rain has risen to a full-blown thunder-and-lightning storm upon reaching the replica's exit. She checks her cell phone. She doesn't have any service.

"There'll be a boardwalk straight ahead," Thalia says, putting her hands on her mother's shoulders. "We're going to go up it, then across the grass toward a courtyard. After that, as long as we don't see Martin, I should be able to dial 911. Then we're going to either . . ." She pauses. Every step of this escape plan is ephemeral at best, but this last stage seems too improbable to even consider. She forces herself to continue. "We'll either stay hidden under the courtyard overhang, or keep going, around the side of the house. Toward the driveway and away from the mansion."

There's so much that could go wrong, it makes her head hurt, but Maureen nods. Thalia places a hand on the door handle. Rain pelts the earth. The ocean crashes. At the next boom of thunder, Thalia braces herself and pushes open the door.

At first, there is so much rain that Thalia can't be sure what she is looking at. The nonstop precipitation over the last week has caused the ground leading up to the boardwalk to degrade into a mess of mud and foaming water. Maureen almost goes down in the soft, squishy soil. Thalia grabs her by the back of the hospital gown. The thin fabric is already soaked, and her mother's hair is plastered to her head. Thalia blinks water from her eyes and steps forward, guiding them forward as quickly as possible while maintaining their footing.

The boardwalk is maybe thirty steps away. No. Not thirty. Just one. Then another. Thirty times. Like Blake did with her sobriety, one moment stacked on top of another. Thalia owes it to her mother to stay focused, to get them out of this, to protect her; Maureen has suffered too much at the hands of her monster.

Her monster! When Thalia looks up, Martin is there, in the expanse of grass separating the lower level of the courtyard from the start of the boardwalk. He lets out a shout that might be manic glee or grim determination. Whether gleeful or grave, he'll cut them off at the pass, if not at the top of the boardwalk, then at the bottom of it.

Maureen goes rigid. Martin has progressed halfway down the lawn and is nearing the mouth of the boardwalk, pushing them into making a decision: they can go back to the tunnels—and get locked in—or over the side of the clay cliffs into the ocean. They could try for the beach, but if the tide is high, they'll be swept out to sea the same as if they jump over the bluff.

Unless . . . Thalia spins left. The entrance to the mulberry forest is maybe fifty yards away. She turns Maureen in the direction of the trees and takes her hand. "We have to make it!" Maureen, hospital gown whipping in the wind, allows Thalia to lead her.

Martin shouts again from behind them, sounding closer than before. But when Thalia risks a look back, she is shocked to see Monty Daniels sprinting over the last few feet of grass toward Martin. *Please,* she wants to shout. *Help us.* But she can't suck in enough breath, and she's not sure he would hear her anyway. For a moment, it looks as if Martin is moving too fast; the groundskeeper isn't going to reach him. *Fall,* she thinks desperately. *Trip on a loose board and impale yourself on an exposed nail.* Monty launches himself into the air and tackles Martin onto the boardwalk. The two men grapple. Monty seems to be gaining the upper hand. Then, to Thalia's horror, Martin rolls on top of Monty and pins the man's arms with his knees. He delivers blow after blow to Monty's face.

She turns away and runs faster. Lightning shoots through the sky. They enter the mulberry forest and keep running.

How long until Martin incapacitates Monty and has us in his sights again? How much ground do we need to gain before we can attempt to throw him off course? Thalia runs straight until she can almost feel Martin's presence behind them, until to wait another moment would be to lose any advantage they might still hold. She darts left, pulling Maureen with her. They run straight, then cut right. Run straight, cut right again. Branches slice at their arms.

The forest lacks the verdant, hanging coverage that full-leafed trees would have afforded them, but the number of trees is so plentiful, their root systems so close together, Thalia's pumping arms and Maureen's billowing gown can't help but get lost in the fold. Still, the next time they hear Martin, Thalia is horrified by how close he is. Maureen lags, her slick fingers coming closer and closer to slipping from Thalia's grasp. She can't go on much longer, sprinting through the root-choked forest. And there's no chance of getting her *out* of the forest and to the mansion without Martin catching them.

Thalia pulls Maureen forward another twenty feet then cuts hard to the left, angling them back in Martin's direction but farther east. She searches for the thickest conglomeration of mulberry trunks, spots a fortuitously large copse, and leads Maureen to it. When they circle the grove, Thalia can hardly believe their luck. The middle two trunks are grown together and hollowed out, vines hanging, moss and leaves sunk into the ground like a blanket, bark jutting to form a tiny eave. Thalia guides Maureen to the recess. Her mother collapses inside it. Thalia looks around, but there's no sign of Martin. She tucks her mother's feet up, removes her jacket and lays it over her, then squeezes in beside her.

Thalia breathes and lets the wind whip around them. Maureen's face is flushed despite the cold; Thalia pulls the jacket up to her chin. They can't hide forever, but she needs a minute to think. A minute to figure how the hell to get out of this.

"Do you have any idea how much I loved it when you used to read to me?" Thalia asks suddenly. Maureen looks up, startled, and Thalia smiles and burrows under her arm, the way she used to when she was a little girl and Maureen would allow her to crawl up into her bed. "You were always so strict. You only let me go to the library because of Ethel, and never to Island Bound books by myself, but you had hundreds of books on the shelves at home, and despite how protective you were in real life, you'd read me whatever I wanted, regardless of how terrifying or disturbing it was."

The wind howls, and Thalia pulls her knees up as a shield, however weak. Her mother is watching her intently.

"It turns out books ended up being important to Blake too," she continues. "I told you how she wrote me a letter before she died? In it, she mentions how reading *Jane Eyre* and *Wuthering Heights* helped her survive growing up in an orphanage. Those books helped me survive in the same way. They took me beyond myself, beyond the island, to a place where the uncertainty and horror were far worse than any I'd ever known. Because, while you were strict and unyielding, distant and unknowable, you also sheltered me from a horror I had no idea was lurking around the corner.

"Those novels taught me that the mind is capable of withstanding even the strongest emotions. Jane Eyre survives her aunt. Isabella survives the whims of Castle Otranto's lords. Rebecca survives Maxim de Winter and Mrs. Danvers. Eleanor Vance doesn't physically survive, but her consciousness does. She becomes one with Hill House, possessing it as much as it possesses her."

Her mother—her broken, weak mother, ailing yet persevering—suddenly smiles. "I'm glad I did something right," Maureen says.

"I love you," Thalia whispers. She leans out of her mother's embrace.

"I love you too."

"Stay here," Thalia says. "I'm going to lead him out of the forest."

"No!" Maureen throws an arm across Thalia's chest. There is terror and grief and pleading in her voice. "Stay here. Please, Thalia, stay here with me."

"He'll find us here eventually," Thalia says. She lowers her mother's arm. "I'm not giving up. I'm going to use the rules to triumph over Martin." Before her mother can protest a second time, Thalia is darting away, out of the rotted-out hollow, around the copse, and back in the direction they came. She stays along the same path, hoping Martin remains centered where they went left. Her feet slap against saturated ground held more or less in place by exposed mulberry roots.

Filtered through the forest, the wind sounds like a wounded beast. She cuts too close to a tree with as many swaying, haphazard branches as a coral polyp has tentacles. One of the reedier branches whips across her cheek. She doesn't stop running, but when she brings a hand to her face, the driving rain washes away the blood smearing her fingers.

I've had enough of this shit, Thalia thinks, and veers toward the center path. Even when she hits it, she doesn't stop running.

"Come and get me, you bastard!" she screams. If Martin is the quintessential villain, her brazenness will have to be too much for him. She's maybe fifty feet from the forest entrance when Martin roars something behind her. She digs deeper, pushing her muscles to remember crisp afternoons spent jogging along the Boston Commons.

She's almost out of the forest, and after that will be the boardwalk, the possibility of leading Martin farther away from Maureen. But there's nothing but silence behind her. No pounding footsteps. No yelling. No panting breath carried to her on the wind. She's at the tree line now. So close to where they started when Martin appeared. That's when she hears her mother's scream.

Thalia skids to a halt so abruptly, her feet dig into the wet earth, but her momentum carries her forward. She tumbles the rest of the way out of the forest, landing in a muddy, bloody heap. The maze of intertwining branches no longer blots out the sky. She sees swirling clouds overhead, an endless nothing. From behind her in the mulberry forest, her mother screams again. Thalia pats her pockets, the ground, looking for a branch, a rock, a shard of bark, but there's nothing she might use as a weapon. There are only puddles and mud and a wintry sludge of earth and half-decayed leaf matter.

She crawls to her feet and takes a step toward the forest, but she can already hear Martin coming toward her. He breaks from the cover of a skeletal copse, dragging a near-unconscious Maureen. "No," Thalia says. Blinking away tears of anger, she steps toward Martin but slips and sinks back into the sludge.

Martin drags Maureen out of the forest and across the expanse of muddy terrain at the forefront of the replica. Thalia forces herself to her feet. She looks behind her. Monty's crumpled form obscures the entrance to the boardwalk. She looks ahead. The fence separating the cliff's edge from more solid ground seems to sway in the wind like the pitiful barrier it is. It did not stop Thalia from retrieving Blake's bottle of mulberry wine. It will not stop Martin from reaching the edge. But being outside the cover of splayed tree branches seems to reinvigorate Maureen.

She fights Martin's grip, though her flailing has no effect. She tries to bite him, but he's better dressed for the weather than she is, and her teeth don't penetrate the rainproof jacket. Thalia sees her mother being dragged to the highest point of the bluffs through a misty haze of crimson, as if the sky is shedding blood, for her anger has turned the pounding rain red.

Martin Dempsey has ruined so many lives. His family has terrorized generations of women on Block Island. He killed her sister. He's about to kill her mother. He'll kill Aileen, and he will kill her too. And if he doesn't kill her, what will Thalia have left? Regret for not having saved them, despite following the "rules"? A shattered life to walk through alone?

"Martin!" she screeches, lurching forward, blinded by red rage, red rain. "Stop!"

Then it hits her. Martin *will* stop. He is the quintessential gothic villain: reprehensible, lustful, devoid of guilt, full of fear. He's bound by the rules as much as she is. He's not throwing Maureen over the edge until he's basked in the perceived success of his chaotic evil.

And it will be in that moment that Thalia must make her move.

Chapter 46

Martin is at the fence now, pushing Maureen through the slats. Maureen reaches up to grasp the wood, but Martin lifts a boot and slams it down on her fingers. Her mother keens. Or else it's the wind. Or the ocean. Or a voice in Thalia's own head. Nothing is distinguishable from anything else. Everything has fused together—the mansion, the monster, the past, the present. And it's then Thalia decides that if the only option afforded to her in the final moment is to tackle Martin over the edge of the cliff, she will do so. With any luck, he'll fall short of the water and land on the rocks. That's the fate he deserves, to suffer for days—like Ambrosio, the worst villain in all gothic fiction—before dying alone, damned for eternity. If Thalia's fate is to die saving the mother who spent her life protecting her, so be it.

Martin has his back to her, three feet from the fence, only several inches from the cliff's edge. Maureen's hospital gown is torn, but Martin has gathered enough fabric in one fist to have yanked her to her feet. He has full control to toss her in whatever direction he chooses. For now, he holds her hostage and stares out over the crashing ocean.

Thalia creeps onto the bottom fence slat. She can't tackle Martin with any sort of forward momentum while he's holding her mother. But Thalia doesn't see him letting go of Maureen, so she'll have to make him. She climbs to the top slat in a crouch, her right hand on the fence post. She hovers there for no more than a second then stands and jumps, aiming her feet at Martin's shoulders.

He goes down with a violent folding of limbs and torso, head thrown back, a startled shout bursting from his lips. Mercifully, he drops Maureen's gown and falls hard on his upper back. Thalia can practically hear the air whooshing from his lungs in a painful burst. He clutches his chest and rolls onto his elbow, already getting to his feet.

Thalia's fall was painful, but she was expecting it. She scrabbles up and yanks Maureen toward the fence. *Kick him when he's down. Maybe I can*—her idea to slam into him a second time is hijacked by an explosion of pain in her left ankle. Martin has both hands around her leg and is squeezing so hard Thalia fears the bones there will break.

His arms are strong enough that he can pull her toward the cliff's edge with the same motion as someone helping an item along a conveyor belt while standing indifferently to one side of it. She grabs for something, anything, but her fingers find only mud, slick and useless. A sharp bit of root jabs into her ribs, and Thalia lets out a scream. The sense of rushing backward adds to her terror. He's yanking her with such speed and intensity that—once her lower body has cleared the edge—he needs only to let go of her. Thalia flies over reedy thatches of flattened beach grass and dead roots from a nearby shrub.

Through some sheer stroke of good fortune, Martin's efforts don't send her all the way over the cliff. She is in the exact same position as when she retrieved Blake's bottle of wine, but without the tether of her jacket. To crawl back up would be impossible without assistance, and even then, she's losing millimeters with every second. Martin looks displeased she's already hung on this long. His lip curls, and he shakes his head, relieved to almost be done with this. He turns away from Thalia, bends down, and reappears with Maureen once again in his clutches, one large, mud-coated hand around the back of her neck.

"There's no reason it had to be this difficult," Martin says. He frowns down at Thalia, but when he turns to Maureen, the frown turns into a sneer. "For twenty-seven years, you did the one thing I asked of you. You kept quiet. The spaced-out, friendly-enough local waitress whose daughter had moved off the island for a better life was all but invisible. I don't know how that junkie daughter of yours—oh, hell, let's call a spade a spade at this point, that junkie daughter of *ours*—found out about you, but her coming here almost derailed everything.

"As it turns out, she actually made things better for me." He laughs. "I made Blake disappear, got rid of Fiona, and set my sights on a new business venture with far better potential. Everything should have returned to normal. Fiona was in jail. Maureen, you were in your usual haze." He pauses to spit at her mother. Maureen flinches, and when Thalia's rage manifests as a growl, she slips down the side of the cliff another few inches. Martin looks down at her and laughs.

This is it, then. The moment. He thinks he has them. Thalia has to do something. She presses herself as close to the cliff as possible and feels around for something, anything, with one foot. She hardly breathes, too terrified the tiny movement will send her over the edge.

"Aileen is smitten," Martin continues. "Marriage is on the horizon, as is the long-awaited—and rightful—ownership of White Hall by a Dempsey. And not just any Dempsey. But me. The worthiest of five generations."

Thalia's foot catches something. A root. Not a dead free-floating root, but one with depth and determination, growing in the side of the cliff as it has. She pushes herself up, only slightly, but it's enough that, if she can find one more root or branch to grab on to, she might be able to launch herself high enough to reach him.

"I'm the only one to succeed against you bitches," Martin says. He laughs and jerks his chin at the mansion behind him. "And against the Searles bitches." Thalia raises even higher on the thin, shuddering root. Her foot is cramping, the muscles shaking. She walks her fingers forward. It might be . . . no, it's not going to be enough.

"But this is it. I'm sick of the weather, and I'm sick of dealing with you." He pulls Maureen back so as to push her over the edge with as much force as possible. "Goodbye, Maureen. Say hello to the other Mulberry Maidens for me, parading around the tunnels in a hell of their own creation. They can have it. You can have it. Those dark, dank passageways. Me, I'll be staying up here. Now that White Hall is mine."

He regrips Maureen's neck, then thrusts her forward. Thalia uses every last bit of strength to push herself up off the root and lift her arms. Martin throws Maureen off the cliff at the same moment the shot rings out.

Chapter 47

Maureen falls, hospital gown floating behind her. The fabric grazes Thalia's fingers. She's going to miss it. There's not enough to grab on to. Then, her fingers find a tear in the fabric, and she latches on and draws her arm in at the same time. She's got her. Somehow, she has her mother, and though she's stopped Maureen from plunging down the side of the cliff to the ocean below, her mother's body still hits the cliffside with a horrible thud.

Thalia looks up. Martin hovers, tilted. His feet are too far behind him to stay upright, and there's a hole in his khaki-colored jacket. A crimson hole that's spreading even as Thalia watches Martin fall. "Duck!" Thalia shouts, though she's unsure if Maureen can hear, let alone understand, her. Thanks to Martin's height and the angle of his fall, he topples over them, rather than crashing into and pulling them down.

Thalia looks beside her. Maureen's left cheek is pressed into the cliff, the burnt red of the clay accentuating the whiteness of her face. "Mom," Thalia says, "hang on. We have to crawl up." She's inching her fingers out of the tear in Maureen's gown and across her shoulder. She doesn't dare release the pressure she's exerting against her mother's body.

"Here," a voice says, and a wet sleeve of fabric is smacking the mud by Thalia's face. She looks up to see Aileen's bruised visage, chestnut hair plastered to her head. Thalia grabs the sleeve and ties it around her mother's right wrist. She pulls a few more inches of fabric toward them and tucks it into her mother's hand.

"Can you hoist her up with your arm?" Thalia calls. Though Aileen isn't hanging over a cliff, she's in hardly any better condition than Thalia or Maureen. *How did she get all the way out here and fire a gun?* A moment later, another voice answers Thalia's question.

"I'm going to help her," Sarah calls down to them. "Maureen, are you ready?"

Maureen takes a shuddering breath but nods.

"Ready!" Thalia yells. Then, to her mother, she says, "Don't you dare let go." As Sarah and Aileen drag her up, Thalia keeps one hand on her mother, convinced she might float away, still not entirely believing that Maureen is alive, that she's going to be okay.

In less than twenty seconds, her mother's not only off the cliff, but back far enough from the edge that Thalia can no longer see her. Aileen, too, is out of sight. Sarah throws the jacket sleeve down again, and Thalia grabs it like the life raft it is. For one terror-inducing second as she's pulled up, she sees Sarah's feet slide forward in the muck and thinks they're both going over. But then her friend is catching hold of the fence rail, and Thalia continues up and over the lip of the cliff without incident. When both feet are on relatively solid ground, she stumbles forward and collapses into Sarah. The two of them slide to the ground.

"I found Aileen in the parlor loading her gun," Sarah says. "I think she had half a mind to use it against you and Maureen. But we got out here in time to hear Martin's little speech."

Thalia nods, unable to respond. Aileen is, despite her injuries, tending to Maureen. When she's helped Maureen into the jacket, she goes to Monty on the boardwalk. The groundskeeper is conscious, and Aileen helps him up.

They need to get Monty and the two women inside, and then to the hospital, as quickly as possible, but Thalia allows herself these few seconds to breathe. To feel immense, heart-palpitating relief. None of them should be alive, and yet here they all are. Each freed from their role in Martin's plot, in the Dempseys' century-long reign of terror.

Somewhere below, in the black, unyielding, freezing, great-white-shark-infested waters, the villain's body disappears beneath a series of frothing, unforgiving waves.

∽

She's not sure how they make it to the courtyard, to the moment when police officers and EMTs appear along the mansion's east garden, large ponchos billowing out around them like tents. Aileen and Maureen are immediately whisked away, into separate but adjacent ambulances. Sarah is in the back of a third, but Thalia refuses to tolerate the medical technicians' poking and prodding. She speaks only with Bill Kiste, the island's sole detective who, in response to Sarah's inspired phone call to the Coast Guard—members of which are also present—came along to see what was going on at White Hall.

"We should go down to the station," Detective Kiste says after several minutes.

Thalia nods. She knows her five-minute condensed version of events sounds, well, like the plot of a novel. Something for which suspension of disbelief and a penchant for the macabre is essential to glean any sort of understanding. As she walks toward the police car, she passes the ambulance where Sarah is being treated for minor cuts and scrapes. "You all right?" Sarah calls out to her.

Thalia stops and looks back to where the two forensic specialists are cordoning off the area around the cliff's edge. There'd been no conversation among the women about altering the story. Aileen had simply handed over the pistol to the first officer who reached her, and told him she'd shot Martin Dempsey when he tried to throw Maureen over the cliff. After that, Aileen had gone into shock, and refused to answer any more questions. Thalia knows it's going to be a long night, much like preparing for a court case. The results of this briefing, however, will bring a measure of peace to *her*, not some distant client. Peace and, hopefully, closure.

"I'm okay," Thalia says, and smiles at her friend. "But I'll be a whole lot better when there's an ocean separating me from this mansion."

"That's a real shame," Sarah says. "Hilda and Willow wanted to throw a 'Welcome home' party for you. I thought we could do it at White Hall."

"Rather than a 'Welcome-back-to-Block-Island' party for me," Thalia says, "how about I invite you, Patrick, and the girls to Boston? My apartment building has a guaranteed 'No trapdoors, no oceanside cliffs, and no mulberry-forest-mazes' policy."

"That sounds like a great idea," Sarah says, then sees that Detective Kiste is waiting for Thalia. "You better go."

"I'm going." But she doesn't move. "Sar?"

"Yeah, Thal?"

"Thank you. I couldn't have done this without you. My sister."

Her best friend nods, and something hits her: a painful truth she's only realizing now. Sarah *has* been her sister for twenty-five years, and while she wouldn't trade her for anything, she had a real sister that same amount of time. The relationship she has with Sarah, she could have had with Blake too. And Blake could have had with her.

"Can you give me a minute?" Thalia asks Detective Kiste. The detective nods and lights a cigarette. Thalia walks to the end of the courtyard and looks out over the sprawling mulberry forest, the boardwalk, the miniature White Hall that, once she tells the police of Helen's remains, will become a full-on crime scene excavation. She knows the detective's eyes are on her, but she doesn't care. She has something to say. To Blake.

"I told you I'd confirm or disprove every last statement made against you." Her voice is low, but steady. "That I'd get to the bottom of our mother's fears, of the connection between you and Martin. The odds of you getting out of this unscathed were insurmountable. You couldn't have known how intertwined you were with the history of this island, especially when you'd gone through so much tragedy in Boston. But I hope I proved to you that I was always on your side. From the beginning. From your letter. From the second I knew about you. And I'll continue to be on your side in death.

"Martin was a narcissistic sociopath, but if he was right about anything, I hope it's that you are with Mary Hopkins Searles and Helen Gilbert Brown, and that the three of you will continue to make yourselves known at White Hall. You don't need me anymore. You're free of your addiction. Free from those chains, those ghosts, you built the foundation of your decaying castle on. Free to, finally, rest in peace."

She stands at the edge of the courtyard for another few seconds.

"Ms. Mills?" Detective Kiste asks. "Are you ready?"

Thalia follows the detective through the mansion, out the front door, and around the circular drive to his car. She looks up to the sky. The sun doesn't come out. Not yet. That would be a cliché unworthy of the dark, terrifying story they've somehow lived through. But Thalia thinks it will.

If not today, or tomorrow, then soon.

Epilogue

Seven Months Later

Thalia drives up Route 95 toward Boston, on her way back from the Point Judith ferry terminal in Galilee. Her mother is seated beside her, dressed in a ribbed black sweaterdress and running the fingers of one hand over the smooth shellac nail polish on the other. It's a nervous, but preferable, habit she picked up when she quit smoking over the summer. The doctors had advised her not to take on too much at once, so Maureen had waited almost two months after being discharged from an inpatient substance abuse treatment center before tossing the remaining cartons in the garbage.

Thalia had told her not to be too hard on herself if she slipped up, but Maureen was steadfast in her abstinence; she hadn't relapsed with a single cigarette—or pill or drink—once in the ensuing months.

"So what did you think?" Maureen asks. "It's pretty unbelievable, right?" She's referring, of course, to the transformation of White Hall to which Thalia had just been witness. Gone are the rows of extralarge wine barrels, the cooling units, the fermenters, and the twisting mazes of siphon tubing. Gone, too, is any mention of bed-and-breakfast on the front sign or printed menus. The Searleses will no longer permit guests to schedule a vacation on their website or show up after missing the last ferry and request a room for the night. Despite this, the mansion is more crowded than ever.

"It *is* unbelievable," Thalia replies. And really, she is having trouble believing it. That after being released from prison, Fiona was able to not only forgive Aileen but return to their Dream House. To turn the mansion into a home for domestic violence and other sexual assault survivors.

Maureen is quiet. Thalia knows, from speaking with Aileen, that Maureen has been helping out at White Hall often, though she's only just started opening up to Thalia about her work there. After Above the Rocks closed down, Maureen was hesitant to look for another serving job on the island. She has told Thalia that she thinks she'll find it much easier to maintain her sobriety long term working at White Hall as opposed to in a restaurant.

"I'm glad they're keeping Monty on as groundskeeper," Thalia says.

"Montague Daniels, Corrine Daniels's ex-husband and *Martin and Michael's first cousin*." Maureen shakes her head incredulously. "You know, Monty left Corrine only about one year after she was my labor-and-delivery nurse, right after they moved back to the island. If her drinking had progressed faster, and he'd left her sooner, he might never have known about Blake." Maureen shakes her head again. "Corrine's always been a gabber, so it doesn't surprise me that, all those years ago when they *were* still together, she told him what happened, the circumstances surrounding Blake's conception."

"What exactly did she tell him?" Thalia asks. This is the first time she and Maureen have spoken about Monty's part in things.

"That Maureen Mills had a baby girl she gave up for adoption," Maureen clarifies. "But not why I gave her up or that I'd been . . ." She pauses, then says quietly, "He didn't know Blake was in danger until it was too late."

"I still can't believe he overheard that first conversation between Aileen and Martin," Thalia says. She'd wondered how Monty knew who Blake was and what she was doing on the island until Aileen told her that Monty was in the foyer while she was on the phone with Martin in the parlor. She saw him slipping out the front door after hanging up but didn't realize he'd heard *everything* until much, much later. Thalia is quiet, contemplating all the connections and coincidences that have led them to this moment.

"Sarah's been phenomenal," Maureen says, shifting the conversation back to more positive topics.

Thalia keeps her eyes on the road but smiles. Sarah sold her taxi to Dr. Maddox's daughter and drives solely for Aileen and Fiona now—in a nice new Subaru—helping the women get to their appointments, jobs, the ferry terminal for off-island commitments. "No surprise there," she says. "I know she really loves the new job." Thinking of her best friend, she adds, "Sarah's one of the best people I know."

Maureen puts a hand on Thalia's arm. "Second only to you." Thalia doesn't say anything, and Maureen continues, "Are you okay? With . . . everything? Is there anything you want to ask me? We've hardly talked about your father."

Thalia squints a little, not wanting to let the tears come. "I am okay. And whenever *you* need to talk about something, I'll listen. But I don't need to know anything about who he was. Everything I am, I am because of you."

They drive in silence until something occurs to Thalia. "Actually, there is something I want to ask."

"Of course."

"Were you ever with Timmy Graham?"

Maureen bursts out laughing. "You know, I was, actually. Ages ago. Before he was such a slimeball." She sobers. "You know, much of what makes Timmy *Timmy* can probably be attributed to Martin. The games they played, the little competitions they had."

Thalia nods. Yet another poisonous offshoot to be traced back to the Dempseys. She turns left onto Forest Hills Avenue. A minute later, Maureen says, more to herself than to Thalia, "There it is. Yale Terrace."

Thalia turns and slows the car, following the narrow, winding road to a section she no longer needs a map to locate. After several minutes, she pulls over alongside an immaculately manicured, circular lot. The early fall foliage—shades of cider, goldenrod, sandstone, and bronze—cuts a sharp contrast to the cloudless, cyan-blue sky.

There are no other visitors at this tier. She shuts the car off, and she and Maureen get out. Thalia straightens the hem of her long, slouchy sweater, adjusting what's stowed within a deep, wide front pocket. She no longer has much interest in fashionable jumpsuits or fringy blouses. She no longer needs a shield to protect her from the past.

Columns of marble obelisks herald them forward, guiding their passage like stern, silent ushers. Crows caw to one another among the branches of a massive honey locust, their black feathers against the cadmium-yellow leaves like something from the cover of a New England travel guide. They pass stone mausoleums draped with vines and shadowed with moss, their pointed arches, towers, and spires as ornate as any English cathedral a hundred times their size.

In the tier ahead, there's a row of slant markers, bevel headstones, and monuments. "Up here," Thalia says to Maureen. She leads her to a large upright monument, and Maureen breathes in sharply.

The headstone is as tall as Thalia and made of bronzy-green granite, the top portion of which extends into twin, curling scrolls. Above the scrolls are two carved skulls, and centered at the very top is a winged cherub face. About a third of the way down is another winged cherub, and below that is Blake's name, date of birth, and date of death. The lower cherub's cape falls down around the words in stone billows. On the other side of the cape is an arched column that matches the double border of the headstone's base.

"Thalia," Maureen says softly, "I'm so glad you brought me here."

Thalia nods. She's forgiven her mother for the rigid, occasionally ruthless upbringing. Of course she has; Maureen was trying to protect them—both her first daughter and her second. Thalia's even started talking with Laura more seriously about the possibility of adopting a daughter of their own. But she hasn't forgiven Maureen for keeping

Blake from her, and she's not sure she ever will, though she knows this isn't fair.

Thalia turns to reexamine the headstone she commissioned. Once it was installed—and she'd visited Blake's gravesite alone—she called Maureen and told her the plot was ready for whenever she was up for a visit. Maureen had requested they make the trip the following weekend. Now she is seeing the quiet, secluded, ethereal cemetery herself.

"I know neither one of us ever really met her. Not truly," Thalia says. "But from everything I know about her, this headstone seems fitting. The scrolls are representative of the Book of Life. Blake felt as if her deeds, the things she'd done, were carved in stone, never to be rewritten. But Laura and I visited Blake's AA group the Wednesday before I finalized the design. Her sponsor, Chris, gave a memorial speech in honor of Blake.

"She quoted Revelation 20:12: 'The books were opened: and another book was opened, which is the book of life: and the dead were judged out of those things which were written in the books, according to their works.' I felt like Blake would have appreciated that. She wanted so badly to write her own story. To be her own heroine, not simply acted upon by addiction and abandonment and men."

"It's perfect," Maureen says. "And not only that, it belongs on the grounds of a desolate abbey, half hidden by a wall of mist."

"Like this one," Thalia says and takes the thick, tattered novel—featuring a mist-cloaked abbey—from her sweater pocket. She opens it, ensures the paper within is tucked close to the spine, then shuts it and places *The Mysteries of Udolpho* at the base of Blake's tombstone. Her mother nods and smiles. Thalia smiles back.

But her smile fades, for this tombstone, while an ending, is not a happy one. Despite following the rules, White Hall didn't burn to the ground, Blake didn't get whisked away by a wealthy nobleman, and while Martin did fall to his death, Thalia doesn't believe he suffered nearly as much as he deserved. Nor has he, as far as she knows, been damned for all eternity.

But like all endings, it is also a beginning. And Thalia will have to take whatever solace there is in that. Blake, the sister whom—to Thalia's bitter grief—she was never permitted to know, is dead. But through a mere letter, Thalia understands that she would have loved her.

And that she did dare much for her sake.

AFTERWORD

The Daughters of Block Island began in January 2020 as a short-story retelling of a popular murder ballad, "The Twa Sisters," sometimes called "The Dreadful Wind and Rain." In the ballad, a young woman is drowned by her older sister after they are two-timed by a suitor; in some versions, the older sister's affections are unrequited, but she's spurred to murder all the same. I took the story—then in epistolary format—to one of my MFA residencies for critiquing and found that it wasn't working on multiple levels; readers weren't connecting with either the characters or the series of emails being used to tell the tale. My fellow MFA candidates thought the setting might be worth keeping, however. They also wondered—if the complex synopsis was any indication—if the story might warrant a full-length novel.

I trunked the story rather than making any of the changes suggested. I'd never abandoned a project for which I'd completed an at least semicoherent first draft, but I couldn't envision where I wanted the characters to end up. I wasn't even sure whose story it was, Blake's or Thalia's.

Cut to November 2021 and my sudden desire to write a new novel. I'd recently finished a manuscript about New England's "last vampire," tuberculosis victim Mercy Brown, and was keen to write another novel set in Rhode Island and with a dark historical bent. *What about Block Island?* I asked myself. *What about my little epistolary experiment about two sisters being used as pawns by two other sisters, all of whom were being master-manipulated by a villain straight from the pages of Ann Radcliffe or Matthew Lewis?*

I revisited the story, as well as the feedback from the critique session, and was instantly discouraged. The thing was a mess. Even in conjunction with the synopsis, the mystery was garbled, the characters' motivations were muddy, and worst of all, the gothic elements felt predictable, melodramatic, and trite.

With no other ideas, I set out to rewrite it as a novel anyway. As the days passed and the word count grew, the plot and character motivations became clearer. The gothic elements, however, weren't faring so well. They became triter, more predictable, and more melodramatic. But I *wanted* the crumbling castle set against a backdrop of perpetual rain, goddammit! I wanted an orphan returning to her ancestral village to get to the bottom of a long-buried secret, and I wanted ghosts haunting the mansion halls! How could I lean into the trappings of the gothic without it coming across as a cliché? How could I make gothic fiction new?

I'm a big fan of the *Scream* franchise, so it didn't take long to come up with the answer . . . I needed to make gothic meta! Blake's shaky sobriety and fragile disposition meant that she was the perfect character to believe she'd become trapped in a gothic novel. After that, I was free to employ whatever staple of the genre I wished, so long as I acknowledged the ridiculousness of the nonstop rain or the absurdity of a castle on the edge of a tiny island harboring secret passageways, a mulberry tree forest, and at least one ghost.

While doing research for the novel, I discovered that a castle-like mansion off the coast of rugged, nautical Rhode Island wasn't as absurd as I had once thought when I found myself gazing upon White Hall in a little historical volume of Block Island lore and legends. My initial reaction to the structure made its way into *The Daughters of Block Island* when Blake muses that the mansion was "entirely out of place on an island very much one with the culture of New England." The author of the volume, Ethel Colt Ritchie, called White Hall an "outstanding landmark" that took two full years to construct. In a *Block Island Times* article, New Shoreham resident and historian Martha Ball described a building that "seemed to sit on a full story of weathered, windowless gray, easy to draw in memory, difficult to explain even with photos at hand," and an 1890s Block Island guidebook described it as follows:

> The most magnificent of these [summer cottages], and indeed, one of the finest in the world is the elegant mansion of Mr. Edward F. Searles of Methuen, Mass., who has here exhausted all the resources at command of almost fabulous wealth in the erection of a stately pile of oriental splendor. Every stranger approaching the Island asks about the imposing structure, whose noble dome glistens in the sunlight on the southern slope of the Corrugated Bluffs of the Neck.

Here was the solution to the question, What type of manor should I situate at the center of *The Daughters of Block Island*? For what could be better than one born of history, one whose "stately pile of oriental splendor" I could regularly observe—and obsess over—in sepia-toned photographs?

White Hall was built between 1888 and 1890 by—as the guide-book states—Edward F. Searles of Methuen, Massachusetts, an interior and architectural designer, and his wife, Mary Hopkins, the widow of railroad tycoon Mark Hopkins. Mark Hopkins had been one of the "Big Four" railroad czars, and Mary Searles was often referred to as "the richest woman in America" (Mark and Mary were also first cousins). Mary had no children but had adopted her housekeeper's son. Edward and Mary met after Edward helped furnish her San Francisco mansion in Nob Hill. They worked together again on another of Mary's baronial homes, the Kellogg Terrace (known today as the John Dewey Academy in Great Barrington, Massachusetts).

Edward and Mary's business partnership blossomed into romance, and a fair amount of gossip surrounded their relationship (and what were believed to be the ulterior motives of each), as Mary was twenty-three years Searles's elder. In 1887, upon visiting Block Island, they purchased sixty-five acres of land on the northern part of Corn Neck, extending from the Great Salt Pond to the Atlantic. A few months later, Edward and Mary were married. Upon returning from their European honeymoon, Mary took pains to change her will to exclude her adopted son, leaving all her earthly possessions upon her death to her new husband.

Edward Searles went back to Block Island in 1888 and enlisted prolific church architect Henry Vaughan to design and build his dream house, christened *White Hall*. The mansion followed the English Mannerist tradition, with massive, identical, bilaterally symmetrical wings, separated from one another by a three-story central hall that rose to a belvedere ceiling. The earliest photographs show a crowning domed lantern that was removed after just one year of winter winds (according to Martha Ball, fifty years later the mansion had been reduced to "white house flat roof" on nautical charts). Edward and Mary lived at White Hall—in opposite wings—only minimally, and islanders started calling the opulent structure *Searles' Folly*. Upon Mary's death in 1891, Edward never lived at the mansion again, though he paid for its upkeep until his own death in 1920.

The mansion underwent several changes in ownership—and a brief stint as a nightclub—between 1929 and 1959. In 1963, Searles' Folly mysteriously burned to the ground. Islanders who watched the fire described a feeling much like the climax of Edgar Allan Poe's "The Fall of the House of Usher," and said there had "long been a doomed feel to the place beginning with the death of [Mary Searles]." In 1984, the bulldozed and neglected property was purchased by the Town of New Shoreham, and the site functions as an area of public access to what is now known as Mansion Beach. Today, all that remains of White Hall are parts of the two brick entry pillars and a skeletal bit of foundation.

The real history of White Hall, then, is as complex and scandalous as the fictionalized one, and while many details of this novel—the mulberry trees, the underground tunnels, the proximity of the mansion to the ocean and clay cliffs—were fabricated to pave Blake's descent into gothic hell, I relished being able to include so much of White Hall's architectural idiosyncrasies and misplaced charm. I took many liberties with the real cast of characters who orbited in and out of White Hall's sphere too: in *The Daughters of Block Island*, Edward Searles is Mary's father rather than her husband, and Mary is courted by the fictional son of a fictionalized version of Henry Vaughan. My pondering over the real Mary Searles's inexplicable disowning of her adopted son contributed to Blake's low self-esteem and feelings of worthlessness at being abandoned by her own mother. All things considered, there are as many echoes of Edward and Mary Searles—and White Hall—resonating from the pages of *The Daughters of Block Island* as there are the gothic novels from which the manuscript is inspired.

And I do so hope that *this* gothic novel finds its way into your heart in the way that *The Haunting of Hill House*, *Rebecca*, and all the others mentioned in these pages found their way into mine.

—Christa Carmen
December 7, 2022

ACKNOWLEDGMENTS

There are many individuals without whom the writing of this novel would not have been possible. Special thanks go to Robert Levy and Nancy Holder for convincing me that the characters in the first, short-story version of *The Daughters of Block Island* had a lot more to say, as well as to the inimitable Gwendolyn Kiste for her unending wisdom, humor, talent, and friendship.

Shouts from the (peaked and gabled) rooftops for Joshua Rex, Belicia Rhea, Elise Bryant, Christine Granfield, Jean Colistra, and Allan Patch for reading early drafts and commenting astutely on everything from the number of times *gothic horror* was mentioned to the most realistic state of the 130-year-old wallpaper on White Hall's walls.

Big thanks, as well, to the members of the Monday Night Write Group—Larry Hinkle, Valerie B. Williams, Terry Emery, Ken Godfrey, Jessica McMahan, Stephen Cords, Tom Deady, and John Buja—for their invaluable critiques, and to my dear friend Sarah Itteilag for fielding numerous medical field–related questions.

Heartfelt cheers for my perpetual writing/friend crew: Jessica Wick, Elissa Sweet, Julia Rios, Claire Cooney, Carlos Hernandez, Lazaryn McLaughlin, Mary Robles, Lauren Elise Daniels, Aron Beauregard, and all the members of the Rhode Island "We Are Providence" group. They make the already-pleasurable pursuit of writing—and living—an absolute joy.

Much love and appreciation go to the wonderful women who provided early praise for *The Daughters of Block Island*: Nancy Holder, V. Castro, Jo Kaplan, Cynthia Pelayo, Hailey Piper, and Gwendolyn Kiste; thank you for being true supporters and truer friends.

To Jill Marr, my endlessly optimistic and enthusiastic agent, for believing in *The Daughters* from the moment I first mentioned my little tale of murder and mulberry forests on Block Island. Whether Mercy Brown or the meta-gothic, her unwavering support has meant all the difference.

To Grace Doyle, Charlotte Herscher, and everyone at Thomas & Mercer for offering their thoughts along the way. Grace's vision for the final version of this story—and her command of all its moving pieces in order to get us there—was indispensable, and Charlotte's sensibility and expertise were a great fit for the colorful, Romantic figures populating this book.

Thank you to the real Ethel, Ethel Colt Ritchie, and to Vincent P. de Luise, MD, whose detailed research, records, and collection of photographs kick-started my obsession with Edward Searles, Mary Frances Hopkins, and White Hall. And my gratitude to columnist Martha Ball and editor Renee Meyer at the *Block Island Times* for allowing my use of several quotations within the afterword of this novel.

I'm so appreciative of my loving family—both immediate and extended—who fully support my obsession with writing and the macabre: the Colistras (Jean, Jerry, Lori, Josh, Elsie, Cory, Pam, Cali, Luca, godson Joey, Nico, James, Chrissy, Arden, and Avery); the Granfields (Kevin, Christine, Kevin, and Catherine); the Forenzas (Mike, Michael, and Amelia); the Beauchamps (Doc and Marian); the Intrieris (Sal, Rachel, Salvatore, and Gianluigi); the Cohens (Eric, Kaitlin, Arthur, Zelda, and godson Perry); the Williams (John, Jill, and Beau); and the Quattromanis (Barry, Barbie, Thomas, and Andrew).

Lastly, thank you to my parents, Rick and Jeanne Quattromani, for *everything*, from instilling in me a love of reading to providing me with—or preparing me for—every opportunity I've ever had. With regard to this novel, thank you to my father for taking my sister and me out on the water constantly when we were kids. I cannot count the number of times, while writing this story, I pictured Block Island as I remembered it from the bow of his Grady White: a distant, fog-encased town, secretive and seductive. And thank you to my mother for her appreciation for *The Monk*, *Rebecca*, and the work of Victoria Holt, which challenged me to write a novel that would honor the great gothic novels of the past.

Thank you to my sister, Lauren Quattro Forenza, for being such a pillar of steadfastness and support that my murder-ballad-inspired tale of two (sets of) sisters could *only* be tempestuous and catastrophic, since I have no basis for toxic or codependent sibling relationships in real life. A thank you, as well, to my dear, departed beagle, Maya. Though I couldn't see her, I know she was there for the penning of this one too.

Thank you to my patient and quick-witted husband, John Beauchamp, who's the best at weathering my narrative-plot-point-working-out-rants and whose delight in any writing success I've ever had is so absolute, it causes me to appreciate those accomplishments that much more. This one's not a clear-cut horror novel, so I'll channel my best Byronic hero and lord my knowledge of gothic "rules" over him while I can . . . at least until the next one comes out.

Finally, thank you to my brilliant and beguiling daughter, Eleanor Rose, a beam as bright as the lens of the loftiest lighthouse. Her inquiries of "Can *I* write a book?" and her infinite fascination with words and stories, wicked stepmothers and sea serpents, inspire me every minute of every day. I look forward to boarding the ferry with her on some sunny afternoon in the not-so-distant future and traveling the twelve nautical miles across the Atlantic to Block Island. There, we'll admire the two-hundred-foot-tall clay cliffs of the Mohegan Bluffs on our way to the island's northern shore, where we'll run our hands along what remains of the two brick entry pillars that, once upon a time, marked the entrance to White Hall. We'll dig our bare feet into the sand and listen to the waves crash along the shore of Mansion Beach. Upon returning home, I'll give her *The Daughters of Block Island* and explain that fiction, as Stephen King once wrote, is the truth inside the lie.

Thank you to Eleanor, and to everyone else, who helped me search for that truth.

ABOUT THE AUTHOR

Photo © 2022 by Joshua Behan

Christa Carmen lives in Rhode Island and is the Bram Stoker Award–nominated author of the short story collection *Something Borrowed, Something Blood-Soaked.* She has a BA from the University of Pennsylvania, an MA from Boston College, and an MFA from the University of Southern Maine.

When she's not writing, she keeps chickens; uses a Ouija board to ghost-hug her dear, departed beagle; and sets out on adventures with her husband, daughter, and bloodhound–golden retriever mix. Most of her work comes from gazing upon the ghosts of the past or else into the dark corners of nature, those places where whorls of bark become owl eyes, and deer step through tunnels of hanging leaves and creeping briars only to disappear. Visit her at www.christacarmen.com.